"Todd [is] the biggest literary phenom of her generation."
—*Cosmopolitan*

"I was almost at the point like with *Twilight* that I just stop everything and my sole focus was reading the book . . . Todd, girl, you are a genius!!!"
—*Once Upon a Twilight*

"The Mr. Darcy and Lizzy Bennet of our time . . . If you looked up 'Bad Boy' in the fiction dictionary, next to it would be a picture of Hardin alongside *Beautiful Bastard* and Mr. Darcy."
—*That's Normal*

"The one thing you can count on is to *expect the unexpected*."
—*Vilma's Book Blog*

"Anna Todd manages to make you scream, cry, laugh, fall in love, and sit in the fetal position . . . Whether you have read the Wattpad version or not, *After* is a can't-miss book—but get ready to feel emotions that you weren't sure a book could bring out of you. And if you have read the Wattpad version, the book is 10x better."
—*Fangirlish*

"A very entertaining read chock-full of drama drama drama . . . This book will have you from the first page."
—*A Bookish Escape*

"I couldn't put this book down! It went with me everywhere so I could get my Hessa fix every spare moment I had. Talk about getting hooked from page one!"
—*Grown Up Fangirl*

ANNA TODD

AFTER EVER HAPPY

**SIMON &
SCHUSTER**

London · New York · Sydney · Toronto · New Delhi

A CBS COMPANY

First published by Gallery Books, an imprint of Simon & Schuster Inc., 2015
First published in Great Britain by Simon & Schuster UK Ltd, 2015
A CBS COMPANY

10

Simon & Schuster UK Ltd
1st Floor
222 Gray's Inn Road
London WC1X 8HB

www.simonandschuster.co.uk

Simon & Schuster Australia, Sydney
Simon & Schuster India, New Delhi

A CIP catalogue record for this book
is available from the British Library

Paperback ISBN: 978-1-5011-0684-2
eBook ISBN: 978-1-5011-0685-9

Printed and bound by CPI Group (UK) Ltd, Croydon, CR0 4YY

To everyone out there who has ever fought
for someone or something they believe in.

prologue

HARDIN

Many times in my life I felt unwanted, out of place in the worst way. I had a mum who tried, she really, honestly tried, but it just wasn't enough. She worked too much; she slept during the days because she was on her feet all night. Trish tried, but a boy, especially a lost boy, needs his father.

I knew Ken Scott was a troubled man, an unpolished wanna-be man who was never pleased or impressed by anything I did. The little Hardin who was pathetic in the way he tried to impress the tall man whose shouts and stumbles filled the cramped space of our shitty house would be pleased at the possibility that the cold man isn't his father. He would sigh, grab his book from the table, and ask his mum when Christian, the nice man who made him laugh by reciting passages from old books, was coming over.

But Hardin Scott, the adult man struggling with addiction and anger passed down by the shitty excuse for a father he was given, is fucking livid. I feel betrayed, confused as fucking hell, and fucking angry. It makes no sense, the cheesy plot of the switched fathers that every shitty sitcom uses couldn't possibly be my life. Buried memories resurface.

My mum, on the phone the morning after one of my essays was chosen for the local paper: "I just thought you would want to know, Hardin is brilliant. Like his father," she softly praised into the line.

I looked around the small living room. The man with the dark hair, passed out on the chair with a bottle of brown liquor at his feet, wasn't brilliant. *He's a fucking mess,* I thought as he stirred in the chair, and my mum quickly hung up the phone. There were numerous times like this, too many to count, that I was too stupid, too young, to understand why Ken Scott was so distant with me, why he never hugged me the way my friends' dads would their sons. He never played baseball with me or taught me anything except how to be a fucking drunk.

Was all of that a waste? Is Christian Vance actually my father?

The room is spinning, and I stare at him, the man who supposedly fathered me, and I see something familiar in his green eyes, the line of his jaw. His hands are shaking as he pushes his hair back from his forehead, and I freeze, realizing that I'm doing the exact same thing.

chapter **one**

TESSA

That's impossible."

I stand but quickly sit back down on the bench when the grass underneath me seems to sway unsteadily. The park is filling with people now. Families with small children, balloons and presents in their arms despite the cold weather.

"It's true, Hardin is Christian's son," Kimberly says, her blue eyes bright and focused.

"But Ken . . . Hardin looks just like him." I remember the first time I met Ken Scott, inside a yogurt shop. I immediately knew he was Hardin's father; his dark hair and his height brought me to the easy conclusion.

"Does he? I don't really see it, except the hair color. Hardin has the same eyes as Christian, the same facial structure."

Does he? I struggle to picture the three faces. Christian has dimples like Hardin and the same eyes . . . but it just doesn't make sense: Ken Scott is Hardin's father—he has to be. Christian looks so young compared to Ken. I know they're the same age, but Ken's alcoholism took its toll on his appearance. He's still a handsome man, but you can see where the liquor has aged him.

"This is . . ." I struggle for words and air.

Kimberly looks at me apologetically. "I know. I've wanted to tell you so bad. I hated keeping this from you, but it wasn't my place." She puts her hand on mine and squeezes gently. "Christian assured me that as soon as Trish gave him permission, he would tell Hardin."

"I just . . ." I take a deep breath. "That's what Christian is doing? Telling Hardin *now*?" I stand up again and Kimberly's hand drops away. "I have to go to him. He is going to—" I can't even begin to fathom how Hardin will react to the news, especially after finding Trish and Christian together last night. This will be too much for him.

"He is." Kim sighs. "Trish hasn't agreed fully, but Christian said she was close enough and things were getting out of hand."

As I pull out my phone, my only thought is that I can't believe Trish would hide this from Hardin. I had thought more of her, much more as a mother, and now I feel as if I've never met the woman.

My phone is already pressed to my cheek, Hardin's line ringing in my ear, when Kimberly says, "I told Christian that he shouldn't separate you two when he told Hardin, but Trish recommended that if he does it, he needed to do it alone . . ." Kimberly's mouth presses into a hard line, and she looks around the park, then up at the sky.

I reach the dull tone of the automated system on Hardin's voicemail. I dial again while Kimberly sits silently, only to get his voicemail for the second time. I shove my phone into my back pocket and start wringing my hands. "Can you take me to him, Kimberly? Please?"

"Yes. Of course." She jumps to her feet, calling for Smith.

Watching the little kid walk toward us with what I can only call a cartoon butler's stride, it occurs to me that Smith is Christian's son . . . and Hardin's brother. Hardin has a little brother. And then I think about Landon . . . what does it mean for Landon and Hardin? Will Hardin want anything to do with him now that he doesn't have a real family tie to him? And Karen, what about sweet Karen and her baked goods? Ken—what about the man who tries so hard to make up for the terrible childhood of a boy who isn't his son. Does *Ken* know? My head is spinning, and I need to see Hardin. I need to make sure that he knows I am here for him, and we will figure this out together. I can't imagine how he feels right now; he must be so overwhelmed.

"Does Smith know?" I ask.

After a few beats of silence, Kimberly says, "We thought he did because of the way he is with Hardin, but he couldn't possibly."

I feel for Kimberly. She already had to deal with her fiancé's infidelity, and now this. When Smith gets to us, he stops and gives us a mysterious look, as if knowing exactly what we've been talking about. That's not possible, but the way he leaves ahead of us and goes to the car without saying a word, it does make me wonder.

As we drive through Hampstead to find Hardin and his father, the panic in my chest rises and falls, rises and falls.

chapter two

HARDIN

The crack of snapping wood sounds throughout the bar.

"Hardin, stop!" Vance's voice echoes through the space, from somewhere.

Another snap, followed by the sound of breaking glass. The sound pleases me, heightening my thirst for violence. I need to break things, to hurt something, even if it's an object.

And I do.

Screams erupt, breaking me out of my trance. I look down at my hands and find the splintered end of an expensive chair leg. I look up at the blank faces of the alarmed strangers, searching for one face: Tessa's. She isn't here, though, and in this moment of rage I can't decide if that's a good thing or not. She would be afraid; she would be worried for me, panicking in a rushed way and calling my name to drown out the gasps and shouts ringing in my ears.

I drop the wood quickly as if it had burned my skin. And feel arms around my shoulders.

"Get him out of here before they call the police!" Mike says, his voice louder than I've ever heard it before.

"Get the fuck off of me!" I shrug away from Vance and glare at him through the red filling my vision.

"You want to go to jail?!" he shouts, only inches from my face.

I want to shove him to the ground, wrap my hands around his neck . . .

But a couple more women scream, making sure I don't go back down that black hole again. I look around the expensive bar, noting the shattered tumblers on the floor, the broken chair, the horrified expressions of patrons expecting to glide above this kind of carnage. It'll be only moments before their shock turns to anger over my disrupting their overpriced pursuit of happiness.

Christian is by my side again as I storm past the hostess and outside. "Get in my car and I'll explain everything to you," he huffs out.

Worried that the cops really might be showing up any moment, I do what he says, but I'm not sure how to feel or what to say. Despite the confession, I can't wrap my mind around this. The impossibility of it all is ridiculous.

I get in the passenger seat just as he hits the driver's side. "You can't be my father, it's not possible. It doesn't make a bit of sense—none of it." Looking at the expensive rental, I wonder if this means Tessa is stranded at that damn park where I dropped her off. "Kimberly has a car, right?"

Vance looks at me incredulously. "Yes, of course she does." The low purr of the engine grows louder as he zips through traffic. "I'm sorry that you found out this way. Everything was coming together for a while, but then it started to slip." He sighs.

I stay silent, knowing I will lose my shit if I open my mouth. My fingers dig into my legs; the slight pain keeps me calm.

"I'm going to explain it to you, but you have to keep an open mind, okay?" He glances over at me, and I can see the pity in his eyes.

I won't be pitied. "Don't fucking talk to me like a goddamned child," I snap.

Vance looks at me, then back at the road. "You know that I grew up with your dad, Ken—we were mates since I can remember."

"Actually I *didn't* know that." I glare at him. Then I turn to watch the landscape zooming by. "I don't know shit about anything, apparently."

"Well, it's true. We grew up almost as brothers."

"Then you fucked his wife?" I say, interrupting his bedtime story.

"Look," he nearly growls. His hands are white-knuckled on the steering wheel. "I'm trying to explain this to you, so please just let me speak." He takes a deep breath to calm his own temper. "To answer your question, it wasn't like that. Your mum and Ken began dating in high school when your mum moved to Hampstead. She was the most beautiful girl I had ever seen."

My stomach turns at the memory of Vance's mouth on hers.

"But Ken swept her off her feet immediately. They spent every moment of every day together, just like Max and Denise did. The five of us had formed a little clique, you could say." Lost in the ridiculous memory, he sighs. and his voice becomes distant. "She was witty, smart, and head over heels for your dad—fuck. I'm not going to be able to stop calling him that . . ." He groans. His fingers tap on the steering wheel, as if to goad him on.

"Ken was smart—quite brilliant, really—and when he got into university with a full scholarship and early admission, he became busy. Too busy for her. He would spend hours upon hours at the school. It quickly became the four of us without him, and things between your mum and I . . . well, my feelings grew tremendously and hers began."

Vance takes a momentary break to switch lanes and turn the vent so more air comes in. The air is still heavy and thick, and my mind is a fucking whirlwind when he starts up again.

"I always loved her—she knew that—but she loved him, and he was my best friend." Vance swallows. "As the days and nights went by, we became . . . intimate. Not sexually at this point, but we were both giving in to our feelings and not holding back."

"Spare me the fucking details." I clench my fists on my lap, forcing my mouth to close so he can finish.

"Okay, okay, yeah." He stares out the windshield. "Well, one thing led to another, and we were having a full-blown affair at this point. Ken had no idea. Max and Denise suspected something, but neither of them spoke up. I begged your mum to leave him for neglecting her—I know it's fucked-up, but I loved her."

His brows knit together. "She was the only escape I had from my own self-destructive behaviors. I cared about Ken, but I couldn't see past my love for her. I never could see past it." He blows out a hard breath.

"And . . ." I press after a few seconds of silence.

"Yes . . . Well, and so when she announced that she was pregnant, I thought we would run away together and that she would marry me instead of him. I promised her that if she chose me, I would quit fucking off and would be there for her . . . for you."

I feel his eyes on me, but I refuse to look into them.

"Your mum felt I wasn't stable enough for her, and I sat there biting my tongue while she and your—Ken—announced that they were expecting and that they would be married that same week."

What the fuck? I look over at him, but he's clearly lost in the past as he stares at the road ahead.

"I wanted the best for her, and I couldn't drag her through the mud and ruin her reputation by telling Ken or anyone the truth of what happened between us. I kept telling myself that he had to know deep down that it wasn't his child growing inside of her. Your mum swore that he had not touched her in months." Vance's shoulders shake lightly as an evident chill runs through him. "I stood there in my suit at their small wedding as his best man. I knew he would give her what I couldn't. I wasn't even planning to go to university. All I did with my time was pine after a married woman and memorize pages from old novels that would never become my life. I had no plan, no money, and she needed both of those things." He sighs, trying to escape the memory.

Watching him, I'm surprised by what comes to mind and what I feel compelled to say. I form a fist, then relax, trying to resist.

Then I form a fist again, and I don't recognize my voice as I ask, "So basically my mum used you for her entertainment and tossed you aside because you had no money?"

Vance lets out a deep breath. "No. She didn't use me." He glances in my direction. "I know it seems that way, and it's such a fucked-up situation, but she had to think of you and your future. I was a complete and utter fuckup—complete rubbish. And I had nothing going for me."

"And now you have millions," I bitterly remark. How can he defend my mum after all this shit? What is wrong with him? But then something in me turns, and I think about my mother, losing two men who later turned out to be rich, while she toils away at her job, coming home to her sad little house.

Vance nods. "Yes, but there was no way to know how I would turn out. Ken had his shit together, and I didn't. Period."

"Until he started getting shit-faced every night." My anger starts building again. I feel as if I will never escape this anger as the sharp sting of betrayal cuts through me. I spent my childhood with a fucking drunk while Vance was living the high life.

"That was another one of my fuckups," says this man who I was so sure for so long that I knew, that I really *knew*. "I went through a lot of shit after you were born, but I enrolled in university and loved your mum from afar . . ."

"Until?"

"Until you were about five years old. It was your birthday, and we were all there for your party. You came running into the kitchen, yelling for your daddy—" Vance's voice cracks, and I ball my fist tighter. "You had a book clutched to your chest, and for a second I forgot that you weren't talking about me."

I slam my fist on the dashboard. "Let me out of the car," I demand. I can't listen to this anymore. This is so fucked-up. It's too much for me to comprehend at once.

Vance ignores my outburst and keeps driving along this residential street. "I lost it that day. I demanded that your mum tell Ken the truth. I was sick of watching you grow up, and by then I had already secured my plans to move to America. I begged her to come with me, and to bring you, my son."

My son.

My stomach lurches. I should just jump out of the car, moving or not. I look out at the pleasant little houses we travel past, thinking I will take physical pain over this any day.

"But she refused and told me that she had some testing done and . . . and that you weren't my child after all."

"What?" I reach up to rub my temples. I would crack the dashboard with my skull if I thought it would help.

I look over at him and see him looking left and right quickly. Then I notice the speed we're traveling at and realize that he's running every stoplight and stop sign, trying to make sure I don't jump out. "She panicked, I guess. I don't know." He eyes me. "I knew she was lying—she admitted there were no tests many years later. But at the time, she was adamant; she told me to leave it alone and apologized for making me think you were mine."

I focus on my fist. Flex, release. Flex, release . . .

"Another year went by, and we began speaking again . . ." he starts, but something is off in his tone.

"You mean *fucking* again."

Another hard exhale escapes his mouth. "Yes . . . every time we were near one another, we made the same mistake. Ken was working a lot, studying for his master's by that point, and she was home with you. You were always so much like me; every time I came over, you had your face buried between pages. I don't know if you remember, but I would always bring books to you. I gave you my copy of *The Great Gats*—"

"Stop." I cringe at the adoration in his voice while distorted memories fog my mind.

"We kept this going on and off for years, and we thought everyone was oblivious. It was my fault; I could never stop loving her. No matter what I did, she haunted me. I moved closer to their house, directly across the street. Your father knew; I don't know how he knew, but it became clear that he did." After a pause and a turn down another street, Vance adds, "He started drinking then."

I sit up, slamming my palms against the dashboard. He doesn't even flinch. "So you left me with an alcoholic father who was only an alcoholic because of you and my mum?" The anger in my voice fills the car, but I can barely breathe.

"I tried to convince her, Hardin. I don't want you blaming her, but I tried to tell her to bring you to live with me—but she wouldn't." His hands run over his hair, and he tugs at the roots. "His drinking became heavier and more frequent every week, but she still wouldn't admit that you were mine—not even to me—so I left. I had to leave."

He stops talking, and when I look over at him, his eyes are blinking rapidly. I reach for the door handle, but he accelerates and presses the power locks several times in a row, the *click-click-click* seeming to echo around the car.

Vance's voice is hollow when he starts talking again. "I moved to America, and I didn't hear from your mum for years, not until Ken finally left her. She had no money and was working herself to the bone. I had already started bringing in money, not nearly as much as I have now, but enough to spare. I came back here and got a place for us, the three of us, and I took care of her in his absence, but she grew more and more distant from me. Ken sent divorce papers from wherever the hell he'd run off to, and still she didn't want anything permanent from me." Vance frowns. "After all I did, I still wasn't enough."

I remember his taking us in after my dad left, but I never thought too much into it. I had no idea that it was because he had a history with my mum, or that I could be his son. My already tattered view of my mum is completely shredded now. I've lost all respect for her.

"So when she moved back into that house, I still took care of both of you financially, but I went back to America. Your mum started returning my checks each month and wouldn't answer my calls, so I started to assume that she'd found someone else."

"She didn't. She just spent every hour of every day working." My teenage years were lonely at home; that's why I found company with the wrong crowd.

"I think she was waiting for him to come back," Vance says quickly, then pauses. "But he never did. He stayed a drunk year after year until something made him finally decide he had had enough. I didn't talk to him for years until he contacted me when he moved to the States. He was sober, and I had just lost Rose.

"Rose was the first woman since your mum that I could look at and not see Trish's face. She was the sweetest woman, and she made me happy. I knew I would never love anyone as bright as I did your mum, but I was content with Rose. We were happy, and I was building a life with her, but I've been damned . . . and she grew sick. She gave birth to Smith, and I lost her . . ."

I gape at the thought. "Smith." I've been too busy trying to put the fucked-up pieces together to even think about the boy. What does this mean? *Fuck.*

"I thought of that little genius as my second chance to be a father. He made me whole again after his mother died. I was always reminded of you as a boy; he looks just like you did when you were young, only with lighter hair and eyes."

I remember Tessa claiming the same thing after we met the

kid, but I don't see it. "This is . . . this is fucked-up" is all I can think to say. My phone vibrates in my pocket, but I just look at my leg, like it's some phantom sensation, and I can't seem to move myself to answer the call.

"I know it is, and I'm sorry. When you moved to America, I thought I would be able to be close with you without being a father figure. I stayed in contact with your mum, hired you on at Vance, and tried to grow as close to you as you would let me. I repaired my relationship with Ken, even though there will always be hostility. I think he pitied me after I lost my wife, and by that point he had changed so much. I only wanted to be close to you—I would take anything I could get. I know you hate me now, but I would like to think I accomplished that for a little while at least."

"You've been lying to me my entire life."

"I know."

"So have my mum and my . . . Ken."

"Your mum is still in denial," Vance says—another excuse for her. "She will barely admit it even now. And as for Ken, he always had his suspicions, but your mum has never confirmed it. I believe that he still focuses on the slight chance that you are his son."

I roll my eyes at the absurdity of what he's said. "You're telling me that Ken Scott is stupid enough to believe that I'm his child after all the years of you two fucking around behind his back?"

"No." Stopping the car at the side of the road, he puts it in park and looks over at me, serious and intense. "Ken is *not* stupid. He's hopeful. He loved you—he still loves you—and you are the only reason he stopped drinking and went back to finish his degree. Even though he knew the possibility was there, he still did all of that for you. He regrets all the hell he put you through and all the shit that happened to your mum."

I flinch as the images haunting my nightmares flow behind

my eyes. As I relive what those drunken soldiers did to her all those many years ago.

"There wasn't any testing done? How do you know you're even my father?" I can't believe this question is being asked.

"I know it. You know it, too. Everyone always said how much you looked like Ken, but I know it's my blood that runs through your veins. The timeline doesn't add up for him to be your father. There is no way that she was pregnant by him."

I focus on the trees outside, and my phone starts to buzz again. "Why now? Why are you telling me this now?" I ask, my voice rising, my barely existent patience evaporating.

"Because your mum has grown paranoid. Ken mentioned something to me two weeks ago, asking you to get some blood testing done to help Karen, and I brought it up to your mum—"

"Testing for what? What does Karen have to do with any of this?"

Vance glances down at my leg, then at his own cell phone resting on the middle console. "You should answer that. Kimberly is calling me as well."

But I shake my head. I'll call Tessa as soon as I'm out of this car.

"I really am sorry for all of this. I don't know what the hell I was thinking, going to her house last night. She called me, and I just . . . I don't know. Kimberly is to be my wife. I love her more than anything—even more than I ever loved your mum. It's a different type of love; it's reciprocated, and she is everything to me. I made a huge mistake seeing your mum again, and I will spend my life making up for that. I won't be surprised if Kim leaves me."

Oh, spare me the sad-sack act. "Yeah, Captain Obvious. You probably *shouldn't* have been trying to fuck my mum on the counter."

He glares at me. "She sounded *panicked* and she said she wanted to make sure her past was in the past before her wedding, and I'm a poster boy for terrible decisions." He taps his fingers on the steering wheel, shame clear in his voice.

"So am I," I mumble to myself, and reach for the door handle.

He reaches for my arm. "Hardin."

"Don't." I pull my arm away and get out of the car. I need time to process all of this shit. I've just been bombarded with too many answers to questions I never even knew to ask. I need to breathe, I need to calm down, I need to get away from him and get to my girl, my salvation.

"I need you to get away from me. We both know that," I tell him when he doesn't move his car. He stares at me momentarily, then nods, leaving me on the street.

I look around the street and notice a familiar storefront halfway down the block, meaning I'm only blocks from my mum's house. My blood is pounding behind my ears as I reach into my pocket to call Tess. I need to hear her voice, I need her to bring me back to reality.

As I watch the building, waiting for her to answer, my demons battle inside me, pulling me into the comfortable darkness. The pull is stronger and deeper with each unanswered ring, and soon I find my feet carrying me across the street.

Pushing my phone back into my pocket, I open the door and walk into the familiar scenery of my past.

chapter three

TESSA

Broken glass crunches under my feet as I shift side to side, waiting patiently. Or as close to patiently as I can manage.

At last, when Mike is done talking to the police, I go up to him. "Where *is* he?" I ask, and not nicely.

"He left with Christian Vance." Mike's eyes are void of all emotion. His look makes me calm down a bit, recognize that this isn't his fault. This is his wedding day, and it's been ruined.

I look around at the broken wood and ignore the whispers coming from the nosy onlookers. My stomach is in knots, and I try to hold myself together. "Where did they go?"

"I don't know." He buries his head in his hands.

Kimberly taps my shoulder. "Look, when the police are done with those guys, if we stick around, they might want to talk to you, too."

I glance back and forth between the door and Mike. I nod, then follow Kimberly outside to prevent drawing any of the cops' attention to me.

"Can you try Christian again? I'm sorry, I just need to talk to Hardin." I shiver in the chill air.

"I'll try again," she promises, and we walk across the parking lot to her rental car.

A slow, sinking feeling sets in my stomach as I watch yet another police officer enter the swanky bar. I'm terrified for Hardin, not because of the police, but because I'm afraid of how he will handle all this when he's alone with Christian.

I see Smith sitting quietly in the backseat of the car and lean my elbows onto the trunk and close my eyes.

"What do you mean, you don't know?" Kimberly shouts, breaking me out of my thoughts. "*We'll* find him!" she snaps and ends the call.

"What's happening?" My heart is pounding so loud that I'm afraid I won't hear her answer.

"Hardin got out of the car and Christian lost track of him." She gathers her hair and pulls it into a ponytail. "It's almost time for that damn wedding," she says, looking toward the door of the bar where Mike stands, alone.

"This is a disaster," I groan, sending a silent prayer that Hardin is on his way back here.

I grab my phone again, and some of the panic decreases when I see his name on the missed-call list. With shaking hands, I dial him back and wait. And wait. And get no answer. I call back again and again, only to get his voicemail each time.

chapter four

HARDIN

Jack and Coke," I bark.

The bald bartender glares at me as he pulls an empty glass from the rack and fills it with ice. Too bad I didn't think to invite Vance; we could have shared a father-son drink.

Fuck, this is all so fucked-up. "Double, actually," I modify the order.

"Got it," the big man sarcastically responds. My eyes find the old television on the wall, and I read the captions on the bottom of the screen. The commercial is for an insurance company, and the screen is covered by a giggling baby. Why they choose to put babies in every damn commercial, I will never know.

The bartender wordlessly slides my drink across the wooden bar just as the baby makes a sound that's presumably supposed to be even more "adorable" than giggling, and I bring the glass to my lips, allowing my mind to take me far away from here.

"WHY DID YOU BRING HOME baby products?" I had asked.

She sat down on the edge of the bathtub and pulled her hair into a ponytail. I started to worry if she had an obsession with children—it sure as hell seemed like it.

"It's not a baby product," Tessa had said and laughed. "It just has a baby and a father printed on the package."

"I really don't understand the appeal there." I lifted the box of shaving products Tessa had brought home for me, examining the chubby cheeks of a baby and wondering what the hell a baby has to do with a shaving kit.

She shrugged. "I don't really get it either, but I'm sure putting a baby's image on it will help with sales."

"Maybe for women buying their boyfriend's or husband's shit," I corrected her. No man in his right mind would've grabbed that thing off the shelf.

"No, I'm sure fathers would buy it, too."

"Sure." I had ripped open the box and laid the contents out in front of me, then made eye contact with her through the mirror. "A bowl?"

"Yes, it's for the cream. You'll get a better shave if you use the brush."

"And how do you know that?" I raised a brow at her, hoping she didn't know this from experience with Noah.

Her smile was wide. "I looked it up!"

"Of course you did." My jealousy disappeared, and she playfully kicked her feet at me. "Since you seem to be an expert in the art of shaving, come help me."

I had always just used a simple razor and cream, but since she had clearly put thought into this, I wouldn't deny her. And, frankly, the blooming idea of her shaving my face was a major fucking turn-on. Tessa smiled and got to her feet, joining me in front of the sink. She picked up the tube of cream and filled the bowl before swirling the brush around to create a lather.

"Here." She smiled, handing me the brush.

"No, you do it." I placed the brush back into her hand and wrapped my hands around her waist. "Up you go." I lifted her onto the sink. Once she was settled, I pushed her thighs apart and stood between them.

Her expression was cautious but concentrated as she dipped the brush into the lather and swiped it across my jaw.

"I don't really want to go anywhere tonight," I told her. "I have so much work to do. You've been distracting me." Grabbing a handful of her tits, I squeezed gently.

Her hand jerked, flinging some of the shaving cream onto my neck.

"Good thing the razor wasn't in your hand," I joked.

"Good thing," she mocked, and picked up the brand-new razor. Then she chewed at her full lips and asked, "Are you sure you want me to do it? I'm nervous that I'll cut you by accident."

"Stop worrying." I smirked. "I'm sure you researched this part online, anyway,"

Her tongue peeked out in a childish way, and I leaned forward to kiss her before she began. She didn't say anything, because I was right.

"But know that if you cut me, you should definitely run." I laughed.

She scowled again. "Stay still, please." Her hand was slightly shaky, but quickly grew steady as she gently dragged the razor across my jawline.

"You should just go without me," I said and closed my eyes. Tessa's shaving my face was somehow comforting and surprisingly calming. I didn't feel like going to my father's house for dinner, but Tessa was going stir-crazy being in the apartment all the time, so when Karen had called to invite us, she'd jumped at the request.

"If we stay in tonight, then I want to reschedule and go this weekend. Will you have your work done by then?"

"I guess so . . ." I complained.

"You can call and tell them, then. I'll start dinner after this, and you can work." She tapped my top lip with her finger, signaling for me to tuck my lips in, and she carefully shaved around my mouth.

When she was finished, I said, "You should drink the rest of that wine in the fridge, because the cork has been off for days now. It's going to be vinegar soon."

"I . . . I don't know." She hesitated. I knew why. I opened my eyes, and she reached behind her back to turn the faucet on and wet a towel.

"Tess"—I pressed my fingers under her chin—"you can drink in front of me. I'm not some struggling alcoholic."

"I know, but I don't want it to be weird for you. I don't really need to be drinking so much wine anyway. If you aren't drinking, I don't need to."

"My problem isn't drinking. It's only when I'm pissed-off and drink—that's when there's a problem."

"I know." She gulped.

She did know.

She dragged the warm towel across my face, wiping the excess shaving cream away.

"I'm only an asshole when I drink to try to solve shit, and lately there hasn't been anything to solve, so I'm fine." Even I knew that wasn't an ironclad guarantee. "I don't want to be one of those geezers like my father who drink themselves stupid and endanger the people around me. And since you happen to be about the only person I give a fuck about, I don't want to drink around you anymore."

"I love you," she'd simply replied.

"And I love you."

Breaking the oh-so-serious air of the moment, and because I didn't want to go down this road any further, I stared down at her body perched on the sink. She was wearing one of my white T-shirts, with nothing but black panties underneath.

"I may have to keep you around now that you can properly shave my face. You cook, you clean . . ."

She swatted at me and rolled her eyes. "And what do I get out of this deal? You are messy; you only help me cook once a week, if that. You are grumpy in the morning—"

I cut her off by placing my hand between her legs and pushing her panties to the side.

"I guess you are good at something." She'd grinned as I slid one finger inside her.

"Only one thing?" I added another, and she groaned, her head rolling back.

THE BARTENDER'S HAND thumps against the counter in front of me. "I *said*, 'Do you want another drink?'"

I blink a few times and look down at the bar, then up at him.

"Yeah." I hand the glass over, the memory fading as I wait for my refill. "Another double."

As the old, bald bastard heads down the bar, I hear a woman's voice say with surprise, "Hardin? Hardin Scott?"

I turn my head to see the somewhat familiar face of Judy Welch, my mum's old friend. Well, ex-friend. "Yeah." I nod, noticing that age hasn't been kind to her.

"Holy hell! It's been, what . . . six years? Seven? Are you here alone?" She puts her hand on my shoulder and lifts herself onto the barstool next to me.

"Yeah, around that, and, yes, I'm here alone. My mum won't be chasing after you."

Judy has the unhappy face of a woman who's drunk way too much in her lifetime. Her hair is the same white blond that it was when I was a teenager, and her implants look too large for her small frame. I remember the first time she touched me. I felt like a man—fucking my mum's friend. And now, looking at her, I wouldn't fuck her with the bald bartender's dick.

She winks at me. "You have definitely grown up."

My drink is placed in front of me, and I gulp it down within seconds.

"Talkative as ever." She pats my shoulder again, calling out her drink order to the bartender. Then she turns to me. "Here to drown your sorrows? Love problems?"

"Neither." I roll my glass between my fingers, listening to the ice clink against the glass.

"Well, I'm here to drown out a lot of both. So let's you and I have a shot," Judy says with a smile I remember from deep in the past and orders the two of us a round of cheap whiskey.

chapter five

TESSA

Kimberly curses Christian out so bad over the phone that afterward she has to stop and catch her breath. She reaches a hand out to my shoulder. "Hopefully Hardin's just walking around to clear his head. Christian said he was giving him space." She groans in disapproval.

But I know Hardin, and I know that he doesn't just "clear his head" by walking around. I try to reach him again, but I'm immediately met with his voicemail. He has turned his phone off completely.

"Do you think he would go to the wedding?" Kim looks at me. "You know, to cause a scene?"

I want to tell her that he wouldn't do that, but with the weight of all of this pressing on him, I can't deny it's a possibility.

"I can't believe I'm even suggesting this," Kimberly says delicately. "But maybe you should come to the wedding after all—at least to make sure he doesn't interrupt? Plus, it's likely that he's trying to find you anyway, and if nobody's on their phones, that's probably where he will look first."

The idea of Hardin's showing up to the church and causing a scene makes me nauseous. But selfishly I hope that he does go there, otherwise I will have almost no chance of finding him. That he has turned his phone off makes me worry if he *wants* to be found.

"I guess so. Maybe I should go and just stay outside, out front?" I suggest.

Kimberly nods sympathetically, but her expression hardens when a sleek black BMW pulls into the lot, parking next to Kimberly's rental.

Christian steps out, dressed in a suit. "Any word from him?" he asks as he approaches. He leans in to kiss Kimberly on her cheek—a gesture of habit, I suppose—but she pulls away before his lips can touch her skin.

"I'm sorry," I hear him whisper to her.

She shakes her head and turns her attention to me. My heart aches for her; she doesn't deserve such a betrayal. I guess that's the thing about betrayal, though: it holds no prejudice and preys on those who neither see it coming nor deserve it.

"Tessa's coming with and is going to watch out for Hardin at the wedding," she begins to explain. Then she meets Christian's eyes. "So that while we're all inside, she can make sure nothing else interrupts this precious day." The venom in her tone is clear, but she remains calm.

Christian shakes his head at his fiancée. "We aren't going to that damn wedding. Not after all this shit."

"Why not?" Kimberly asks with dead eyes.

"Because this"—Vance gestures back and forth between the two of us—"and because both of my sons are more important than any wedding, especially this one. I don't expect you to sit there with a smile in the same room as her."

Kimberly looks surprised, but at least partially placated by his words. I watch and keep quiet. Christian's referral to Hardin and Smith as his "sons" for the first time has rattled me. There are so many things I could say to this man—so many hateful words I desperately want to sling at him—but I know I shouldn't. It won't help anything, and my focus needs to stay on figuring out Hardin's whereabouts and how he is handling the news.

"People will talk. Especially Sasha." Kimberly scowls.

"I don't give a shit about Sasha or Max, or anyone. Let them talk. We live in Seattle, not Hampstead." He reaches for her hands, and she lets him gather them between his. "Fixing my mistakes is the only priority I have right now," he says, his voice shaky. The cold anger I feel toward him begins to melt, but only slightly.

"You shouldn't have let Hardin out of the car," Kimberly says, her hands still in Christian's.

"I couldn't exactly stop him. You know Hardin. And then my seat belt got stuck, and I couldn't tell where he went . . . goddammit!" he says, and Kimberly softly nods in agreement.

I finally sense it's time for me to speak. "Where do you think he went? If he doesn't show up at the wedding, where should I look?"

"Well, I just checked both bars I know that are open this early," Vance says with a frown. "Just in case." His expression softens when he looks at me. "I know now I shouldn't have separated him from you while I told him. It was a huge mistake, and I know that you're what he needs right now."

Unable to think of anything remotely polite to say to Vance, I give him a simple nod and pull my phone from my pocket to try Hardin yet again. I know his phone won't be on, but I have to try.

While I call, Kimberly and Christian look at each other silently, hand in hand, each searching the other's eyes for some sign. When I hang up, he looks at me and says, "The wedding is starting in twenty minutes. I can drive you there now, if you want."

Kimberly holds up a hand. "I can drive her. You take Smith and go back to the hotel."

"But—" he begins to argue, but given the look on her face, he wisely chooses not to continue. "You'll come back to the hotel, won't you?" he asks, his eyes filled with fear.

"Yes." She sighs. "I'm not going to leave the country."

Relief replaces Christian's panic, and he lets go of Kimberly's hands. "Be careful and call me if you need anything. You know the address of the church, right?"

"Yes. Give me your keys." She holds out one hand. "Smith's fallen asleep, and I don't want to wake him."

I silently applaud her strong demeanor. I would be a mess if I were her. I *am* a mess now, on the inside.

LESS THAN TEN MINUTES LATER, Kimberly drops me off in front of a small church. Most of the guests have already gone inside, leaving only a few stragglers on the outside steps. I take a seat on a bench and watch the streets for any sign of Hardin.

From where I'm sitting, I can hear the wedding march start up inside the church and picture Trish in her wedding gown, walking down the aisle to meet her groom. She's smiling and bright and beautiful.

But the Trish in my mind doesn't coincide with the mother who lies about the father of her only son.

The steps empty, and the last few guests go inside to watch Trish and Mike wed. Minutes tick by, and I can hear nearly every sound coming from inside the small building. A half hour later, the guests cheer as the bride and groom are pronounced husband and wife, which I take as my cue to leave. I don't know where I'll go, but I can't just sit here and wait. Trish will be exiting the church soon, and the last thing I need is an awkward run-in with the new bride.

I begin walking back the way we arrived, at least I think. I don't remember exactly, but it's not like I have anywhere to go. I pull out my phone again and redial Hardin, but his phone is still off. My battery is less than half-full, but I don't want to power it off, in case Hardin tries to call.

As I continue my search, aimlessly walking the neighborhood and looking inside at restaurant bars here and there, the sun begins to set in the London sky. I should have asked Kimberly to borrow one of their rentals, but I wasn't thinking clearly at the time and she has other things to worry about right now. Hardin's rental is still parked at Gabriel's, but I don't have a spare key.

The beauty and grace of Hampstead diminishes with each step I take into the other side of town. My feet are aching, and the spring air is growing colder as the sun sets. I shouldn't have worn this dress or these stupid shoes. If I had known how today was going to turn out, I would have worn workout clothes and sneakers to make it easier to chase Hardin down. In the future, if I ever leave town with him again, that will be my standard uniform.

After some time, I can't tell if my mind is playing tricks on me or if the street I've wandered onto is actually familiar. It's lined with small houses much like Trish's, but I had been drifting in and out of sleep when Hardin drove us into town, and I don't trust my mind right now. I'm thankful that the streets are mostly empty and all the residents seem to be inside for the night. Otherwise, sharing the streets with the people leaving the bars would make me even more paranoid. I nearly burst into tears of relief when I see Trish's house a little ways off. It's grown dark, but the streetlamps are on, and as I get closer, I'm increasingly positive it's her house. I don't know if Hardin will be there, but I pray that if he isn't, the door will at least be unlocked, so I can sit down and have some water. I've been walking aimlessly around block after block for hours. I'm lucky that I ended up on the only street in this village that could be of any use to me.

As I near Trish's house, a tattered glowing sign in the shape of a beer distracts me. The small bar is set in between a house and an alley. A chill runs through me. It must have been hard for Trish to stay in the same house, so close to the bar her assailants came from to find Ken. Hardin told me once that she simply couldn't afford to move. The way he shrugged it off surprised me. But, sadly, money is vicious that way.

This is where he is, I know it.

I go up to the little place, and when I pull open the iron door, I'm immediately embarrassed by my attire. I look like a complete madwoman walking into this type of bar in a dress and barefoot, my shoes in my hands. I gave up on wearing them an hour ago. I drop my heels onto the floor and slide my feet back into them, wincing at the pain of the straps rubbing against the raw patches of skin on my ankles.

The bar isn't crowded, and it doesn't take me long to scan the room and find Hardin, sitting at the bar with a glass raised to his mouth. My heart plummets to the floor. I knew I would find him this way, but my faith in him is taking a beating right now. I had hoped, with everything in me, that he wouldn't resort to drinking his pain away. I take a deep breath before approaching him.

"Hardin." I tap his shoulder.

He swivels the barstool around to face me, and my stomach turns at the sight in front of me. His eyes are bloodshot, deep, red lines mapping across them so fiercely that the white has nearly disappeared. His cheeks are flushed, and the smell of liquor is so heavy that I can taste it. My palms begin to sweat, and my mouth goes dry.

"Look who it is," he slurs. The glass in his hand is nearly empty, and I cringe at the sight of three empty shot glasses on the bar before him. "How'd you find me, anyway?" He tilts his head back and gulps down the rest of the brown liquor before calling to the man behind the bar, "Another!"

I move my face so that it's directly in front of Hardin's, so he can't look away. "Baby, are you *okay?*" I know that he isn't, but don't know how I should handle him until I can gauge his mood and how much alcohol he's consumed.

"Baby," he says mysteriously, like he's thinking about something else as he talks. But then he snaps to and gives me a killer smile. "Yeah, yeah. I'm fine. Have a seat. Want a drink? Have a drink—barkeep, *another!*"

The bartender looks at me, and I shake my head no. Not noticing that, Hardin pulls out the stool next to him and pats the seat. I glance around the small bar before climbing up onto the stool.

"So how'd you find me?" he asks again.

I'm confused and put on edge by his behavior. He's clearly drunk, but that's not what is bothering me; it's the eerie calm behind his voice. I've heard it before, and it never brings with it good things.

"I've been walking around for hours, and I recognized your mum's house across the street, so I knew . . . well, I knew I should look here." I shiver at the reminder of Hardin's stories of Ken's spending night after night at this exact bar.

"My little detective." Hardin softly says while raising a hand to tuck my hair behind my ear. I don't flinch or pull away, despite the growing anxiety bubbling inside me.

"Will you come with me? I want us to go back to that hotel for the night, and then we can leave in the morning,"

Right then, the bartender brings him his drink, and Hardin gives it a serious look. "Not yet."

"Please, Hardin." I meet his bloodshot eyes. "I'm so tired, and I know you are, too." I try to use my weakness against him without bringing up Christian or Ken. I lean closer to him. "My feet are killing me, and I've missed you. Christian tried to find you and couldn't. I've been walking for a while, and I really want to go back to the hotel. Together."

I know him well enough to be certain that if I start rambling about anything too heavy, he'll lose it and this calmness will evaporate in seconds.

"He didn't look that hard. I started drinking"—Hardin holds up his glass—"at the bar right across from where he left me."

I lean into him, and he begins talking again before I can come up with anything to say. "Have a drink. My friend is here—she'll buy you a shot." He waves a hand at the glasses on the bar. "We ran into each other at that other fine establishment, but then since it seemed like an evening from the past, I decided to bring us here. For old times' sake."

My stomach drops. "Friend?"

"An old friend of the family." He nods toward a woman emerging from the bathroom. She appears to be in her late thirties, early forties and has bleached-blond hair. I'm relieved that she isn't a young woman, since it appears that Hardin has been drinking with her for a while now.

"I really think we should go," I press, and reach for his hand.

He jerks away. "Judith, this is Theresa."

"Judy," she corrects him, at the same time that I say "Tessa."

"Nice to meet you." I force a smile and turn back to Hardin. "Please," I beg again.

"Judy knew that my mum was a whore," Hardin says, and the smell of whiskey bombards my senses again.

"I didn't say that." The woman laughs. She's dressed too young for her age. Her top is low cut, and her flared jeans are too tight.

"She did say that. My mum hates Judy!" Hardin smiles.

The strange woman returns his smile. "Wonder why?"

I begin to feel as if I'm on the outside of a private joke between them. "Why?" I ask without thinking.

Hardin gives her a warning glare and waves his hand, dismissing my question. It takes everything in me not to knock him from the barstool. If I weren't aware that he's only trying to mask his pain, I would do just that.

"Long story, doll." The woman waves for the bartender. "Anyway, you look like you could use some tequila."

"No, I'm okay." The last thing I want is a drink.

"Lighten up, baby." Hardin leans closer to me. "You aren't the one who just found out his entire life is a fucking lie, so lighten up and have a drink with me."

My heart aches for him, but drinking isn't the answer. I need to get him out of here. Now.

"Do you prefer your margaritas frozen or on the rocks? This isn't no fancy place, so you don't have many choices," Judy tells me.

"I said I didn't *want* a *fucking drink*," I snap.

Her eyes widen, but she recovers quickly. I'm almost as surprised by my outburst as she is. I hear Hardin chuckle next to me, but I keep my eyes on this woman, who clearly enjoys her secrets.

"Okay, then. Someone needs to relax." She digs her hands into her purse. She pulls out a pack of cigarettes and a lighter from the oversize bag and lights up. "Smoke?" she asks Hardin.

I look at him, and to my surprise he nods. Judy reaches behind me to hand him the lit cigarette from her mouth. Who the hell is this woman?

The disgusting stick is placed between Hardin's lips, and he takes a puff. Tendrils of smoke swirl between us, and I cover my mouth and nose.

I glare at him. "Since when do you smoke?"

"I've always smoked. Just not since I started at WCU." He takes another drag. The glowing red fire at the end of the cigarette taunts me, and I reach over and snatch it from Hardin's mouth and drop it into his half-full glass.

"*What the fuck?*" he half yells and stares down at his ruined drink.

"We are leaving. Now." I step down from the barstool, grabbing hold of Hardin's sleeve and pulling at him.

"No. We aren't." He twists away from my grip and attempts to get the bartender's attention.

"He doesn't want to leave," Judy chimes in.

My anger is boiling, and this woman is just pissing me off. I stare deep into her mocking eyes, which I can barely find through the anthill of mascara she's caked on. "I don't remember *asking* you. Mind your own business, and find a new drinking partner, because we are *leaving!*" I shout.

She looks at Hardin, expecting him to defend her—and then the sick history between the two of them comes to me. This isn't the way a "friend of the family" would behave with the son of her friend who is half her age.

"I *said* I don't want to leave," Hardin insists.

I've pulled out all the stops here, and he isn't listening. My last option is to play on his jealousy—a low blow, especially in the state he's in, but he's left me no other choice.

"Well," I say as I begin scanning the bar exaggeratedly, "if you won't take me back to the hotel, I will have to find someone else to do it." My eyes settle on the youngest man in the place, who is at a table with his friends. I give Hardin a few seconds to respond, and when he doesn't, I begin walking toward the group of young men.

Hardin's hand is around my arm in mere seconds. "Hell no, you won't."

I spin around, taking note of the barstool he's knocked over in his haste to reach me, and Judy's ridiculously uncoordinated attempts to get it back upright.

"Then take me back," I reply with a tilt of my head.

"I'm wasted," he says, as if that justifies this whole scene.

"I know. We can call a cab to take us to Gabriel's, and I'll drive the rental to the hotel." Inside I say a little prayer that this ruse will work.

Hardin squints at me for a second. "You've got it all figured out, don't you?" he mumbles sarcastically.

"No, but staying here isn't doing a bit of good, so either you go pay for your drinks and take me out of here, or I will leave with someone else."

He releases his light grip on my arm and steps close. "Don't you threaten me. I could just as easily leave with someone else," he says, only inches from my face.

A sting of jealousy pains me, but I ignore it. "Go ahead. Go home with Judy, then. I know you slept with her before. I can tell." I keep my back straight and my voice steady as I challenge him.

He looks at me, then to her, and smiles a little. I flinch, and he frowns. "It wasn't anything too impressive. I barely remember it." He's attempting to make me feel better, but his words have the opposite effect.

"Well? What's it going to be?" I raise my brow.

"Damn it," he grumbles, then half stumbles back to the bar to pay for his drinks. It looks like he just empties his pockets on the bar, and after the bartender extracts some bills, he shoves the rest in Judy's direction. She looks at him and then over at me, sinking a little as if something has deflated her spine.

As we exit the bar, Hardin says, "Judy says bye," and it makes me want to explode.

"Don't talk to me about her," I snap.

"Are you jealous, Theresa?" he slurs, wrapping his arm around me. "Fuck, I hate this place, this bar, that house." He gestures toward the small house across the street. "Oh! You want to know something funny? Vance lived there." Hardin points to the brick house directly next to the bar. A dim light is on upstairs, and a car is parked in the driveway. "I wonder what he was doing the night that those men came into our fucking house." Hardin's eyes scan the ground, and he bends down. Before I realize what's happening, his arm is raised behind his head, a brick in his hand.

"Hardin, no!" I yell and grab his arm. The brick falls to the ground and skids across the concrete.

"Fuck this." He tries to reach for it, but I stand in front of him. *"Fuck all of this! Fuck this street! Fuck this bar and that fucking house! Fuck everyone!"*

He stumbles again and walks into the street. "If you won't let me destroy that house . . ." His voice trails off, and I pull my shoes from my feet and follow him across the street and into the front yard of his childhood home.

chapter six

TESSA

I trip over my bare feet while rushing behind Hardin into the front yard of the house where he spent his painful childhood. One of my knees lands on the grass, but I quickly steady myself and get back on my feet. The front screen door is pulled open, and I hear Hardin fumbling with the doorknob for a moment before he pounds his fist against the wood in frustration.

"Hardin, please. Let's just go to the hotel," I try to convince him as I approach.

Ignoring my presence completely, he bends down to grab something from beside the porch. I assume it's a spare key but am quickly proven wrong when a fist-size rock is pushed through the glass pane on the center of the door. Hardin snakes his arm through, thankfully avoiding the sharp ridges of the broken glass, and unlocks the door.

I look around the quiet street, but nothing seems amiss. No one is outside to notice our disruption, and no lights have flickered on at the sound of the breaking glass. I pray that Trish and Mike aren't staying next door at Mike's house tonight, that they've gone off to some fancy hotel for the night, given that neither of them are well-off enough to go on an extravagant honeymoon.

"*Hardin.*" I'm walking on water here, trying my hardest to keep from sinking under. One slipup, and we both will drown.

"This fucking house has been nothing but a tormentor of mine," he grumbles, stumbling over his boots. He catches himself on the arm of a small couch before he falls. I survey the living room, and I'm grateful that most of the furnishings have been packed into boxes or have already been removed from the house in preparation for the demolition following Trish's move.

He narrows his eyes and focuses on the couch. "This couch here"—he presses his fingers against his forehead before finishing—"that's where it happened, you know? That exact same fucking couch."

I knew he wasn't in his head, but his saying that confirms it. I remember him telling me months ago that he'd destroyed that couch—"the piece of shit was easy to shred," he bragged.

I look at the couch before us, the newness of it evident by the stiff cushions and unmarked fabric. My stomach turns. Both over the memory and the thought of what this mood of Hardin's is building up to.

His eyes close momentarily. "Maybe one of my fucking fathers could have thought to buy a new one."

"I'm so sorry. I know this is so much for you right now." I try to comfort him, but he continues to ignore me.

He opens his eyes and walks into the kitchen, and I follow a few feet behind. "Where is it . . ." he mumbles and drops to his knees to look inside the cabinet under the kitchen sink. "Gotcha." He holds up a bottle of clear liquor. I don't want to ask whose liquor it was—or is—and how it got there in the first place. Given the thin layer of dust that appears on Hardin's black T-shirt when he rubs the bottle against the fabric, I'd say it's been hiding in there for at least a few months.

I follow him as he returns to the living room, unsure of what he will do next.

"I know you're upset and you are completely justified to be angry." I stand in front of him in a desperate attempt to gain his attention. He refuses to even glance down at me. "But can we *please* go back to the hotel?" I reach for his hand, but he pulls away. "We can talk, and you can sober up, please. Or you can go to sleep, whatever you want, but please, we need to leave here."

Hardin ducks around me and walks to the couch, pointing. "She was here . . ." He points to the couch with the bottle of liquor. My eyes prick with tears, but I swallow them down. "And no one came to fucking stop it. Neither of those fuckups." He spits and twists the top off the full bottle. He presses the bottle to his lips and tips his head back, gulping the liquor down.

"Enough!" I shout, stepping closer to him. I'm fully prepared to yank that bottle right from his hands and shatter it against the kitchen tile. Anything so he doesn't drink it. I don't know how much more alcohol his body can stand before he passes out.

Hardin takes another swig before stopping. He uses the back of his hand to wipe the excess liquor from his mouth and chin. He grins and looks at me for the first time since we entered this house. "Why? You want some?"

"No—*yes*, actually, I do," I lie.

"Too bad, Tessie. There isn't enough to share," he slurs, holding up the large bottle. I cringe at the use of my father's nickname for me. It has to be over a liter of whatever liquor it is; the label is worn and half-torn. I wonder how long ago he hid it there—was it during those worst eleven days of my entire life? "I bet you're loving this."

I take a step back and try to think of a plan of action. I don't have many options right now, and I'm becoming a little frightened. I know he would never physically hurt me, but I don't know how he'll treat himself—and I'm not emotionally prepared for another lashing from him. I've gotten too used to the somewhat controlled Hardin that I have been graced with lately: sarcastic and moody, but no longer hateful. The gleam in his bloodshot eyes is all too familiar to me, and I can see the malice brewing behind them.

"Why would I be loving this? I hate seeing you this way. I never want you to be hurting like this, Hardin."

He smiles and softly chuckles before lifting the bottle and pouring some liquor onto the couch cushions. "Did you know that rum is one of the most flammable of spirits?" he says darkly.

My blood runs cold. "Hardin, I—"

"This rum here is one hundred proof. That's pretty damn high." His voice is hazy, slow, and frightening as he continues to douse the couch.

"Hardin!" I exclaim, my voice growing louder. "What are you going to do then? Burn the house down? That isn't going to change anything!"

Waving a dismissive hand toward me, he sneers, "You should go. No kids allowed."

"Don't talk to me like that!" Feeling brave, and slightly afraid, I reach for the bottle and grip the handle.

Hardin's nostrils flare and he tries to loosen my grip. "Let go of it. Now," he says through his teeth.

"No."

"Tessa, don't push me."

"What are you going to do, Hardin? Fight me over a bottle of alcohol?"

His eyes go wide; his mouth opens in surprise when he looks at both of our hands playing tug-of-war.

"Give me the bottle," I demand, tightening my grip on the handle of the large bottle. It's heavy, and Hardin isn't making it any easier, but my adrenaline is pumping, giving me the strength I need. Cursing under his breath, he pulls his hand away. I didn't expect him to give in that easily, so as his weight is removed, the bottle slips from my hand and topples to the floor in front of us, spilling onto aged wood.

I reach for it as I suggest the opposite: "Leave it there."

"I don't see the big deal here." He grabs the bottle before I can and pours more liquor onto the couch, then walks in a circle around the room, leaving a trail of flammable rum behind him. "This shithole is going to be demolished anyway. I'm doing the new owners a favor." He looks at me and shrugs playfully. "This is probably cheaper anyway."

I slowly turn away from Hardin and reach into my purse to find my phone. The battery warning symbol is flashing, but I pull up the only number that could possibly help us at this point. Keeping the phone in my hand, I turn back to Hardin. "The police will come to your mother's house if you do this. You will get arrested, Hardin." I pray that the person on the line can hear me.

"Don't give a fuck," he mumbles, his jaw clenched. He looks down at the couch, his eyes piercing the present to stare into the past. "I can still hear her screaming. Her cries sounded like a wounded fucking animal. Do you know what that sounds like to a little boy?"

My heart aches for Hardin, for both versions of him—the innocent little boy who was forced to watch his mother beaten and violated, and the angry, hurt man who feels like his only recourse is to burn down the entire house to rid himself of the memory.

"You don't want to go to jail, do you? Where would I go? I would be stranded." I don't give a damn about myself, but hope that the idea will make him reconsider his actions.

My beautiful dark prince stares at me for a moment, my words seeming to have rattled him. "Call a cab now. Walk down to the end of the street. I'll make sure you're gone before I do anything." His voice is clearer now than it should be, considering the amount of alcohol in his blood. But all I hear is him trying to give up on himself.

"I don't have any way to pay for a cab." I make a show of digging out my wallet and showing him my American currency.

His eyes pinch closed, and he chucks the bottle against the

wall. It shatters, but I barely flinch. I've seen and heard this too many times in the last seven months to be shaken by it.

"Take my goddamn wallet and *get. Out. Fuck!*" In one swift motion he pulls his wallet from his back pocket and tosses it onto the floor before me.

I bend down and shove it into my purse. "No. I need you to come with me," I say softly.

"You are so perfect . . . you know that, right?" He takes a step toward me and lifts his hand to cup my cheek. I flinch at the contact, and a deep frown sets on his beautifully tormented face. "Don't you know that? That you are perfect." His hand is hot against my cheek, and his thumb begins to move across the skin.

I can feel my lips trembling but I keep a straight face. "No. I'm not perfect, Hardin. No one is," I quietly reply, my eyes staring into his.

"You are. You're too perfect for me."

I want to cry—*are we back to this?* "I'm not going to let you push me away. I know what you're doing: you're drunk, and you are trying to justify this by comparing us. I'm just as fucked-up as you."

"Don't talk like that." He frowns again. His other hand moves up to my jaw and pushes into my hair. "It doesn't sound right, coming from that beautiful mouth." His thumb runs along my bottom lip, and I can't help but notice the contrast between the way his eyes burn with dark pain and rage and his light and gentle touch.

"I love you, and I'm not going anywhere," I say, praying to break through his drunken haze. I search his eyes for any hint of my Hardin.

" 'If two people love each other, there can be no happy end to it,' " he softly replies.

Instantly recognizing the words, I tear my eyes from his.

"Don't quote Hemingway to me," I snap. *Did he think I wouldn't recognize it and know what he was trying to do?*

"It's true, though. There's no happy ending—not for me, anyway. I'm too fucked-up." He drops his hands from my face and turns away from me.

"No, you aren't! You—"

"Why do you do that?" he slurs, his body swaying back and forth. "Why do you always try to find the light in me? Wake up, Tessa! *There isn't any fucking light!*" he screams, and slams both of his hands against his chest.

"I'm nothing! I'm a fucked-up piece of shit with fucked-up parents and a fucked-up head! I tried to warn you, I tried to push you away before I destroyed you . . ." His voice gets lower, and he reaches into his pocket. I recognize the purple lighter as Judy's from the bar.

Hardin doesn't look at me as he strikes the flame.

"My parents are messed up, too! My father is in rehab, for God's sake!" I shout back at him.

I knew this would happen—I knew Christian's confession would be Hardin's breaking point. One person can only handle so much, and Hardin was already so fragile.

"This is your last chance to go before this place burns to the ground," he says without looking at me.

"You'd burn down the house with me in it?" I choke out. I'm crying now, but I don't remember when I started.

"No." His boots are so loud as he crosses the room; my head is spinning, my heart is aching, and I'm afraid I've lost my sense of reality. "Come on." He lifts his hand to me, asking me to take it.

"Give me the lighter."

"Come here." He holds both arms to me. I'm full-on sobbing now. "Please."

I force myself to ignore his familiar beckoning, no matter how much it hurts to do so. I want to run into his arms and take him away from here. But this is no Austen novel with a happy ending and good intentions; this is a Hemingway at best, and I can see right through his gesture. "Give me the lighter, and we can leave together."

"You almost had me believing that I could be normal." The lighter still rests dangerously in his palm.

"No one is!" I cry. "No one is normal—I don't want you to be. I love you now, I love you and all of this!" I look around the living room and back to Hardin.

"You couldn't. No one would, or ever has. Not even my own mum."

As the words leave his lips, the sound of the door slamming against the wall makes me jump. I look toward the noise, and relief floods through me when Christian rushes into the living room. He's out of breath and panicked. He stops in his tracks when he takes in the state of the small room, liquor covering nearly every inch.

"What—" Christian's eyes narrow at the lighter in Hardin's hand. "I heard sirens on my way here. We need to leave, *now!*" he shouts.

"How did you . . ." Hardin looks back and forth between Christian and me. "You called him?"

"Of course she did! What was she going to do? Let you burn the house down and get yourself arrested?" Christian yells.

Hardin throws his hands in the air, still holding that lighter. "Get the fuck out! Both of you!"

Christian turns to me. "Tessa, go outside."

But I stand my ground. "No, I'm not leaving him in here." Has Christian not learned that Hardin and I shouldn't be separated?

"Go," Hardin says, taking a step toward me. He flicks his thumb across the metal of the lighter, igniting the flame. "Take her outside," he slurs.

"My car is parked in the alley across the street—go to it and wait for us," Christian instructs. When I look at Hardin, his eyes are set on the white flame, and I know him well enough to know that he's going to do this whether I leave or not. He's too intoxicated and too upset to stop now.

A cold set of keys is placed into my hand, and Christian leans in close. "I'm not going to let anything happen to him."

After a moment of internal battle, I wrap my fingers around the keys and walk out the front door without looking back. I run across the street and pray that the sirens in the distance have another destination in mind.

chapter seven

HARDIN

As soon as Tessa runs out the front door, Vance starts waving his hands in front of him and yelling, "Go ahead! Go ahead! Go ahead!"

What is he talking about—and why the fuck is he even here? I hate Tessa for calling him. I take that back; I could never hate her, but, *fuck*, she pisses me off.

"No one wants you here," I say, my mouth numb as I speak to this man.

My eyes are burning. *Where is Tessa? Did she leave?* I thought she did, but now I'm confused. *How long ago did she come here? Was she even here to begin with? I don't know.*

"Light the fire."

"Why? You want me to burn with the house?" I ask. A younger version of him leaning against the mantel at my mum's house fills my mind. He was reading to me. "Why was he reading to me?"

Did I say that out loud? I have no fucking idea. Present-day Vance stares at me, expecting something.

"All your mistakes would be gone if I were, too." The metal on the lighter burns the rough skin on my thumb, but I continue to flick the lighter.

"No, I want you to burn the house down. Maybe then you can have some peace."

I think he may be yelling at me, but I can barely see straight, let alone measure the volume of his voice. He's actually giving me his permission to burn this shit down?

Who said I need fucking permission?

"Who are you to give me the okay? I didn't fucking *ask* you!" I lower the flame down to the arm of the couch and wait for it to catch. I wait for the all-consuming fire to destroy this place.

Nothing happens.

"I'm a real piece of work, yeah?" I say to the man who claims to be my father.

"That's not going to work," he says. Or maybe I'm the one speaking—hell if I know.

I reach for an old magazine lying on top of one of the boxes and bring the flame to the corner of the pages. It ignites immediately. I watch the fire travel up the pages and toss the burning magazine onto the couch. I'm impressed by how quickly the fire swallows the couch, and I swear I can feel the fucking memories burning along with the piece of shit.

The trail of rum is next—it's burning in a twisted line. My eyes can barely keep up with the flames as they dance across the floorboards, flicking and cracking, making the most comforting sounds. The colors are bright, fucking mad and they angrily attack the rest of the room.

Over the sound of the flames, Vance shouts, "Are you *satis-fied*?"

I don't know if I am.

Tessa wouldn't be, she would be sad that I destroyed the house.

"Where is she?" I ask, searching the room, which is blurry, and filling with smoke.

If she's in here and something happens to her . . .

"She's outside. She's safe," Vance assures me.

Do I trust him? I fucking hate him. This is all his fault. Is Tessa still here? Is he lying?

But then I realize Tessa is too smart for this. She'd already be gone. Away from this. Away from my destruction. And if this man had raised me, I wouldn't have become this bad a person. I wouldn't have hurt so many people, especially Tessa. I never wanted to hurt her, but I always do.

"Where were you?" I ask him. I wish the flames would grow. At their small size, the house will never burn completely. I may have stashed another bottle somewhere. I can't think clearly enough to remember. The fire doesn't feel big enough. The small flames don't match the size of my fucking anger, and I need more.

"I was at the hotel with Kimberly. Let's go before the fire department arrives, or you get yourself hurt."

"No—where were you *that night*?" The room is beginning to spin, and the heat is suffocating me.

Vance seems genuinely shocked and stops, shifting completely upright. "*What?* I wasn't even here, Hardin! I was in America. I would never let something like that happen to your mum! But, Hardin—we need to go!" he yells.

Why would we go? I want to watch this shit burn.

"Well, it happened anyway," I say, my body getting heavier and heavier. I should probably sit down, but if I have to play these images in my head, so does he. "She was beaten to a bloody fucking pulp. Each of them had their way with her, they fucked her over and over and over . . ." My chest hurts so fucking bad, I wish I could reach inside and yank everything out. Everything was easier before I met Tessa, nothing could hurt me. Even this shit wouldn't hurt me like this. I had learned to suppress it until she made me . . . she made me feel shit that I never wanted to, and now I can't seem to turn it off.

"I'm sorry! I'm so sorry that happened! I would have stopped it!"

I look up, and he's crying. *How dare he fucking cry when he didn't have to watch it*—he *didn't have to see it each time he closed his eyes to sleep, year after year after year.*

Flashing blue lights pour through the windows, scatter across all the glass in the room, interrupting my bonfire. The sirens are fucking loud—holy shit, they're loud.

"Get out!" Vance shouts. "Get out now! Go out the back door and get in my car! Go!" he screams frantically.

Fucking dramatics.

"Fuck you." I stumble; the room is spinning faster now and the sirens are piercing my ears.

Before I can stop him, his hands are on me and he's pushing my drunken body back through the living room, into the kitchen, and out through the back. I try to push back, but my muscles refuse to cooperate. The cold air hits me, making me dizzy, and then my ass lands on the concrete.

"Go to the alley and get in my car," I think he says before he disappears.

I scramble to my feet after falling over a few times and try to open the back kitchen door, but it's fucking locked. Inside I hear multiple voices, all shouting and something buzzing. *What the fuck is that?*

I pull my phone from my pocket and see Tessa's name flashing across the screen. I can either go find his car in the alley and face her, or I can go inside and get arrested. I look at her blurry face on the screen, and the decision is made for me.

I can't for the life of me figure out how the fuck I'm going to get across the street without the cops spotting me. The screen on my phone is duplicated and shifting, but somehow I manage to dial Tessa's number.

"Hardin! Are you all right?" she cries into the speaker.

"Pick me up at the end of the street, in front of the cemetery." I lift the latch on the neighbor's gate and end the call. At least I don't have to go through Mike's yard.

Did he marry my mum today? For his sake, I hope not.

"You wouldn't want her to be alone forever. I know you love her;

she's still your mother," Tessa's voice rings through my head. Great, now I'm hearing voices.

"I'm not perfect. No one is," her sweet voice reminds me. She's wrong though, she's so very wrong, and naïve, and perfect.

I manage to find myself standing at the corner of my mum's street. The cemetery behind me is dark; the only light is coming from the flashing blues in the distance. The black Beemer pulls up moments later, and Tessa stops in front of me. I climb into the car without a word, and the door is barely closed before she floors the gas pedal.

"Where should I go?" Her voice is hoarse and she's trying to stop sobbing, but she's failing miserably.

"I don't know . . . There aren't many"—my eyes are heavy— "places here, it's night and late . . . and there's nothing open . . ."

I close my eyes and everything fades away.

THE SOUND OF SIRENS startles me awake. I jump at the loud noise, and my head slams against the roof of the car.

Car? Why the fuck am I in a car?

I look over and find Tessa sitting in the driver's seat, her eyes closed and her legs curled up against her body. I'm instantly reminded of a sleepy kitten. My head is fucking killing me. I drank way too fucking much.

It's daylight, the sun is hiding behind the clouds, leaving the sky gray and dreary. The clock on the dashboard informs me that it's ten minutes until seven. I don't recognize the parking lot we are parked in, and I try to remember how the hell I got in the car in the first place.

There are no police cars or sirens now . . . I must have been dreaming them in my sleep. My head is throbbing, and when I pull my shirt up to wipe my face, the thick smell of smoke invades my nostrils.

Flickers of a burning couch and Tessa crying play through my mind. I struggle to put them together; I'm still half-drunk.

Beside me, Tessa stirs and her eyes flutter before opening. I don't know what she saw last night. I don't know what I said or did, but I do know that the way she's looking at me right now makes me wish I would have burned . . . with that house. Images of my mum's house flash through my mind.

"Tessa, I—" I don't know what to say to her; my mind isn't working and neither is my fucking mouth.

Judy's bleached hair and Christian pushing me out the back door of my mum's house fill some of the gaps in my memory.

"Are you okay?" Tessa's tone is soft and rough at the same time. I can tell she has nearly lost her voice.

She's asking me if I'm okay?

I search her face, confused by her question. "Uhm, yeah? Are you?" I may not remember most of the night . . . hell, the day or night, but I know she should be upset with me.

She nods slowly, her eyes performing the same searching that mine are.

"I'm trying to remember . . . The cops came . . ." I sift through the memories as they come. "The house was burning . . . where are we?" I look out the window, trying to figure it out.

"We are . . . well, I'm not really sure where we are." She clears her throat and looks straight ahead through the windshield. She must have been screaming a lot. Or crying, or both, because she can barely speak. "I didn't know where to go, and you fell asleep, so I just kept driving, but I was so tired. I had to pull off the road eventually." Her eyes are bloodshot and swollen; black makeup is smeared underneath them, and her lips are dry and cracked. She's barely recognizable. Still beautiful, but I've drained her.

Looking at her right now, I can see the lack of warmth in her cheeks, the loss of hope from her eyes, the missing happiness from her full lips. I took a beautiful girl who lives her life for others, a girl who always found the good in everything, even me, and turned her into a shell whose void eyes are staring back at me now.

"I'm going to be sick," I choke out and yank the passenger door open. All of the whiskey, all of the rum, and all of my mistakes splatter against the concrete, and I repeatedly vomit until I'm left with nothing but my guilt.

chapter eight

Tessa's voice comes through soft and raspy in the gaps between my harsh breathing: "Where should I go?"

"I don't know." Part of me wants to tell her to get on the next plane out of London, alone. But the selfish—and much stronger—part knows that if she did, I wouldn't make it through the night without drinking myself sick. Again. My mouth tastes like vomit, and my throat burns from the brutal way my system expelled all that liquor.

Opening the center console between us, Tessa pulls out a napkin and begins to wipe the corners of my mouth with the rough paper. Her fingers barely touch my skin, and I flinch away at the icy cold.

"You're freezing. Turn the car on." But I don't wait for her to oblige. Instead I lean across and turn the key myself, blasting the air from the vents. The air is cold at first, but this expensive-ass car has some trick to it, and warmth quickly spreads through the small space.

"We need to get gas. I don't know how long I was driving, but the fuel light is on, and that screen says so, too." She points to the lavish navigation screen on the dash.

The sound of her voice is killing me. "You've lost your voice," I say, even though it's incredibly obvious. She nods and turns her head away from me. My fingers wrap around her chin, and I turn her face back to me. "If you want to leave, I won't blame you. I'll take you to the airport right now."

She gives me a puzzled look before opening her mouth. "You're staying here? In London? Our flight is tonight, I thought—" The last word voice comes out as more of a squeak than anything else, and she breaks into a coughing fit.

I check the cup holders for some water or something, but they're empty.

I rub her back until she stops coughing, then I change the subject. "Trade me places; I'll drive over there." I nod toward the filling station across the road. "You need water and something for your throat."

I wait for her to move out of the driver's seat, but she rakes her eyes over my face before shifting the car into drive and pulling out of the parking lot.

"You're still over the legal limit," she finally whispers, careful not to strain her nonexistent voice.

I can't exactly argue with that. There is no way that a few hours of dozing in this car has sobered me completely. I drank enough liquor to black out most of the night, and the resulting headache is massive. I'll probably be drunk for the entire fucking day, or half of it. I can't tell. I can't even remember how many drinks I had . . .

My jumbled counting is cut short when Tessa parks in front of a gas pump and reaches for the door handle.

"I'll go in." I climb out of the car before she can argue.

There aren't many people inside at this early hour, only men dressed for work. My hands are filled with aspirin, water bottles, and bags of snacks when Tessa walks into the small store.

I watch as every head turns to look at the disheveled beauty in her dirty white dress. The men's looks make me even more nauseated.

"Why didn't you stay in the car?" I ask as she approaches.

She waves a hunk of black leather in front of my face. "Your wallet."

"Oh."

Handing it to me, she disappears for a moment, but takes her place next to me just as I reach the counter. In each hand is a large, steaming cup of coffee.

I drop my pile of things on the counter. "Can you check the location on your phone while I pay?" I ask, taking the oversize cups from her small hands.

"What?"

"The location on your phone, so we can see where we are."

Grabbing the aspirin bottle and shaking it before he scans it, the portly man behind the counter remarks, "Allhallows. That's where you are." He nods at Tessa, who politely smiles back.

"Thank you." She widens her grin, and the poor bastard flushes.

Yeah, I know she's hot. Now look away before I rip your eyes from your head, I want to tell him. *And next time you make a god-awful noise when I'm hungover, like you did with that aspirin bottle, it's all over.* After last night, I could use the outlet, and I'm not in the mood for this mopey shit's eyes to be raking across my girl's chest at seven in the fucking morning.

If I weren't immensely aware of the lack of emotion behind her eyes, I would probably have pulled him over the counter, but her fake smile, black-rimmed eyes, and dirt-stained dress stop me and yank me from my violent thoughts. She just looks so lost, so sad, so fucking lost.

What have I done to you? I silently ask.

Her focus shifts to the door, where a young woman and child are entering, hand in hand. I watch her as she watches them, following their movements a little too closely, if you ask me; it's borderline creepy. When the little girl stares up at her mum, Tessa's bottom lip trembles.

What the hell is that about? Because I threw a fit over the new revelation in my family?

The clerk has packed up all of my stuff and holds the bag somewhat rudely in front of my face to get my attention. It seems that as soon as Tessa stopped looking at him, he decided he could be rude to me.

I snatch the plastic bag and lean toward Tessa. "Ready?" I ask, nudging her with my elbow.

"Yeah, sorry," she mutters and grabs the coffees from the counter.

I fill the car up, all the while considering the consequences of driving Vance's rental into the sea. If we're in Allhallows, we're right next to the shore; it wouldn't be hard.

"How far are we from Gabriel's bar?" Tessa asks when I join her in the car. "That's where the car is."

"Only about an hour and a half, traffic considering." *The car slowly sinks in the ocean, costing Vance tens of thousands; we take a cab to Gabriel's for a couple hundred. Fair trade.*

Tessa twists the top off the small bottle of aspirin and shakes three of them into my hand, then frowns and stares down at her screen, which has started to light up. "Do you want to talk about last night? I just received a text from Kimberly."

Questions begin pushing through the muddied images and voices from last night and into the surface of my mind . . . Vance locking me outside and walking back into the burning house . . . As Tessa continues to stare at her phone, I grow increasingly worried.

"He's not . . ." I don't know how to ask the question. It won't seem to pass over the lump in my throat.

Tessa looks at me, and her eyes begin to fill with tears. "He's alive, of course, but . . ."

"What? He's what?"

"She says he was burned."

A slight and unwelcome pain tries to seep through the cracks in my defenses. Cracks that she caused in the first place.

She wipes one eye with the back of her hand. "Only on one leg. Kim said one leg, and that he's to be arrested as soon as he is released from the hospital, which should be soon, any minute, really."

"Arrested for what?" I know the answer before she gives it.

"He told the police that he started the fire." Tessa lifts her shitty phone in front of my face so I can read the long text message from Kimberly for myself.

I read it all, not learning anything new, but getting a good sense of Kimberly's panic. I don't say anything. I have nothing to say.

"Well?" Tessa asks softly.

"Well what?"

"Aren't you even slightly concerned about your father?" Then, taking in my murderous glare, she adds, "I mean Christian."

He's hurt because of me. "He shouldn't have even showed up there."

Tessa looks appalled by my nonchalance. "*Hardin*. That man came there to help me—to help you."

Sensing the beginning of a rambling spell, I interrupt her. "Tessa, I know—"

But she surprises me by holding a hand up to silence me. "I wasn't finished. Not to mention he took the blame for a house fire that you caused and was *injured*. I love you, and I know you hate him right now, but I know you—the real you—so don't sit here and act like you don't give a shit what happens to him, because I know damn well that you do." Violent coughing punctuates her angry speech, and I push the water bottle to her mouth.

I take a moment to mull over her words as she settles her cough. She's right—of course she is—but I'm not ready to face any of the things that she just mentioned. I'm not fucking ready to admit that he did something for me—not after all these years. I'm not ready for him to suddenly be a fucking father to me. Fuck no. I don't want anyone, especially him, to think that this somehow evens the score, that I will somehow forget all of the shit he missed, all of the nights I spent listening to my parents screaming at one another, all of the times I rushed up the stairs at the sound of my father's drunken voice—the way he *knew* and didn't tell me all the while.

No, fuck that. It's not fucking even, and it never will be. "You think because he gets a little burn on his leg and *chooses* to take the blame that I will forgive him?" I run my hands through my hair. "I'm supposed to just forgive him for lying to me for twenty-one fucking years?" I ask, my voice much louder than I intended it to be.

"No, of course not!" she says, raising her voice right back at me. I worry that she might blow out a vocal cord or something, but she goes right on. "But I refuse to allow you to brush this off as some small thing he did. He is going to jail for you, and you act as if you couldn't be bothered to even ask how he is. Absent, lying, father or not, he loves you, and he saved your ass last night."

This is bullshit. "Whose side are you fucking on?"

"There aren't any *sides!*" she shouts, her voice echoing in the small space and not helping my ringing headache one bit. "*Everyone* is on your side, Hardin. I know you feel like it's you against the world, but look around you. You have me, your father—both of them—Karen, who loves you as her own, and Landon, who loves you much more than either of you will ever admit." Tessa half smiles at the mention of her best friend, but continues her lecture. "Kimberly may challenge you, but she cares for you, too, and Smith, you are literally the only person that little boy likes." She gathers my hands in her shaking ones and rubs her thumbs across my palms in gentle caresses.

"It's ironic, really: the man who hates the world is most loved by it," she whispers, her eyes glossy and full of tears. Tears for me, so many tears for me.

I let out a deep breath and grab the bar from her hands, tearing open the wrapper. "You need to eat something. You look like you'll pass out any moment."

"I feel that way," she says quietly, more to herself than me, it seems.

I'm considering shoving the damned thing into her mouth, when she takes it from me for a bite.

"You want to go home, then?" I finally ask her. Not wanting to ask where exactly home will be for her.

She grimaces. "Yes, your father was right. London isn't as I imagined."

"I ruined it for you, that's why."

She doesn't deny it, but she doesn't confirm it either. Her silence and the way she's vacantly staring out at the trees pushes me to say what I need to say. It's now or never.

"I think I should stay here for a while . . ." I say into the open air between us.

Tessa's mouth stops its chewing, and she turns, narrowing her eyes at me. "Why?"

"It doesn't make sense for me to go back there."

"No, it doesn't make sense for you to stay here. Why would you even consider that?"

Her feelings are hurt, just like I knew they would be—but what other choice do I have?

"Because my father isn't my actual father, my mum is a lying"—I stop myself from calling her the name I want to—"and my biological father is going to jail because I caught her house on fire. It's a ridiculous drama series on its own." Then, to try to get a reaction out of her, I wryly add, "All we need is a cast of young girls with too much makeup and impractical clothes, and we would have a hit."

Her sad eyes study mine. "I'm still not seeing why any of this would make you want to stay here. Here, as in away from me—

that's what you want, isn't it? You want to be away from me." She says the last part as if saying it aloud verifies it as truth.

"It's not that . . ." I start, but stumble. I don't know how to put my thoughts into words—that's always been my biggest fucking problem. "I just think if we had some time apart, you could see what I'm doing to you. Just look at yourself." She flinches, but I force myself to continue. "You are dealing with problems that you would've never be faced with if it wasn't for me."

"Don't you *dare* act like you're doing this for me," she snaps, her voice as cold as ice. "You are as self-destructive as they come, and *that's* your only motive behind this."

I am. I know I am. It's what I do: I hurt other people, and then I hurt myself before anyone can hurt me back. I'm fucked-up; that's just the way it is.

"You know what?" she says after getting tired of waiting for me to speak up. "Fine. I'll let you hurt both of us in this self-depriving mission of your—"

My hands are on her hips and she's back on my lap before she can finish. Tessa tries to climb off me, scratching at my arms when I won't let her move an inch.

"If you don't want to be with me, then get off of me," she seethes. No tears, only anger. Her anger I can handle; it's the tears that kill me. The anger dries them away.

"Stop fighting me." I gather both of her wrists behind her back and hold them in only one of my hands. She glares, her eyes warning me.

"You don't get to do this every time something makes you feel bad. You don't get to decide that I'm too good for you!" she shouts in my face.

I ignore her and bring my mouth to the curve of her neck. Her body jolts again, this time out of pleasure, not anger.

"Stop it . . ." she says with absolutely no conviction. She's trying to deny me because she thinks she should, but we both know that this is what we need. We need the physical connection that brings us to an emotional depth that neither of us can explain or deny.

"I love you, you know I do." I suck at the tender skin at the base of her neck, reveling in the way it turns pink from the suction of my lips. I continue to suck and nibble at the skin, just enough to create a cluster of markings, but not hard enough to make them stay for longer than a few seconds.

"You sure aren't acting like it." Her voice is thick, and her eyes follow my free hand as it moves across her exposed thigh. Her dress is bunched up at her waist in the most maddening way possible.

"Everything I do is because I love you. Even the stupid shit." I reach the lace of her panties, and she gasps when I run a single finger across the moisture already collected between her thighs. "Always so wet for me, even now."

I slide her panties over and push two fingers into her wet flesh. She whimpers and arches her back against the steering wheel, and I feel her body relaxing. I move the seat back farther to give us more room inside the small car.

"You can't distract me with—"

I remove my fingers from her and plunge them back in, stopping the words before they can fall from her lips.

"Yes, baby, I can." I bring my lips to her ear. "Will you stop fighting me if I let your hands go?"

She nods. The second I let them go, they move to my hair. Her fingers bury into the thick mess of my hair, and I tug the front of her dress down with one hand.

Her white lace bra is sinful despite its holy coloring. Tessa, whose blond hair and white ensemble contrast in the most extreme manner with my dark hair and dark clothes. Something about the contrast is so fucking erotic: the ink on my wrist as my fingers disappear inside her again, the clean, unmarked skin of her thighs, the way her soft moans and whimpers fill the air as my eyes drag shamelessly up her tight stomach and back to her chest.

I tear my eyes away from her perfect tits long enough to scan the parking lot. The windows are tinted, but I want to be sure we are still alone on this side of the street. I unfasten her bra using one hand and slow the movement of my other. She whines in protest, but I don't bother to hide the smile on my face.

"Please," she begs for me to continue.

"Please what? Tell me what you want," I coax her, the way I have since in the beginning of our relationship. It has always felt like unless she spoke the words aloud, they couldn't be true. She couldn't possibly want me the way I want her.

She reaches down and pushes my hand back between her thighs. "Touch me."

She's swollen and waiting and fucking soaking, wanting me, needing me, and I fucking love her more than she could ever comprehend. I need this, I need her to distract me, to help me escape all of this bullshit, even if only for a little while.

I give her what she wants, and she moans my name in approval, taking her lip between her teeth. Her hand moves under mine to grip me through my jeans. I'm so hard that it hurts, and Tessa's touches and squeezes aren't helping.

"I want to fuck you. Now. I have to." I glide my tongue over one of her breasts. She nods, her eyes rolling back in her head, and I suck at the sensitive tip while kneading its twin with the hand that isn't between her legs.

"*Hard-in . . .*" she groans. Her hands are eager to free me from my jeans and boxers. I lift my hips enough for her to tug my jeans down my thighs. My fingers are still buried in her, moving at a tender pace, just enough to drive her fucking crazy. I remove my fingers from her and bring them to her swollen lips, pressing them into her mouth. She sucks at them, her tongue running slowly up and down my fingers, and I groan, quickly withdrawing them before I come from that alone. I lift her by her hips and lower her back onto me.

We share the same relieved moan, both desperate for one another.

"We shouldn't be apart," she says, pulling me by my hair until my mouth is level with hers. Can she taste the cowardly goodbye on my breath?

"We have to be," I say as she begins to swivel her hips. *Fuck.*

Tessa lifts herself slowly. "I won't force you to want me. Not anymore." I begin to panic, but all my thoughts are lost as she slowly lowers herself back down onto me, only to pull back and then repeat the same torturous movement. She leans forward to kiss me, her tongue lapping around mine as she takes control.

"I want you," I breathe into her mouth. "I always fucking want you, you know that." A low sound rips through me as her hips quicken their movements. Holy fuck, she's going to kill me.

"You are leaving me." She glides her tongue across my bottom lip, and I reach down to where our bodies are joined and bring her swollen clit between my fingers.

"I love you," I say, unable to find any other words, and she's silenced by my pinching and rubbing her sensitive bud of nerves.

"Oh God." Her head falls to my shoulder, and she wraps her arms around my neck. "I *love* you," she practically sobs as she comes, squeezing all around me.

I follow directly after, filling her with every drop of me, literally and metaphorically.

MINUTES OF SILENCE PASS, and I keep my eyes closed and my arms wrapped around her back. We are both covered in sweat; the heat is still pouring from the vents, but I don't want to let her go long enough to turn it off.

"What are you thinking?" I finally ask.

Her head is resting on my chest, her breathing slow and steady. She doesn't open her eyes when she responds, "That I wish you could stay with me forever."

Forever. Have I ever wanted anything less with her?

"Me, too," I say, wishing I could give her the promise of the future that she deserves.

After a few more minutes of silence, Tessa's phone buzzes on the floorboard, and on instinct I reach across and grab it, shifting her body with mine.

"It's Kimberly," I say and hand Tessa the phone.

Two hours later we are knocking on the door of Kimberly's hotel room. I'm almost convinced that we are at the wrong room when I take in Kimberly's appearance. Her eyes are swollen and she doesn't have an ounce of makeup on. I like her better that way, but she just looks so wrecked right now, like she's been crying all her tears plus somebody's else's.

"Come in. It's been a long morning," she says, her normal sass completely absent.

Tessa immediately hugs her, wrapping her arms around her friend's waist, and Kimberly begins to sob. I feel incredibly uncomfortable just standing in the doorway, given that Kim irritates the shit out of me and that she isn't the type that wants an audience while she's vulnerable. I leave them in the sitting room of the grand suite and wander into the kitchen area. I pour a cup of coffee and stare at the wall until the sobs turn into muffled voices in the other room. I'll keep my distance for now.

"Is my dad coming back?" a smooth voice says from somewhere, causing me to jerk in surprise.

Looking down, I see the green-eyed Smith has taken a seat in a plastic chair next to me. I didn't even hear him approaching.

I shrug and take a seat next to him, staring intensely at the wall. "Yeah. I think so." I should tell him just what a fucking great man his father . . . *our* father really is . . .

Holy shit.

This strange little specimen of a kid is my fucking brother. I absolutely can't wrap my head around it. I look over at Smith, which he takes as a cue to continue his line of questioning.

"Kimberly said that he's in trouble, but he can pay his way out of it. What does that mean?"

I can't stop the scoff that comes from my mouth at his intrusive eavesdropping and thorough questioning. "I'm sure that's the case," I mumble. "She just means that he will be out of trouble soon. Why don't you go sit with Kimberly and Tessa?" My chest burns at the sound of her name as it comes from my mouth.

He looks over in the direction of their voices, then assess me sagely. "They're mad at you. Especially Kimberly, but she's more mad at my dad, so you should be okay."

"You'll learn that women are always mad."

He nods. "Unless they die. Like my mom did."

My mouth falls open and I look at his face. "You shouldn't say shit like that. People will find it . . . odd."

He shrugs his shoulders as if to say that people already find him odd. Which is true, I suppose.

"My dad is nice. He's not bad."

"Okay?" I stare down at table to avoid looking into those green eyes.

"He takes me a lot of places and says nice things to me." Smith places a piece of a toy train on the table. What is with this boy and trains?

"And . . ." I say, swallowing the feelings that come with his words. *Why is he rambling about this now?*

"He will take you places, too, and tell you nice things."

I look over at him. "And why would I want that?" I ask, but his green eyes tell me that he knows much more than I assumed.

Smith tilts his head and swallows a little swallow, watching me. It's both the most scientifically detached and the most vulnerably childlike I have ever seen the little oddball. "You don't want me to be your brother, do you?"

Damn it. I desperately search for Tessa, hoping that she will come save me. She would know exactly what to say.

I look at him, trying to appear calm, but certain I'm failing. "I never said that."

"You don't like my dad."

Right then, Tessa and Kimberly enter, saving me from having to answer him, thank God.

"Are you okay, honey?" Kimberly asks him, ruffling his hair slightly.

Smith doesn't speak. He merely nods once, adjusts his hair, and takes his train car with him into the other room.

chapter nine

TESSA

"Just use the shower here—you look like hell, girl," Kimberly says in a kind voice despite the unflattering words.

Hardin is still sitting at the table, a cup of coffee between his large hands. He has barely looked at me since I walked into the kitchen to find him talking to Smith. The idea of the two of them spending time together as brothers warms my heart.

"All of my clothes are in the rental car at that bar," I tell her. I want nothing more than a shower, but I don't have any clothes to wear.

"You can wear something of mine," she suggests, even though we both know I could never fit into her clothes. "Or Christian's. He has some shorts and a shirt you—"

"No, hell no," Hardin interrupts, throwing Kimberly a hard glare as he stands. "I'll go get your shit. You *aren't* wearing his clothes."

Kimberly opens her mouth to argue, but closes it before the words can come. I look at her with thankful eyes, grateful that a war won't be started in the kitchen of her hotel suite.

"How far is Gabriel's from here?" I ask, hoping one of them knows the answer.

"Ten minutes." Hardin holds his hand out for the keys to the car.

"Can you drive?" I made the drive back from Allhallows because the alcohol was still in his system, and his eyes are still glassy.

"Yes," he says tersely.

Wonderful. Kimberly's suggestion that I borrow Christian's clothing has turned Hardin from sullen to pissed-off in under a minute.

"Do you want me to come? I could drive the rental back since you are driving Christian's car—" I begin, but I'm quickly cut off.

"No. I'll be fine."

I don't like his impatient tone, but I bite my tongue, literally, to keep from telling him off. I don't know what has gotten into me lately, but I find it harder and harder to keep my mouth shut. This can only be a good thing for me—maybe not for Hardin, but certainly for me.

He leaves the suite without another word or so much as a glance back to me. I stare at the wall for long, silent minutes before Kimberly's voice breaks my trance.

"How is he handling it?" She leads me over to the table.

"Not well." We both grab a seat.

"I can see that. Burning a house down probably isn't the healthiest way to deal with anger," she says without a single hint of judgment in her words.

I stare at the dark wood on the table, not willing to meet the eyes of my friend. "It's not his anger that I'm afraid of. I can feel him withdrawing with every breath he takes. I know it's childish and selfish of me to even mention this to you, because you are going through all of this and Christian is in trouble . . ."

It's probably best that I keep my selfish thoughts to myself.

Kimberly places her hand on mine. "Tessa. There's no rule that says only one person can feel pain at a time. You're going through this just as much as I am."

"I know, but I don't want to bother you with my prob—"

"You aren't bothering me. Spill."

I look up at her with the intent to stay quiet, to keep my complaints to myself, but she shakes her head as if she can read my mind.

"He wants to stay here in London, and I know if I let him, we will be finished."

She smiles. "You two seem to have a different definition of *finished* than the rest of us." I want to throw my arms around her neck for giving me such a warm smile in the middle of hell.

"I know it's hard to believe me when I say that given our . . . history, but this whole thing with Christian and Trish will either be the nail in our coffin, or our saving grace. I don't see any other outcome, and now I guess I'm afraid of which it'll be."

"Tessa, you have too much weighing on you. Vent to me. Vent and vent some more. Nothing you say will make me think any less of you or anything. Like the selfish bitch I am, I need someone else's problems to distract me from my own issues right now."

I don't wait for Kimberly to change her mind. Instead, the floodgates open and the words pour from my mouth like uncontrollable, rushing waters. "Hardin wants to stay in London. He wants to stay here and send me back to Seattle like some burden that he can't wait to unload. He's withdrawing from me, like he always does every single time he's hurt, and now he's gone off the deep end and burned that house down and has absolutely no remorse. I know he's angry, and I would never say this to him, but he's only making things worse for himself.

"If he would just deal with his anger and admit that he can feel pain—admit that someone other than himself or me is important in this world—he could get through this. He infuriates me, because he tells me that he can't live without me and would rather die than lose me, but as soon as the going gets tough, what does he do? He pushes me away. I'm not going to give up on him—I'm in far too deep for that now. But sometimes I just feel so tired of battling that I start to think about what my life would have been without him." I pull my eyes up to Kimberly's. "But when I start to picture it, I nearly collapse from the pain."

I grab the half-empty cup of coffee from the table and down it. My voice is better than it was a few hours ago, but my ranting has taken its toll on my sore throat.

"It doesn't make sense to me still, after all these months, all this turmoil, that I would rather do all of this"—I wave my hand around the room in a dramatic gesture—"than be without him. The worst of times with him have been nothing, compared to the best. I don't know if I'm delusional or insane. Maybe both. But I love him more than myself, more than I ever thought possible, and I just want him to be happy. Not for me, but for him.

"I want him to look in the mirror and smile, not scowl. I need him to not think of himself as a monster. I need him to see the real him, because if he doesn't pull himself out of the villain role, it will destroy him, and I'll just be left with ashes. Please don't tell him or even Christian any of this. I just needed to get it all out because I feel like I'm drowning, and it's hard to keep myself above water, especially when I'm fighting against the current to save him rather than myself."

My voice cracks at that last bit, and I become a coughing mess. Smiling, Kimberly opens her mouth to speak, but I hold up a finger.

I clear my throat. "There's more. On top of all of this, I went to the doctor to get . . . to get birth control," I say, nearly whispering the last words.

Kimberly tries her best not to laugh but fails utterly. "No need to whisper—spit it out, girl!"

"Fine." I flush. "I got on birth control, and my doctor did a quick scan of my cervix. He said that it's short, shorter than average, and he wants me to come in for more testing, but he mentioned infertility."

I look over to see sympathy in her blue eyes. "My sister has the same thing; they like to call it cervical incompetence, I think. What a horrible term: *incompetence* makes it sounds like her vagina got an F in math or was a shitty lawyer or something."

Kimberly's attempt at humor, and that she knows someone with the same problem I may have, makes me feel better, a little.

"And does she have children?" I ask, but instantly regret it as her face falls.

"I don't know if you want to hear about her right now. I could tell you another time."

"Tell me." I shouldn't want to hear it, but I can't help it. "Please," I beg.

Kimberly takes a deep breath. "She struggled to get pregnant for years; it was terrible for her. They tried fertility treatments. Anything you can find on Google, she and her husband tried."

"And?" I press her to hurry along, reminding myself of Hardin right now, rudely interrupting her. I hope he's on his way back. In this state, Hardin can't be left to his own devices.

"Well, she finally was able to get pregnant, and it was the happiest day of her life." Kimberly looks away from me, and I know she's either lying or leaving something out for my sake.

"What happened? How old is the baby now?"

Kimberly clasps her hands together and looks me square in the eyes. "She was four months along when she miscarried. But that is only what happened to *her*—don't get yourself distraught over her story. You may not even have the same thing. And if you do, things may be different for you."

With a hollow ringing in my ears I say, "I have this feeling, just this gut feeling, that I won't be able to get pregnant. The moment the doctor mentioned infertility, it was like it just clicked."

Kimberly grabs my hand on the table. "You don't know that

for sure. And not to be a downer, but Hardin doesn't want kids anyway, right?"

Even with the small knife twisting into my chest from her words, I feel better now that I have told someone about my worries. "No. He doesn't. He doesn't want children or marriage with me."

"Were you hoping he would change his mind?" She gives me a little squeeze.

"Yes, sadly I was. I was almost sure he would. Not right now of course but years from now. I thought maybe if he was older and we both were finished with college, he would eventually change his mind. But now that seems even more delusional than before." I feel my cheeks flush in embarrassment. I can't believe I'm actually saying these things aloud. "I know I sound ridiculous worrying over children at my age, but being a mother was always something I wanted since I can remember. I don't know if it's because my mother and father weren't the best parents, but I have always felt this urge, this need, to be a mother. Not just a mother, but a really good one—a mother that would love her children unconditionally. I would never judge them or belittle them. I would never pressure them or humiliate them. I wouldn't try to mold them into a better version of myself."

At first, talking about this, I felt insane. But Kimberly is nodding along to everything I'm saying, making me feel like maybe I'm not the only one who feels this way. "I think I would be a good mother, if I was ever given the chance, and the idea of a little brown-haired, gray-eyed little girl running into Hardin's arms brings my heart to my throat. I imagine it sometimes. I know it's stupid, but sometimes I picture them sitting there, both of them with unruly wavy hair." I laugh at the ludicrous vision, one that I have imagined far more times than could possibly be considered normal. "He would read to her and carry her on his shoulders, and she would have him wrapped around her finger."

I force a smile, trying to erase the sweet image from my head. "But he doesn't want that, and now that he has learned about Christian being his father, I know he never, ever will."

Tucking my hair behind my ears, I'm surprised, and more than a little proud of myself, that I made it through all that without a single tear.

chapter ten

HARDIN

I wish you could stay with me forever."

Tessa had said that against my chest. It's what I wanted to hear. It's what I need to hear, forever.

But why would she possibly want forever with me? What would that even be like? Tessa and I in our forties with no children, no marriage—just the two of us?

That would be perfect, for me. That would be my absolute ideal future, but I know that would never be enough for her. We've had the same argument too many times to count, and I know that she would be the first to cave, because I never would. Being an asshole means being the most stubborn. And she would give up having children and a marriage for me.

Besides, what kind of father would I be? A shitty one, that's for damn sure. I can't get through the question in my mind without laughing—it's ridiculous to even consider. As fucked-up as this trip has been, it's been a giant fucking wake-up call for me when it comes to my relationship with Tessa. I've always tried to warn her, tried to keep her from going down with me, but I never tried hard enough. If I'm being honest, I know I could have pushed harder to keep her safe from me, but, selfishly, I couldn't. Now seeing the way that her life will be with me, I have no other choice. This trip has cleared the romantic fog from my head, and miraculously, I have been granted the opportunity to have an easy way out. I can send her back to America, and she can get on with her life.

Tessa's future with me is nothing but a lonely, black hole for her. I would get everything I wanted from her—her constant love and affection for years and years—but she would be left unfulfilled, and as every year passes, she will resent me more and more for depriving her of what she truly wanted. I might as well cut out the middleman and save her the wasted time.

When I arrive at Gabriel's, I quickly throw Tessa's bag into the backseat and head back to Kimberly's hotel. I need a plan, a solid fucking plan that I will actually stick to. She is too stubborn and too in love with me to just give up on me.

That's her problem, she's one of those people who will give and give without taking, and the fucked-up truth is that people like her are the easiest prey for someone like me, who takes and takes until there is nothing left. That's what I have done since the beginning, and that's what I will always do.

She will try to convince me otherwise; I know she will. She will say that marriage isn't important anymore, but she would just be lying to herself to keep me around. That says a lot about me, that I have manipulated her into loving me so unconditionally. The masochist in me starts to doubt her love as I drive.

Does she love me as much as she says, or is she addicted to me? There is a heady difference, and the more shit she puts up with from me, the more it seems like an addiction, the thrill of waiting for me to fuck up again so she can be there to fix me.

That's what this is: she must see me as a project, someone she can fix. The conversation has come up before, more than once, but she refused to admit it.

I fish through my memories for a specific encounter and finally find it floating somewhere in my muddled, hungover brain.

IT WAS RIGHT AFTER MY MUM LEFT to go back to London after Christmas, and Tessa had looked up at me with worried eyes. "Hardin?"

"Yeah?" I had asked, speaking through the pen between my teeth.

"Will you help me take this tree down when you're finished working?"

I wasn't actually working; I was writing, but she didn't know that. We had had a long and interesting day. I had caught her coming back from lunch with fucking Trevor, and then I'd bent her over her desk and fucked her senseless.

"Yes, just give me a minute." I tucked the pages away, afraid that she would see them while cleaning up, and stood to help her take down the tiny tree she'd decorated with my mum.

"What are you working on anyway? Is it anything good?" She reached for the tattered binder she constantly complained about my leaving around the house. The coffee-cup rings and pen marks covering the weathered leather drove her insane.

"Nothing." I jerked it from her hands before she could open it.

She pulled back, obviously surprised and a little hurt by my actions. "Sorry," she said quietly. A deep frown set across her beautiful face, and I tossed the binder on the couch and reached for her hands. "I was just asking. I didn't mean to pry or upset you."

Fuck, I was such a prick.

I still *am*.

"It's fine, just don't mess with my work shit. I don't . . ." I couldn't come up with an excuse as to why, because I hadn't stopped her in the past. Whenever I came across a draft that I knew she would like, I would share it with her. She loved when I did that, and there I was scolding her for doing it now.

"Okay." She turned away from me and started to pull the ornaments off the hideous tree.

I stared at her back for a few minutes, wondering why I was so angry. If she read what I was writing, how would she feel? Would she like it? Or would she be appalled and throw a fit? I didn't know, and I still don't, which is why she still has no clue about it to this day.

"Okay? That's all you have to say?" I picked at her, wanting a fight. Fighting was better than ignoring; shouts were better than silence.

"I won't mess with your things anymore," she said without turning to look at me. "I didn't know you would be so upset."

"I . . ." I struggled to find something to fight about. Then I just went for the bone. "Why are you even with me?" I asked roughly. "After everything that happened—is it the drama that you like?"

"What?" She spun around, a small snowflake ornament in her hands. "Why are you starting a fight with me? I said I wouldn't touch your things anymore."

"I'm not starting a fight," I lied. "I just want to know, because it seems like you are addicted to the drama and ups and downs more than anything." I knew it wasn't fair to say, but I said it anyway. I was in a mood and wanted her to join me.

She stepped toward me, dropping the ornament into the box next to the tree. "You know that isn't true. I love you, even when you are looking for a fight with me. I hate the drama; you know that. I love you for you, end of story." She leaned up on her toes to kiss my cheek, and I wrapped my arms around her.

"Why do you love me, then? I do nothing for you," I argued weakly. The scene I'd caused at Vance's earlier that day was fresh in my mind.

She took a patient breath and rested her head against my chest. "This"—she tapped her index finger over my heart—"that's why. Now please stop trying to fight me. I have a paper to work on, and this tree won't put itself away."

She was so gentle with me, so understanding, even when I didn't deserve it.

"I love you," I said into her hair and moved my hands to her hips. She molded into me, letting me lift her into my arms, and she wrapped her legs around my waist as I carried her across the living room to the couch.

"I love you, always. Don't doubt me, I will always love you," she assured me, her mouth against mine.

I undressed her slowly, savoring every inch of her sexy curves. I loved the way her eyes went wide as I rolled the condom on. That same afternoon she had been nervous about fucking while on her period, but her chest was moving up and down with rapid jerks as I began to stroke myself in front of her. Impatient breaths and a small whine was all it took for me to stop teasing her. I moved between her thighs and pushed into her slowly. She was so wet and tight, I lost myself in her and I still can't remember how that damn tree got stored away.

I HAVE BEEN DOING THIS too much lately, dwelling on happy memories from my time with her. My hands are shaking, gripping the steering wheel as I pull myself from my mind; her moans and whimpers fade away as I force myself back to the present.

I'm waiting in a slow line of traffic, only a few miles away from Tessa. I need to solidify my plan and make sure her ass is on that plane tonight. It's a late flight, not departing until nine, so she will have plenty of time to make it to Heathrow. Kimberly will take her there; I know she will. My head still hurts—the liquor is making a slow departure from my body, and I still feel a little tipsy. Not so much so that I can't drive, but my mind isn't all there.

"Hardin!" a familiar voice says. The voice is muffled by my window, so I quickly roll it down. Every time I turn around, someone from my past is there, calling my name.

"Holy shit!" I yell to the car next to me. My old friend Mark is in the next lane. If this isn't a sign from above, I don't know what is.

"Pull over!" he shouts back, a wide grin spreading across his face.

I pull Vance's rental into the lot of an ice-cream shop, and he parks next to me. He's out of his piece-of-shit car before I am and rushes over to yank my door open.

"You're back and you didn't even tell me?" he yells, patting me on the shoulder. "And, damn, tell me this Beemer is a rental, or did you get rich on me?"

I roll my eyes. "Long story, but it's a rental."

"Are you back for good, or what?" His brown hair is cropped short now, but his eyes are just as glazed over as they always were.

"Yeah, I'm back for good," I answer, settling it. I'm staying here and she's going back, simple as that.

He studies my face. "Where are your fucking rings? You took them out?"

"Yeah, I got sick of them." I shrug, but examine his face. When he turns his head a little, the light catches two little studs beneath his lips. Damn, the kid got snakebites.

"Damn, Scott, you look so different. It's fucking crazy. It's been, what, two years?" He throws his hands up. "Three? Hell, I've been high for the last ten years, so I couldn't tell you." He laughs and digs into his pocket to pull out a pack of smokes.

I decline when he offers me one, which earns me a raised brow. "What, you like straight edge now?" he accuses.

"No, I just don't want a fucking cigarette," I snap.

He laughs the way he always did when I would get this way. He was always the leader of our little group of delinquents, older than me by a year, but enough that I always looked up to him in a way and wanted to be like him. That's why when an even older guy named James came along and he and Mark started the games, I jumped right in. It didn't bother me the way they treated girls, even when they taped them without their knowledge.

"You're a bitch now, aren't you?" He smiles, his lit cigarette between his teeth.

"Fuck off. You're high right now, aren't you?" I knew he would always remain this way, always high and stuck in his glory days of fucking loads of chicks and staying high.

"Nah, I'm coming off of a long night, though." He grins, obviously proud of himself as he remembers whatever, or *who*ever, he did last night. "Where you headed now? You staying at your mum's?"

My chest tightens at the mention of my mum and the house that I burned to the ground. I can feel the hot smoke on my cheeks and see the bright flames swallowing the house when I looked back before climbing into the car with Tessa. "No, I'm staying between places."

"Oh, got it." He doesn't get it, though. "If you need a place to crash, you can stay at my place. James is my roommate now—he'd get a kick out of seeing your grown ass, too. All Americanized and shit."

I can hear Tessa's voice in my head now, begging me not to go down this familiar, easy road, but I ignore her protests and nod at Mark. "I need a favor, actually."

"I can find you anything you need—James sells now!" Mark responds with some pride.

I roll my eyes. "That isn't what I mean. I need you to follow me to my hotel so I can drop something off, then take me to Gabriel's to get my car."

I will have to extend the rental time, if they'll allow it. I choose to ignore that an entire apartment and a car are back in Washington. I'll figure that shit out later.

"Then you'll come to my flat?" He stops. "Wait, who are you dropping shit off to?" Even high, he didn't miss that detail.

There is no fucking way in hell I'm telling Mark about Tessa, no fucking way. "Just some chick." I feel the burn in my throat as I lie about who Tessa is to me, but I need to protect her from this.

He walks back over to his car, pausing before he gets in. "She hot? I can wait outside if you need to fuck her again. Or maybe she'll let me—"

My vision goes red and I take a few breaths to calm down. "No. Fuck no. Not happening. You'll stay in the car. *I'm* not even going inside." When he doesn't look convinced, I add, "I mean it. If you get out of the fucking car and go anywhere near—"

"Dude, chill the fuck out! I'll stay in the car!" he shouts, and holds up his hands like I'm a cop.

He's still laughing and shaking his head as he follows me out of the parking lot and back onto the street.

chapter eleven

TESSA

I check my phone where it's plugged into the wall. "He's been gone for over an hour." I try to call him again.

"He's probably just taking his time," Kimberly says, but I can see the doubt in her eyes as she tries to comfort me.

"He's not answering. If he went back to that bar . . ." I stand up and being pacing.

"He'll probably pull up any minute." She opens the door and peeks out, looking left and right, then down. She says my name quietly, but her voice sounds off. Something's not right.

"What? What is it?" *Is Hardin in the hallway?* I zip over to where Kimberly is just as she bends down . . . and grabs my suitcase.

Dread takes over, bringing me to my knees. I barely feel Kimberly's arms around me as I open the front pocket of the suitcase.

An airline ticket, a single airline ticket, is there. Next to it, Hardin's key chain with the keys to his car and apartment still attached.

I knew this was coming. I knew he would back away from me the moment he could. Hardin can't handle any type of emotional trauma, he just isn't equipped. I could have, should have, been preparing for this, so why does this ticket feel so heavy in my hand and my chest feel like it's on fire? I hate him for doing this to me, so quickly and out of anger, and I hate myself for not preparing for this. I should be tough right now; I should pick up the tiny scrap of dignity I haven't lost and stand tall. I should take this ticket, grab my damn suitcase, and get the hell out of London. That's what any self-respecting woman would do. It's simple, isn't it? I keep this thought in my head as my knees buckle below me, my hands shake, covering the embarrassment on my face as I break into pieces over this man, again.

"He's an ass," Kimberly insults Hardin, as if I didn't already know he's an asshole. "You know he will come back; he always does," she says against my hair. I look at her, and I can see the anger and the protective-friend threat in her eyes.

I gently pull myself out of her arms and shake my head. "I'm okay. I'm fine. I'm okay," I chant, more so to myself than to Kim.

"You aren't," she corrects me, tucking a wild strand of my hair behind my ear.

I get a glimpse of Hardin's hands doing that exact gesture, and I pull away. "I need a shower," I say to my friend, just before I lose it.

NO, NOT BROKEN. I'm not broken; I'm defeated. What I feel right now is purely defeat. I've spent months and months fighting against the inevitable, pushing against a current that was much too big to brave alone, and now I've been swallowed into it with no lifeboats in sight.

"Tessa? Tessa, are you okay?" Kimberly yells from the other side of the bathroom door.

"I'm fine," I manage, the words sounding as weak as I feel. If I don't feel an ounce of strength, I can attempt to hide some of the weakness.

The water is cold now, it's been cold for minutes . . . maybe even an hour. I haven't the slightest idea of how much time I've been in here, crouched down on the floor of the shower, my knees folded against my chest, the cold water spraying down on me. It was borderline painful a while ago, but my body went numb a few Kimberly checkups ago.

"You have to get out of that shower. Don't think I won't break the door down."

I don't doubt for a second that she would do just that. I've ignored that threat a few times already, but this time I reach up and turn the shower off. Still, I make no move to leave my spot on the floor.

Seemingly satisfied that the water's gone off, I don't hear from Kimberly for another little while. But the next time she pounds, I call back to her, "I'm getting out."

By the time I stand up, my legs are wobbly and my hair is almost dry. I dig into my bag and go through the mechanics of pulling on my jeans, one leg, then the next, lift arms above head, pull shirt down over stomach. I feel like a robot, and when I wipe my hand across the mirror, I see that I look like one, too.

How many times will he do this? I silently ask my reflection.

No, how many times will I let him do this? That's the real question.

"No more," I say out loud to the stranger looking back at me. I will find him, this last time, and only for the sake of his family. I will drag his ass out of London and do what I should have done a long time ago.

chapter twelve

HARDIN

Damn, Scott! Look at you—you're a fucking mammoth!" James stands up from the couch and moves toward me. It's true. Compared to both him and Mark, I'm fucking huge. "What are you, six foot fucking ten?" James's eyes are glassy and bloodshot. It's barely one in the afternoon.

"Six-three," I correct, and receive the same friendly greeting Mark gave, a firm hand on my shoulder.

"This is fucking awesome! We need to get the word out that you're back. Everyone's still here, man." James rubs his hands together like he's plotting something big, and I don't even want to know what that might be.

Has Tessa found the bag outside of the door yet? What did she think about it? Did she cry? Or is she beyond that now?

I sure as hell don't want the answer to that question. I don't want to picture her face when she opened the door. I don't even want to think about the way she felt when she saw only one ticket stuffed into the front pocket of that suitcase. All my clothes have been removed from it and tossed into the backseat of my rental.

I know her well enough to know that she's going to expect a goodbye from me. She's going to try to find me before she gives up. But after her one last effort, she *will* give up. She won't have a choice, because she will never be able to find me before the flight, and by tomorrow she'll be far, far gone from me.

"Dude!" Mark's voice is loud and his hand is waving in front of my face. "Are you fucking zoning out?"

"My bad," I say with a shrug. But then it occurs to me: if Tessa gets lost in London looking for me, what will I do? Anything?

Mark puts his arm around me, pulling me into the conversation he and James have broken into as they decide who to invite over. They name loads of familiar names and a few that I haven't heard and start making phone calls for a midday party, barking out times and liquor orders.

I pull away and go into the kitchen to look for a glass for some water, looking around the apartment for the first time since I walked through the door. It's a fucking mess. It looks the way the frat house did every Saturday and Sunday morning. Our apartment never looked this way, not when Tessa was around, at least. The counters were never covered in old pizza boxes, and the tables were free of beer bottles and bongs. I'm backsliding, and I fucking know it.

Speaking of bongs, I don't even have to look over at Mark and James to know what they're doing now. I hear the bubbling noise of the water in the bong, then the distinct smell of pot starts filling the place.

Masochist that I am, I pull my phone out of my pocket and turn the power back on. The picture I have set as my wallpaper is my new favorite of Tess. For now, at least. My favorite changes every damn week, but this one is fucking perfection. Her blond hair is down, hanging over her shoulders, and the light is shining on her, making her glow. A true smile fills her entire face, and her eyes are screwed shut, her nose crinkled in the most adorable fucking way. She was laughing at me, scolding me, really, for smacking her ass in front of Kimberly, and I'd snapped the picture just as she burst into laughter after I whispered to her the other, much-dirtier things I could do in front of her obnoxious friend.

I wander back into the living room, and James snatches my phone from my hand. "Give me some of whatever you're on!"

I'm quick to take it back before he can get a glance at the picture.

"Touchy, touchy," James mocks me as I change the background. No need to fuel these fuckers.

"I invited Janine," Mark says, sharing a laugh with James.

"I don't know why you two are laughing." I point to Mark. "She's *your* sister." Then I point at James. "And *you* fucked her, too." Not like this is surprising; Mark's sister is known for fucking every single one of her little brother's friends.

"Fuck you, man!" James takes another hit from the bong and passes it to me.

Tessa would fucking kill me. She would be so disappointed; she doesn't approve of me drinking, let alone smoking pot.

"Hit it or pass it," Mark urges.

"If Janine is coming over, you'll need it. She's still hot as fuck," James tells me, earning a glare from Mark and a laugh from me.

Hours pass this way, smoking, dwelling, drinking, dwelling, smoking, and before I know it, the place is full of people, including the girl in question.

chapter thirteen

TESSA

I may not have much, but I still have a little pride, and I would rather face Hardin by myself and have this conversation one-on-one. I know exactly what he's going to do. He's going to tell me that I am too good for him and that he is no good for me. He's going to say something hurtful, and I will try to convince him otherwise.

I know Kimberly must think I'm a fool for chasing after him after his cold dismissal, but I love him, and this is what you do when you love someone: you fight for him—you chase after him when you know he needs you. You help him fight the battle against himself, and you never give up on him, even when he gives up on himself.

"I'm fine. If I find him and you're with me, he will feel cornered, and it will make things worse," I tell Kimberly for the second time.

"Be careful, please. I don't want to have to kill that kid, but, at this point, nothing is off the table." She half smiles at me. "Wait, one more thing." Kimberly raises a finger and rushes over to the coffee table in the center of the room. She digs through her purse and then waves me over to her.

Kimberly, being Kimberly, brushes a shiny, colorless gloss across my lips and hands me a tube of mascara. She grins. "You want to look your best, right?"

Despite the ache in my chest, I smile at her effort to help me look decent. Of *course* that is part of the equation to her.

* * *

TEN MINUTES LATER, my cheeks are no longer red from crying. The puffiness around my eyes is less noticeable, thanks to concealer and a little shadow. My hair is brushed and somewhat controlled into large waves. Kimberly gave up after a few minutes, sighing, then saying that "beach waves" are in right now anyway. I don't remember her changing me out of my T-shirt and into a tank top and cardigan, but she has transformed me from a zombie in a remarkably short time.

"Promise me that you will call if you need me," Kimberly insists. "Don't think I won't come looking for you."

I nod in agreement, knowing that she won't hesitate. She hugs me twice more before giving me the keys to Christian's rental, which Hardin left in the parking lot.

When I get into the car, I plug my phone into the charger and roll the window all the way down. The car smells like Hardin, and the empty coffee cups from this morning are still in their holders, reminding me of the way he made love to me only hours ago. That was his goodbye to me—I realize now that part of me knew it then but just wasn't ready to accept it. I didn't want to admit the defeat that was skimming around the surface, waiting to encase me. It doesn't seem possible that it's almost five o'clock. I have less than two hours to find Hardin and convince him to come back home with me. The flight boards at eight thirty, but we have to arrive a bit before seven to go through security, just to be safe.

Will I be flying home alone?

I look at myself in the rearview mirror, facing that same girl who had to pull herself up off that bathroom floor. I acknowledge the sick feeling that tells me I'll be on that airplane alone.

I only know one place to look for him, and if he isn't there, I have no idea what I will do. I start the car up, but pause with my hand on the gearshift. I can't drive aimlessly around London with no money and nowhere to go.

Desperate and worried, I try to call him again, and I nearly burst into happy tears when he picks up the phone.

"Hellooo, who is this?" an unrecognizable male voice says. I pull the phone away to be sure I called the right number, but Hardin's name is clear across the screen. "Hellooo," the man says louder, drawing out the word again.

"Uhm, hi. Is Hardin there?" My stomach twists; it knows that this guy is bad news although I don't have a clue who he is.

Laughter and multiple voices echo in the background; more than one of them are female voices. "Scott is . . . disposed at the moment," the man tells me.

Disposed?

"It's *indisposed,* you idiot," a woman yells in the background, laughing.

Oh God. "Where is he?" I can tell I've been put on speaker-phone, the way the noise changes.

"He's busy," another guy says. "Who's this? You coming to the party? Is that why you called? I like your American accent, birdie, and if you're a friend of Scott's . . ."

A party? At only five? I try to focus on that useless fact rather than the multiple female voices bursting through my phone and the fact that Hardin is "busy."

"Yeah," my mouth answers before my brain agrees. "I need the address again."

My voice is shaky and unsure, but they don't seem to notice.

The man who answered the phone gives me an address, and I quickly type it into the navigation on my phone. It crashes twice, and I have to ask him to repeat himself, but he obliges and tells me to hurry, bragging proudly that there is more liquor there than I've ever seen in my life.

* * *

TWENTY MINUTES LATER I'm in the small lot adjoining a run-down brick building. The windows are large, and the three of them are covered in what looks like white tape or possibly garbage bags. The lot is full of cars; the BMW that I drove here sticks out like a sore thumb. The only car even close in resemblance is Hardin's rental. It's near the front, blocked in, meaning he's been here longer than most of the others.

When I reach the door of the building, I take a deep breath to gather my strength. The stranger on the phone said it was the second door on the third floor. The shady building doesn't seem large enough to have three floors, but as I climb the stairs, I'm proven wrong. Loud voices and the thick smell of marijuana hit me before I even reach the top of the staircase on the second floor.

Looking up, I have to wonder why Hardin would be here. Why would he come to this place to deal with his issues? As I reach the third floor, my heart is racing and my stomach is tied in knots as my mind flips through all of the possible things that could be happening behind the scarred and graffitied door number two.

I shake my head, clearing all the doubts. Why am I so paranoid and nervous? This is Hardin I'm talking about, my Hardin. Even mad and withdrawn, beyond cruel words he would never do anything to purposely hurt me. He is going through a hard time with all of his family issues, and he just needs me to stomp in there and take him home with me. I'm psyching myself out and getting worked up for nothing.

The door opens just before I reach up to knock, and a young guy wearing all black walks past me without stopping or closing the door behind him. Waves of smoke roll out into the hallway, and I have to fight the urge to cover my nose and mouth. I step across the threshold, coughing.

And stop in my tracks at the sight in front of me.

Shocked by the sight of a half-naked girl sitting on the floor, I look around the room and notice that nearly everyone is half-naked.

"Lose the top," a young guy with a beard says to a bleach-blond girl. She rolls her eyes but quickly disposes of her shirt, leaving her in only a bra and panties.

Staring at the scene a little longer, I realize that they are playing some sort of card game that involves taking their clothes off. This realization is much better than the initial conclusion my mind went to, but only a little.

I'm slightly relieved that Hardin isn't in the group of increasingly naked cardplayers, and I scan the crowded living room but don't see him.

"You coming in, or what?" someone asks. I look around, searching for the source of the voice. "Close the door behind you and come in," he says, stepping forward from behind someone at my left. "Have I met you before, Bambi?"

He chuckles, and I shift uncomfortably as his bloodshot eyes rake over my body, staying too long on my chest to be considered anything but vulgar. I don't like his chosen nickname for me, but I can't seem to find a way to tell him my real name. Given the sound of his voice, I'm sure he's the person that answered Hardin's phone.

I shake my head; all words have dissolved on my tongue.

"Mark," he introduces himself, reaching for my hand, but I flinch away. Mark . . . I instantly recognize the name from Hardin's letter and other stories about him. He's friendly enough, but I know how he really is. I know what he did to all those girls. "This is my flat. Who invited you?"

At first I think he's mad because of the question, but his face just reads bravado instead. His accent is thick, and he *is* attractive. Somewhat frightening, but attractive. His brown hair is sticking up at the front, and his facial hair is messy yet groomed, a "douche-bag, hipster look," as Hardin calls it, but I find it decent. His arms are bare of any tattoos, but two piercings stick out below his bottom lip.

"I'm . . . uhm . . ." I struggle to get a grip on my nerves.

He laughs again and grabs hold of my hand. "Well, Bambi, let's get you a drink to relax you." He smiles. "You're freaking me out."

As he leads me to the kitchen, I'm beginning to wonder if Hardin is even here. Maybe he dropped the car here and his phone before going someplace else. Maybe he's in the car. Why didn't I check it? I should probably go down and do that; he was so tired he just might be napping—

Then my breath is knocked clear from my chest.

If anyone were to ask me how I feel right now, I'm not sure what I would say. I don't think I'd have an answer. There's pain and heartache and panic and rejection, but at the same time I feel numb. I feel nothing and everything at once, and it's the worst sensation I have ever felt.

Leaning against the counter with a joint between his lips and a bottle of liquor in one hand is Hardin. But that's not what makes my heart stop. What stole my breath is the woman sitting on the counter behind him, her bare legs wrapped around his waist, her body around him like it was the most natural thing in the world.

"Scott! Give me the damn vodka. I need to make my new friend Bambi here a drink," Mark yells.

Hardin's bloodshot eyes turn to Mark, and Hardin smiles nastily, a dark look that I have never before seen from him. As he turns from Mark to me, to find out who Bambi is, I'm close enough to see his dilated pupils blow out, instantly wiping away that foreign expression.

"What . . . what are you . . ." He fumbles the words. His eyes follow down my arm and somehow grow even larger as he takes in the sight of Mark's hand over mine. Pure rage fills Hardin's face, and I pull my hand away.

"You two know each other?" my party host asks.

I don't respond. Rather, my eyes narrow in on the woman whose legs are still wrapped around Hardin's waist. He still hasn't made any move to remove her from him. She's wearing only panties and a T-shirt. A plain black T-shirt.

Hardin is wearing his black sweatshirt, but I don't see the familiar peek of a faded T-shirt collar underneath. This random girl is oblivious of the tension, focused only on the joint she just pulled from Hardin's mouth. She even smiles at me, a clueless, obviously intoxicated smile.

I have been rendered silent. Stunned to even imagine that I know this person now before me. I don't think I could speak even if I wanted to. I know Hardin is in a dark place right now, but seeing him like this, high and drunk and with another woman, is too much for me. It's too fucking much, and all I can think of doing is getting as far away as possible.

"I'll take that as a yes." Mark laughs and pulls the bottle of liquor from Hardin's hand.

Hardin still hasn't spoken either. He's just staring at me like I'm a ghost, like I'm an already-forgotten memory that he never expected to have to revisit.

I turn on my heel and push through anyone who gets in my path on my way out of hell. When I make it down one flight of stairs, I lean against the wall and slide down it, out of breath. My ears are ringing and the weight of the last five minutes is crashing down on me—I don't know how I will make it out of this building.

I listen in vain for the sound of boots slamming against the steel stairs, and each silent minute cuts deeper than the last. He didn't even come after me. He let me see him that way and didn't bother to chase after me with an explanation.

I don't have any more tears to give him, not today; but it turns out that crying without tears is much more painful than with, and impossible to control. After all this, all the fights, all the laughs, all the time spent together, this is how he chooses to end it? This is how he tosses me to the side? He has so little respect for me that he's getting high and letting that other woman touch him and wear his clothing after doing God knows what with her?

I can't even allow myself to indulge that thought—it will cripple me. I know what I saw, but knowing and accepting are two different things.

I am good at making excuses for his behavior. I have mastered that talent in the long months of our relationship, and I have been loyal to those excuses to a fault. But now there is no excuse. Even the pain he feels from the betrayal of his mother and Christian doesn't give him a pass to hurt me this way. I have done nothing to him to warrant what he's doing right now. My only mistake was trying to be there for him and putting up with his displaced anger for far too long.

The humiliation and pain is transforming into anger the longer I sit in this empty staircase. It's a heavy, thick, overbearing fucking anger—and I'm done making excuses for him. I'm done letting him do this shit and letting it go with just a simple apology and promise to change.

No. Hell no.

I'm not going out without a fight. I refuse to walk away and let him think it's okay to treat people this way. He obviously has no regard for himself, or for me right now, and as the angry thoughts fill my head, I can't stop my feet from pounding back up those shitty stairs and back into that hellhole of an apartment.

Pushing open the door so that it slams into someone, I make my way back to the kitchen. My anger surges further when I find Hardin still in the same exact spot, the exact same whore still attached to his back.

"No one, man. She's just some random . . ." he's saying to Mark.

I can barely see straight I'm so angry. Before he can register me, I grab the bottle of vodka from Hardin's hand and throw it against the wall. It shatters, and the room falls silent. I feel detached from my body; I'm watching an angry, outrageous version of myself losing her mind, and I can't stop her.

"What the *fuck*, Bambi?" Mark shouts.

I turn to him. "My name is Tessa!" I yell.

Hardin's eyes close, and I watch, waiting for him to speak up, to say anything.

"Well, *Tessa*. You didn't have to break the vodka!" Mark sarcastically replies. He's too high to even care about the mess I made; apparently his only issue is the liquor spilt.

"I learned how to smash bottles against walls from the best." I glare at Hardin.

"You didn't tell me you had a girlfriend now," the skank latched onto Hardin says.

I look back and forth between Mark and the woman. There is an obvious resemblance . . . and I've read that letter too many damn times to not know who she is.

"Leave it to Scott to bring a crazy-ass American chick into my flat, throwing bottles and shit," Mark says, clearly amused.

"Don't," Hardin says, stepping toward us.

I give him my best poker face. My chest is rising and falling with deep, panicked breaths, but my face is a mask, a front devoid of any emotion. Just like his.

"Who is this chick?" Mark asks Hardin as if I were not standing there.

Hardin dismisses me again by saying, "I already told you," not even having the balls to look at me while degrading me in front of a room full of people.

But I've had enough. "What the hell is *wrong with you*?" I

scream. "You think you can slum it here and smoke pot all day long to forget about your problems?"

I know how crazy I'm acting, but, for once, I couldn't care less what anyone thinks of me. I don't give him a chance to answer before I continue. "You are so selfish! You think pushing me away and closing yourself off is good for me? You know damn well how this goes by now! You can't last without me—you'll just be miserable, and so will I. You aren't doing me any good by hurting me, yet I find you like *this*?"

"You don't know what you're even talking about," Hardin says, his voice low and intimidating.

"I don't?" I throw my hands up. "She's wearing your fucking shirt!" I scream, and point at the fucking whore, who hops down from the counter, tugging at the hem of Hardin's shirt to cover her thighs. She's much smaller than me and the shirt looks gigantic on her. The image will be burned into my memory until my last day, I know it will. I can feel it burning into me now, my entire body is burning, on fire with rage, and in this moment of pure, raw, fucking anger . . . it all clicks.

Everything makes sense to me now. My earlier thoughts regarding love and not giving up on the one you love couldn't be further from the truth. I was wrong this entire time. When you love people, you don't let them destroy you along with themselves, you don't allow them to drag you through the mud. You try to help them, try to save them, but the moment that your love is one-sided or selfish, if you keep trying, you are a fool.

If I loved him, I wouldn't let him ruin me, too.

I have tried and tried with Hardin. I have given him chance after chance after chance, and this time I thought everything would be fine. I actually thought this would work. I thought if I loved him enough, if I only tried harder, it could work and we could be happy.

"Why are you even here?" he asks, interrupting my epiphany.

"What? You thought I would let you get away with being a coward?" Behind the pain, the anger begins to sizzle. I'm terrified for its departure, but I almost welcome the resolve as it settles over me. For the last seven months, I have been weakened by Hardin's words and this cycle of rejection, but now I see our volatile relationship for what it is.

Inevitable.

It's always been inevitable, and I can't believe that it took me all this time to see that, to accept it.

"I'll give you one last chance to leave with me now and go back home, but if I walk out of this door without you, that will be it."

His silence and the smug look in his impaired eyes pushes me further over the edge.

"Thought so." I'm not even yelling anymore. There is no point. He isn't listening. He never has. "You know what? You can have all of this, you can drink and smoke your fucking life away"—I step closer, stopping only a few feet from him—"but this is all you will ever have. So I hope you enjoy it while it lasts."

"I will," he responds, cutting through me. Again.

"So, if she isn't your girlfriend . . ." Mark says to Hardin, reminding me that we aren't alone in the room.

"I am *no one's* girlfriend," I snap.

My attitude seems to spur Mark further; his smile grows, and his hand moves to my back in an attempt to lead me back into the living room. "Good, it's settled, then."

"Get off of her!" Hardin's hands push against Mark's back, not hard enough to knock him down, but with enough force to push him away from me. "Outside, now!" Hardin snaps while walking past me through the living room and out the door. I follow him out into the hallway and slam the door behind me.

He tugs at his hair, his temper rising. "What the fuck was that?"

"What was *what*? Me calling you out on your shit? You think you can just shove a plane ticket and a key chain into a suitcase and I'll go away?" I shove at his chest, pushing him against the wall. I almost apologize, I almost feel guilty for pushing him, but when I look up into his dilated eyes, every trace of remorse dissolves. He reeks of pot and liquor; there's no hint of the Hardin I love.

"I'm so fucking lost in my own head right now that I can't think straight, let alone give you a fucking explanation for the thousandth goddamn time!" he yells, slamming a fist into the cheap drywall, cracking it.

I have witnessed this scene one too many times. This one will be the last. "You didn't even try! I did nothing wrong!"

"What more do you need, Tessa? Do you need me to fucking spell it for you? Get out of here—go back where you belong! You have no business in this place, you don't fit in." By the time he gets to the last word, his voice is neutral—soft, even. Disinterested, almost.

I don't have any fight left in me. "Are you happy now? You win, Hardin. You win yet again. You always do, though, don't you?"

He turns, looking me straight in the eyes. "You know that better than anyone, wouldn't you say?"

chapter fourteen

TESSA

I don't know how I manage to make it to Heathrow on time, but I do.

Kimberly gives me a goodbye hug when she drops me off, I think. I do remember Smith just watching me, calculating something unknowable.

And here I sit on the plane, next to an empty seat, with an empty mind, and an empty heart. I couldn't have been more wrong about Hardin, and that really does just go to show that people can only change themselves, no matter how hard you try. They have to want it as bad as you do or there is no hope.

It's impossible to change people who have their mind set on who they are. You can't support them enough to make up for their low expectations, and you can't love them enough to make up for the hate they feel for themselves.

It's a losing battle, and finally after all this time, I am ready to surrender.

chapter fifteen

HARDIN

James's voice rings in my ear, and his bare foot is rubbing against my cheek. "Dude! Get up. Carla's almost here, and you're hogging the only bathroom."

"Fuck off," I groan, closing my eyes again. If I *could* move, what I would do is break his toes.

"Scott, get the fuck up. You can crash on the couch, but you're a fucking giant and I need to piss and at least attempt to brush my teeth." His toes press against my forehead, and I attempt to sit up. My body feels like a fucking bag of bricks, and my eyes and throat burn.

"He's alive!" James calls.

"Shut the fuck up." I cover my ears and walk past him into the living room. Empty beer bottles and red cups are being tossed into trash bags by a half-naked Janine and an overenthusiastic Mark.

"So, how was the bathroom floor?" Mark lilts through the cigarette between his lips.

"It was ace." I roll my eyes and sit down on the couch.

"You were fucking *wrecked*," he says quite proudly. 'When was the last time you drank like that?"

"I don't know." I rub my temples, and Janine hands me a cup. I shake my head, but she pushes it closer.

"It's only water."

"I'm fine." I don't mean to be a dick to her, but, fuck, she's annoying.

"You were so fucked-up," Mark says. "I thought that American . . . what was her name, Trisha?" My heart pounds in my chest at the mention of her name, even if he got it wrong. "I thought she was going to tear the place down! She was a feisty little thing."

Images of Tessa screaming at me, throwing a bottle against the wall, and walking away from me flood my memory. The weight of the pain in her eyes presses me farther into the couch, and I feel like I'm going to get sick again.

It's for the best.

It is.

Janine rolls her eyes. "Little? I wouldn't say she was little."

"I *know* you're not insulting her looks," I say coolly, despite the burning urge to throw the cup of water in Janine's face. If Janine thinks she's anywhere near as beautiful as Tessa, she's been snorting more cocaine than I thought.

"She's not as skinny as me."

One more bitchy comment, Janine, and I'll tear your self-confidence to shreds.

"Sis, no offense, but that chick was way hotter than you. That's probably why Hardin is so in loo-ove." Mark draws out the last word.

"In *love*? Please! He kicked her ass out of here last night." Janine laughs, and the knife twists in my stomach.

"I'm not—" I can't even finish the sentence with a steady voice. "Don't bring her up again. I'm not fucking around," I threaten the pair.

Janine mumbles something under her breath, and Mark chuckles while emptying an ashtray into a trash bag. I lay my head against the cushion behind my back and close my eyes. I'm not going to be able to be sober, ever. Not if I want this pain to go away; not if I have to sit here with a hollowed-out fucking chest.

I feel antsy and impatient, nauseated and exhausted, and it's the worst fucking combination.

"She will be here in twenty minutes!" James says. I open my eyes and find him dressed and walking in circles in the small living room.

"We know. Shut up, already. We go through this once a month." Janine lights a joint, and I reach for it the moment she exhales.

I have to self-medicate; there is no other option for a coward like me, hovering in a corner and hiding from the throbbing ache of having my entire life ripped away from me.

I cough on the first hit. My lungs haven't missed the dry burn from forcing too much pot on them. After the third hit, the ache dims, the numbness taking over. Not completely the way it should, but I'm getting there. I'll be back in form.

"Give me that, too." I reach for the bottle in Janine's hand.

"It's not even noon," she says, screwing the lid on.

"I didn't ask you for the time and temperature. I asked for the vodka." I rip it from her hands, and she huffs in annoyance.

"So you dropped out of uni, then?" Mark asks, blowing circles with the smoke leaving his mouth.

"No . . ." *Shit.* "I don't know. I haven't gotten that far yet." I take a swig of the liquor, welcoming the burn as it travels down into my empty body. I have no fucking idea what I'll do about school. I only have half a semester left until I graduate. I've already turned in the graduation paperwork and opted out of the damn ceremony. I also have an apartment with all my shit in it and a car parked at Sea-Tac Airport.

"Janine, go make sure the sink is empty of dishes," Mark says.

"No, I always get stuck doing your fucking dishes—"

"I'll buy your lunch. I know you're broke," he says, which works, and she leaves us alone in the living room. I can hear

James shuffling around in his bedroom; it sounds like he's redecorating the place.

"What's with this Carla chick?" I ask Mark.

"She's James's girlfriend. She's real cool, actually, but she's a bit of a snob. Not like bitchy or anything, she's just not into all this shit." Mark waves his hands around the dingy apartment. "She's in med school and her parents have money and shit."

I laugh. "Then what the hell is wrong with her that she's with James?"

"I can hear you, cunts!" James yells from his bedroom.

Mark's laughing now, much harder than I am. "I don't know, but he's fucking pussy-whipped and panics every time she comes to visit. She lives in Scotland, so it's only like once a month, but this is how it always is. He's always trying to impress her. That's why he enrolled in uni, even if he already failed two classes."

"And that's why he fucks your sister all the time?" I raise a brow. James was never a one-woman man, that's for damn sure.

James pops his head around the corner to defend himself. "I only see Carla once a month, and I haven't fucked Janine in weeks!" He disappears again. "Now stop talking shit before I kick both your asses out!"

"Fine! Go shave your balls or something," Mark taunts him, and passes the joint to me. He taps the label on the vodka bottle resting between my legs. "Look, Scott, I'm not into all this relationship-drama bullshit, but you're not fooling anybody here with this whole act."

"It's not an act," I snap.

"Sure, sure. All I'm getting at is that you show up here in London after being gone for three years, not to mention that chick you brought with you." His eyes move from my face to the bottle, to the joint. "And you're bingeing. Plus, I think your hand is broken."

"It's none of your business. Since when do you give a fuck

about bingeing? You do it every day." I'm growing more and more annoyed with Mark and his sudden need to pry into my fucking life. I ignore his comment about my hand, which admittedly is turning purple and green. But that shitty drywall couldn't have broken my hand.

"Don't be a dick; you can indulge all you want. I don't remember you being this sensitive; you were fucking ruthless before."

"I'm not sensitive; you're just making something out of nothing. That chick is some random girl from my college in America. I met her and fucked her. She wanted to see England, so she paid our way here, and I fucked her again in the queen's realm. End of story." I take another drink of vodka to drown the bullshit I'm spewing.

Mark still doesn't look convinced. "Sure." He rolls his eyes—a pesky habit he picked up from his sister.

Annoyed, I turn and face him, but even before I speak, I feel bile rising in my throat. "Look, when I met her, she was a virgin, and I fucked her to win a bet worth a good chunk of fucking change, so, no, I'm not sensitive. She's no one to me—"

This time I can't swallow it down. I cover my mouth and dash past James, who ends up cussing me out for puking all over the bathroom floor.

chapter sixteen

TESSA

"This thing is like a little laptop." I press another button on my new gadget. My new iPhone has more functions than a computer. I run my finger over the large screen, tapping on the small squares. Tapping on the small camera box, I jump back when an unflattering angle of me cringes back at me. I quickly close it, pressing down on the Safari icon. I type Google because, well, that's my first instinct. This phone is so odd. It's more than confusing, but I'm in no hurry to learn how to navigate the thing. I've only had it for ten minutes and haven't even left the store yet. Everyone makes it seem so simple, tapping and sliding their fingers across the gigantic screen, but there are so many options. Too many, really.

Still, I suppose it's fun to have so many options to occupy my time. This thing could keep me busy for hours, days maybe. I scroll through the music choices and am amazed by the idea of having endless songs at the tap of a finger.

"Did you want me to help you transfer your contacts and pictures and stuff to your new phone?" the young girl behind the counter asks. I had forgotten that she and Landon were here; I was so entranced by attempting to learn how to use this phone.

"Uhm, no, thank you," I politely decline.

"Are you sure?" Her heavily lined eyes are surprised. "It only takes a sec." She chews her gum.

"I have all the numbers I need memorized."

She shrugs her shoulders and stares at Landon.

"I need yours," I say to him. My mother and Noah's numbers were always the only ones of necessity. I need a fresh start, a new beginning. My shiny new phone with only a few numbers saved in it will help that. As much as I always refused to get a new phone before, I'm glad I did now.

It feels surprisingly refreshing to start over: no contacts, no pictures, nothing.

Landon guides me through saving a new number, and we leave the store.

"I'll show you how to get your music back. It's easier on this phone anyway," Landon says, smiling as he turns onto the freeway. We are on our way back from the mall, where I had to spend too much money on a week's worth of clothes.

A clean break, that's what this needs to be. No reminiscing, no scrolling through photo after photo. I don't know where to go, what to do next, but I do know that holding on to something that was never mine will only hurt more.

"Do you know how my father is doing?" I ask Landon over lunch.

"Ken called in on Saturday, and they told him that Richard was adjusting. The first few days are going to be the worst." Landon reaches across the table to steal fries from my plate.

"Do you know when I can visit him?" If all I have is my estranged-until-only-a-month-ago father and Landon, I want to hold on to both of them as closely as I can.

"I don't know for sure, but I will ask when we get back to the house." Landon looks over at me. I hold on to my new phone, bringing it to my chest without thinking about it. Landon's eyes fill with sympathy. "I know it's only been one day, but have you given New York any thought?" he asks cautiously.

"Yes, a little."

I'm waiting to make the decision until I talk to Kimberly and Christian in person. I heard from her this morning, and she said they will be leaving England on Thursday. I'm still trying to figure out how it's only Tuesday. It feels much longer than two days since I left London.

My mind goes to *him* and what he's doing . . . or who he's with. Is he touching that girl right now? Is she wearing his shirt again? Why am I torturing myself with thoughts of him? I've been avoiding him, and now I can see his bloodshot green eyes, I can feel the tips of his fingers brushing across my cheek.

I was both hurt and pathetically relieved when I found a dirty black T-shirt while rummaging through my suitcase at Chicago O'Hare. I started off looking for my phone charger and ended up finding his last blow. I couldn't bring myself, no matter how many times I tried, to walk over and throw it into the nearest trash can. I couldn't. Instead, I shoved it back into the suitcase and buried it under my clothes.

So much for a clean break, but I'm giving myself a break, given how hard all this feels. How my entire world has been ripped apart, and I'm left alone to sort out the pieces . . .

No. As I resolved on the plane, I won't indulge in such thinking. These thoughts are getting me nowhere. Feeling sorry for myself only makes it worse.

"I'm leaning towards New York, but I need a little more time to decide," I tell Landon.

"Good." His smile is contagious. "We would leave in about three weeks at the end of the semester."

"I hope so." I sigh, desperately wanting time to pass. A minute, an hour, a day, a week, a month, any time that passes can only be a good thing for me at this point.

And so it does, time passes, and somehow I find myself moving along with it. The problem is, I haven't decided if that's a good thing or not.

chapter seventeen

HARDIN

Opening the front door of the apartment, I'm surprised when I find all the lights on. Tessa usually doesn't keep them all running at once; she's a stickler for keeping our electricity bill low.

"Tess, I'm home. Are you in the room?" I call out. I can smell dinner in the oven, and soft music is playing on our little stereo.

I toss my binder and keys onto the table and go in search of her. I quickly notice that the bedroom door's slightly open, and then I hear voices snaking out through the opening, as if riding the music out into the hallway. The moment I hear *his* voice, I shove the door open with anger.

"What the fuck!" I scream, the sound booming through the small bedroom.

"Hardin? What are you doing here?" Tessa asks as if I'm intruding. She pulls the comforter up to cover her bare body, a faint smile resting on her lips.

"What am I doing here? What is *he* doing here?" I point an accusatory finger at Zed, who scrambles off the bed and begins pulling his boxers on.

Tessa continues to glare at me like I'm the one fucking some shithead in our bed. "You can't keep coming here, Hardin." The tone of her voice is so dismissive, so mocking. "This is the third time this month." She sighs, lowering her voice. "Have you been drinking again?" The question is laced with sympathy and annoyance.

Zed crosses in front of the bed and protectively stands in front of her, his arm hovering over her . . . her swollen belly.

No . . .

"Are you?" I choke out. "You're . . . you and him?"

She sighs again, tightening the blanket around her. "Hardin, we have been over this so many times. You don't live here. You haven't lived here for, I forget, something like over two years now." She's so matter-of-fact about it all, and the way her eyes search Zed's face for help with my intrusion isn't lost on me.

Confused, the air taken out of me, I crumple to my knees in front of the two of them. And then quickly feel a hand on my shoulder.

"I'm sorry, but you have to go. You're upsetting her." Zed's voice gently mocks me.

"You can't do this to me," I beg her, reaching my hand toward her pregnant belly. It can't be real. It *can't* be real.

"You did this to yourself," she says. "I'm sorry, Hardin, but you did this."

Zed rubs her arms to calm her, and rage rips through me. I dig into my pocket and pull out my lighter. Neither of them notice; they just cling to each other as my thumb flicks over the lighter. The small flame is familiar, an old friend now, as I bring the flame to the curtain. My eyes close as Tessa's face is illuminated by the angry flames consuming the room.

"HARDIN!" MARK'S FACE is the first thing I see when my eyes fly open. I push his face away and fling myself from the couch and fall onto the floor in a panic.

Tessa was . . . and I was . . .

"You were having one hell of a dream, man." Mark shakes his head at me. "Are you okay? You're soaked."

I blink a few times and run my hands through my sweat-drenched hair. My hand is killing me. I figured the bruising would lighten up by now, but it hasn't.

"Are you okay?"

"I . . ." I have to get out of here. I have to go somewhere or do something. The image of the room in flames is burned into my memory.

"Take this and go back to sleep; it's four in the morning." He pulls the top off a plastic bottle and drops a single pill into my sweaty palm.

I nod, unable to speak. I dry-swallow the pill and lie back on the couch. Eyeing me one last time, Mark disappears back into his bedroom, and I pull my phone from my pocket and look at Tessa's picture.

Before I can stop myself, my finger is running over the call button. I know I shouldn't, but if I can just hear her voice once, maybe I'll sleep peacefully.

"Your call cannot be completed as dialed . . ." a robotic voice intones coldly. *What?* I check my screen and try again. Same message. Again and again.

She couldn't have changed her number. She wouldn't . . .

"Your call cannot be . . ." I hear for the tenth time.

Tessa changed her number. She changed her phone number, to make sure I can't reach her.

When I fall asleep again, hours later, I'm met with a different dream. It begins the same, with me coming home to that apartment, but this time no one is home.

chapter eighteen

HARDIN

Y ou still haven't let me finish what I started on Sunday." Janine leans into me, resting her head on my shoulder. I move over on the couch a little to get away from her, but taking it as a sign that maybe we're going to lie down together or something, she only moves closer.

"I'm good." I turn her down for the hundredth time in the past four days. Has it really been only four days?

Fuck.

Time needs to move faster, or I don't know if I'll survive.

"You need to loosen up. I can help you with that." Her fingers trail down my bare back. I haven't showered in days, or worn a shirt. I couldn't bring myself to put the damn thing back on after Janine wore it. It smelled like her, not like my angel.

Fucking Tessa. I'm going crazy. I can feel the hinges holding my mind in one piece being pulled farther, ready to snap completely.

This is what happens every time I sober up—she creeps into my mind. The nightmare I was tortured with last night still haunts me. I would never hurt her, not physically. I love her. Loved her. Fuck, I still love her and I always will, but there isn't shit I can do about it.

I can't fight every day of my life to be perfect for her. I'm not what she needs, and I never will be.

"I need a drink," I tell Janine. She gets up from the couch languorously and goes into the kitchen. But when another unwelcomed thought of Tessa intrudes, I yell out, "Hurry up."

She walks in holding a bottle of whiskey, but stops and gives me a look. "Who the hell do you think you're talking to? If you're going to be an asshole, you can at least make it worth my while."

I haven't left this apartment since I arrived, not even to walk down and get a change of clothes from my rental car.

"I still say your hand is broken," James says as he walks into the living room, interrupting my thoughts. "Carla knows what she's talking about. You should just go to the clinic."

"No, I'm fine." I ball my fist and splay my fingers to prove the point. I flinch and curse at the ache. I know it's broken, I just don't want to do shit about it. I have been self-medicating for four days now; a few more won't hurt.

"It's never going to heal if you don't. Just go real quick, and when you get back, you can have that bottle to yourself," James insists. I miss the asshole James. The James who would fuck a chick and show the tape to the chick's boyfriend an hour later. This concerned-for-my-health James is annoying as fuck.

"Yeah, Hardin, he's right," Janine butts in, moving the whiskey behind her back.

"Fine! Fuck," I grumble. I grab my keys and phone and leave the apartment. I grab a shirt from the backseat of the rental and throw it on before heading to the hospital.

THE WAITING ROOM is crowded with too many noisy children, and I'm stuck in the only empty seat, which is next to a whiny homeless man who got his foot run over.

"How long have you been waiting?" I ask the man.

He smells like garbage, but I can't say shit, because I probably smell worse than he does. He reminds me of Richard, and I wonder how he is doing in rehab. Tessa's father is in rehab, and here I am drowning myself in liquor and clouding my mind with excessive amounts of pot and the occasional pill from Mark. The world is an amazing place.

"Two hours," the man responds.

"Fucking hell," I mumble to myself and stare at the wall. I should have known not to come here at eight at night.

Thirty minutes later, my homeless companion's name is called, and I'm relieved to be able to breathe from my nose again.

"My fiancée is in labor," a man announces as he enters the lobby. He's dressed in a neatly pressed button-down shirt and khaki pants. He looks oddly familiar.

When a petite and very pregnant brunette steps out from behind him, I sink lower in the plastic chair. Of course this would be happening. I would be on a bender, getting my broken hand looked at, at the exact moment *she* goes into labor and arrives at the hospital.

"Can you help us?" he says, pacing back and forth frantically. "She needs a wheelchair! Her water broke twenty minutes ago, and her contractions are only five minutes apart!"

His antics are making the other patients in the waiting room start to get a little anxious, but the pregnant woman just laughs and wraps her hand around her man's. But then, that's Natalie for you.

"I'm okay to walk, I'm fine. It's okay." Natalie explains to the nurse that her fiancé, Elijah, is more panicked than necessary. While he continues to pace, and she remains calm, almost hostesslike, I laugh from my seat, and Natalie looks over to find me staring.

A big smile fills her face. "Hardin! What a coincidence!" Is this the pregnant-woman glow people are always going on about?

"Hey," I say, looking everywhere except her fiancé's face.

"I hope you're well." She comes closer to me while her guy

talks to the nurse. "I met your Tessa just the other day. Is she here with you?" Natalie asks, searching the lobby.

Shouldn't she be like screaming in pain or something? "No, she's, uhm . . ." I begin to make up an explanation, but right then another nurse steps from behind the check-in station and says, "Miss, we're ready for you."

"Oh, hear that? The show must go on." Natalie turns, but then looks over her shoulder and waves at me. "It was good to see you, Hardin!"

I sit there, my mouth agape.

This must be some sick joke from above. I can't help but be a little happy for the girl; her life wasn't completely ruined by me . . . Here she is, smiling and madly in love, ready to have her first child while I sit alone, smelling and wounded in the crowded waiting room.

Karma has finally caught up to me.

chapter nineteen

TESSA

Thank you for following me here. I just wanted to drop the car off and grab the last of my things," I tell Landon through the passenger window of his car.

I was conflicted when it came to where to leave the car. I didn't want to leave it parked at Ken's house, because I was afraid of what Har—*he* . . . will say or do when he eventually shows up to get it. Parking it in the lot at the apartment makes more sense; it's a nice, well-patrolled area, and I don't think anyone will mess with it without being caught.

"Are you sure you don't want me to come up there with you? I could help you carry stuff down," Landon offers.

"No, I'll go alone. I only have a few things anyway. It will only take one trip. Thank you, though." All of which is the truth, but the truth-truth is that I just want to say goodbye to our old place on my own. On my own: it feels more natural that way now.

When I walk into the lobby, I try not to let old memories flood my mind. I think of nothing—blank white spaces and white flowers and white carpet and white walls. No thoughts of him. Only white spaces and flowers and walls, not him.

My mind has another plan for me, however, and slowly the white walls are streaked with black, the carpet is soiled with black paint, and the flowers rot into black waste leaves and flake away.

I'm only here to grab a few things, only one box of clothes and a folder from school, that's it. I'll be in and out in five minutes. Five minutes isn't long enough to get sucked back into the darkness.

It's been four days now, and I'm only growing stronger. It's getting easier to breathe with each second that passes without him. Going back here, to this place, could end up being a terrible blow to my progress, but I need to get this over with if I want to move on and never look back. I'm going to New York.

I'm going to forgo summer-semester classes, like I'd been considering, and get to know the city that will be my home, at least for a few years. Once I'm there, I'm not leaving until I graduate from college. Another transfer on my transcripts will only make me look bad, so I have to stay in one place until I finish. And that place will be New York City. It's a scary thought, and my mother won't be happy about the move, but it's not up to her. It's up to me, and I'm finally making decisions based solely on *my* needs and *my* future. My father will be finished with his rehab program by the time I get settled in, and if it's possible, I'd love for him to come visit me and Landon.

I begin to panic just thinking about my lack of preparations for this move, but Landon is going to help me sort out all of the details; we have spent the last two days applying for grant after grant. Ken has drafted and sent out a recommendation letter, and Karen has been helping me google part-time jobs. Sophia has been over every day, too, filling me in on the hottest spots in town and warning me of the dangers of living in such a massive city. She was sweet enough to offer to speak with her boss about helping me get a job as a hostess at the restaurant she'll be at herself.

Ken, Karen, and Landon recommended that I just transfer to the new Vance Publishing branch that will be opening within the next few months. Living in New York City without an income will be impossible, but it's just as impossible to get a paid internship without graduating college first. I still haven't talked to Kimberly about my move, but she has so much going on right now and they just returned from London. I've barely heard from her, only a text

here and there, but she assures me she will call as soon as everything settles down.

Pushing my key into the lock of our apartment, it hits me that
a hatred for the space has taken root since I was last here, making it hard for me to believe that I ever loved this place so much.
Entering, I see the light is on in the living room: just like him to
leave it on before going on an international trip.

I guess it was only a week ago, though. Time is tricky when
you're in hell.

I walk straight to the bedroom and into the closet to grab
the folder I came for. No reason to draw this out any longer than
needed. The manila folder isn't on the shelf where I remember its
being, so I'm left sifting through piles of Hardin's work. He probably shoved the folder into the closet while attempting to clean the
messy room.

That old shoe box is still on the shelf, and my curiosity gets
the best of me. I reach for it, pull it down, and sit cross-legged on
the floor. I lift the top off and set it aside. The box is full of page
after page of his handwriting scribbled in random lines, covering
the front and back of the pages. I notice that some of the pages
are typed, and I choose one of those to read.

> *You pierce my soul. I am half agony, half hope. Tell me
> not that I am too late, that such precious feelings are gone
> for ever. I offer myself to you again with a heart even more
> your own than when you almost broke it, eight years and a
> half ago. Dare not say that man forgets sooner than woman,
> that his love has an earlier death. I have loved none but you.*

I immediately recognize the words of Austen. I read through
a few pages, recognizing quote after quote, lie after lie, so I reach
for one of the handwritten pages instead.

That day, day five, is when the weight appeared on my chest. A constant reminder of what I have done, and most likely lost. I should have called her that day while staring at her pictures. Did she stare at mine? She only has one to this day, and ironically I found myself wishing I would have allowed her to take more. Day five was when I threw my phone against the wall in the hopes of smashing it, but I only managed to crack the screen. Day five is when I desperately wished she would call me. If she called me then it would be okay, everything would be okay. We would both apologize and I would go home.

As I read through the paragraph for the second time, my eyes threaten to spill tears.

Why am I torturing myself by reading this? He must have written this long ago, right after he returned from London the last time. He has changed his mind completely and wants nothing to do with me, and finally I'm okay with that. I have to be. I'll read one more paragraph and I'll put the lid back on the box, only one more, I promise myself.

Day six I woke with swollen and bloodshot eyes. I couldn't believe the way I broke down the previous night. The weight on my chest had magnified and I could barely see straight. Why am I such a fuckup? Why did I continue to treat her like shit? She is the first person who has ever been able to see me, inside of me, the real me, and I treated her like shit. I blame her for everything when in reality it was me. It was always me, even when I wasn't doing anything wrong, I was. I was rude to her when she tried to talk to me about things, I yelled at her when she called me out on my bullshit, and I lied to her repeatedly. She has forgiven

me for everything, always. I could always count on that and
maybe that's why I treated her the way I did, because I knew
I could. I smashed my phone under my boot on day six.

That's it. I can't read any more without breaking every ounce
of strength I have built since I left him in London. I toss the
pages back into the box and slam the lid down. Unwelcome
tears spill from my traitorous eyes, and I can't get out of here fast
enough. I would rather call the administrative office and get re-
prints of all my transcripts than spend another minute in this
apartment.

I leave the shoe box on the floor of the closet and walk across
the hall to the bathroom to check my makeup before I go back
downstairs and face Landon. Pushing the door open, I turn the
light on, yelping in surprise when my foot catches on something.

Someone . . .

My blood turns to ice, and I try to focus on the body on the
floor of the bathroom. This isn't happening.

Please, God, don't let it be . . .

And when my eyes focus, half of a prayer is answered. It's not
the boy who left me that's lying still on the floor at my feet.

It's my father, with a needle sticking out of his arm and no
color in his face. Which means half of my nightmares have been
fulfilled instead.

chapter twenty

HARDIN

The pudgy doctor's glasses are hanging from the bridge of his nose, and I can practically smell the judgment radiating off him. I assume he's still mad that I flew off the handle after being asked "Are you sure you hit a wall?" for the tenth time. I know what he's thinking, and he can fuck off.

"You have a metacarpal fracture," he informs me.

"English, please?" I mumble. I've calmed, for the most part, but I'm still beyond pissed-off by his questioning and hard stares. Working in the busiest clinic in London, he has surely seen worse than me, but he still glares at me every chance he gets.

"Bro-ken," he says in a slow voice. "Your hand is broken, and you'll need to wear a cast for a few weeks. I'll give you a prescription to help manage the pain, but you'll just have to wait it out, wait for the bones to knit back together."

I don't know which is more laughable, the idea of wearing a cast or that he seems to think I need help managing my pain. There's nothing that any pharmacist can dole out that'll help with my pain. Unless they've got a selfless blonde with blue-gray eyes on their shelves, they've got nothing for me.

AN HOUR LATER my hand and wrist are covered in a thick plaster. I tried not to laugh in the old man's face when he asked me what color cast I wanted. I remember being young and wishing to have a cast for all my friends to sign their names and draw stupid pictures in permanent marker across; too bad I didn't have any friends until I found my place with Mark and James.

Those two are so different now than they were as teens. I mean, Mark is still a dipshit, his brain fried from too many drugs. Nothing will reverse that. But the changes in both men are quite evident. James is pussy-whipped by some med student, which is something I would never have expected. Mark is still wild, still living in a world without consequence, but he's softer now, more relaxed, and comfortable with living the way he is. Sometime in the last three years they both lost the hardness that used to cover them like a blanket. No, like a shield. I don't know what caused that change in them, but given my current *situation*, I don't welcome it. I expected the same assholes from three years ago, but those blokes are nowhere to be found.

Yes, they still do more drugs than humanly possible, but they're not the same malicious delinquents they were when I left London years ago.

"Stop by the chemist, and you'll be good to go." The doctor gives me a quick nod and leaves me alone in the exam room.

"Fuck." I tap on the hard surface of the stupid cast. This is such bullshit. Will I be able to drive? To write?

Fuck no, I don't need to write anything anyway. That shit needs to stop now; it has gone on long enough, and my sober mind keeps fucking with me, slipping thoughts and memories in when I'm too distracted to keep them out.

Karma keeps fucking with me, and true to her bitchy reputation, she continues the mockery as I pull my phone from my pocket to find Landon's name across the screen. I ignore the call and shove the thing back into my jeans.

What a fucking mess I've made.

chapter twenty-one

TESSA

"How long will she be like this?" Landon says to someone somewhere. Everyone is acting like I can't hear them, like I'm not even present, but I don't mind. I don't want to be here, and it feels good to be here but feel invisible at the same time.

"I don't know. She's in shock, honey," Karen's sweet voice answers her son.

Shock? I'm not in shock.

"I should have gone inside with her!" Landon chokes out through a sob.

If I could look away from the cream-colored wall in the Scotts' living room, I know that I would see him in his mother's arms.

"She was up there alone with his body for almost an hour. I thought she was just getting her stuff, and maybe even some closure—but I let her sit up there with his dead body for an hour!"

Landon's crying so much, and I should comfort him; I know I should, and I would if I could.

"Oh, Landon." Karen's crying, too.

Everyone seems to be crying except me. What is wrong with me?

"It's not your fault. You couldn't have known he was there; you couldn't have known that he left his program."

At some point during the hushed whispers and sympathetic attempts to get me to move from my spot on the floor, the sun has gone down and the attempts come less often, until finally they stop completely, and I'm left alone in the oversize living room with my knees hugged tightly against my chest and my eyes never, ever leaving the wall.

Through the paramedics' and police officers' rushed voices and orders, I learned that my father was in fact dead. I knew it when I saw him, when I touched him, but they confirmed it. They made it official. He died by his own hand, from pushing the needle into his vein. The bags of heroin found in the pocket of his jeans spoke of his intent for the weekend. His face was so pale and whitewashed that the image behind my eyelids looks more like a mask than a human face. He was alone in the apartment when it happened, and he had been dead for hours when I stumbled onto his body. His life bled out as the heroin seeped in through the syringe, further damning that hell disguised as an apartment.

That's exactly what that place is—as it had been from the moment I entered it. Bookshelves and a brick wall veiled the evil there, hiding the cursed place with pretty details, masking an evil that every demon in my life seems to point back to, that damn apartment. If I had never stepped across that threshold, I would still have everything.

I would have my virtue; I wouldn't have given it to a man who would never love me enough to stick around.

I would still have my mother; she's not much, but she's the only family I have now.

I would still have a place to live, and I would never have reconnected with my father only to find his lifeless body on the bathroom floor two months later.

I'm well aware of the dark place that my thoughts are dragging me into, but I don't have the strength to fight anymore. I've been fighting for something, for what I thought was everything, for too damn long and I can't do it anymore.

* * *

"HAS SHE SLEPT AT ALL?" Ken's voice is low and cautious.

The sun has come up now, and I can't find the answer to Ken's question. *Have* I slept? I don't remember falling asleep, or waking up, but it doesn't seem possible that an entire night has passed while I've been staring at this blank wall.

"I don't know, she hasn't moved much since last night." The sadness in my best friend's voice is deep and painful.

"Her mum called again an hour ago. Have you heard from Hardin?"

That name coming from Ken's mouth would have just killed me . . . if I weren't already dead.

"No, he won't answer my calls, and I called the number you gave me for Trish, but she hasn't answered either. I think they're still on their honeymoon. I don't know what to do, she's so . . ."

"I know." Ken sighs. "She just needs time; that had to be traumatizing for her. I'm still looking into what the hell happened and why I wasn't informed when he left the facility. I gave them strict orders, along with a healthy amount of money, to call me if something happened."

I want to tell Ken and Landon to stop blaming themselves for my father's mistakes. If anyone is to blame, it's me. I should never have gone to London. I should have been there to keep watch over him. Instead, I was across the world dealing with another loss, and Richard Young was fighting and losing the battle with his own demons, all alone.

KAREN'S VOICE WAKES ME, or jars me out of my trance. Or whatever this is.

"Tessa, please have some water. It's been two days, dear. Your mom's coming here to get you, sweetheart. I hope that's okay," the person I consider closest to being my real mother says softly, trying to get through to me.

I attempt to nod, but my body just won't respond. I don't know what's wrong with me, but I'm screaming from the inside out and no one can hear me.

Maybe I'm in shock after all. Shock isn't a bad place, though. I'd like to stay here as long as I can. It hurts less.

chapter twenty-two

HARDIN

The apartment is full again, and I'm working on my second drink and first joint. The constant burn of liquor on my tongue and smoke in my lungs is starting to get to me. If being sober didn't hurt so fucking bad, I wouldn't touch the shit again.

"It's been two days, and this shit's already itching," I complain to whoever will listen.

"Sucks, man, but next time you won't be putting holes in walls, will you?" Mark taunts me with a smirk.

"Yes, he will," James and Janine say at the same time.

Janine holds her hand out to me. "Give me another one of your pain pills." The fucking junkie has already eaten half the bottle in less than two days. Not that I care—I don't have a use for them, and I sure as fuck don't care about what she puts into her body. At first I thought the pills would help me, get me higher than the shit James has, but they don't. They make me tired, and being tired leads to sleep, which leads to nightmares, which always involve *her*.

I roll my eyes and stand to my feet. "I'll just give you the damn bottle." I walk to Mark's room to get the pills from under my small pile of clothes. It's been almost a week, and I have only changed my clothes once. Before she left, Carla, the annoying chick with a savior complex, sewed some hideous black patches over the holes in my jeans. I would have cussed her ass out if James wouldn't have kicked me out on the spot for doing so.

"Hello, Hardin Scott. Phone!" Janine's high-pitched voice echoes from the living room.

Fuck! I left my phone on the table in the living room.

When I don't respond immediately, I hear Janine say cheekily, "Mr. Scott's busy at the moment; can I ask who's calling?"

"Give me the phone, *now*," I say, darting back into the room and tossing the pills for her to catch. I try to stay calm when she just gives me her middle finger and continues talking, letting the bottle hit the floor. I'm getting fucking tired of her shit.

"Ooohh, Landon sounds like a hot name, and you're American. I love American men—"

All subtlety lost, I snatch the phone from her hand and press it to my ear. "What the hell do you want, Landon? Don't you think if I wanted to talk to you, I would have answered the last . . . I don't know, thirty fucking times you called?" I bark.

"You know what, Hardin?" His voice is equally as harsh as mine. "Fuck you. You're a selfish asshole, and I should have known better than to call you. She will get through this without you, just the way she always has to."

The line goes dead.

Get through what? What the hell is he talking about? Do I even want to know?

Who am I kidding—of course I fucking do. I immediately dial him back and push past a couple of people and go into the empty hallway for some privacy. Panic rises within me, and my fucked-up mind travels to the worst possible scenario. When Janine slinks into the hallway, clearly to eavesdrop, I head out to the rental car I've been hanging on to still.

"What?" he snaps.

"What are you talking about? What happened?" *She's okay, right? She has to be.* "Landon, tell me she's okay." I have no patience for his lack of words.

"It's Richard, he's dead."

Whatever I might have been expecting to hear, that was not it. Through the haze I'm in, I feel it. I feel the sting of loss inside me, and I fucking hate it. I shouldn't feel this, I barely even knew the junk—the man.

"Where's Tessa?" This is why Landon called me so many times. Not to give me a lecture about leaving Tessa, but to let me know her father's dead.

"She's here at the house, but her mother is on her way to get her. She's in shock, I think; she hasn't spoken since she found him."

The last part of his sentence has me reeling and clutching my chest. "What the fuck? She found him?"

"Yeah." Landon's voice breaks at the end and I know he's crying. It doesn't bother me like it usually does.

"Fuck!" *Why did this happen? How could this happen to her just after I sent her away?* "Where was she, where was his body?"

"Your apartment. She went there to get the last of her stuff and drop your car off."

Of course, even after that, and even after how I treated her, she's considerate enough to think of my car.

I force out the words I both want to and don't want to say: "Let me speak to her." I've wanted to hear her voice, and I've hit rock bottom, falling asleep for the last two nights to the robotic message reminding me that she has changed her number.

"Did you not hear me, Hardin?" Landon says, exasperated. "She hasn't spoken or moved in two days except to use the restroom, and I'm not even sure about that. I haven't seen her move at all. She won't drink anything, she won't eat."

All the shit I've been pushing back, trying to ignore, floods over me and pulls me under. I don't care what the repercussions will be, I don't care if the last shred of sanity I have left disappears: I need to talk to her. I reach the car and get in, immediately clear on what I have to do.

"Just try to put the phone to her ear. Listen to me and just do it," I tell Landon and start the car up, silently pleading with whoever is listening up there that I don't get pulled over on the way to the airport.

"I'm just worried that hearing your voice may make it worse," his voice sounds through the speakerphone. I turn the volume all the way up and set the phone on the center console.

"Goddammit, Landon!" I hit my cast against the steering wheel. It's hard enough to drive with a fucking cast as it is. "Put the phone to her ear, *now*, please." I try to keep my voice calm, despite the cyclone ripping me apart from the inside out.

"Fine, but don't say anything to upset her. She's already been through enough."

"Don't talk to me like you know her better than I do!" My anger toward my know-it-all stepbrother has reached a new high, and I nearly run into the median, yelling at him.

"I may not, but you know what I do know? I know that you're a freaking idiot for whatever you did to her this time, and you know what else I know? That if you weren't so damn selfish, you would have been here with her and she wouldn't be in the state she's in now," he spews. "Oh, and one more thing—"

"*Enough!*" I hit my cast against the steering wheel again. "Just put the phone to her ear—you being an asshole isn't going to help anything. Now *give her the fucking phone.*"

Silence is followed by Landon's gentle voice: "Tessa? Can you hear me? Of course you can." He half laughs. I can hear the pain in his voice as he tries to coax her to speak. "Hardin is on the phone, and he . . ."

Soft chanting comes through the speaker, and I lean toward the phone in an attempt to hear the noise. *What is that?* For the next few seconds, it continues, low and haunting, and it takes me too long to realize it's Tessa's voice repeating the same word over and over and over. "No, no, no," she says, not stopping, not slow-ing, "no, no, no, no, no . . ."

What was left of my heart snaps into too many pieces to count.

"No, please, no!" she cries on the end of the line.

Oh God.

"Okay, it's okay. You don't have to talk to him—"

The line goes dead, and I call back, knowing that no one is going to pick up.

chapter twenty-three

TESSA

I'm going to pick you up now," the familiar voice I haven't heard in too long says, trying to comfort me as strong arms lift me from the floor and cradle me like a child.

I bury my head into Noah's solid chest and close my eyes.

My mother's voice is here, too. I don't see her, but I can hear her: "What's wrong with her? Why isn't she talking?"

"She's just in shock," Ken starts to say. "She'll come around soon—"

"Well, what am I supposed to do with her if she won't even speak?" my mother bites back.

Noah, able to deal with my callous mother in a way that no one else can, softly says, "Carol, she just found her dad's body a few days ago. Be easy on her."

I've never been so relieved to be near Noah in my entire life. As much as I love Landon, and as thankful as I am for his family right now, I need to be taken away from this house. I need someone like my oldest friend now. Someone who knew me *before*.

I'm going crazy; I know I am. My mind hasn't been functioning properly since my foot hit the very solid, and very still, body of my father. I haven't been able to process a single rational thought since I cried his name and shook him so hard that his jaw fell open and the needle popped out of his arm, landing with a clinking noise that still echoes inside my broken mind. Such a simple sound. Such a horrific sound.

I felt something inside me snap when my father's hand jerked in mine, an involuntary muscle spasm that I still can't decide about, whether it actually happened or if it was my mind creating a false sense of hope. That hope quickly vanished when I checked his pulse again, only to feel nothing, only to leave me staring into his dead eyes.

Noah's stride gently rocks me as we move through the house.

"I'll call her phone later to check on her. Please answer so I can see how she's doing," Landon softly requests. I want to know how Landon is; I hope he didn't see what I saw, I just can't remember.

I know I was holding my father's head in my hands, and I think I was screaming or crying, or both, when I heard Landon enter the apartment. I remember him trying to fight with me to let go of the man who I was only beginning to know, but after that my mind jumps straight to when the ambulance arrived and blanks out again until I was sitting on the floor at the Scotts' home.

"I will," Noah assures him, and I hear the screen door opening. Cool drops of rain land on my face, washing away days' worth of tears and filth.

"It's okay. We're going home now; it's all going to be okay," Noah whispers to me, his hand pushing my rain-soaked hair off my forehead. I keep my eyes closed and rest my cheek against his chest; its heavy beat only reminds me of when I pressed my ear against my father's chest, only to find no heartbeat, no breathing.

"It's okay," Noah says again. This is just like old times, his coming to my rescue after my father's addictions wreak havoc.

But there are no greenhouses to hide in, not this time. This time there is only darkness and no escape in sight.

"We're going home now," Noah repeats as he places me into a car.

Noah's a dear, sweet person, but doesn't he know that I have no home?

* * *

THE HANDS ON MY CLOCK move so slowly. The longer I stare at them, the more they mock me, slowing down with each click of their hands. My old bedroom is so big—I could have sworn it was a small room, but now it feels massive. Maybe it's me that feels small? I feel light now, lighter than I did the last time I slept in this bed. I feel like I could float away and no one would notice. My thoughts aren't normal; I know this. Noah tells me this each time he tries to talk me back into reality. He's here now; he hasn't left since I lay down in this bed, Lord knows how long ago.

"You're going to be okay, Tessa. *Time heals all.* Remember our pastor always said that." Noah's blue eyes are worried for me.

I nod, staying silent, and stare at the provoking clock hanging on the wall.

Noah drags a fork along the untouched plate of food from hours ago. "Your mother is going to come in and make you eat dinner. It's late, and you still haven't touched your lunch."

I glance toward the window, noting the darkness outside. *When did the sun disappear? And why didn't it take me with it?*

Noah's soft hands gather mine in them, and he asks me to look at him. "Just take a few bites so she will let you rest."

I reach for the plate, not wanting to make things more difficult for him, knowing he's just doing my mother's bidding. I bring the stale bread to my mouth and try not to gag on the rubbery lunchmeat as I chew. I count the time it takes to force myself to take five bites and swallow them down with the room-temperature water left on the nightstand from this morning.

"I need to close my eyes," I tell Noah when he tries to offer me some grapes from the plate. "No more." I gently push the plate away. The sight of food is making me want to vomit.

I lie down and bring my knees to my chest. Noah being Noah reminds me of the time we got in trouble for throwing grapes at each other during Sunday service when we were twelve.

"That was our most rebellious thing we did, I think." he says with a soft laugh.

The sound puts me to sleep.

"YOU'RE NOT GOING IN THERE. The last thing we need is you setting her off. She's sleeping for the first time in days," I hear my mother's voice say from down the hall.

Who is she talking to? I'm not sleeping, am I? I lean up on my elbows, and the blood rushes to my head. I'm so tired, so tired. Noah is here, in my childhood bed with me. It all feels so familiar, the bed, the messy blond hair sticking up from Noah's head. I feel different, though, out of place and disoriented.

"I'm not here to hurt her, Carol. You should know that by now."

"You—" my mother attempts to fight back, but she's interrupted.

"You should also know that I still don't give a fuck what you say." My bedroom door opens, and the last person I thought I'd see pushes past my irate mother.

Noah's arm is heavy across me, weighing me into the bed. His grip tightens on my waist in his sleep, and my throat burns at the sight of Hardin. His green eyes are furious at the sight in front of him. He crosses the room and forcefully yanks Noah's arm from my body.

"What the—" Noah wakes with a startle and jumps to his feet. When Hardin takes another step toward me, I scramble across the twin bed and my back hits the wall, hard. Hard enough to knock the wind from me, but I still try to get away from him. I cough and Hardin's eyes soften.

Why is he here? He can't be here, I don't want him here. He's done enough damage, and he doesn't get to just show up here and pick at the scraps.

"Fuck! Are you okay?" His inked arm reaches for me, and I do the first thing that comes to my twisted mind: I scream.

chapter twenty-four

HARDIN

Her screams fill my ears, my empty chest, my lungs, until they finally rest somewhere inside me that I wasn't quite sure could be reached anymore. A place only she can access, and always will.

"What are you doing here?" Noah jumps to his feet and moves between me and the small bed like some fucking white knight designated to protect her . . . from me?

She's still screaming; why is she screaming?

"Tessa, please . . ." I'm not sure what I'm asking for, but her screams turn to coughs, and her coughs turn to sobs, and her sobs turn to choking sounds that I simply can't handle. I take a cautious step toward her, and she finally catches her breath.

Her haunted eyes still rest on me, burning a hole into me that only she can fill.

"Tess, do you want him here?" Noah asks.

It's taking every ounce of my self-control to ignore that he's here in the first place, and he's really pushing it.

"Get her some water!" I tell her mum. She ignores me.

Then, unbelievably, Tessa's head moves swiftly back and forth, denying me.

That triggers her makeshift protector to raise his hand to me and grow bold. "She doesn't want you here."

"She doesn't know what she wants! Look at her!" I throw my hands in the air and immediately feel Carol's manicured nails digging into my arm.

She's lost her shit if she thinks I'm going anywhere. Doesn't she know by now that she can't keep me away from Tessa? Only I can keep myself away from her—a stupid fucking idea that I can't seem to hold to.

Noah leans in toward me a little. "She doesn't want to see you and you would be best to leave."

I don't give a fuck that the kid has seemed to grow in size and muscle mass since the last time I've seen him. He's nothing to me. He will soon learn why people don't bother to even attempt to come between Tessa and me. They know better, and he will, too.

"I'm not leaving." I turn to Tessa. She's still coughing, and no one seems to care. "Someone get her some goddamn water!" I yell in the small room, and the noise echoes from wall to wall.

Tessa whimpers and pulls her knees to her chest.

I know she's in pain, and I know that I shouldn't be here, but I also know that her mum and Noah will never be able to truly be there for her. I know Tessa better than the two of them combined, and I've never seen her this way, so surely neither of them will have a clue what to do with her while she's in this state.

"I'll call the police if you don't leave, Hardin," Carol says, low and threatening, from behind me. "I don't know what you did this time, but I'm sick of it, and you have no place here. You never have, and you never will."

I ignore the two interlopers and take a seat on the edge of Tessa's childhood bed.

To my horror, she moves away again, this time scuttling back with her hands—until she hits the edge and falls hard to the floor. I'm on my feet in seconds to bring her into my arms, but the sounds she makes when my skin touches hers are even worse than the horrified screams that sounded from her minutes ago. I'm not sure what to do at first, but after endless seconds of this a broken scream of "Get off of me!" leaves her cracked lips and slices clear through my body. Her small hands pound at my chest and claw at my arms, trying to break my embrace. It's hard to try to comfort her this way with this cast on. I'm afraid it will hurt her, and that's the last thing I want.

As much as it kills me to see her so desperate to get away from me, I'm so fucking happy to see her react at all. The mute Tessa was the worst, and instead of yelling at me, like she is now, her mum should be thanking me that I brought her girl out of that phase in her grief.

"Get off!" Tessa screams again, and Noah begins to protest behind me. Tessa's hand hits my solid cast, and she cries out again. "I hate you!"

Her words burn me, but I still hold her flailing body in my arms.

Noah's deep voice breaks through Tessa's screams: "You're making things worse!"

Then she goes mute again . . . and does the worst thing she could do to my heart. Her hands break free of my hug—it's harder than hell to hold her with one hand—and she reaches for Noah.

Tessa reaches for Noah to help her, because she can't stand the sight of me.

I let go of her immediately, and she rushes into his arms. One of his arms hooks around her waist, and one rests at the base of her neck, pulling her head to his chest. Fury wrestles with sense, and I'm fighting my hardest to stay calm, watching his hands on her. If I touch him, she will hate me even more. If I don't, I'll be driven crazy watching this.

Fuck—why did I come here in the first place? I should have stayed away, just like I had planned. Now that I'm here, I can't seem to force my feet out of this goddamn room, and her cries only trigger my need to keep her near. I can't fucking win for losing, and it's making me crazy.

"Make him go," Tessa sobs into Noah's chest.

The splintering pain of rejection seeps in, making me motionless for a few seconds. Noah turns to me, silently begging in the most civil way for me to leave the room. I hate that he's become her comfort; one of my biggest insecurities has slapped me in the face, but I can't think of it that way. I have to think of her. Only what's best for her. I back away clumsily, reaching and scrambling for the door handle. Once I'm outside the small room, I lean against the door to catch my breath. How did our life together spiral down so much in such a short time?

I find myself in Carol's kitchen filling a glass with water. It's awkward, since I only have one usable hand, and it takes longer to get the cup, fill it, and turn off the faucet, all the while the huffing woman behind me grating my nerves.

I turn to face her, waiting for her to tell me she called the police. When she just glares at me silently, I say, "I don't care about the trivial shit right now. Go ahead and call the police, or do whatever you have to do, but I'm not leaving this shithole of a town until she talks to me." I take a drink from the glass and cross the small but immaculate kitchen to stand before her.

Carol's voice is hard. "How did you get here? You were in London."

"It's called a fucking plane, that's how."

She rolls her eyes. "Just because you fly across the world and show up before the sun comes up doesn't mean you have a place with her," she says, seething. "She made that clear—why won't you leave her? You're only hurting her, and I won't continue to stand around and allow it."

"I don't need your approval."

"She doesn't need you," Carol fires back, grabbing the glass from my hand as if it were a loaded gun. She slams it onto the counter and meets my eyes.

"I know you don't like me, but I love her. I make mistakes—way too fucking many of them—but, Carol, if you think I'm going to leave her with you after she saw what she saw, experienced

what she experienced, then you're even crazier than I thought."
I pick the glass back up just to spite her and take another drink.

"She will be fine," Carol remarks coolly. She pauses for a minute, and something inside her seems to crack. "People die, and she will get over it!"

She says it loudly. Too loudly: I hope that Tessa couldn't hear her mother's cold remark.

"You're serious? She's your fucking *daughter*, and he was your *husband* . . ." I trail off, remembering the two weren't actually legally married. "She's hurting, and you're being a heartless bitch, which is exactly why I won't leave her here with you. Landon shouldn't have let you come get her in the first place!"

Carol cocks her head back indignantly. "*Let* me? She's my daughter."

The glass in my hand shakes and the water laps over the side and onto the floor. "Maybe you should act like it, then, and try to be there for her!"

"Be there for her? Who's here for me?" Her emotionless voice cracks, and I'm shocked when the woman who I was convinced was made of stone crumbles and leans against the counter to keep herself from falling to the floor. Tears roll down her face, which is heavily made-up despite that it's only five in the morning. "I didn't see that man for years . . . He left us! He left me after making promise after promise of a good life!" Her hands swipe across the counter, knocking jars of utensils to the floor. "He lied—he lied to me—and he left Tessa and ruined my entire life! I could never even look at another man after Richard Young, and he left us!" she screams.

When she grasps my shoulder and digs her head into my chest, sobbing and screaming, for a flash she looks so much like the girl I love that I can't bring myself to push her away. Not knowing what else to do, I wrap one arm around her and stay silent.

"I wished for this—I wished he would die," she admits

through her tears. I can hear the shame in her voice. "I used to wait for him, I used to tell myself that he would come back for us. For years I did this, and now that he's dead, I can't even pretend anymore."

We stay this way for a long time, her crying into my chest, telling me in different ways with different words that she hates herself because she's glad that he's dead. I can't find words to comfort this woman, but for the first time since I met her, I can see the broken woman behind the mask.

chapter twenty-five

TESSA

After a few minutes of sitting with me, Noah gets up, stretches, and says, "I'm going to get you something to drink. You need food, too."

My fists wrap around his shirt, and I shake my head, begging him not to leave me alone.

He sighs. "You'll get sick if you don't eat something soon," he says, but I know I've won the battle. Noah has never been one to hold his ground.

The last thing I want is something to drink or to eat. I only want one thing: for *him* to leave and never come back.

"I think your mom is giving Hardin an earful." Noah attempts a smile but fails.

I hear her yelling, and something crashes in the distance, but I refuse to let Noah leave me alone in the room. If I'm left alone, he will come in. That's what he does, he preys on people when they are at their weakest. Especially me, who has been weak since the day I met him. I lay my head back on my pillow and block out everything—my mother screaming, the deep, accented voice yelling back at her, and even Noah's comforting whispers in my ear.

I close my eyes and drift between nightmares and reality, trying to decide which is worse.

WHEN I WAKE UP AGAIN, the sun is bright through the thin curtains tacked over the windows. My head is pounding, my mouth is dry, and I'm alone in the room. Noah's tennis shoes are on the floor, and after a moment of peaceful confusion, the weight of the last twenty hours knocks the breath out of me, and I bury my face in my hands.

He was here. He was here, but Noah and my mother helped—

"Tessa," his voice says, startling me out of my thoughts.

I want to pretend this is a phantom, but I know it's not. I can *feel* his presence here. I refuse to look up at him as I hear him enter the room. *Why is he here? Why does he think he can toss me aside, then swoop back in when it's convenient?* That's not happening anymore. I've already lost him and my father, and I don't need either loss shoved in my face right now.

"Get out," I say. The sun disappears, hiding behind the clouds. Even the sun doesn't want to be near him.

When I feel the bed shift under his weight, I hold my ground and try to hide the shiver that passes through me.

"Have some water." A cold glass is pressed against my hand, but I swat it away. I don't even flinch when I hear it fall to the floor. "Tess, look at me." Then his hands are on me—icy, his touch almost foreign—and I jerk away.

As much as I want to crawl into his lap and let him comfort me, I don't. And I won't, not ever again. Even with my mind in the place it is now, I know that I won't ever let him in again. I can't, and I won't.

"Here." Hardin hands me another glass of water, from the bedside table, this one not as cold.

Instinctively I grab it. I don't know why, but his name echoes in my mind. I didn't want to hear his name, not in my own head, that's the only place I am safe from him.

"You'll drink some water," he softly demands.

I stay silent as bring the glass to my lips. I don't have the energy to refuse the water out of spite, and I am beyond thirsty. I finish the entire glass within seconds, my eyes never leaving the wall.

"I know you're angry at me, but I just want to be here for you," he lies.

Everything he says is a lie—always has been, always will be. I stay quiet, a low snort coming from my mouth at his claim.

"The way you acted when you saw me last night . . ." he begins. I can feel his eyes on me, but I refuse to look at him. "The way you screamed . . . Tessa, I've never felt pain like that—"

"Stop it," I snap. My voice doesn't sound like my voice, and I begin to wonder if I'm even awake right now, or if this is another nightmare.

"I just want to know that you're not afraid of me. You aren't, are you?"

"This *isn't about you*," I manage. And it's true, absolutely true. He's tried to make this about him—his pain—but this is about my father's death and that I can't take any more heartache.

"Fuck." He sighs, and I just know that he's running his hands over his hair. "I know it's not. That's not what I meant. I'm worried about you."

I close my eyes and hear thunder in the distance. *He's worried about me?* If he was so worried about me, maybe he shouldn't have sent me back to America alone. I wish I hadn't made it home; I wish something had happened to me on the trip back—so *he* could deal with the loss of *me*.

Then again, he probably wouldn't want to be bothered. He would be too busy getting high. He wouldn't even notice.

"You aren't yourself, baby."

I begin to shake at the use of the sick nickname.

"You need to talk about this, everything with your dad. It will make you feel better." His voice is too loud, and the rain is pounding against the old roof. I wish it would just cave in and let the storm outside sweep me away.

Who is this person sitting here with me? I sure as hell don't know him, and he doesn't know what he's talking about. I should talk about my father? Who the hell is he to sit here and act like he cares about me, like he could help me? I don't need help. I need silence.

"I don't want you here."

"Yes, you do. You're just mad at me right now because I acted like an asshole and I fucked up."

The pain I should feel isn't there, nothing is. Not even when my mind flashes with the images of his hand on my thigh as we drive in his car, his lips gently sliding over mine, my fingers threading through his thick hair. Nothing.

I feel nothing as the pleasant memories are replaced with ones of fists flying through drywall and that woman wearing his shirt. He slept with her only days ago. Nothing. I feel nothing, and it feels so good to finally feel nothing, to finally have control over my emotions. I'm realizing, as I stare at the wall, that I don't have to feel anything I don't want to. I don't have to remember anything I don't want to. I can forget it all and never allow the memories to cripple me again.

"I'm not." I don't clarify the words, and he tries to touch me again. I don't move. I bite my cheek, wanting to scream again, but not wanting to give him the satisfaction. The calming ease that sweeps over me from his fingers on mine proves just how weak I am, right after I'd just settled on a path of perfect numbness.

"I'm sorry about Richard, I know how—"

"No." I pull my hand away. "No, you don't get to do this. You don't get to come here and pretend like you're here to help me when you're the one who has hurt me the most. I won't tell you again." I know my voice is flat—I hear it sounding as unconvincing and as empty as I feel inside. "Get out."

My throat hurts from speaking so much; I don't want to talk anymore. I just want him to go away, and I want to be left alone. I focus on the wall again, not allowing my mind to taunt me with images of my father's dead body. Everything is messing with me, fucking with my mind, and threatening the tiny bit of reason left inside me. I'm grieving two deaths now, and it's tearing me apart piece by tiny piece.

Pain isn't remotely kind in that way: pain wants its promised pound of flesh, ounce for ounce. It won't settle until you're left with nothing but a flaky shell of who you were. The burn of betrayal and the sting of rejection hurt, but nothing compares to the pain of being empty. Nothing hurts worse than not hurting at all, and that that makes no sense and perfect sense at the same time convinces me I'm going fucking crazy.

And I'm actually okay with that.

"Do you want me to get you something to eat?"

Did he not hear me? Does he not understand that I don't want him here? It's impossible to think that he can't hear the chaos inside my mind.

"Tessa," he presses when I don't respond. I need him to get away from me. I don't want to look into those eyes, I don't want to hear any more promises that will be broken when he begins to let his self-hatred take over again.

My throat burns—it hurts so bad—but I yell for the person who really cares: "Noah!"

As soon as I do, he's rushing through the bedroom door, looking determined to be the force of nature that will finally move the immovable Hardin out of my room, out of my life. Noah stands in front of me and looks at Hardin, who I finally spare a glance at. "I told you if she called for me, that was it."

Instantly moving from soft to enraged, Hardin's shooting bullets at Noah, and I know he's trying hard to rein in his temper. There's something on his hand . . . a cast? I look again, and sure enough, a black cast covers his hand and wrist.

"Let's get something clear," Hardin says as he stands and looks down at Noah. "I'm trying not to upset her, and that's the only reason I haven't snapped your fucking neck. So don't push your luck."

In my damaged, chaotic mind, I can see my father's head snapping back, jaw popping open. I just want silence. I want silence in my ears, and I need silence in my mind.

I start gagging as the image multiplies as their voices get louder, angrier, and my body begs me to just let it all go, to just let everything out of my stomach. The problem is that there's nothing inside me but water, and so acid burns my throat when I vomit onto my old comforter.

"Fuck!" Hardin exclaims. "Get out, damn it!" He shoves at Noah's chest with one hand, and Noah stumbles back, bracing himself against the frame of the door.

"You get out! You're not even wanted here!" Noah fires back and rushes forward, pushing Hardin.

Neither of them notice as I stand from the bed and wipe vomit from my mouth with one sleeve. Because all either of them can see is red and their infinite "loyalty" to me, I make it out of the room, down the hall, and out the front door without either of them noticing.

chapter twenty-six

HARDIN

F uck you!" My cast connects with Noah's jaw, and he rears back, spitting blood.

He doesn't stop, though. He charges me again and knocks me to the floor. "You son of a bitch!" he yells.

I roll on top of him. If I don't stop now, Tessa will hate me even more than she already does. I can't stand this asshole, but she cares for him, and if I do any real damage to him, she will never forgive me. I manage to get to my feet and put some distance between this fucking newfound linebacker and myself.

"Tessa . . ." I start and turn to the bed, but my stomach drops when I find it empty. A wet stain from her getting sick is the only evidence that she was there at all.

Without a glance at Noah, I stalk down the hallway, calling her name. *How could I be so stupid? When will I stop being such a fuckup?*

"Where is she?" Noah asks from behind me, following me like a suddenly lost puppy.

Carol is still asleep on the couch. She hasn't moved from the spot I laid her in last night after she fell asleep in my arms. The woman may hate my fucking guts, but I couldn't deny her comfort when she needed it.

To my horror, the screen door is open and hanging on the hinges, blowing back and forth in the wind from the storm. Two cars are parked in the driveway: Noah's and Carol's. The $100 cab ride I took here from the airport was worth the time I would have wasted going all the way to Ken's house for my car. At least Tessa hasn't tried to drive anywhere.

"Her shoes are here." Noah picks up one of Tessa's flimsy shoes and tosses it back onto the floor.

Blood is smeared across his chin, and his blue eyes are wild, filled with worry. Tessa is walking around alone in the middle of a massive storm because I let my fucking ego take over.

Noah disappears for a moment while I scan the landscape outside, trying to catch a glimpse of my girl. When Noah returns from searching her room again, her purse is in his hand. She has no shoes on, no money, and no phone. She couldn't have gone far—we were only fighting for a minute, tops. How could I let my temper distract me from her?

"I'll get in my car and check around the block," Noah says, pulling his keys from the pocket of his jeans and walking out the door.

He has the advantage here. He grew up on this street; he knows this place and I don't. I look around the living room and then walk to the kitchen. I glance out the window and realize that I have the advantage, not him. I'm surprised he didn't think of this himself. He may know the town, but I know my Tessa, and I know exactly where she is.

The rain is still coming down in large, unforgiving sheets as I descend the back porch steps with one stride and cross the grass to the small greenhouse in the corner, hiding between a cluster of swaying trees. The metal door is cracked open, proving my instincts right.

I find Tessa huddled on the floor, dirt covering her jeans and her bare feet layered in mud. Her knees are pulled to her chest, and her shaky hands are covering her ears. It's a heartbreaking sight, seeing my strong girl reduced to a shell. Pot after pot of dirt lines the poor excuse for a greenhouse; it's obvious that no one has been in here since Tessa left home. A few cracks are in the ceiling, sending streams of rain down in random spots throughout the small space.

I don't say anything, but I don't want to surprise her, and I hope she can hear the sloshing of my boots against the mud covering the floor. When I look down again, I see that there is no floor after all. That explains all the mud. Taking her hands away from her ears, I lean down to force her eyes to mine. She thrashes away like a cornered animal, and I flinch at her reaction but keep my grip on her hands.

She digs her hands into the mud and uses her legs to kick at me. The moment I let go of her wrists, she covers her ears again, a terrible whimper falling from her full lips. "I need quiet," she begs, slowly rocking back and forth.

I have so many things to say, so many words to throw at her in hopes that she will listen to me and come out of hiding within herself, but one look into her desperate eyes, and I lose them all.

If she wants quiet, I will give her that. Fuck, at this point I will give her anything and everything she wants as long as she doesn't force me to leave.

So I move closer to her, and we sit on the muddy floor of the old greenhouse. The greenhouse that she used to hide away from her father, the greenhouse that she's now using to hide from the world, to hide from me.

We sit here as the rain pounds against the glass roof. We sit here as her whimpers turn to quiet sobs and she stares into the empty space in front of her, and we sit in silence with my hands over her small fingers covering her ears, blocking her from the noise around us, giving her the silence she needs.

chapter twenty-seven

HARDIN

As I sit here listening to the sounds of the unforgiving storm outside, I can't help but draw comparisons to the shitstorm I've made out of my life. I'm an asshole, the biggest one, the worst possible fucking kind of dickhead there is.

Tessa finally fell still only minutes ago; her body leaned toward me and she allowed herself to rest against me for physical support. Her swollen eyes closed, and now she's asleep despite the rain pounding loudly on the flimsy greenhouse.

I shift slightly, hoping that she won't wake when I lay her head down onto my lap. I need to get her out of here, out of the rain and away from the mud, but I know what she will do when she opens her eyes. She's going to cast me away, tell me that I'm not wanted here, and, fuck, I'm not ready to hear those words again.

I deserve them—all of them and then some—but that doesn't change that I'm a goddamned coward, and I want to enjoy the silence while it lasts. Only here in the sweet silence can I pretend to be someone else. I can, just for a minute, pretend that I'm Noah. Well, a less annoying version of him, but if I were him, things would have been different. Things would be different now. I would have been able to use words and affection to win Tessa over from the beginning, instead of some stupid game. I would have been able to make her laugh more often than cry. She would have trusted me wholly and completely, and I wouldn't have taken that trust, crumbled it into ash, and watched it blow away. I would have savored her trust and maybe even been worthy of it.

But I'm not Noah. I'm Hardin. And being Hardin doesn't mean shit.

If I didn't have so many fucking issues vying for attention inside my head, I could have made her happy. I could have shown her the light in life, just as she has done for me. Instead, here she sits, broken and completely fucked-up. Her skin is streaked with dark mud, the filth on her hands has now begun to dry, and her face, even in sleep, is twisted into a painful frown. Her hair is wet in some places, dry and matted in others, and I begin to wonder if she has changed her clothes more than once since she left London. I would have never sent her back here if I could even have imagined she would find her dad's body in my apartment.

When it comes to Tessa's father himself and his death, the confusion I feel is overwhelming. The instinct to brush it off as a nonevent happening to a misfit who wasted his life away comes first, but then immediately the loss of him is heavy on my chest. I didn't know him long, and I barely tolerated the man, but he was decent enough company. I would be hard-pressed to admit it, but I sort of liked him. He was obnoxious, and I absolutely loathed the way he emptied box after box of my cereal, but I adored something about the way he loved Tessa and his optimistic outlook on life, even though his own life fucking sucked.

And the irony is that as soon as he finally had something, someone worth living for, he's gone. Like he couldn't handle that much goodness. My eyes burn to release some sort of emotion, grief maybe. Grief for losing a man I barely knew or liked, grief for losing the idea of a father I thought I had with Ken, grief for losing Tessa, and just a tiny bit of hope that she will come around and not be lost forever.

My selfish tears mix with the drops of moisture falling from my rain-soaked hair, and I bow my head, fighting the urge to bury my face into her neck for comfort. I don't deserve her comfort, I don't deserve anyone's comfort.

I deserve to sit here alone and weep like a pitiful rogue amid silence and desolation, my oldest and truest friends.

The pathetic sobs that leave my mouth are lost in the sound of the rain, and I'm thankful that this girl I adore is asleep and unable to witness the breakdown that I can't seem to control. My own actions are the driving force behind every fucked-up thing that's happening right now, right down to Richard's death. If I hadn't agreed to take Tessa to England, none of this shit would have happened. We would be blissful and stronger than ever, just like we were a week ago. *Fuck, has it only been that long?* It seems impossible that such few days have come and gone, yet it seems like a damn lifetime since I've touched her, held her, and felt her heart beating under my palm. My hand hovers there, across her chest, wanting to touch her, but afraid to wake her.

If I can just touch her once, just feel the steady beat of her heart, it will anchor mine and calm me. It will bring me out of this breakdown and stop these disgusting tears from rolling down my cheeks and stop the violent heaves of my chest.

"Tessa!" Noah's deep voice rumbles through the rain outside, then thunder booms through the air like an exclamation mark. I wipe at my face furiously, praying to disappear into the chill spring air before he comes bursting in here.

"Tessa!" he calls again, this time louder, and I know he's right outside the greenhouse.

I grit my teeth and hope that he doesn't yell her name again, because if he wakes her up, I . . .

"Oh, thank God! I should have known she was in here!" he exclaims when he bursts in. His voice is loud, his expression wild with relief.

"Would you shut the fuck up? She's just fallen asleep," I whisper harshly and glance down at Tessa's sleeping form. He's the last person that I wanted to walk in on me like this, and I know he can see my bloodshot eyes, the messy evidence of a breakdown clear in the redness of my cheeks.

Fuck, I don't think I can even hate this motherfucker, because he's making it a point not to stare at me, not to embarrass me. It makes part of me hate him more, that he's *that* unfailingly *good*.

"She . . ." Noah looks around the muddy greenhouse and back to Tessa. "I should have known she would be in here. She always used to come in here . . ." He brushes his blond hair back from his forehead and surprises me by taking a step toward the door. "I'll be in the house," he says wearily. Then, his shoulders sagging, he leaves without even so much as a rough closing of the screen door.

chapter twenty-eight

TESSA

He's been pestering me for the last hour, staring into the mirror, watching me apply my makeup and curl my hair, groping me every chance he gets.

"Tess, baby," Hardin groans for the second time, "I love you, but you have got to hurry up or we will be late to our own party."

"I know, I just want to look decent. Everyone will be there." I give him an apologetic smile, knowing he won't stay annoyed long and secretly loving the unpleasant expression on his face. I love the way a dimple appears on his right cheek when he has that adorable grumpy scowl.

"*Decent?* You'll be the center of everyone's attention," he whines, his jealousy clear.

"What's the party for, again?" I swipe a thin layer of gloss across my lips. I can't remember what's going on—I only know everyone is excited, and we are going to be late if I don't finish grooming myself soon.

Hardin's strong arms wrap around me, and just like that I suddenly remember what everyone's celebrating. It's such a horrible thought, I drop the tube of gloss into the sink and let out a little gasp just as Hardin whispers, "Your father's funeral."

I SIT UP and, finding myself wrapped around Hardin, quickly untangle myself from him.

"What's wrong? What happened?" he exclaims.

Hardin's here, right beside me, and my legs were intertwined with his. I shouldn't have fallen asleep—why did I do that? I don't even remember falling asleep; the last thing I remember was Hardin's warm hands on mine, covering my ears.

"Nothing," I croak. My throat burns, and I take in my surroundings while my brain catches up with me. "I need water." I rub my neck and attempt to stand. Stumbling, I glance down at Hardin.

His face is tight and his eyes are red. "Did you have a dream?"

The nothing quickly creeps back inside me, settling just below my breastbone and setting up camp there, in the deepest and emptiest spot.

"Sit down." He reaches for me, but his fingers burn on my skin and I pull away.

"Please, don't," I quietly beg. The grumpy, adorable Hardin from my dream was just that, a pointless dream, and I am now faced with this Hardin, the one who keeps coming back for another hit after tossing me aside. I know why he does it, but that doesn't mean I'm willing to deal with it right now.

He lowers his head in defeat and drops his hand to the ground to lift himself up. His knee slides farther into the mud, and I look away while he catches himself on the railing. "I don't know what to do," he says softly.

"You don't have to do anything," I mutter and attempt to pull all of my strength into forcing my legs to take me out of here and into the pouring rain.

I'm halfway across the yard when I hear him behind me. He's keeping a safe distance behind me, and I'm grateful. I need space from him, I need time to think and breathe, and I need him not to be here.

I pull the back door open and step inside the house. Mud instantly streaks the rug, and I cringe at the reaction that this mess will pull from my mother. Instead of waiting to hear her complaints, I undress down to my bra and panties, leaving my clothes in a muddy pile on the back porch and try my best to rinse my feet in the rain before trudging across the clean tile floor. My feet squeak with each step, and I flinch as the back door opens and Hardin's boots track mud in with them.

Such a silly thing to worry about, mud? Out of all the things on my mind, mud seems so trivial, so small. I miss the days when a mess was a concern.

A voice breaks through my inner discussion. "Tessa? Did you hear me?"

I blink and look up to find Noah standing in the hallway with damp clothes and no shoes on his feet. "I'm sorry, I didn't."

He nods sympathetically. "It's okay. Are you all right? Do you need a shower?"

I nod and he steps into the bathroom, starting the water. The noise from the shower draws me closer, but Hardin's hard voice stops me.

"He's not helping you take a shower."

I don't respond. I don't have the energy to. *Of course he's not going to—why would he?*

Hardin walks past me, trailing mud behind him. "I'm sorry, but this isn't going to happen."

My mind is disconnected from me, or maybe it just feels that way, but I laugh ruefully at the mess he's left behind him. Not only in my mother's house but everywhere he goes, he leaves a mess behind. Including me—I'm the biggest mess of all.

He disappears into the bathroom and says to Noah, "She's half-naked and you're running her a shower. Fuck no. You aren't going to stay in here while she bathes. Nope, not going to fucking happen."

"I'm only trying to help her, and you're causing a problem when—"

I step into the doorway and push past the two brooding men.

"Both of you leave." My voice is monotone, robotic and flat. "Go fight somewhere else."

I push them out and shut the door. As the lock clicks into place, I pray that Hardin won't add this thin bathroom door to his list of destruction.

Stripping the rest of the way down and stepping into the water, I find it hot, so hot, against my back. I'm covered in filth, and I hate it. I hate the way the mud is crusted under my nails and into my hair. I hate the way that no matter how furiously I scrub, I can't seem to get clean.

chapter twenty-nine

HARDIN

I can't help that she was undressed. All of this stuff going on, and you're concerned about me seeing her body?" The judgment in Noah's tone makes me want to strangle him with my good hand.

"It's not just . . ." I take a deep breath. "It's not that." It's a whole lot of shit that I'm not going to tell him. I fold my hands over my lap, then go to put them in my pockets before realizing the cast isn't going to fit. Awkwardly, I fold my hands over my lap again.

"I don't know what happened between you two, but you can't blame me for wanting to help her. I've known her my whole life, and I've never seen her like this." Noah shakes his head in disapproval.

"I'm not discussing anything with you. You and I aren't on the same team here."

He sighs. "We don't have to be rivals either. I want the best for her, and so should you. I'm not a threat to you. I'm not stupid enough to think she would ever choose me. I've moved on. I still love her, because, well, I think I always will, but not in the way you love her."

His words would be much more acceptable if I hadn't despised his ass for the past eight months. I stay quiet, my back leaning against the wall in front of the bathroom while I wait for the shower to shut off.

"You two broke up again, right?" he asks nosily. He doesn't know when to shut up.

"Obviously." I close my eyes and let my head fall back slightly.

"I'm not getting into your business, but I do hope you'll tell me about Richard and how he ended up in your apartment. I don't get it."

"He was staying at my place after Tessa left for Seattle. He didn't have anywhere else to go, so I let him stay with me. When we left for London, he was supposed to go to rehab, so imagine the surprise when he ends up dead as a fucking doornail on the bathroom floor."

The bathroom door clicks open, and Tessa walks straight past both of us, dressed only in a towel. Noah has never seen her naked before—no other man has—and selfishly I'd like to keep it that way. I know I shouldn't be worried about shit like that, but I can't help it.

I GO INTO THE KITCHEN for some water, and am enjoying the silence when I hear Carol's soft, timid voice: "Hardin, can I talk to you for a minute?"

I'm already confused by her tone, and the woman has barely started speaking.

"Uhm, sure." I stand back a little, keeping a safe distance from her. My back is against the wall in the small kitchen by the time I stop moving.

Her expression is tight, and I know this is just as awkward for her as it is for me. "I just wanted to talk about last night."

I pull my eyes from her and glance at my feet. I don't know how this is going to go, but she's already pinned her hair back and cleaned the mess of makeup that was smeared under her eyes last night.

"I don't know what got into me," she says. "I should have never acted that way in front of you. It was incredibly stupid, and I—"

"It's fine," I interrupt, hoping she'll just stop.

"No, it's really not fine. I want to be clear that nothing has changed here—I still feel strongly about you staying away from my daughter."

I look up to meet her eyes. It's not like I expected anything different from her. "I wish I could say I will listen to you, but I can't. I know you don't like me." I pause and can't help but laugh at my understatement. "You hate me, and I get that, but you know your opinion doesn't mean shit to me. I mean that in the nicest way possible. That's just the way it is."

She catches me off guard by laughing along with me. Like mine, hers is a pained, low-ringing sound. "You're just like him—you speak to me the same way he spoke to my parents. Richard never cared what anyone thought about him either, but look where that got him."

"I'm not him," I snap. I really am trying to be as nice to her as possible, but she's making it difficult. Tessa has been in the shower for so long, and it's taking everything in me not to check in on her, especially given Noah's presence.

"You have to try to see this entire thing from my perspective, Hardin. I was in the same type of toxic relationship, and I know how these things end. I don't want that for Tessa, and if you loved her the way you claim, you wouldn't want that for her either." She looks at me, seeming to expect a reaction from me, but then continues. "I want the best for her. You may not believe me, but I always raised Tessa not to depend on a man, the way I did, and look at her now. She's nineteen years old, and she's reduced to nothing each and every time you decide to leave her—"

"I—"

She holds up her hand. "Let me finish." She sighs. "I envied her, actually. It's pathetic, but a part of me was envious that you always came back for her the way Richard never came back for me. But the more you left, the more I realized that you two will have the same ending that we did, because even though you come back, you never stay. If you want her to end up like me—alone and hateful—then you keep doing what you're doing, and I can assure you that's exactly what will happen to her."

I hate the way Carol sees me, but even more than that, I hate the way that she's right. I do always leave Tessa, and even though I come back, I wait until she's comfortable and then I leave again.

"It's up to you. You're the only person she seems to listen to, and my daughter loves you too much for her own good."

I know she does—she loves me, and because she loves me, we won't end up like her parents.

"You can't give her what she needs; you're only holding her back from finding someone who will," she says, but mostly what I hear is Tessa's old bedroom door closing, meaning that she's out of the shower.

"You'll see, Carol, you'll see . . ." I say and pull an empty glass from the cabinet. Filling it with water for Tessa, I tell myself I can change our course and prove everyone wrong, myself included. I know that I can.

chapter thirty

TESSA

I feel slightly less insane after the shower, or maybe the short nap in the greenhouse, or maybe the silence I was finally granted. I don't know, but I can see the world with more clarity, only slightly more, but it's helping me not feel so delusional and giving me a little hope that each day will bring more clarity, more peace.

"I'm coming in," Hardin says and opens the door before I can respond. I pull a clean T-shirt down over my stomach and sit on the bed. "I brought you more water." He places a full glass on the small nightstand and sits on the opposite side of the bed.

I came up with a speech in the shower, but now that he's here in front of me, I can't remember any of it. "Thank you" is all I can think to say.

"Are you feeling better?"

He's being cautious. I must look so frail, so weak to him. I feel it, too. I should feel defeated and angry and sad and confused and lost. The thing is, there's still nothing. There's the deep throb of nothing, though I'm growing used to it as each minute passes.

During each long minute in the shower while the water turned cold, I thought of things from a new perspective. I thought of the way my life has turned into this dark hole of absolutely nothing, and I thought about how much I hated feeling that way, and I thought of the perfect solution, but now I can't get the jumbled words into a proper sentence. This must be what it feels like to lose your mind.

"I hope you are."

He hopes I'm what . . . ?

"Feeling better," he adds, answering my thoughts. I hate the way he's so connected to me, the way he knows what I'm feeling and thinking even when I don't.

I shrug and focus on the wall again. "I am, sort of."

The wall is easier to focus on than the brilliant green of his eyes, the green that I was always so terrified of losing. I remember that when we would lie in bed together, I was always hoping I would get another hour, another week, maybe even another month, with those eyes. I would pray that he would come around and want me permanently, the way I wanted him. I don't want to feel that anymore, I don't want that desperation rolling off me when it comes to him. I want to sit here with my nothing and be content and quiet, and maybe, one day, I can become someone else, someone I thought I would be before I started college. If I'm lucky, I could at least once again be the girl I was before I left home.

That girl is long gone, though. She took a ticket straight to hell, and here she sits, silently burning.

"I want you to know how sorry I am for everything, Tessa. I should have come back here with you. I shouldn't have ended things with you because of my own problems. I should have let you be there for me like I want to be for you. Now I know how you must feel, constantly trying to help me when I pushed and pushed you away."

"Hardin," I whisper, not sure what I will say next.

"No, Tessa, let me say this. I promise you, this time it will be different. I'll never do that again. I'm sorry that it took your dad dying to make me realize how much I need you, but I won't run off again, won't neglect you again, won't disappear into myself again—I swear it." The desperation in his voice is all too familiar: I've heard this same tone and these same words many, many times from him.

"I can't," I say calmly. "I'm sorry, Hardin, but I really can't."

He moves to my side in a panic and drops to his knees in front of me, ruining the carpet there. "Can't what? I know it will take some time, but I'm prepared to wait for you to come out of this, this state of grief you're in. I'm willing to do everything; I mean *everything*."

"We can't, we never could." My voice is flat again. I guess robotic Tessa is here to stay. I don't have enough energy to push any emotion into my words.

"We can get married . . ." he rambles, then seems surprised by his own words, but he doesn't take them back. His long fingers wrap around both of my wrists. "Tessa, we can get married. I'll marry you tomorrow, if you'll agree. I'll wear a tux and everything."

The words that I've been hysterically wishing and waiting for have finally fallen from his lips, but I can't feel them. I heard them clear as day, but I can't feel them.

"We can't." I shake my head.

He grows more desperate. "I have money, more than enough money to pay for a wedding, Tessa, and we could have it wherever you choose. You can get the most expensive dress and flowers, and I won't complain about any of it!" His voice is loud now, echoing through the room.

"It's not about that—it's not right." I wish I could engrave into my heart his words and the way his voice sounds so frantic— excited even—and take them with me into the past. A past where I couldn't see how destructive our relationship really was, when I would have given anything to hear those words from him.

"What is it, then? I know you want this, Tessa; you've told me so many times." I can see the battle behind his eyes, and I wish I could do something to ease his pain, but I can't.

"I don't have anything left, Hardin. I don't have anything left to give you. You've already taken it all, and I'm sorry, but there's just nothing left." The hollowness inside me grows, taking my entire being with it, and I've never been so thankful to feel nothing. If I could feel this, any of this, it would kill me.

It would surely kill me, and I decided only a little while ago that I want to live. I'm not proud of the dark thoughts that crossed my mind in that greenhouse, but I'm proud that they were brief and that I overcame them on my own, on the floor of a cold shower after the hot water ran out.

"I don't want to take anything from you. I want to give you exactly what you want!" He gasps for air, and the sound is so troubled that I almost agree with everything he's saying just so I won't ever have to hear that sound again.

"Marry me, Tess. Please just marry me, and I swear I'll never do anything like this again. We could be together forever—we would be husband and wife. I know you're too good for me, and I know you deserve better, but now I know that you and I, we aren't like anyone else. We aren't like your parents or mine; we are different and we can fucking make it, okay? Just listen to me one more time—"

"Look at us." I wave my hand weakly through the space between us. "Look at who I've become. I don't want this life anymore."

"No, no, no." He stands up and paces across the floor. "You do! Let me make it up to you," he begs, tugging at his hair with one hand.

"Hardin, please calm down. I'm sorry for everything I've done to you, and most of all I'm sorry that I complicated your life, and I'm sorry for all the fighting and back-and-forth, but you have to know this wouldn't work. I thought"—I smile a pitiful smile—"I thought that we could make it. I thought ours was a love of the novels, a love that no matter how hard and fast and tough it was, I thought we would survive anything and everything and live to tell the story."

"We can, we can survive it!" he chokes out.

I can't look at him, because I know what I would see. "That's just it, Hardin, I don't want to have to survive. I want to *live*."

My words strike something in him, and he stops pacing, stops tugging at his hair. "I can't just let you go. You know that. I always come back to you—you had to know that I would. I would have come back from London eventually and we—"

"I can't spend my life waiting for you to come back to me, and it would be selfish of me to want you to spend yours running from me, from us." But I'm confused again. I'm confused because I don't remember ever having these thoughts; all of my thoughts have always been geared toward Hardin and what I could do to make him better, to make him stay. I don't know where these thoughts and words are coming from, but I can't ignore the resolve I feel when I say them.

"I can't be without you," he declares—another sentiment he's proclaimed a million times, yet he does everything in his power to keep me away, to shut me out.

"You can. You'll be happier and less conflicted. It would be easier, you said so yourself." I mean it. He will be happier without me, without our constant back-and-forth. He can focus on himself and his anger toward both of his fathers, and one day he could be happy. I love him enough to want his happiness, even if it's not with me.

He brings his hands in fists to his forehead and clenches his teeth. "No!"

I love him, I'll always love this man, but I've run out. I can't continue to be the fuel to his fire when he's constantly coming back with bucket upon bucket of water to extinguish it. "We've fought so hard but I think it's time to stop."

"No! No!" His eyes search the room, and I know what he's going to do before he does it. That's why I'm not surprised when the small lamp goes flying across the room and shatters against the wall. I don't move. I don't even blink. It's all too familiar, and this is why I'm doing what I'm doing.

I can't comfort him, I can't. I can't even comfort myself, and I don't trust myself enough to wrap my arms around his shoulders and whisper promises into his ear.

"This is what you wanted, remember? Go back to that, Hardin. Just remember why you didn't want me. Remember why you sent me back to America alone."

"I can't be without you; I need you in my life. I need you in my life. I *need*. *You*. In my life," he chants.

"I can still be in your life. Just not like this."

"You're seriously suggesting we be friends?" he spits out venomously. The green of his eyes is almost gone now, replaced by black as his anger builds. Before I can respond, he continues: "We can't go back to being friends after everything. I could never be in the same room as you and not be with you. You are everything to me, and you're going insult me by suggesting *we be friends*? You don't mean that. You love me, Tessa." He looks into my eyes. "You have to. Don't you love me?"

The nothing begins to chip away, and I fight desperately to hold on to it. If I begin to feel this, it will take me down. "Yes," I breathe.

He kneels down in front of me again.

"I love you, Hardin, but we can't keep doing this to each other."

I don't want to fight with him, and I don't want to hurt him, but the weight of this is on his back. I would have given him everything. Hell, I did give him everything, and he didn't want it. When times got hard, he didn't love me enough to fight his demons for me. He gave up, each and every time.

"How will I survive without you?" He's crying now, right in front of my face, and I blink back my own tears and swallow the heavy lump of guilt in my throat. "I can't. I won't. You can't just throw this away because you're going through some shit. Let me be here for you, don't push me away."

Once again, my mind detaches from my body and I laugh. It's not an amused laugh; it's a sad and broken laugh at the irony of what he's said. He's asking of me what I've asked of him, and he doesn't even realize it.

"I've been begging for the same since I met you," I softly remind him. I love him and I don't want to hurt him, but I've got to end this cycle once and for all. If I don't, I won't make it out alive.

"I know." His head falls onto my knees, and his body shakes against me. "I'm sorry! I'm sorry!"

He's hysterical, and the nothing is slipping too fast for me to stop it. I don't want to feel this, I don't want to feel him crying against me after promising and offering the things I've waited what feels like an eternity to hear.

"We will be okay. When you snap out of this, we will be okay," I think he says, but I'm not sure, and I can't ask him to repeat it, because I can't handle hearing it again. I hate this about us. I hate that no matter what he does to me, I somehow find a way to blame myself for his pain.

I catch a glimpse of movement at the door, and I nod at Noah, letting him know that I'm fine.

I'm not fine, but I haven't been for a while, and unlike before, I don't feel the need to be fine. Noah's eyes move to the broken lamp, and he looks worried, but I nod again, silently pleading with him to leave, to let me have this moment. This last moment to feel Hardin's body against mine, to feel his head on my lap, to memorize the black swirls of ink across his arms.

"I'm sorry that I couldn't fix you," I tell him while softly stroking his damp hair.

"Me, too," he cries against my legs.

chapter thirty-one

TESSA

"Mother, who *is* paying for the funeral?" I ask.

I don't want to come off as insensitive or rude, but I have no living grandparents, and both of my parents were born as lone children. I know my mother can't afford a funeral, especially for my father, and I worry that she has taken this on just to prove a point to her friends at church.

I don't want to wear this black dress that Mother bought me, I don't want to wear these black, high-heeled shoes that she surely can't afford, and most of all I don't want to see my father buried.

My mother hesitates; the tube of lipstick in her hand floats just above her lips as she makes eye contact with me in the mirror. "I don't know."

I turn to her in disbelief—I mean, if I could muster enough energy for the feeling to actually be called disbelief. Maybe it's more like numb curiosity. "You don't know?" I watch her. Her eyes are swollen, the evidence that she has been taking his death harder than she will ever admit.

"We don't need to be discussing financials, Theresa," she scolds, ending the conversation by walking off into the living room.

I nod in agreement, not wanting to start a fight with her. Not today. Today will be hard enough. I feel selfish and a little twisted that I can't bring myself to understand what he was thinking when he pushed that last needle into his vein. I know he was an addict, and he was only doing what he'd spent years doing, but

I still can't wrap my mind around what it would take to do that, knowing how deadly it is.

In the last three days since seeing Hardin, I have began to get my sanity back. Not completely, and part of me is terrified that I'll never be the same again.

He's been staying at the Porters' house for the last three nights. This was a massive surprise to me, and to Mr. and Mrs. Porter, I'm sure; they surely haven't spent much time around anyone who doesn't have a membership to the country club in town. I would have loved to have seen the expression on Mrs. Porter's face when Noah brought Hardin home to stay with them. I can't imagine Hardin and Noah getting along well, or at all, so I know how hurt Hardin must have been by my rejection if he was willing to take Noah up on his hospitality.

The heavy weight of my grief is still there, still hiding behind the barrier of nothingness. I can feel it pushing at the wall, trying desperately to ruin me and push me over the edge. I was terrified that after Hardin's breakdown, the pain would win, but I am thankful that it's been the opposite.

It's an odd thing, knowing that he's so close to this house but he hasn't tried to come by. I need the space, and Hardin usually isn't good at giving me space. Then again, I never wanted it before. Not like this. A knock on the front door has me adjusting my black tights faster, and I glance in the mirror one last time.

I lean in closer, examining my eyes. Something about them is different that I can't quite describe . . . they look *harder*? *Sadder*? I'm not sure, but they match the pathetic excuse for a smile I try to give. If I weren't half-mad, I would be more concerned about the difference in my appearance.

"Theresa!" my mother calls in annoyance just as I reach the hallway.

Given the sound of her voice, I expect to see Hardin. He's given me the space I've asked for, but I suspected that he would come by today, the day of my father's funeral. But when I turn the corner, my body freezes; I'm surprised, pleasantly so, to see in the front doorway none other than Zed.

When his eyes meet mine, he looks unsure of himself, but when I feel my lips turning into a grin, his face splits into a bright smile—the one I love, the one where his tongue appears between his teeth and his eyes shine.

I invite him in. "What are you doing here?" I ask right as my arms wrap around his neck. He hugs me, too tight, and I cough dramatically before he lets up.

He grins. "Sorry, it's been a while." He laughs, and my mood is instantly brightened by the sound. I haven't been thinking of him—I feel almost guilty that his face hasn't entered my mind once in the last few weeks—but I'm glad he's here. His presence is a reminder that the world hasn't stopped since my incredible loss.

My loss . . . I don't want to admit even to myself which loss has been harder for me to cope with.

"It has," I say. Then the reason for the distance between Zed and me pops into my mind, interrupting our greeting, and I cautiously look past him out the front door. The last thing I need is a brawl on my mother's perfectly groomed lawn.

"Hardin is here. Well, not here in this house, but he's a few doors down."

"I know." Zed doesn't look the least bit intimidated despite their history.

"You do?"

My mother gives me a quizzical look, then disappears into the kitchen to leave Zed and me alone. My mind begins to catch up with the realization that Zed is here. I haven't called him—how could he have known about my father? I suppose it's remotelly possible it could have been on the news and online, but even so, would Zed have noticed that?

"He called me." At Zed's words my head snaps up so I can

look into his eyes. "He's the one who told me to come here and see you. You disconnected your phone, so I had to take his word for it."

I'm not sure what to say to that, so I just look at Zed silently, trying to figure out the secret math involved here.

"That's okay, right?" He reached out an arm, but stops short of actually touching me. "You don't mind me coming here, do you? I can go, if it's too much for you. He just said you needed a friend, and I knew it had to be bad if he was calling *me*, out of all people." Zed ends with a little laugh, but I know he's being serious.

Why would Hardin call him instead of Landon? Actually, Landon is on his way here anyway, so why would Hardin request Zed to come to me?

I can't help but feel that this is some sort of setup, as if Hardin is testing me in some way. I hate the idea of that, that he would do that type of thing right now, but he's done worse. I can't allow myself to forget that he's done worse things, and there is always some sort of motive behind his actions. He always has an angle, a hidden equation to how he approaches me.

I'm more hurt than anything by his proposal of marriage. He'd denied me the chance of marriage since the beginning of our relationship, only to bring it up twice—two times when he wanted something. Once when he was too drunk to know what he was saying, and once in an attempt to make me stay. If I had woken up next to him the next morning, he would have taken it back just like before. Like he always does. He's been nothing but broken promises since I've met him, and the only thing worse than being with someone who doesn't believe in marriage is being with someone who would marry me only to win a momentary victory, not because he truly wants to be my husband.

I need to remember that, or I will keep having these ridiculous thoughts. These thoughts that sneak in throughout my days of Hardin in a tuxedo. The image causes me to laugh, and tuxedo

Hardin quickly shifts into jeans and boots, even on his wedding day, but I think I would be okay with that.

Would have been. I have got to stop these fantasies; they're not helping my sanity. Another one creeps in, though. This time Hardin is laughing, holding a glass of wine . . . and I notice a silver wedding band on his ring finger. He's laughing loudly, his head tilted back in that charming way.

I push it back.

His smile creeps through, a vision of him spilling wine on his white T-shirt. He would probably insist on wearing white, instead of the usual black, just to humor himself and horrify my mother. He would gently push my hands away as I patted the stain with a napkin. He would say something like "Should have known better than to wear white anyway." And he would laugh and bring my fingers to his lips, kissing each fingertip softly. His eyes would linger on my wedding ring, and a proud smile would take over his face.

"Are you all right?" Zed's voice breaks through my pitiful thoughts.

"Yeah." I shake my head to rid the perfect image of Hardin smiling at me as I approach Zed. "I'm sorry, I'm a little out of it lately."

"That's okay. I would be worried if you weren't." He wraps a comforting arm around my shoulders.

When I think about it, I shouldn't be surprised that Zed came all the way here to support me. The more I think of it, the more I remember. He was always there, even when I didn't need him to be. He was in the background, always in Hardin's shadow.

chapter thirty-two

HARDIN

Noah is so damn annoying. I don't know how Tessa could stand him for all those years. I'm beginning to think she was hiding from *him* in that greenhouse instead of from Richard.

I wouldn't blame her, I'm tempted to do the same right now.

"I don't think you should have called that guy," Noah says from the couch across the massive living room of his parents' house. "I really don't like him. I don't like you either, but he's even worse than you."

"Shut up," I groan and go back to staring at this weird pillow that's on the plush, oversize chair I've claimed these past few days.

"I'm just saying. I don't understand why you called him if you hate him so much."

He doesn't know when to shut up. I hate this town for not having a hotel within twenty miles of Tessa's mum's house. "Because"—I let out an annoyed breath—"she doesn't hate him. She trusts him even though she shouldn't, and she needs some kind of friend right now, since she won't see me."

"What about me? And Landon?" Noah pulls at the tab of a can of soda, and it opens with a loud pop. Even the way he opens soda is obnoxious.

I don't want to tell Noah that what I'm really worried about is that Tessa will run back to *him*, wanting the safe relationship instead of giving me another chance. And when it comes to Landon, well, I'll never admit it, but I sort of need him to be *my* friend. I have none, and I kind of need him, in a way. A little.

A lot. I need him a fucking lot, and except for Tessa, I have no one else, and I barely have her, so I can't lose him, too.

"I still don't understand. If he likes her, why would you want him around her? You're obviously the jealous type, and you know about stealing people's girlfriends better than anyone."

"Ha-ha." I roll my eyes and glance out the expansive windows covering the front wall of the house. The Porters' house is the biggest on this street, probably the biggest in this entire shithole of a town. I don't want him getting the wrong impression here. I still hate his ass, and I'm only allowing him to be around me because I need to give Tessa her space without going too far. "Why do you care anyway? Why are you suddenly playing nice with me? I know you despise me, just the way I do you." I look over at him, dressed in his stupid fucking cardigan and brown dress shoes that should have a penny stuck on the top of them.

"I don't care about you; I care about Tessa. I just want her to be happy. It took me a long time to come to terms with everything that happened between us because I was so used to her. I was comfortable and conditioned to be that way, so I couldn't understand why she would possibly want someone like you. I didn't get it, and I still don't, really, but I see how much she has changed since she met you. Not in a bad way either, it's a really good change." He smiles at me. "Excepting this week, obviously."

How could he think that? I have done nothing but hurt her and tear her down since I crashed into her life.

"Well"—I shift uncomfortably in the chair—"that's enough bonding for today. Thanks for not being a dick."

I stand and walk toward the kitchen, where I can hear Noah's mum working the blender. In my stay here, I've found *vast* entertainment in the way she fumbles with words and traces her fingernails over the cross around her neck each time I'm in the same room with her.

"Leave my mom alone, or I'll kick you out," Noah warns

mockingly, and I almost laugh. If I didn't miss Tessa so damn much, I would laugh along with the asshole. "You're going to the funeral, right? You can ride with us if you want; we aren't leaving for another hour," he offers, which makes me stop.

I shrug my shoulders and pick at the fringe along the bottom of my cast. "No, I don't think that's a good idea."

"Why not? You did pay for it. You were his friend, kind of. I think you should go."

"Stop talking about it, and remember what I said about spreading it around that I paid for the shit," I threaten. "I.e., don't fucking do it."

Noah rolls his stupid blue eyes at me, and I leave the room to torture his mum and get my mind off Zed's being in the same house as Tessa.

What was I thinking?

chapter thirty-three

HARDIN

I can't remember the last time I attended a funeral. Come to think of it, I'm pretty sure I've never been to one.

When my mum's mum died, I simply didn't feel like going. I had booze to drink and a party that I just couldn't miss. I never had the urge to say a final goodbye to a woman I barely knew. One thing I did know about the old woman was that she didn't care much for me. She could barely stand my mum, so why would I spend my time sitting in a pew, pretending to be upset about a death that, in reality, didn't affect me at all?

Yet here I sit years later in the back of a tiny church, mourning the death of Tessa's father. Tessa, Carol, Zed, and what appears to be half the damn congregation all crowd the front rows. Only me and an old woman, who I'm pretty sure doesn't actually know where she is, sit in the lone pew near the back wall.

Zed is sitting on one side of Tessa and her mother on the other.

I don't regret calling him . . . Well, I do, but I can't ignore the flicker of life that seems to have been revived since his arrival earlier today. She still doesn't look like my Tessa, but she is getting there, and if that asshole is the key to that light, then so fucking be it.

I've done a lot of fucked-up shit in my life, a lot. I know this, Tessa knows this, hell, everyone in this church probably fucking knows it thanks to her mother, but I will make this right with my girl. I don't give a fuck about making amends with any of the other shit from my past or present; I only care about fixing what was broken within her.

I broke her . . . she says she couldn't fix me . . . that she will never be able to. But my damage wasn't caused by her. I was healed by her, and while she was healing me, I was splintering her beautiful soul into too many pieces. Essentially, I single-handedly broke her, broke her fucking brilliant spirit, while selfishly being stitched back together. The most fucked-up part of this massacre is that I refused to see just how much I was hurting her, just how much of her light I had dimmed. I knew it; I knew it all along, but it didn't matter, it only mattered when I finally got it. When she denied me, once and for all, I got it. It hit me like a damn truck, and I couldn't move out of the way even if I tried.

It took her father's death to make me see just how stupid my plan to save her from me actually was. If I had thought about it, really thought this mess through, I would have known how stupid it all was. She wanted *me*—Tessa has always loved me more than I deserve, and how did I repay her? I pushed and pushed until she was finally done with my shit. Now she doesn't want me; she doesn't want to want me, and I have to find a way to remind her how much she loves me.

Now here I sit, watching as Zed loops his arm around her shoulder and pulls her into his side. I can't even look away. I'm stuck watching them. Maybe I'm punishing myself, maybe not, but either way, I can't stop staring at the way she leans into him and he whispers something in her ear. The way his thoughtful expression somehow calms her and she sighs, nodding once, and he smiles at her.

Someone slides in next to me, temporarily interrupting my self-torture.

"We're nearly late . . . Hardin, why are you sitting back here?" Landon asks.

My father . . . Ken, sits down next to him, while Karen takes it upon herself to walk to the front of the small church to approach Tessa.

"You may as well go up there, too. The front row is only for people who Tessa can stand," I complain, glancing at the line of people, who, from Carol to Noah, I can't stand.

And that includes Tessa. I love her, but I can't stand being so close to her while she's comforted by Zed. He doesn't know her the way I do; he doesn't deserve to be sitting next to her right now.

"Stop that. She can 'stand' you," Landon says. "This is her father's funeral, try to remember that."

I catch my father—*fuck*—Ken, I catch *Ken* staring at me.

He's not even my father. I knew this, I've known for the last week, but now that he's in front of me, it's like I'm finding out for the first time again. I should tell him right now, I should affirm his longtime suspicions and just let the truth out about my mum and Vance. I should tell him right here, right now, and let him feel as fucking disappointed as I was. Was I disappointed? I don't know for sure; I was mad. I still am mad, but that's about as far as I've gotten.

"How are you feeling, son?" His arm reaches across Landon to rest his hand on my shoulder.

Tell him. I should tell him. "I'm fine." I shrug, wondering why my mouth won't cooperate with my mind and just say the words. Like I always say, misery loves company, and I'm as miserable as it gets.

"I'm sorry about all of this, I should have called the facility more. I promise you that I had checked on him, Hardin. I did, and I had no clue that he left until it was too late. I'm sorry." The disappointment in Ken's eyes silences me from forcing him to join my pity party. "I'm sorry that I always fail you."

My eyes meet his and I nod, deciding in this moment that he doesn't need to know. Not right now. "It's not your fault," I quietly remark.

I can feel Tessa's eyes on me, calling my attention from so many feet away. Her head is turned toward me, and Zed's arm is no longer around her shoulders. She's staring at me, the way I was her, and I grip the wooden pew with everything I have, to restrain myself from rushing across the church to her.

"Either way, I'm sorry," Ken says and removes his hand from my shoulder. His brown eyes are glossy, like Landon's.

"It's fine," I mumble, still focusing on the gray eyes holding mine.

"Just go up there, she needs you," Landon suggests, his voice soft.

I ignore him and wait for her to give me some sort of signal, any tiny, little fragment of emotion to show me that she does need me. I will be next to her in seconds.

The preacher steps to the podium, and she turns away from me without beckoning me to her, without a real indication that she was actually seeing me at all.

But before I can feel too sorry for myself, Karen smiles down at Zed and he slides down, allowing her to take the seat next to Tessa.

chapter thirty-four

TESSA

I give another fake smile to another faceless stranger and move on to the next, thanking each of them for attending. The funeral was short; apparently this church doesn't take kindly to celebrating the life of an addict. A few stiff words and phony praises were given, and that was that.

Only a few more people; a few more simulated thanks and forced emotions as condolences are given. If I hear what a great man my father was one more time, I think I'll scream. I think I'll scream right in the middle of this church, in front of all my mother's judgmental friends. Many of them have never even met Richard Young. Why are they here, and what lies has my mother told them about my father if they are praising him?

It's not that I don't think my father was a good man. I didn't know him well enough to judge his character accurately. But I do know the facts, and the facts are that he left me and my mother when I was a child, and he only came back into my life a few months ago by chance. If I hadn't been with Hardin at that tattoo parlor, chances are I would never have seen him again.

He didn't want to be in my life. He didn't want to be a father or a husband. He wanted to live his own life and make choices that revolved around him and him alone. That's fine, it is, but I can't understand it. I can't understand why he would run away from his responsibilities only to live the life of a drug addict. I remember how I felt when Hardin mentioned my father's drug use; I couldn't believe it. Why was I so accepting of his being an alcoholic, but not a drug addict? I just couldn't wrap my head around it. I think I was trying to make him better, in my mind. I'm slowly realizing that, like Hardin always says, I'm naïve. I'm naïve and foolish to keep trying to find the good in people when all they do in return is prove me wrong. I'm always proven wrong, and I'm sick of it.

"The ladies want to come over to the house when we leave here, so I need you to help prepare for that as soon as we get home," my mother says after the last hug is given.

"Who are the ladies? Did they even know him?" I snap. I can't help the harsh tone of my voice, and I feel slightly guilty when my mother frowns. The guilt is pushed back when she glances around the church to make sure none of her "friends" caught my disrespectful tone.

"Yes, Theresa. Some of them did."

"Well, I'd love to help as well," Karen interrupts as we walk outside. "If that's okay, of course?" She smiles.

I am so thankful for Karen's presence. She's always so sweet and thoughtful; even my mother seems to like her.

"That would be lovely." My mother returns Karen's smile and walks away while waving at an woman unfamiliar to me in the small crowd across the lawn of the church.

"Do you mind if I come, too? If not, I get it. I know Hardin's here and all, but since he's the one that called me in the first place . . ." Zed says.

"No, of course you can come. You drove all the way here." I can't help but scan the parking lot in search of Hardin at the mention of his name. Across the lot, I spot Landon and Ken getting into Ken's car; as far as I can see, Hardin isn't with them. I wish I had gotten a chance to speak to Ken and Landon, but they were sitting with Hardin and I didn't want to take them away from him.

During the funeral I couldn't help but worry that Hardin

would tell Ken the truth about Christian Vance right in front of everyone. Hardin would be feeling bad, so he might want someone else to feel bad, too. I pray that Hardin has enough decency to wait until he can find the right time to disclose the hurtful truth. I know he's decent; deep down Hardin is not a bad person. He's just bad for me.

I turn to Zed, whose fingers are picking at the dots of fuzz on his red button-down shirt. "Do you want to walk back? It's not a far walk, twenty minutes at most."

He agrees, and we slip away before my mother can shove me into her small car. I can't stand the thought of being trapped in an enclosed space with her right now. My patience with her is growing thin. I don't want to be rude, but I can feel my frustration grow with every stroke of her hands over her perfectly curled hair.

Zed breaks the silence ten minutes into the walk through my small hometown. "Do you want to talk about it?"

"I don't know. Anything that I say probably won't make any sense." I shake my head, not wanting Zed to know just how crazy I've become during the last week. He hasn't asked about my relationship with Hardin, and for that I'm thankful. Anything involving Hardin and me isn't open for discussion.

"Try me," Zed challenges with a warm smile.

"I'm mad."

"Upset mad or crazy mad?" he teases, playfully touching his shoulder to mine as we wait for a car to pass before crossing a street.

"Both." I try to smile. "Mostly just upset mad. Is it wrong that I feel sort of angry at my father for dying?" I hate the way the words sound. I know it's wrong, but it feels so right. The anger feels better than the nothing, and the anger is a distraction. A distraction that I'm in desperate need of.

"It's not wrong to feel that way, but then again it sort of is. I don't think you should be mad at him. I'm sure he didn't know what he was doing when he did what he did." Zed looks down at me, but I look away.

"He did know what he was doing when he brought those drugs into that apartment. Sure, he didn't know he was going to die, but he knew it was a possibility, and all he cared about was getting high. He didn't think about anyone except himself and his high, you know?" I swallow the guilt that comes with the words. I loved my father, but I need to be truthful. I need to let my feelings out.

Zed frowns. "I don't know, Tessa. I don't think it was like that. I don't think I could be mad at someone who died, especially my parent."

"He didn't raise me or anything. He left when I was a little girl."

Did Zed already know that? I'm not sure. I'm so used to talking to Hardin, who knows everything about me, that sometimes I forget that other people only know what I let them.

"Maybe he left because he knew it was better for you and your mom?" Zed says, trying to comfort me, but it's not working. It's only making me want to scream. I'm tired of hearing this same exact excuse from mouth after mouth. Those same people claim they want the best for me, yet they make excuses for my father, who left me, acting like he was doing it for my own good. What a selfless man, leaving his wife and daughter all alone.

"I don't know." I sigh. "Let's just not talk about it anymore."

And we don't. We stay silent until we arrive at my mother's house, and I try to ignore the annoyance in her voice when she scolds me for taking so long to get home.

"Luckily Karen is here to help," she says as I walk past her and enter the kitchen.

Zed stands uncomfortably, unsure whether to help. Quickly though, my mother hands him a box of crackers, ripping open the top and pointing wordlessly to an empty tray. Ken and Landon have already been put to work chopping vegetables and arranging fruit on my mother's best serving trays. The ones she uses when she wants to impress people.

"Yeah, luckily," I say under my breath. I thought the spring air would help cool my anger, but it hasn't. My mother's kitchen is too small, too stuffy, and it's filling with overly dressed women with something to prove.

"I need air. I'll be back, just stay here," I say to Zed when my mother rushes down the hallway for something. As thankful as I am that he drove all the way here to comfort me, I can't help but hold our conversation against him. I'm sure once I clear my head I'll see it differently, but right now I just want to be alone.

The back door opens with a creak, and I curse at myself, hoping that my mother doesn't come flying out into the yard to drag me back into the house. The sun has worked magic on the thick mud that covered the floor of the greenhouse. Dark, wet patches still cover half the space, but I'm able to find a dry spot to stand. The last thing I need is to ruin these high-heeled shoes my mother couldn't afford to buy me in the first place.

A movement catches my eye, and I begin to panic until Hardin comes into view from behind a shelf. His eyes are clear, and beneath them dark circles shadow his pale skin. The usual glow, the warm tan, of Hardin's skin has vanished and been replaced with a fragile, haunted ivory.

"Sorry, I didn't know you were here," I say, quick to apologize and immediately backing out of the small space. "I'll go."

"No, it's fine. It was *your* hiding space to begin with, remember?" He gives me a small smile, and even the tiniest of smiles from him feels more real than the countless fakes I've received today.

"True, but I need to go inside anyway."

I grab the handle of the screen door, but he reaches out to stop me from opening it. I jerk away the moment his fingers graze my arm, and he sucks in a harsh breath from my rejection. He quickly recovers and reaches past me to hold on to the door handle, making sure I can't leave.

"Tell me why you came out here," he softly demands.

"I just . . ." I struggle for the words. After my conversation with Zed, I lost the urge to discuss my terrible thoughts about my father's death. "It's nothing."

"Tessa, tell me." He knows me well enough to know that I'm lying, and I know him well enough to know he isn't going to let me leave this greenhouse until I tell him the truth.

But can I trust him?

My eyes look him over, and I can't help but focus on the new dress shirt he's wearing. He must have purchased it solely for the funeral because I know every shirt he owns, and there is no way he could fit into Noah's clothes. Not that he would ever wear them . . .

The black sleeve of the new shirt is ripped open from the cuff, making room for his cast.

"Tessa," he presses, bringing me from my inner distraction. The top button on his shirt is undone and the collar is crooked.

I take a step back from him. "I don't think we should do this."

"Do what? *Talk?* I just want to know what it is you're hiding from."

What a simple yet loaded demand. I'm hiding from everything. I'm hiding from too many things to name, him being the most important of those things. I want to vent my feelings to Hardin, but it's just too easy to slide back into our pattern, and I'm not willing to play these games anymore. I can't take another round. He has won, and I'm learning to be okay with that.

"You and I both know you're not leaving this greenhouse until you spill, so save us both the time and energy and tell me." He attempts this line as a joke, but I can see the flicker of desperation behind his eyes.

"I'm mad," I finally admit.

He nods sharply. "Of course you are."

"I mean I'm really mad, like pissed-off."

"You should be."

I look over at him. "I should be?"

"Hell yeah, you should be. I'd be pissed off, too."

I don't think he gets what I'm trying to say. "I'm mad at my father, Hardin. I'm so mad at him," I clarify and wait for Hardin's response to change.

"So am I."

"You are?"

"Hell yeah, I am. And you should be, too; you have every right to be pissed-off at his ass. Dead or not."

I can't stop the laugh that falls from my lips at the serious expression covering Hardin's face while he speaks such ridiculous words. "You don't think it's wrong that I can't even be sad anymore because I'm so damn mad at him for killing himself?" I pull my bottom lip between my teeth and pause before continuing, "That's what he did. He killed himself, and he didn't even think about how it would affect anyone. I know that's selfish of me to say that, but that's how I feel."

My gaze drops to the dirt floor. I'm ashamed to say these things, to mean them, but I feel so much better now that they are out there floating around. I hope the words stay here, in this greenhouse, and I hope that if my father is up there somewhere, he can't hear me.

Hardin's fingers press under my chin and he tilts my head up. "Hey," he says, and I don't flinch from his touch, but I am grateful when he drops his hand. "Don't be ashamed to feel that way. He did kill himself, and it's no one's fault but his own. I saw how fucking excited you were when he came back into your life, and he's an idiot for throwing that away just to get high." Hardin's tone is harsh, but his words are exactly what I need to hear right now.

He softly chuckles. "But I'm one to talk, right?" He closes his eyes and slowly shakes his head back and forth.

I quickly direct the conversation away from our relationship. "I feel bad for feeling this way. I don't want to disrespect him."

"Fuck that." Hardin waves his cast-covered hand through the air between us. "You are allowed to feel how you want to fucking feel, and no one can say shit about it."

"I wish everyone felt that way." I sigh. I know confiding in Hardin isn't healthy, and I have to tread lightly here, but I just know he's the only one who actually understands me.

"I mean it, Tessa. Don't you let any of those snobby fuckers make you feel bad for how you feel."

I wish it were that simple. I wish I could be more like Hardin and not care what anyone thought of me or how other people feel, but I can't. I'm just not made that way. I feel for others, even when I shouldn't, and I would like to think that eventually that trait will stop being my downfall. Caring is a good trait to have, but it hurts me too often.

In the few short minutes I've been in the greenhouse with Hardin, almost all of my anger has disappeared. I'm not sure what has replaced it, but I no longer feel the burn of fury, just the steady burn of pain that I know will be a longtime companion of mine.

"Theresa!" my mother's voice sounds through the yard, and Hardin and I both wince at the interruption.

"I have no problem telling any of them, her included, to fuck off. You know that, don't you?" His eyes search mine, and I nod. I know he doesn't, and part of me wants to unleash him on the crowd of chatty women who have no business being here.

"I know." I nod again. "I'm sorry for venting like this. I just—"

The screen door opens and my mother steps into the greenhouse. "Theresa, please come inside," she says authoritatively. She's trying her best to mask her anger toward me, but her façade is slipping, and fast.

Hardin looks from my mother's angry face to mine before stepping past both of us. "I was just leaving anyway."

The memory of my mother's finding him in my dorm room all those months ago passes through my mind. She was so mad and Hardin looked so defeated when I left with her and Noah. Those days feel so ancient now, so simple. I had no clue what was ahead, none of us did.

"What are you doing out here anyway?" she asks as I follow her through the yard and up the porch steps.

It's none of her business what I was doing. She wouldn't understand my selfish feelings, and I would never trust her enough to reveal them. She wouldn't understand why I was talking to Hardin after avoiding him for three days. She wouldn't understand anything that I could tell her, because she fundamentally doesn't understand me.

So instead of answering her question, I stay quiet and wish that I would have had the chance to ask Hardin what *he* came to my greenhouse to hide from.

chapter thirty-five

HARDIN

"Hardin, please. I've got to get ready," Tessa had whined into my chest one day. Her naked body was sprawled across me, distracting every brain cell I have left.

"You're not convincing me, woman. If you actually wanted to leave, you would be out of bed by now." I pressed my lips against the shell of her ear, and she wiggled against me. "You certainly wouldn't be rubbing yourself against my cock right now."

She giggled and slid against me, deliberately making contact with my erection.

"Now you've done it," I groaned, wrapping my fingers around her curvy hips. "You'll never make it to class now." My fingers slid to the front of her, sliding into her as she gasped.

Fuck, she always felt so fucking tight and warm around my fingers, even more so around my cock.

Without a word, she had rolled onto her side and wrapped her hand around me, jerking slowly. Her thumb swiped across the bead of moisture already present, betraying the cool smirk on my face, as she whined for more.

"More what?" I teased her, praying that she would take the bait. Either way I knew what was coming next; I just loved to hear her say it.

Her desires became more substantial, more tangible, when said aloud. The way she whined and whimpered for me was more than for my satisfaction or a plea of lust. The words signified her trust in me; the movements of her body engraved her loyalty to me; and the promise of her love for me filled me, body and soul.

I was completely consumed by her, completely fucking lost in her, every single time I made love to her, even when I was being dishonest with her. This time was no exception.

I had pressed her for the words that I wanted. The words that I needed. "Tell me, Tessa."

"More *everything*, just . . . just all of you," she moaned, running her lips along my chest, and I lifted one of her thighs to wrap it around my own. It would be more difficult this way, but much deeper, and I could watch her easily. I could watch what only I could do to her, and I would fucking revel in the way her mouth fell open and she came, calling my name alone.

You already have all of me, I should have said. Instead, I reached in front of her and pulled a condom from the nightstand and slid it on, pressing between her legs. Her satisfied groan had me almost burst right then, but I held it together long enough to bring her to the edge with me. She whispered how much she loved me and how good I made her feel, and I should have told her that I felt the same way, even more than she could ever imagine, but instead, I spoke only her name as I emptied myself into the condom.

There were so many things I should have said, could have said, and sure as hell would have said if I had known my days in heaven were numbered.

Had I known that I would be cast out so soon, I would have worshipped her the way she deserves.

"Are you sure you don't want to stay here another night? I heard Tessa telling Carol that she was around one more night," Noah says, pushing me out of my mind and back into reality in that annoying way he has. After a minute of staring at me like Mr. Rogers, he asks, "Are you okay?"

"Yeah." I should tell him what was happening in my head, the bittersweet memory of Tessa wrapped around me as she clawed at my back and came. Then again, I don't want that image in his head.

He raises a blond brow at me. "So?"

"I'm leaving. I need to give her some space." I wonder just how the actual fuck I got myself into this situation to begin with. I'm a fucking idiot, that's how. My stupidity is incomparable. Except for my fathers', my mum's, too, I suppose. I must get this stupidity from them. The three of them must be where I acquired the need to sabotage myself, to destroy the only good in my life.

I could blame them.

I could, but blaming everyone else hasn't gotten me anywhere so far. Maybe it's time I do something different.

"Space? I didn't know you knew the word," Noah tries to joke. He must notice my glare, because he quickly adds, "If you need anything—I don't know what that could be, but just anything in general—you can call me." He awkwardly glances around the vast living room of his family home, and I stare at the wall behind him to avoid looking at him.

After an uncomfortable back-and-forth with Noah and more than a few nervous glances from Mrs. Porter, I take my small bag and head out of the house. I don't have shit with me, just this tiny bag of a few dirty clothes and my cell-phone charger. Even worse, much to my annoyance, it's only now, now that I'm outside in the drizzling rain, that I remember where my car is. *Fuck.*

I could walk down to Tessa's mum's and catch a ride with Ken if he's still there, but I don't think that's a good idea. If I get anywhere near her, if I even so much as breathe the same air as my girl, no one will be able to tear me away from her. I let Carol easily dismiss me in the greenhouse, but that won't be happening again. I was so close to breaking through to Tessa. I felt it, and I know she did, too. I saw her smile. I saw the empty, sad girl smile for the sad boy who loves her with all of his broken soul.

She still holds enough love for me to waste another smile on me, and that means the fucking world. She's my fucking world. Maybe, just maybe, if I give her the space she needs for now, she will continue to toss me scraps. I'll take those scraps with fucking pleasure. A small smile, a one-word text response—hell, if she doesn't get a restraining order against me, then I'll gladly settle for anything she can give until I can remind her of what we have together.

Remind her? I suppose it's not much of a reminder, since I've never actually shown her the way I could be. I've only been selfish and afraid, letting my fear and self-loathing run the show, always taking my attention from her. I could only focus on myself and my disgusting habit of taking every ounce of her love and trust and throwing it in her face.

The rain is picking up now, and really it's okay. The rain would usually help me bask in my self-hatred, but not today; today the rain isn't so bad. It's almost cleansing.

You know, if I didn't fucking hate metaphors.

chapter thirty-six

TESSA

The rain has returned, falling in a heavy, lonely sheet across the lawn. I'm leaning against the window now, staring out at it as if I'm mesmerized by it. I used to like the rain; it was a sort of comfort as a child, and that comfort carried out into my teenage and now adult years, but now it only reflects back the loneliness inside me.

The house has cleared now. Even Landon and his family have gone back home. I can't seem to decide if I'm happy that they left, or if I'm sad to be alone.

"Hey," a voice and a soft knock sound at the bedroom door, reminding me that I'm not alone after all.

Zed offered to stay at my mother's tonight, and I couldn't turn him down. I sit down near the headboard and wait for him to open the door.

When a few seconds pass and he hasn't entered the room, I call, "You can come in."

I guess I'm used to a certain someone barging in before I grant him permission. Not that I ever really minded . . .

Zed enters the small room, dressed in the same clothes he wore to the funeral, only now some of the buttons on his dress shirt are unfastened and his gelled hair has flattened, taking on a softer, more comfortable look.

He takes a seat on the edge of the bed and shifts toward me. "How you feeling?"

"Well, I'm okay. I don't know how I'm supposed to feel," I answer honestly. I can't tell him that I'm mourning the loss of two men tonight, not only one.

"Do you want to go somewhere? Or maybe watch a movie or something? To take your mind off of things?"

I take a moment to think about his question. I don't want to go anywhere or do anything, even though I probably should. I was fine standing by the window and obsessing over the desolate rain.

"Or we could just talk? I've never seen you like this, you aren't yourself." Zed rests his hand on my shoulder, and I can't help but lean into him. It was unfair of me to be so harsh on him earlier today. He was only trying to comfort me; he just said the opposite of what I wanted to hear. It's not Zed's fault that I've recently taken a turn for Crazyville—it's mine and mine alone. Population two: only me and my emptiness. It gets its own number, since it's the only thing left standing with me after the battle.

"Tessa?" Zed's fingers touch my cheek to gain my attention.

Embarrassed, I shake my head at him. "I'm sorry; I told you, I'm feeling a little mad." I attempt a smile, and he does the same. He's worried for me; I can see it in the golden brown of his eyes. I can see it in the weak smile he's pushing across his full lips.

"It's all right. You have a lot going on. Come over here." He pats the empty space next to him, and I scoot closer. "I have something to ask you." His tanned cheeks give an obvious flush.

I nod for him to go on. I have no idea what his question could be, but he's been such a great friend to me, coming all the way here to comfort me.

"Okay, well . . ." He pauses, drawing out a long breath. "I was wondering what happened between you and Hardin." He bites down on his bottom lip.

I quickly look away. "I don't know if we should discuss Hardin, and I . . ."

"I don't need specifics. I just want to know if it's really, truly over this time?"

I swallow. It's hard to say, but I reply, "It is."

"You're sure?"

What? I turn back to look at him. "Yes, but I don't see what—"

I'm cut off by Zed's lips pressing against mine. His hands move to my hair and his tongue pushes through my closed mouth. I gasp in surprise and he takes that as an invitation to push further and press his body against me, forcing me back against the mattress.

Confused and caught off guard, my body reacts quickly and my hands shove against his chest. He hesitates for a moment, still trying to melt his mouth to mine.

"What are you doing?" I gasp, the moment that he finally lets up.

"What?" His eyes are wide and his lips are swollen from the pressure against mine.

"Why did you *do* that?" I jump to my feet, completely thrown by his affections, and I'm trying desperately not to overreact.

"What? Kiss you?"

"Yes!" I shout at him before quickly covering my mouth. The last thing I need is my mother coming in.

"You said that you and Hardin were finished! You just said that!" His voice comes out louder than mine, but he makes no move to silence himself the way I did.

Why would he think this is okay? Why would he kiss me?

Instinctively, I cross my arms over my chest, and I realize I'm trying to cover myself up. "That wasn't an invitation for you to make a move or something! I thought you were here to comfort me *as a friend.*"

He scoffs. "A friend? You know how I feel about you! You've always known how I felt about you!"

I'm baffled by the roughness of his tone with me. He's always been so understanding. What's changed?

"Zed, you agreed that we would be friends—you know how I

feel about him." I keep my voice as calm and neutral as I possibly can despite the panic inside my chest. I don't want to hurt Zed's feelings, but he is way out of line.

He rolls his eyes. "No, I don't know how you feel about him, because you two go back and forth, back and forth. You change your mind on a weekly basis, and I'm always waiting, waiting, waiting."

I shrink back. I barely recognize this Zed; I want the old one back. The Zed that I trust and care for isn't here.

"I know that. I know that's what we do, but I thought that I made myself clear about—"

"Hanging all over me doesn't exactly send that message." His voice is flat, cold, and a set of chills run down my spine at the difference in him that has appeared in the last two minutes.

I'm offended and confused by his accusation. "I wasn't hanging all over you." *He couldn't possibly believe that!* "You put your arm around me to comfort me at my father's funeral. I thought it was a lovely gesture; I didn't mean for you to take it any other way. I certainly didn't. Hardin was there—you couldn't have possibly thought that I would be affectionate with you in front of him?"

The echo of a cabinet closing sounds through the small house, and I'm infinitely relieved when Zed makes an effort to lower his voice. "Why not? You have used me to make him jealous before," he whispers harshly.

I want to defend myself, but I know he's right. Not about everything, but his point is valid here. "I know I have in the past, and I'm sorry for that. I really am. I've told you how sorry I was before, and I'll say it again: you have always been there for me, and I appreciate you so much, but I thought we talked about this. I thought you understood that you and I could only have a friendship, if that."

He waves his hands through the air. "You're so whipped by

him that you don't even see just how in deep you are." The warm glow of his eyes has dropped in temperature, settling at a chilled amber.

"Zed," I sigh in defeat. I didn't want to fight with him, not after the week I've had. "I'm sorry, okay? I really am, but you are behaving completely inappropriately right now. I thought we were *friends*."

"We aren't," he spits. "I thought you just needed more time, I thought this would be my shot at finally having you, and you threw me away. Again."

"I can't give you what you want—you know I can't. It's impossible for me. Right or wrong, Hardin has left his mark on me, and I wouldn't be able to give myself to you, to anyone, I fear."

The moment the words leave my mouth, I regret them.

The look in Zed's eyes when I'm finished with my pathetic speech has me reeling, grasping, for any hint of the harmless but hopeful Mr. Collins I thought I knew. Instead, I'm standing in this bedroom staring at the pushy and fake Wickham, who pretended to be charming and loyal to gain affections, hurt by Darcy in the past, when he was really a liar.

I make my move for the door. How could I have been so foolish? Elizabeth would grab me by the shoulders and shake sense into me. I spent so much time defending Zed against Hardin, making his worries about Zed out to be a dramatic rambling out of jealousy, when Hardin was right the entire time.

"Tessa, wait! I'm sorry!" he calls behind me, but I'm already opening the front door and rushing out into the rain by the time his voice travels down the hallway, drawing my mother's attention.

But I'm gone, gone, already gone into the night.

chapter thirty-seven

My bare feet splash along the concrete, and my clothes are soaked by the time I make it to the Porters' house. I don't know the time—I couldn't even guess the hour—but I'm grateful that the lights in the foyer are on. Relief washes over me like the cool rain when Noah's mother answers my knocking at the door.

"Tessa? My dear! Are you okay?" She rushes me inside, and I cringe at the sound of the water rolling off me and onto their clean hardwood flooring.

"I'm sorry, I just . . ." As I stare around the expansive and practically spotless living room, I instantly regret coming here.

Hardin wouldn't want to see me anyway—what was I thinking? He isn't mine to rush to anymore—he isn't the man I thought he was.

My Hardin disappeared in England, that place of all my fairy tales, and a stranger took his place and ruined us. My Hardin would never get high and touch another woman, let another woman wear his clothes. My Hardin wouldn't mock me in front of his friends and send me packing back to America, tossing me away like I was nothing. I *am* nothing—to him, anyway. The more offenses that I list, the more foolish I sound inside my own mind. The truth of the matter is, the only Hardin I knew has done all of the above, over and over again, and even now, when I'm the only one in on the conversation, I'm still defending him.

How pathetic am I.

"I'm so sorry, Mrs. Porter. I shouldn't have come here. I'm sorry," I frantically apologize. "Please don't tell anyone I was here." And like the unstable person I've become, I rush back into the rain before she can stop me.

By the time I stop running, I'm near the post office. I always hated this corner as a child. The small, brick post office rests alone in the very back of the town. Not a single other house or business is near, and at times like this, when it's dark and raining, my eyes play tricks on me, and the small building blends into the trees. I always ran past it as a child.

My adrenaline has worn off now, and my feet are aching from repeatedly smacking the concrete. I don't know what I was thinking, coming this far into town. I wasn't thinking, I suppose.

My already questionable sanity is at play again as a shadow emerges from underneath the awning of the post office. I begin to back away, slowly, just in case I'm not imagining things.

"Tessa? What the fuck are you doing?" the shadow says in what sounds like Hardin's voice.

I turn on my heel to run, but he's quicker than me. His arms wrap around my waist, and he pulls me to his chest before I can take off. A large hand forces me to look up at him, and I try to keep my eyes open and focused, despite the heavy drops of rain clouding my vision.

"Why the hell are you out here in the rain, alone?" Hardin scolds through the noise of the storm.

I don't know how to feel. I want to take Hardin's advice and just feel however I want to—but it's not that simple. I can't betray the tiny scrap of strength left inside me. If I allow myself to feel the overwhelming relief of Hardin's hand on my cheek, I will be letting myself down.

"Answer me. Has something happened?"

"No." I shake my head, lying. I step back from him and try to regain my breathing. "Why are you here this late, out in the middle of nowhere? I thought you were at the Porters'." For a minute I panic, thinking that Mrs. Porter somehow told him about my embarrassing and desperate lapse in judgment.

"No, I left there about an hour ago. I'm waiting for a cab. The asshole was supposed to be here twenty minutes ago." Hardin's clothes are saturated, his hair is drenched, and his hand is shaking against my skin. "Tell me why you are out here, barely dressed and barefoot."

I can tell he's making a conscious effort to stay calm, but his mask isn't intact the way he believes it to be. Clear as day, I can see the panic behind the green of his eyes. Even in the dark, I can see the storm brewing behind them. He knows; he always seems to just know everything.

"It's nothing. Not a big deal." I take a step away from him, but he isn't having it. He steps toward me, even closer than before. He's never been anything less than demanding.

Headlights break through the veil of rain, and my heart begins to pound inside my chest when the shape of a truck comes into view. My brain catches up to my heart, and I realize *I know that truck.*

When it stops, Zed jumps out and rushes toward me, leaving his truck running. Hardin steps between us, silently warning him not to come any closer. Yet another scene that I've become too accustomed to and would rather not see again. Every aspect of my life seems to be a cycle, a vicious one, one that takes a piece of me with it each time that history repeats itself.

Hardin's voice is loud and clear, even through the rain: "What *did you do?*"

"What did she tell you?" Zed counters.

Hardin steps closer to him. "Everything," Hardin lies.

I struggle to make out the expression on Zed's face. It's impossible to see clearly, even with the help of his headlights shining on us.

"She told you that she kissed me then?" Zed sneers, his voice an awful mixture of malice and satisfaction.

Before I can defend myself against Zed's lies, another set of headlights breaks through the night and joins the chaos.

"She *what*?" Hardin shouts.

His body is still turned toward Zed, and the taxi's headlights shine across the space, giving me a glimpse of the smug grin spread wide across Zed's face. How could he lie to Hardin like that about me? Will Hardin believe him? More important, does it matter if he does or not?

Does any of this actually matter?

"This is about Sam, isn't it?" Hardin asks before Zed can respond.

"No, it's not!" Zed wipes his hand across his face, pushing water away.

Hardin points a damning finger at him. "Yes, it is! I knew it! I fucking knew you were going after Tessa because of that whore!"

"She wasn't a whore! And this isn't only about her—I care about Tessa! Just the way I did Samantha, and you had to fuck it up! You always have to come in and fuck everything up for me!" Zed screams.

Hardin takes a step closer to him, but says to me, "Get in the cab, Tessa."

I stand in place, ignoring him. *Who is Samantha?* The name sounds slightly familiar, but I can't place it.

"Tessa, get in the cab and wait for me. Please," Hardin says though clenched teeth. His patience is running thin, and by the look on Zed's face, his has already evaporated.

"Please don't fight him, Hardin. Not again," I beg. I am sick of the fighting. I don't think I can take watching another violent scene after finding my father's body lifeless and cold.

"Tessa—" he begins, but I interrupt.

The last bit of my sanity has officially disappeared as I beg Hardin to leave with me, "Please, this week has been so terrible, and I can't watch it. Please, Hardin. Just get in the cab with me. Take me away from here, please."

chapter thirty-eight

HARDIN

Tessa hasn't spoken a word since I got into the cab, and I'm too busy trying to reel my temper in to comment. Seeing her out here, in the dark and running from something—running from Zed—drives my anger full force, and it would be all too easy to give in to it. To set it free.

I can't do that, though. Not this time. This time, I will prove to her that I can control my mouth, my fists, too. I got into this cab with her instead of smashing Zed's skull against the concrete, like he deserved. I hope she recognizes that; I hope that helps my case, even if by the slightest bit.

Tessa hasn't tried to escape yet, and she didn't speak up when I told the driver to take us by her mum's to get her shit. That's a good sign. It's got to be. Her clothes are soaked, clinging to every inch of her body, and her hair is matted to her forehead. She pushes the mess back with her hand, sighing when the unruly strands won't stay put. It takes every ounce of my self-control not to reach over and tuck her hair behind her ears.

"Wait here while we go inside," I tell the driver. "We will be back in less than five minutes, so don't move this cab."

He was late to pick me up in the first place, so he shouldn't mind waiting. Not that I'm complaining; if he hadn't been, I wouldn't have run into Tessa walking alone in the damn rain.

Tessa opens the door and walks across the yard. She doesn't flinch as the rain pours down on her, shielding her body and nearly taking her from me. After reminding the driver to stay put a second time, I rush after her before the rain can separate us further.

I hold my breath, forcing myself to ignore the red truck parked in front of the house. Somehow Zed got back here first, like he knew where I would take her. But I can't lose my temper. I have to show Tessa that I can hold myself together and put her feelings before my own.

She disappears into the house, and I follow only seconds behind. But already Carol is on her when I enter.

"Theresa, how many times are you going to do this? You're dragging yourself right back into something that you know isn't going to work!"

Zed is standing in the center of the living room, dripping water onto the floor. Tessa's fingers are pinching the bridge of her nose, a sign of pure distress, and once again I struggle to keep my damn mouth shut.

It will only take one wrong word from me to make her stay here, to keep her hours away from me.

Tessa holds up one hand, somewhere between commanding and pleading. "Mother, can you please just stop? I'm not doing anything, I just want to leave here. Being here isn't helping anything, and I have a job and classes in Seattle."

Seattle?

"You're going back to Seattle tonight?" Carol exclaims at her daughter.

"Not tonight, but tomorrow. I love you, Mother, and I know where you are coming from, but I really just want to be close to my . . . well"—Tessa gazes at me, uncertainty clear in her gray eyes—"Landon. I want to be with Landon right now."

Oh . . .

Zed opens his goddamn mouth: "I'll drive you."

I just can't stop myself from cutting in at that suggestion. "*No*, you won't."

I'm trying to be patient and shit, but this is too much. I should have barged in here, grabbed Tessa's bag, and carried her out to the cab before Zed could so much as look at her.

The smirk on his face right now, that same fucking smirk he gave me only minutes ago, is taunting me. He's trying to push me, trying to make me snap in front of Tessa and her mum. He wants to play games with me, like he always does.

But not tonight. I won't give him the satisfaction of being his pawn.

"Tessa, grab your bag," I say. But the mirrored scowl on both women's faces makes me reconsider my choice of words. "Please, please grab your bag?"

Tessa's hard expression softens, and she pads down the hallway and turns into her old bedroom.

Carol's eyes move back and forth between Zed and me before she speaks. "What happened to make her run out into the rain? Which of you caused that?" Her glare is murderous, almost comical, really.

"He did," the two of us answer and point simultaneously, like children.

Carol rolls her eyes and turns to follow her daughter down the narrow hallway.

I focus on Zed. "You can go now."

I know Carol can hear me, but honestly, I don't give a fuck at this point.

"Tessa didn't want me to go; she was only confused. She came on to me, she begged me to stay here with her," he spits. I shake my head, but he continues. "She doesn't want you anymore. You've spent your last dollar where she's concerned, and you know it. You see how she looks at me, how she wants me."

I ball my fists, taking deep breaths to calm myself. If Tessa doesn't hurry out with her bag, the living room will be painted red by the time she returns. That fucker and his fucking smirk.

She wouldn't kiss him. She wouldn't do that.

Visions from my nightmares swirl behind my lids, bringing me one step closer to my breaking point. His hands on her pregnant belly, her nails raking down his back. They way he's always mixed up with other people's girls . . .

She wouldn't do that. She wouldn't kiss him.

"This isn't going to work," I say, forcing the words out. "You aren't going to antagonize me into attacking you in front of her. Not again."

Fuck, I want to smash his fucking head open and watch his brain matter pour out. I want to so fucking bad.

He sits on the arm of the couch and smiles. "You've made it so easy for me. She told me how much she wants me, she told me less than a half hour ago." He glances down at his empty wrist as if he is checking the time on a watch. He's a dramatic motherfucker, always has been.

"Tessa!" I call to gauge how many more seconds I have to tolerate this asshole's presence.

Silence fills the house, followed by the murmuring voices of Tessa and her mum. I close my eyes momentarily, hoping that Carol hasn't convinced Tessa to stay in this shithole of a town for another night.

"That drives you crazy, doesn't it?" Zed mocks, continuing to goad me. "How do you think I felt when you fucked Sam? It was one thousand times worse than the petty jealousy you feel right now."

As if he could possibly fathom the depth of what I feel regarding Tessa. I give him a bored look. "I told you to shut the fuck up and leave. No one gives two fucks about you and Sam. She was easy, too fucking easy for my liking, really, and that was that." Zed takes a step toward me, and I straighten my back, reminding him that my height is one of my many advantages against him.

It's my turn to fuck with him. "What? You don't like hearing about your precious Samantha?"

Zed's eyes turn dark, warning me to stop, but I refuse. He has the fucking nerve to kiss Tessa and try to use her feelings as ammunition against me? He obviously doesn't know that I have an entire arsenal up my fucking sleeve.

"Shut up," he snaps, pushing me further. I may keep my hands to myself this time, but my words will make more of an impact anyway.

"Why?" I glance down the hallway to make sure Tessa is still occupied by her mum while I torture Zed with my words. "You don't want to hear about the night I fucked her? I can barely remember it, really, but I understand it was so new a feeling for her that she was writing about it in that little diary of hers. She wasn't very memorable, I suppose, but at least she was *eager.*"

. I knew how into her he was, and at the time I assumed their relationship would make her more of a challenge. The joke was on me when she ended up being more of a hassle than a toy. "I fucked her brains out, though, I can assure you that. That must be why she pulled that pregnancy shit afterwards. You remember that, don't you?"

For a moment—a brief moment—I pause and consider how he must have felt when he found out. I try to remember what was going through my mind when I decided to pursue her. I knew they were dating. I'd heard her mention his name in the copy room at Vance, and I was instantly intrigued. I had only known Zed for a few weeks, and I thought it would be fun to fuck with him.

"You were supposed to be my friend." His pathetic words fall between us.

"Your friend? None of those degenerates were your friends. I barely knew you; it was nothing personal." I look down the hallway, to make sure Tessa isn't around, then I step closer and wrap my fist around the collar of his shirt. "Just like it was nothing personal when Stephanie introduced Rebecca to you, even though she knew Noah was seeing her. Personal is what you're aiming for by fucking with Tessa. You know what she means to me—more than any office whore could ever mean to you."

I'm caught off guard when he pushes back, slamming me against the wall. Picture frames rattle and fall to the ground, causing Tessa and her mum to rush into the hallway.

"Fuck you! I could have fucked Tessa, too—she would have easily given herself to me tonight if you wouldn't have shown up!" His fist connects with my mouth, and Tessa shrieks in horror. The harsh taste of copper fills my mouth, and I swallow the blood in a quick gulp before wiping my sleeve across my lips and chin.

"Zed!" Tessa scolds, rushing to my side. "Leave! Now!" She shoves her small fists against his chest and I grab hold of her, gently putting space between them.

The pure experience of Tessa hearing him speak of her that way makes me fucking ecstatic. This is what I've been warning her of all along: He has never been the sweet, innocent man she was manipulated into thinking he was.

Granted, I do know that he has some feelings for her—I'm not completely blind to that—but his intentions were never pure. He just proved that to her, and I couldn't be happier. I'm a selfish bastard, but I never claimed otherwise.

Without another word, Zed walks out the front door and into the rain. Headlights flash through the front windows as he peels off and disappears down the street.

"HARDIN?" TESSA'S VOICE IS SOFT and laced with exhaustion. We've been in the backseat of this cab for almost an hour without a single word between the two of us.

"Yeah?" My voice breaks and I clear my throat.

"Who's Samantha?"

I have been waiting for her to ask this question since we pulled away from her mum's house. I could lie to her, I could make up a bullshit story to make Zed look like the piece of shit he is, or I could be honest for once.

"She's a girl who had an internship at Vance. I fucked her while she was dating Zed." I decide not to lie, but regret the harsh words when Tessa flinches. "Sorry, I just want to be honest," I add in an attempt to soften the words.

"You knew she was his girlfriend when you slept with her?" She stares straight into me in that way only she can.

"Yeah, I knew. That's why I did it." I shrug, ignoring the pinch of remorse threatening to surface.

"Why?" Her eyes search mine for a decent answer, but I don't have one. I only have the truth. The filthy, fucked-up truth.

"I have no excuse, it was just a game for me." I sigh, wishing I weren't such a piece of shit. Not for Zed's sake, or Samantha's, but for this beautiful, sweet girl who even now doesn't have a hint of judgment in her eyes as she looks at me, waiting for further explanation.

"You forget that I wasn't the same before I met you. I was nothing like the man you know. Well, I know you think I'm fucked-up now, but trust me, you would hate me even more if you knew me then." I look away from her and out the window. "I know it doesn't seem like it, but you really have helped me so much, you've given me a purpose, Tess."

I hear her sharp exhale of breath and I cringe at the thought of how my words must sound. Pathetic and insincere, I'm sure.

"And what's that purpose?" she asks timidly in the sudden stillness of the night.

"I'm still trying to figure that out. But I will figure it out, so please try and stick around long enough for me to find the answer?"

She looks at me but stays quiet.

I'm thankful for that, I don't think I could handle her rejection right now. I turn my head and look out into the black-black darkness of the landscape around us and am glad that nothing final and devastating came from her mouth.

chapter thirty-nine

TESSA

I wake up to arms wrapping around my waist as I'm lifted out of the car. The white light on top of the cab reminds me of the night I've had. I take in my surroundings, panicking for a moment before realizing that we are in Ken's driveway, not, not . . .

"I would never take you back there," Hardin says into my ear, knowing exactly what I would worry about before the thought can even gel in my mind.

I don't protest as Hardin carries me up the driveway and into the house. Karen is awake, sitting in a chair by the window, a recipe book in her lap. Hardin places me on my feet, and I feel a little wobbly.

Karen stands, walking across the room to hug me. "What can I get you, dear? I made some caramel cakes; you'll love them." She smiles and wraps a warm hand around mine, leading me toward the kitchen without a peep from Hardin.

"I'll take your bag upstairs," I hear him say.

"Is Landon asleep?" I ask his mother.

"I think so, but I'm sure he won't mind if you wake him. It's still early." Karen smiles and places a small, caramel-topped cake on a plate before I can stop her.

"No, it's okay. I can see him tomorrow."

Landon's mother's eyes are on me, soft with her familiar tenderness. Her fingers are nervously twisting her wedding ring on her thin finger. "I know this is terrible timing, and I'm so sorry, but I wanted to talk to you about something." Her warm brown eyes flash with concern and she waves for me to take a bite of the dessert as she pours two glasses of milk.

I nod for her to continue, my mouth full of the delicious cake. I couldn't eat earlier—I was too overwhelmed, and the day has been too long. I reach for another slice.

"I know you have so much going on already, so if you want me to leave you be, just tell me. I promise I understand, but I would really like your opinion on something."

I give her another nod, enjoying the dessert.

"It's about Hardin and Ken."

My eyes go wide, and immediately I start choking on the cake and reach for the milk. *Does she know? Has Hardin said something?*

Karen pats my back while I drink the cold milk down, rubbing in circles as she continues, "Ken's so happy that Hardin has finally started to tolerate him. It makes him so happy that he is finally building a relationship with his son; it's something he's always wanted. Hardin is his biggest regret, and it hurt me for years seeing him that way. I know he's made his mistakes—many, many mistakes—and I am in no way making excuses for those mistakes." Her eyes fill with tears, and she dabs at the corners with her fingers. "Sorry," she says with a smile. "I'm a mess."

After a couple of deep breaths she adds, "He isn't the same man now that he was then. He's had years of sobriety and therapy, years of reflection and remorse."

She knows. Karen knows about Trish and Christian. My chest tightens, and my eyes fill, too. "I know what you're going to say." I feel for this family. I love them as my own, and I feel for everyone in this family that's full of secrets, addictions, and regrets.

"You do?" She blows out a ragged breath that speaks a little of her relief. "Landon told you about the baby? I should have known he would. So I'm assuming Hardin knows, too, then?"

I start coughing again. After an awkward fit, during which

Karen keeps watching my expression, I finally speak. "*What? A baby?*"

"So you didn't know." She laughs softly. "I know I'm much older than you would expect a pregnant woman to be, but I'm only in my early forties, and my doctor has assured me that I'm healthy enough . . ."

"A baby?" I'm relieved that she doesn't know about Christian being Hardin's father, but this is *beyond* a surprise.

"Yes." She smiles. "I was just as shocked as you are. Ken, too. He's been so worried about me. Landon nearly had a breakdown; he knew about all of my appointments, but I didn't tell him what they were for, so the poor thing thought I was sick. I felt terrible, and I had to come clean. This wasn't planned"—her eyes search mine—"but we are happy now that we've gotten over the initial shock of having another child so late in life."

My arms wrap around her, and for the first time in days I feel joy. Where there was nothing dominating my core, there is joy. I love Karen and am thrilled for her. This feels so good. I was beginning to worry that I would never feel this way again.

"This is amazing! I'm so happy for you two!" I gush, and her arms tighten around my back.

"Thank you, Tessa. I knew you would be, and it is quite exciting, the more and more I live with the reality of it." She pulls back and kisses my cheek, then looks me in the eye. "I'm just worried about how this will make Hardin feel."

And like that, my joy for her is cut short and instantly replaced by worry for Hardin. His entire life has been a lie, and he hasn't exactly handled the news well. The man he believed to be his father is now having another child, and Hardin will be forgotten. Whether that's true or not, I know him well enough to know that's where his mind will go. And Karen knows it, which is why she was so worried about bringing it up.

"Do you mind if I'm the one who tells him?" I ask. "If not, I understand."

I don't allow myself to think too far into this. I know that I'm blurring the lines here, but if I'm leaving Hardin, I need to make sure I'm not leaving a mess behind.

That's an excuse, part of me warns.

"No, of course not—to be honest, I was hoping you'd want to. I know this puts you in a terrible position, and I don't want you to feel *obligated* to get in the middle of this, but I *am* afraid of how Hardin will react if Ken is the one to tell him. You have a way with him that no one else does."

"It's fine, really. I will talk to him tomorrow."

She hugs me again. "Today has been a tough day for you. I'm sorry for bringing this up. I should have waited—I just want to avoid the news being a surprise to him, especially since I feel like I'm starting to show a little bit. He's had a hard enough life already, and I want to do whatever I can to make things easier on him. I want him to know that he's a part of this family, and that we all love him so much, that this baby won't change that."

"He knows," I promise. He may not be willing to accept it yet, but he knows.

Footsteps reach the bottom of the stairs, and Karen and I pull away from each other reflexively. We both wipe our cheeks, and I take another bite of the cake as Hardin enters the kitchen. He's showered and changed his clothes. He's now wearing a pair of sweatpants, the legs of which are too short; the WCU logo stitched along his thigh is a dead giveaway that he's wearing Landon's clothing. No way is he a booster like that.

If we were in a different place, I would tease him about the pants. But we aren't. We are in the worst place, yet in the best place for me; it's all confusing and skewed. Then again, a healthy balance and order has never been a factor in our relationship; why would our breakup be any different?

"I'm going to bed. Do you need anything?" he asks, his voice rough and low.

I look up at him but he's staring at his bare feet. "No. Thank you, though."

"I put your stuff in the guest room, your room."

I nod. The insane, untrustworthy part of me wishes Karen weren't in the kitchen with us, but the rational, bitter, and much larger part of me is glad that she is. He disappears up the staircase, and I say good-night to Karen before going up myself.

In short order I find myself outside the room where I've spent some of the best nights of my life. I raise my hand to the knob, but quickly pull away as if the cold metal might burn my skin.

This cycle has got to stop, and if I give in to every impulse, every fiber of my being, that desperately craves to be close to him, I'll never make it out of this continuous loop of mistake after mistake, fight after fight.

I finally let out a breath as I close the guest-room door behind me and turn the lock. I fall asleep wishing that the younger me had known just how dangerous love could be. If I had known it would hurt this bad, if I had known the way it would rip me apart, then sew me back together, only to tear me into pieces again, I would have stayed as far away from Hardin Scott as I possibly could.

chapter forty

TESSA

"Tessie! In here, come in here!" my father calls down the hall, excitement clear in his loud voice.

I climb out of my small bed and rush out to him. The loose ties on my robe nearly trip me in my haste, and I fumble to bind them again as I burst into the living room . . . where my mother and father are standing next to a beautifully decorated and lit-up tree.

I've always loved Christmas.

"Look, Tessie, we got you a gift. I know you're an adult now, but I saw this and had to get it for you." My father smiles and my mother leans into him.

An adult? I look down at my feet, trying to decipher his words. I'm not an adult, at least I don't think I am.

A small box is placed into my hand, and without so much as a thought I eagerly rip the shiny bow off the gift. I love gifts. I don't get them often, so when I do, it's special for me.

As I tear at it, I look up at my parents, but my mother's excitement throws me off. I've never seen her smile this way, and my father, well, I feel as if he shouldn't be here, but I can't remember why that is.

"Hurry and open it!" my father urges as I lift the lid off the box.

I nod excitedly and reach inside . . . only to pull my hand back when something sharp pricks my finger. I nearly curse from the pain and drop the box to the floor. A needle falls onto the carpet. When I look back up at my parents, my father's skin has lost all color and his eyes have gone void.

My mother's smile is bright again, brighter than I've ever seen it before—as bright as a blinding sun, it suddenly seems. My father bends down and grabs the needle from the floor. He takes a step toward me, needle in hand, and I try to back away, but my feet won't move. They won't move no matter how hard I try, and I'm left helpless, only to scream as he pushes the weapon into my arm.

"TESSA!" LANDON'S VOICE is frantic, loud, and frightening as he shakes my shoulders.

I'm sitting up somehow, and my shirt is stained with sweat. I look at him, then back down to my arm, searching like a lunatic for puncture marks.

"Are you *okay*?" he exclaims.

I gasp for breath, my chest aching as I struggle to find air and my voice. I shake my head, and Landon tightens his grip on my shoulders.

"I heard you scream, so I—" Landon is rendered silent when Hardin barges into the room.

Hardin's cheeks are flushed a deep red, and his eyes are wild. "What happened?" He brushes Landon off me and sits next to me on the bed. "I heard you scream—what happened?" His hands move to my cheeks, and his thumbs brush over the tearstains there.

"I don't know. I had a dream," I manage to say.

"What sort of dream?" Hardin's voice is nearly a whisper, and his thumbs are still gliding, slowly as ever, across the skin just under my eyes.

"The kind that you have," I reply, my voice equally hushed.

A sigh leaves his lips, and he frowns. "Since when? Since when do you have my sort of dreams?"

I take a moment to collect my thoughts. "Only since I found him, and it's only been twice. I don't know where they're coming from."

His distressed hand runs over his hair, and my heart twists at the sight of the familiar gesture. "Well, I'm sure finding the body of your dead father would cause anyone to—" He stops midsentence. "I'm sorry, fuck, I need a filter." He sighs in frustration.

He shifts his eyes from mine and looks over to the bedside table. "Do you need anything? Water?" He tries to smile, but it's forced, sad even. "I feel like I've offered you water a thousand times in the last few days."

"I just need to go back to sleep."

"I'll stay?" he half demands, half asks.

"I don't think . . ." I look over at Landon. I almost forgot he was in the room with us.

"It's cool." Hardin's eyes stare past me at the wall behind my head. "I get it."

When he shrugs his shoulders in defeat, it takes everything inside me, every ounce of my self-respect, not to wrap my arms around his neck and beg him to sleep with me. I need his comfort; I need his arms around my waist and my head on his chest as I fall asleep. I need him to give me the peace in sleep that I have always provided for him, but he's no longer the safety net I relied on. Then again, has he ever been? He's been on and off, always just out of reach, constantly running from me and our love. I can't chase him again. I simply don't have the strength to chase after something so unattainable, so unrealistic.

By the time I manage to break free from my thoughts, only Landon remains in the room with me.

"Scoot over," he quietly instructs.

I do just that and fall back asleep, regretting my earlier thoughts of wishing I had stayed away from Hardin.

Even in the midst of the inevitable tragedy that was our relationship, I would never take a second of it back. I wouldn't do it again, but I don't regret a moment I spent with him.

chapter forty-one

HARDIN

The weather here is much better than in Seattle. The rain is nowhere to be found, and the sun has come out for a rare appearance. It's April now: it's about damn time that the sun is out.

Tessa has been in the kitchen with Karen and that Sophia chick all day. I'm trying to show her that I can give her space, that I can wait until she's ready to talk to me—but it's harder than I could have imagined. Last night was hard for me—really damn hard, to see her so distraught, so afraid. I hate that my nightmares have rubbed off on her. My horrors are contagious, and I would take them from her if I could.

When Tessa was mine, she always slept peacefully. She was my anchor, my comfort in the night, fighting off my demons for me when I was too weak, too distracted by self-pity, to help her battle them. She was there, shield in hand, fighting every image that threatened my fucked-up mind. She bore the burden on her own, and that's what finally broke her.

Then I remind myself that she's still mine; she's just not ready to admit it again.

She has to be. There is no other way.

I park my car in front of my father's house. The leasing agent gave me shit when I called to tell him that I'm moving out. He fed me some bullshit about charging me two months' rent for breaking the lease, but I hung up midconversation. I don't care what I have to pay, I'm not living there anymore. I know it's an impulsive decision, and I don't exactly have another place to live, but

I'm hoping I can stay at Ken's for a few days with Tessa until I can convince her to move in with me, in Seattle.

I'm ready for this. I'm ready to live in Seattle if that's what she wants, and my offer of marriage isn't going anywhere. Not this time. I'll marry that girl and live in Seattle until I die if that's what she wants, if that's what makes her happy.

"How long is that chick staying?" I ask Landon, pointing out the window at the Prius parked next to his car. It was kind of cool of him to offer to take me to get my car, especially after I chewed him out for sleeping in the room with Tessa. I wouldn't have been able to unlock the door, he pointed out, but I would have broken the damn thing down if I had the energy. The idea of the two of them sharing a bed has been driving me fucking crazy since I heard their hushed voices from outside the door. I ignored the puzzled look on his face when he found me half-asleep, sitting on the floor outside the door.

I tried to fall asleep in the empty bed in my designated room, but I just couldn't. I had to be closer to her just in case something happened and she screamed again. At least that's what I kept telling myself as I struggled to stay awake in the hallway the entire night.

"I don't know. Sophia is leaving to go back to New York later this week." His voice comes out high-pitched and awkward as hell.

What the hell's that all about? "What?" I press him as we walk inside the house.

"Oh, nothing."

But Landon's cheeks flush, and I follow him into the living room, where Tessa is standing near the window, staring off into space while Karen and mini-Karen share a laugh.

Why isn't Tessa laughing? Why isn't she at least engaged in the conversation?

The woman smiles at Landon. "There you are!"

She's pretty enough, nowhere near Tessa's beauty, but she's easy on the eyes for sure. As she approaches, I look over and notice that, again, Landon is blushing . . . a pastry is in his hand . . . she's smiling wide . . . and it *clicks*.

Why didn't I see it before? He fucking likes her! A million jokes and embarrassing comments flood my mind, and I literally have to bite my tongue to prevent myself from torturing him with this information.

I ignore the start of their conversation and walk straight to Tessa. She doesn't seem to notice my presence until I'm directly in front of her.

"What's going on?" I ask.

There's a fine line between space and . . . well . . . my normal behavior, and I'm trying my best to find a good balance even if it's hard to break the habit.

I know that if I give her too much space, she will withdraw from me, but if I suffocate her, she will run. This is new for me, completely uncharted territory. I hate to admit this to myself, but I had gotten a little too used to her being my emotional punching bag. I hate myself for the way I've treated her, and I know she deserves better than me, but I need this last chance to become someone better for her.

No, I need to be myself. Just a version of me who is worthy of her love.

"Nothing, just baking. The usual. Well, taking a little break from baking, actually." A faint smile crosses her lips, and I grin at her. These small affections, these minuscule hints of adoration toward me, fuel my hope. A hope that's both new and very much out of my comfort zone, but I'll gladly spend my time figuring it out.

Karen and Landon's number one spank-bank chick come over and signal to Tessa, and within seconds they're all back in the kitchen while Landon and I are forgotten and left alone in the living room.

As soon as I'm sure the women can't hear me, a devilish grin stretches across my face and I accuse Landon, "You're hot for her."

"How many times do I have to tell you? Tessa and I are just friends." He sighs an annoyed and overdramatic sigh while scowling at me. "I thought you understood that after cussing me out for an hour this morning."

I waggle my eyebrows. "Oh, I'm not talking about Tessa. I mean Sarah."

"Her name is Sophia."

I shrug and keep smiling. "Same thing."

"No." He rolls his eyes. "It's not. You act like you can't remember any woman's name except Tess."

"Tessa," I correct him with a frown. "And I don't need to remember any other women's names."

"It's disrespectful. You've called Sophia every name that begins with an S, except her actual name, and it drove me insane when you called Dakota *Danielle*."

"You're annoying." I sit down on the couch, smiling at my step . . . Actually, he's not actually my stepbrother anymore. Never was. Realizing that fact, I'm not really sure how I feel about that.

He fights a smile. "So are you."

Would he care if he knew? Probably not, he would probably be relieved that we aren't related, even by marriage.

"I know you like her, admit it." I taunt.

"No, I don't. I don't even know her." He looks away. *Busted.*

"But she'll be in New York with you, and you can explore the streets there together and get caught under an awning during a dramatic downpour—how romantic!" I pull my lip between my teeth to stifle a laugh at his horrified expression.

"Would you stop? She's much older than me and way out of my league."

"She's too hot for you, but you never know. Some girls don't care about looks," I tease. "And who knows? She may be looking for a younger man. How old is your old lady there?"

"Twenty-four. Leave it alone," he begs, and I decide to do just that. I could go on and on with this, but I have other things to focus on anyway.

"I'm going to move to Seattle." I feel sort of almost giddy as I blurt out the news. Sort of.

"What?" He leans in, a little too surprised.

"Yeah, I'm going to see what Ken can do about helping me finish the semester through distance learning, and I'm going to get an apartment in Seattle for Tessa and me. I already dropped my grad packet, so it shouldn't be too big of a deal."

"What?" Landon's eyes dart away from mine.

Did he not just hear what I said? "I'm not repeating myself. I know you heard me."

"Why now? You and Tessa aren't together and she—"

"We will be; she just needs a little time to think it through, but she'll forgive me. She always does. You'll see."

As the words leave my mouth, I look up to see Tessa standing in the doorway, a deep frown etched onto her beautiful face.

A beautiful face that instantly disappears as she turns on her heel and walks back into the kitchen without a word.

"Fuck." I close my eyes and lay my head against the couch cushion, cursing at myself for my awful timing.

chapter forty-two

TESSA

N ew York is the best city in the world, Tessa—it's incredible. I've lived there for five years now, and I still haven't seen all of it. I bet that even in a lifetime you never could," Sophia says while scrubbing at a baking pan that I burned a batch of dough in.

I hadn't been paying attention. I was too lost in my own mind after hearing Hardin's arrogant, uncaring words to notice the smoke coming from the oven. Only when Sophia and Karen came rushing into the kitchen from the pantry was my attention brought to the burnt dough. Neither of them chastised me, though, and Sophia just sprayed it under cold water to cool it down and then started scrubbing.

"Seattle is the largest city I've been to, but I'm ready for New York. I need to get away from here," I tell them. Hardin's face just won't disappear from my mind as I say the words.

Karen gives me a smile as she pours each of us a glass of milk. "Well, I live close to NYU, so I can show you around if you want me to. It's always good to know someone, especially in such a big city."

"Thank you," I tell her, meaning it. Landon will be there, but he will be just as lost as I will surely be, so we could both use a friend out there. The thought of living in New York City is so intimidating, it's almost overwhelming, but I'm sure everyone feels like that before moving across the country. If Hardin were coming along . . .

I shake my head to rid it of the useless thoughts. I couldn't even convince Hardin to move to Seattle for me—he would laugh in my face at New York. And he takes my plans, what I want, so for granted that he thinks I'll forgive him just because I have in the past.

"Well"—Karen smiles, lifting her glass of milk to mine— "here's to New York and new adventures!" She beams. Sophia raises her glass, and I can't help but play Hardin's words in my head as we toast.

"She'll forgive me, she always does. You'll see," he told Landon.

The fear of moving across the country lessens with each word of his as they play on a loop through my thoughts, each syllable a smack in the face to the tiny scrap of dignity I have left.

chapter forty-three

To say that I've been avoiding Hardin would be an understatement. As the days have passed—only two of them, though it feels like forty—I have avoided him at all costs. I know he's here in this house, but I can't bring myself to see him. He's knocked on my door a few times but was met with a weak excuse from me on why I'm not answering.

I just wasn't ready.

However, I've put off what I need to tell him too long now, and Karen is bound to get restless, I know it. She is bursting at the seams with happiness, and I know she doesn't want to keep the addition to their family a secret for long. She shouldn't have to; she should be happy and proud and excited. I can't ruin that for her by being a coward.

So when I hear those heavy boots outside my door, I wait silently, pathetically, both hoping for a knock and wishing for him to go away. I'm still waiting for the day when my mind clears, when my thoughts go back to making sense. The more time that passes, the more I begin to question how clear my thoughts have ever been. Have I always been this confused, this unsure of myself and my decisions?

I wait on my bed, eyes closed and lip throbbing between my teeth, for him to leave before knocking. I'm disappointed, yet relieved, when I hear his door slam across the hall.

Gathering all my strength and my phone in my hand, I check my reflection in the mirror one last time and then cross the hall.

Just as I lift my hand to knock, the door opens, and there stands Hardin, shirtless and looking down at me.

"What's wrong?" he immediately asks.

"Nothing, I—" I ignore the twist in my stomach as his brows pull together in worry. His hands touch me, thumbs gently pressing into my cheeks, and I just stand in the doorway, blinking up at him, not a coherent thought within reach.

"I need to talk to you about something," I finally say. The words come out muffled, and he's looking down at me with confusion clouding his brilliant green eyes.

"I don't like the sound of that," he remarks somberly and drops his hands from my face.

Going to sit on the edge of the bed, he beckons for me to join him. I don't trust the lack of distance between us, and even the thick air in the stuffy room seems to be taunting me.

"So? What is it?" Hardin spreads his hands out behind his head and leans back into them. His athletic shorts are tight; the waistband of them hangs so low that I can tell he is not wearing boxers underneath.

"Hardin, I'm sorry that I've been so distant from you. You know I just need some time to figure everything out," I say by way of a preamble. That wasn't what I had planned to talk to him about, but my mouth apparently has different plans than my head.

"It's okay. I'm glad you came to me because we both know that I'm shit at giving you space, and it's been driving me fucking crazy." He seems relieved now that the words are between us. His eyes rest on mine, and I can't look away from the intensity behind them.

"I know." I can't deny the control he has seemed to gain over his own actions during the past week. I like that he's become a little less unpredictable, but the shield that I've built is still present, still lurking in the background, waiting for him to turn on me, the way he always does.

"Have you talked to Christian?" I ask, needing to move back to the topic at hand before I'm too far lost in the endless mess of us.

Immediately he tenses, scoffing, "No." He squints at me.

This isn't going well. "I'm sorry, I don't mean to be insensitive. I just want to see where your head is right now."

He doesn't respond for a few moments, and the silence stretches between us like a never-ending road.

chapter forty-four

HARDIN

Tessa's eyes are on me. The worry in them builds a gnawing worry in me in return. She's been through so much, a lot of which was at my hand, so worrying about me is the last thing she should be doing. I want her to focus on herself, on being herself again and not putting any more effort into fretting over me. I love the way her compassion for others, especially me, overrides her own troubles.

"You aren't being insensitive. I'm lucky you're even speaking to me." It's the truth, but whatever's supposed to come next in this conversation, I'm unsure of.

Tessa nods slowly. And pauses before gently asking the question that I'm sure was her main reason for coming in here. "So, do you plan on telling Ken about everything from London?"

I lie back on the bed with my eyes closed and think about her question before answering. I have been thinking over this a lot the last few days, going back and forth between telling him in a rushed confession or doing the opposite and keeping the information to myself. Does Ken *need* to know? And if I tell him, am I willing to accept the changes that will come from this? *Will* there be any changes, or am I just being a bitch about it? It seems fitting that the moment I start to tolerate and possibly forgive the man, I find out he's not my father to forgive after all.

I open my eyes and sit up. "I'm still deciding. Actually, I sort of wanted to get your opinion on that."

My girl's blue-gray eyes aren't shining the way I've become so used to, but they hold more life today than the last time I saw her. It was pure fucking torture being under the same roof with her without being *near* her, not in the way I need to be.

Everything has seemed to shift in an ironic twist of fate, and I'm now the one begging for attention, begging for simply anything that she will offer me. Even now, the thoughtful expression in her eyes is enough to soothe the constant ache that I refuse to learn to live with no matter how far she pushes herself away from me.

"Would you like to have a relationship with Christian?" she asks softly, her small fingers tracing the frayed stitching on the comforter.

"No," I quickly respond. "Hell, I don't know," I backtrack. "I need you to tell me what I should do."

She nods, and her eyes meet mine. "Well, I think you should only tell Ken if you think it will help you deal with some of the pain from your childhood. I don't think you should tell him if your only reason to do so is out of spite or anger; and as far as Christian goes, I think you have a little bit of time to make that decision. Just see where things go, you know?" she suggests in that understanding tone she has.

"How is it that you do that?"

She tilts her chin, confused. "Do what?"

"Always say the right thing."

"I don't." A soft laugh falls between us. "I don't say the right things."

"You do." I reach my hand out for her, but she pulls away. "You do say the right things; you always have. I just couldn't hear you before."

Tessa looks away from me, but that's okay. It will take some time for her to get used to hearing these things from me, but she will get used to it. I've made a vow to tell her how I feel and to stop being selfish and expecting her to decipher my every word and intention.

The vibration of her cell phone breaks the stillness, and she pulls it from the pocket of her oversize sweatshirt. I force myself to pretend that she bought the WCU sweatshirt and that she's not wearing Landon's clothing. I have been subjected to wearing every embroidered piece of WCU merchandise known to man, but I hate the idea of his clothes touching her skin. It's irrational and fucking stupid, but I can't stop the thoughts from entering and taking root in my mind.

She swipes her thumb across the screen, and it takes a moment for me to realize what I'm seeing.

I snatch the phone from her hands before she can stop me. "An iPhone? You're shitting me!" I stare down at the new phone in my hands. "This is yours?"

"Yeah." Her cheeks flush, and she reaches for the phone, but I stretch my arms above my head, out of her reach.

"Oh, so *now* you get an iPhone, but when I wanted you to, you absolutely refused!" I tease. Her eyes are wide, and she takes a nervous breath. "Why the change of heart?" I smile at her, easing her discomfort.

"I don't know. It was time, I guess." She shrugs her shoulders, still nervous.

I don't like how she looks unsettled, but I'm hoping that a little playfulness is all that's needed. "What's the pass code?" I ask while hitting the numbers that I'm guessing she'll have used.

Ha—got it on the first try, and I'm welcomed in by her home screen.

"Hardin!" she squeals, attempting to grab the phone from me. "You can't just go through my phone!" She leans across and grabs my bare arm with one hand and reaches for the phone with the other.

"Yes, I can." I laugh. The simplest touch from her has me buzzing; every cell beneath my skin is alive from her skin on mine.

She smiles and holds out a demanding little hand to match

that sweet little grin that I've missed so much. "All right. Give me yours, then."

"Nope, sorry." I continue to tease her while obsessively scrolling through her text messages.

"Give me the phone!" she whines and moves closer to me, but then her smile disappears. "There are probably a lot of things on your phone that I don't want to see." And like that, I can feel her guard sliding back into place.

"No, there isn't. There are over a thousand pictures of you and an entire album of your bullshit music, and if you really want to see how pathetic I am, you could check the call logs and see how many times I've called your old number just to hear that robotic bitch voice tell me that your number is no longer in service."

She glares at me, obviously not believing me. Not that I blame her. Her eyes soften but only momentarily before she says, "None of Janine?" Her voice is so low that I barely catch the accusation.

"What? No! Go on, look at it. It's on the dresser."

"I'd rather not."

I lean up onto my knees and press my shoulder into hers. "Tessa, she's nothing to me. Never will be."

Tessa's trying hard not to care. She's fighting within herself to show me that she has moved on from me, but I know her better than that. I know that she's stewing over the idea of me with another woman.

"I need to go." She stands to leave, and I reach for her. My fingers gently grab her arm, softly asking for her to come back to me. She hesitates at first, and I don't force her. I wait for her, my fingers rubbing small circles into the soft skin above her wrist.

"I know what you think happened, but you're wrong," I try to convince her.

"No, I know what I saw. I saw her in your shirt," she snaps. She pulls her hand away from me but stands closer.

"I was out of my mind, Tessa, but I didn't fuck her." I wouldn't have. Having her touch me was bad enough. For a moment I wonder if I should tell Tessa the way I couldn't stand Janine's cigarette-flavored lips on mine, but that seems like it would only set her off.

"Sure." She rolls her eyes defiantly.

"I miss you and your attitude." I try to lighten the mood, but she only rolls her eyes again. "I love you."

That gains her attention, and she pushes at my chest to put some space between our bodies. "Stop doing that! You can't just decide you want me now and expect me to come running back to you."

I want to tell her that she's going to come back to me because she *belongs with me*, that I will never stop trying to convince her of this. But instead I smile at her and shake my head. "Let's change the subject. I just wanted you to know that I miss you, okay?"

"Okay." She sighs. She brings her fingers to her lips and pinches them, making me forget what I was going to change the subject to.

"An iPhone." I turn her phone in my hand again. "I can't believe you got an iPhone and weren't going to tell me." I glance over and watch as her frown turns into a half smile.

"It's not a big deal. It helps a lot with my schedule, and Landon is going to show me how to download music and movies." Landon's offer as we were leaving the cell-phone store seems so long ago. So much has happened in such a short time.

"I can help you."

"It's okay, really," she says, trying to dismiss me.

"I will help you. I can show you now." I pull up the iTunes Store.

We spend an hour this way, me going through the catalog choosing all of her favorite music and showing her how to download those cheesy Tom Hanks romantic comedies that she seems to love. Tessa is nearly silent the entire time, only a few *Thank yous* and *No, not that songs* are given, and I try not to push her for conversation.

I did this to her, I turned her into the quiet, unsure woman before me, and it's my fault that she doesn't know how to act right now. It's my fault that every time I lean into her, she pulls away, taking a piece of me with her each time.

It seems impossible that I would have anything left to give her, that she doesn't already consume and own every single part of me, but somehow, when she smiles at me, my body comes up with a little more of myself to let her steal away. It's all for her, and it will always be that way.

"Do you need me to show you how to download the best porn, too?" I joke, and I'm awarded another flush of her cheeks.

"Oh, I'm sure you know all about that," she teases back. I love this. I love being able to tease her the way I used to, and I fucking love that she's letting me.

"Not really, actually, I have plenty of images up here." I tap at my forehead with my cast, and she grimaces. "Only of you."

Her frown doesn't waver, but I refuse to allow her to think this way. It's insane thinking—that I would be interested in anyone but her. I'm starting to think she's as crazy as I am. Maybe that would explain why she stayed with me as long as she did.

"I mean it. I only think of you. It's always you." My tone is serious now, too fucking serious, but I don't care enough to change it. I've tried the joking, friendly shit, and I hurt her feelings.

She surprises me by asking, "What types of things do you think about me?"

I bring my bottom lip between my teeth as images of her flash through my mind. "You don't want me to answer that."

Tessa spread out on the bed, her thighs pushed apart and her fingers clawing at the sheets as she comes against my tongue.

Tessa's hips moving in slow, torturing circles as she rides my cock, her moans filling the room.

Tessa kneeling in front of me, her full lips parting as she takes me into her warm mouth.

Tessa leaning forward, her naked skin glowing in the soft light of the room. She's in front of me, facing away from me as she lowers her body onto me. I fill her as she gasps my name . . .

"You're probably right," she laughs, then sighs. "We always do this, we always slip right back into this." She waves her hand back and forth between us.

I know exactly what she means. I'm in the middle of the worst week of my life, and she has me laughing and smiling over a damn iPhone. "This is us, baby. This is how we are. We can't help it."

"We can help it. We have to. I have to." Her words may sound convincing in her mind, but she's not fooling me.

"Stop overthinking everything. You know this is how it should be, us teasing one another over porn, me thinking about all the dirty things I have done, and the still more I want to do, to you."

"This is literally insane. We can't do this." She leans in closer to me.

"Do what?"

"Everything isn't about sex." Her eyes focus on my crotch, and I can tell she's trying to look away from the bulge there.

"I never said it was, but you can do us both a favor and stop acting like you aren't thinking the same things that I am."

"We can't."

But then I notice our breathing has synchronized. And ever-so-subtly her tongue peeks out and caresses her bottom lip.

"I didn't offer," I remind her.

I didn't offer, but I sure as hell wouldn't refuse. I'm not that lucky, though, there is no way she will let me touch her. Not anytime soon . . . right?

"You were suggesting." She smiles.

"When aren't I?"

"True." She fights a giggle. "This is so confusing. We shouldn't be doing this. I don't trust myself around you."

Fuck, I'm glad she doesn't. I don't trust me half the time. But I say, "What could be the worst to happen?" and move a hand to her shoulder. She flinches at the touch, but it's not the same repellent flinch that I've been dealing with for the last week.

"I could continue to be an idiot," she whispers, and I move my hand slowly up and down the length of her arm.

"Stop thinking, just shut your mind off, and let your body control this. Your body wants me, Tessa, it needs me."

She shakes her head, denying the simple truth.

"Yes, yes, it does." I continue touching her, closer to her chest now, waiting for her to stop me. If she does, I will cease all contact. I would never push this on her. I've done a lot of fucked-up shit, but that's never an option.

"See the thing is . . . is that I know every single place to touch you." I look into her eyes for approval, and they're flashing like a neon sign. She's not going to stop me; her body still craves me as it always has. "I know how to make you come so hard that you'll forget everything else."

Maybe if I can please her body, her mind will follow suit. Then, once I can break through to both mind and body, her heart will follow their lead.

I've never been shy when it comes to her body and pleasing her: Why start now?

I take her silence and the way she can't seem to take her eyes off mine for a yes and reach for the hem of her sweatshirt. Damn this thing, it's heavier than it should be, and the damn string is tangled into Tessa's hair. She swats at my bad hand and removes the sweatshirt and detaches her hair from the thing.

"I'm not forcing you into anything here, am I?" I have to ask.

"No," she breathes. "I know it's a terrible idea, but I don't want to stop." I nod. "I need an escape from everything; please distract me."

"Shut your mind off. Stop thinking about all of the other shit and focus on this." I run my fingers along her neckline, and she shivers under my touch.

She catches me off guard and presses her lips to mine. Within seconds the slow, unsure kiss vanishes and is replaced by us. The timid gestures evaporate, and suddenly we are in our own place. All the other bullshit's gone, and it's only me and Tessa and her lips crushing against mine, her tongue making hurried swipes across my own, her hands in my hair, tugging at the roots and driving me fucking wild.

I wrap my arms around her and press my hips into hers until her back reaches the mattress. Her knee is bent, lifted, level with my crotch, and I shamelessly rub myself against her. She gasps at my desperation and removes a hand from my hair to bring down to her own chest. I could burst at the feeling of having her under me again—it's too fucking much, yet not enough, and I can't form a thought aside from her.

She touches herself, gripping one of her large breasts, and I look down like I've forgotten how to do anything else except stare at her perfect body and the way she's finally letting loose with me. She needs this even more than I do. She needs the distraction from the real world, and I will gladly serve in that role.

Our moves aren't calculated—pure passion is fueling us. I'm the fire, and she's the damn gasoline, and there's no sign of stopping or slowing until something is sure to explode. I'll be waiting then, ready to fight the flames for her, keeping her safe so she doesn't get burned by me, again. Her hand travels down her body, and she grips me, rubbing her hand over me, and I have to concentrate not to come from her hand alone. I shift my hips, resting them between her parted legs as she tugs at the waistband of my shorts. I tug at hers with one hand until both of us are naked from the waist down.

The groan that escapes her lips matches my own when I rub against her, skin to skin. I shift slightly, entering her partially, and she groans again. This time she presses her mouth to my bare shoulder. She's licking and sucking at my skin as I push farther inside her. My vision blurs as I try to savor every second of this, every moment that she's willing to be with me in this way.

"I love you," I promise her.

Her mouth stops moving, and her grip on my arms loosens. "Hardin . . ."

"Marry me, Tessa. Please." I push my cock inside her, filling her, hoping to catch her in an unfair moment of weakness.

"If you're going to say things like that, then we can't do this," she says softly. I can see the hurt in her eyes, the lack of self-control she has when it comes to me, and I instantly feel guilty for bringing up fucking marriage while fucking her. *Great fucking timing, you selfish asshole.*

"I'm sorry. I'll stop." I assure her with a kiss. I will give her this time to think, and I will lay off the heavy shit while I'm thrusting in and out of her hot, wet—

"Oh God," she moans.

Instead of confessing my undying love for her, I'll only say the things she wants to hear. "You feel so fucking tight around me. It's been so long," I say against her neck, and one of her hands presses against the bottom of my back, pressing me deeper into her.

Her eyes pinch shut, and her legs begin to tighten. I know she's already close, and even though she hates me right now, she loves my filthy mouth. I'm not going to last long, but neither is she. I've missed this—not only the pure fucking perfection that it is to be inside her, but being close to her in this way is something I need, something she needs.

"Come on, baby. Come around me, let me feel you," I say through gritted teeth.

She obeys, clenching one of my arms and whimpering my name as she pushes her head back into the mattress. She comes apart, stitch by beautifully constructed stitch, and I watch her. I watch her beautiful mouth fall open as she whimpers my name. I watch the way her eyes find mine just before they close in pleasure. It's too much, the beauty of her coming for me, allowing me to have her. I push myself into her once more, grabbing onto her hip as I spill into her.

"Fuck." I drop to my elbows next to her, careful not to crush her with the weight of my body.

Her eyes are closed, her lids heavy as she struggles to open them. "Mhmm," she agrees.

I prop myself up onto my elbow and stare at her while she's not looking. I'm afraid of what will happen when she comes to, when she begins to regret this and her anger toward me grows.

"You okay?" I can't help but trace the curve of her bare hip with my finger.

"Yeah." Her voice is thick and sated.

I'm so fucking glad she came to my door. I don't know how much longer I could have gone without seeing her or hearing her voice.

"You're sure?" I push. I need to know what this meant to her.

"Yes." She opens one eye, and I can't fight the stupid smile on my face.

"Okay." I nod. As I look at her, relaxing in her afterglow, it feels so nice to have her back, even if only for a few moments. She closes her eyes again, and right then I remember something. "So, what did you come here for in the first place?"

Immediately the sated, sleepy look disappears from her beautiful face, and for a moment she opens both eyes wide before regaining her composure.

"What is it?" I ask, Zed's face surfacing in my demented thoughts. "Tell me, please."

"It's Karen." She rolls onto her side, and I force my eyes away from her perfect tits on display.

Why the hell are we discussing Karen while naked? "Okay . . . what about her?"

"She's . . . well . . ." Tessa stops for a moment, and my chest fills with an unexpected panic for the woman, for Ken, too.

"She's *what*?"

"She's pregnant."

What? The fuck? "By who?"

This obliviousness amuses Tessa, and she laughs. "Your father," she says, but quickly corrects herself, "by Ken. Who else?"

I don't know what I was expecting to hear, but Karen's being pregnant was sure as hell not it. "What?"

"I know it's a little surprising, but they're very happy about it."

A little surprising? This is more than a little fucking surprising.

"Ken and Karen are having a baby?" I speak the ridiculous words.

"Yes." Tessa eyes me carefully. "How do you feel about it?"

How do I feel about it? I don't fucking know. I barely know the man, we are just starting to build something here, and now he's having a baby? Another kid he'll actually be sticking around to help raise.

"I guess it doesn't matter how I feel, does it?" I say in a vain attempt to shut both of us up. I lie on my back and close my eyes.

"Yes, it does. It matters to them. They want you to know that the baby won't change anything, Hardin. They want you to be part of the family. You'll be a *big brother again*."

A big brother?

Smith and his weird, adultlike personality come to mind, and I feel nauseated. This is too much for anyone to handle, and it's sure as hell too much for someone as fucked-up as me.

"Hardin, I know it's hard to wrap your head around, but I think—"

"I'm fine. I need a shower." I climb out of the bed and grab the shorts from the floor.

Tessa sits up, confused and hurt, as I pull the shorts up my legs. "I'm here if you want to talk about it. I wanted to be the one to tell you about all of this."

It's too much. She doesn't even want me.

She refuses to marry me.

Why can't she see what we are? What we are together? We cannot be apart. Ours is a love of the novels, better than any Austen or Brontë she has memorized.

My heart is pounding out of my chest—I can barely breathe.

She feels as if she isn't living? I can't understand that. I just can't. I only live when it comes to her. She's the only breath of life inside of me, and without it I will be nothing. I will neither survive nor live.

I wouldn't want to even if I could.

Fuck, the dark thoughts are fighting their way back into my head, and I'm overwhelmed by the struggle to hold on to the little bit of light Tessa has given back to me.

When will this end? When will shit not keep popping up each and every fucking time I finally feel like I have a grasp on my own mind?

chapter forty-five

TESSA

Here I am, here we are, in this endless loop of happiness, lust, passion, overwhelming love, and pain. The pain seems to win, it always wins, and I'm tired of fighting.

I watch, forcing myself not to care, as he crosses the room. The moment the door closes, I smack my hands to my forehead and rub at my temples. What is wrong with me that I can't seem to see anything but him? Why did I wake up this morning ready to face life without him, only to find myself in his bed hours later?

I hate that he has this power over me, but for the life of me I can't stop it. I can't blame him for my weakness, but if I was going to, I would have to argue that he makes it difficult to see the clear lines of right and wrong. When he smiles at me, those lines blur and mix and it's literally impossible to fight the sensation that pulls at my whole body.

He makes me laugh just as often as he makes me cry, and he makes me feel again when I was convinced that my fate was the nothingness inside me. I fully believed that I would never feel anything again, but Hardin pulled me out of that; he grabbed my hand when no one else seemed to care enough to do so, and he pulled me up onto the surface.

Not that any of this changes that we just can't be together. We simply don't work, and I can't allow myself to get my hopes up again, only to be crushed when he pulls back again, when he takes back everything he has confessed, and I refuse to be ripped apart, again and again, by the only hand that helps me.

Here I am, face in hands, obsessively overthinking the mistakes made—my mistakes, his mistakes, our parents' mistakes—and how mine seem to be eating away at me, refusing to allow me any peace.

I got a hint of it, a hint of serenity and calm when his hands were on me, his mouth hot on mine, his fingers digging into the sensitive skin covering my hips, but minutes later the fire's extinguished, and I'm alone. I'm alone and hurt and embarrassed, and it's the same story, only with an even more pathetic ending than the last installment.

I get to my feet, refasten my bra, and tug Landon's sweatshirt over my head. I can't be here when Hardin returns. I can't spend the next ten minutes preparing myself for whichever Hardin decides to make an appearance. I've done this too many times, and I finally got myself to a place where my need for him wasn't so overpowering. Where he wasn't consuming my every thought, he wasn't responsible for my every breath, and I was finally able to see a life after him.

This was a relapse. That's all it was. This was a terrible lapse in judgment, and I'm harshly reminded of that by the silence of the room.

I'm dressed and in my room by the time I hear him opening the bathroom door. His footsteps grow louder as he passes by, and it only takes him a few seconds to realize that I'm no longer in his room.

He doesn't knock—I knew he wouldn't—before he enters my room.

I'm sitting on the bed, legs crossed and held in front of me, protecting myself. I must look pathetic to him: my eyes are burning with regretful tears and my skin smelling of him.

"Why did you leave?" His hair is wet, dripping water down his forehead, and his hands are resting on his bare hips, his shorts hanging too low.

"I didn't. You did," I stubbornly point out.

He blankly stares at me as a few seconds pass. "I guess you're right. Come back?" He forms the demand like a question, and I fight myself not to get up from the bed.

"I don't think that's a good idea." I look away from his gaze, and he treads across the room to sit across from me on the bed.

"Why's that? I'm sorry I freaked out, I just didn't know what to think, and if I'm being totally fucking honest, I didn't trust myself not to say the wrong thing to you, so I figured I would leave the room and clear my head."

Why couldn't he have behaved this way before? Why couldn't he be honest and levelheaded when I needed him to be? Why did it take me finally pulling away for him to want to change?

"I wish you would have at least indicated that instead of just leaving me alone in there." I nod, gathering the tiny scrap of strength inside me. "I don't think we should be alone together."

His eyes go wild. "What are you talking about?" he growls. So much for levelheaded.

I keep my arms crossed. "I want to be here for you, and I will be—if you need to talk about anything or vent, or if you just want someone to be there—but I really think we should stay in common areas. Like the living room or the kitchen."

"You're not serious," he scoffs.

"I am."

"Common areas? Like with Landon serving as our Eleanor Tilney? This is ridiculous, Tess. We can be in the same room without a damn chaperone."

"I didn't say anything about chaperones. I just think with how everything is now"—I sigh—"I think I'm going back to Seattle for a few days." I hadn't fully decided that until now, but now that I've spoken the words, they make sense. I have to get my things ready to move to New York, and I miss Kimberly. I have a doctor's appointment that I've been trying not to think about, and I don't see any good coming from playing house at the Scott residence. Yet again.

"I'll come with you," he offers plainly, like it's the simplest solution.

"Hardin . . ."

Without asking, he takes a seat on the bed, bare chested and all. "I was going to wait to bring this up, but I'm moving out of that apartment and am moving to Seattle, too. That's what you wanted all along, and I'm ready to do it. I don't know what took me so long." He swipes his hand across his hair, pushing the drying strands so they stand up in a messy wave.

I shake my head at him. "What are you talking about?" *Now he wants to move to Seattle?*

"I'll get us a nice place. It won't be a mansion like you're used to at Vance's, but it will be nicer than anywhere you can afford on your own."

Though I know his words weren't meant as an insult, that's how they *feel*, and instantly I'm on edge. "You don't get it," I accuse, flinging my arms up. "You're missing the entire point of everything!"

"What point? Why does there have to be a point to any of this?" He scoots a little closer. "Why can't we just be, and why can't you just let me show you who I can be for you? It doesn't have to be about points and keeping score and making yourself miserable because you love me and won't allow yourself to be with me." He covers my hand with his own.

I pull mine away. "I want to agree with you, and I would love to buy into this fantasy world where we could work, but I've done that for too long and I can't do it anymore. You tried to warn me before, and you gave me chance after chance to see the inevitable, but I was in denial. I can see it now, though—I see that we have been doomed from the start. How many times will we have this conversation?"

He looks at me with those penetrating green eyes. "As many times as it takes to change your mind."

"I never could change yours; what makes you think you could change mine?"

"What just happened between us didn't make it obvious to you?"

"I want you to be a part of my life, just not in that way. Not as my boyfriend."

"Husband?" His eyes are full of humor and . . . *hope?*

I stare at him, amazed that he would *dare* . . . "We aren't together, Hardin! And you can't throw marriage in my face because you think it will change my mind—I wanted you to *want* to marry me, not offer it as a last resort!"

His breathing accelerates, but his voice comes out smooth. "It's not a last resort. I'm not playing games with you—I've learned my lesson there. I want to marry you because I can't imagine living my life any other way, and you can go ahead and tell me I'm wrong, but you know we may as well get married now. We won't be apart, and you know it."

He sounds so sure of himself and sure of our relationship, and again I'm confused and can't decide if I should be angry or if I should be happy about his words.

Marriage doesn't hold the same value as it did only months ago. My parents were never married; I could barely believe it when I found out that they pretended to be to appease my mother and my grandparents. Trish and Ken were married, and that legal binding couldn't save their sinking ship. *What's the point of being married, really?* It almost never works anyway, and I'm beginning to see that it's a ridiculous concept. It's messed up, the way the idea is drilled into our heads that we should promise ourselves to another and depend on that person as our source of happiness.

Lucky for me, I've finally learned that I can't depend on anyone else for my happiness. "I don't think I even want to be married, ever."

Hardin sucks in a harsh breath and his hand moves to my chin, "What? You don't mean that." His eyes search mine.

"Yes, I do mean that. What's the point? It never works, and divorce isn't cheap." I shrug my shoulders and ignore the horrified expression covering Hardin's face.

"What the hell are you saying? Since when are you so cynical?"

Cynical? I don't believe that I'm cynical. I just need to be realistic and not keep holding out for a storybook ending that I will obviously never have. But it's also not like I'm going to put up with his back-and-forth all the time.

"I don't know, since I realized how hopelessly stupid I was. I don't blame you for ending things with me. I was obsessed with having a life I could never have, and it had to drive you insane."

Hardin tugs at his hair in that frustrated way he does. "Tessa, you're talking crazy shit. You weren't obsessed with anything. I was just an asshole." He groans in frustration and kneels in front of me. "Fuck, now look what I've got you thinking! This is all backwards."

I stand up, hating feeling guilty for saying the truth about how I feel. I'm so internally conflicted, and being in this small room with Hardin isn't helping. Near him I can't focus, and I can't stick to my defenses when he's looking at me like each of my words is a weapon against him—no matter how true that is, it still makes me feel sympathy for him when I don't think I should.

I was always so quick to judge women who felt this way. While watching an overly dramatic relationship on-screen, I was quick to label the woman as "weak," but it's not that simple or that cut-and-dried.

There are so many things to take into consideration when labeling someone, and I'll admit before I met Hardin, I did this far too often. Who am I to judge people based on their feelings? I never knew how strong those foolish emotions could be; I couldn't comprehend the magnetic pull that could be felt. I never understood the way love overpowers common sense and passion overtakes logic, or how unnerving it is that no one else really knows how you feel—no one can judge me for being weak or stupid, no one can put me down for the way I feel.

I will never claim to be perfect, and I am struggling every second to keep myself above water, but it's not as easy as people assume. It's not so easy to walk away from someone when he has made his way into every cell, when he has taken over every thought, and he has been responsible for the best and worst feelings I've ever had. No one, not even the doubting part of me, can make me feel bad for loving passionately and hoping desperately that I could have that great love that I've read about in novels.

By the time I finish justifying my actions to myself, my subconscious has taken her hair down and closed her eyes, relieved that I've finally stopped beating myself up for the way that my emotions have been playing me.

"Tessa, I'm coming to Seattle. I won't try and force you to live with me, but I want to be where you are. I'll keep my distance until you're ready for more, and I'll play nice with everyone, even Vance."

"That's not the issue." I sigh. His determination is admirable, but it's never been consistent. He will get bored eventually and move on with his life. We are too far gone this time.

"Like I said before, I will try to keep my distance, but I'm coming to Seattle. If you won't help me decide on an apartment, I'll have to choose it myself, but I'll make sure you'll like it, too."

He doesn't need to know my plans. I use my thoughts to drown out his words. If I hear them, if I really listen to them, they will break down the barrier I've built. The surface split open only an hour ago, and I let my emotions control my body, but I can't let that happen again.

HARDIN LEAVES THE ROOM after another ten minutes of me trying to ignore his promises, and I start packing my bag for Seattle. I've been going back and forth, traveling too much lately, and I look forward to the day when I finally have a place to call home. I need the security, I need the stability.

How is it that I spent my entire life planning for stability only to be out in the world swaying along with no base to call my own, no safety net, nothing at all?

When I reach the bottom of the stairs, Landon is leaning against the wall, and he stops me with a gentle hand on my arm. "Hey, I wanted to talk to you before you leave."

I stand in front of him and wait for him to speak. I hope he's not changing his mind on letting me tag along to New York.

"I just wanted to check with you and see if you've changed your mind about coming with me to NYU. If you did, that's okay. I just need to know so I can tell Ken about the flight arrangements."

"No, I'm still coming. I just need to go to Seattle and say goodbye to Kim and—" I want to tell him about my appointment, but I don't think I'm ready to face that just yet. Nothing is certain, but I'd rather not think about it just yet.

"Are you sure? I don't want you to feel like you have to go, I'll understand if you want to stay here, with him." Landon's voice is so kind, so understanding, that I can't help but throw my arms around his shoulders.

"You are amazing; you know that, right?" I smile up at him.

"I haven't changed my mind. I want to do this; I have to do this for myself."

"When are you going to tell him? What do you think he will do?"

I haven't put much thought into what Hardin will do when I tell him my plans to move across the country. I don't have time to let Hardin's opinion shape my plans, not anymore.

"I honestly don't know how he will react. Up until my father's funeral, I don't think he would have cared one bit."

Landon nods noncommittally. Then noises from the kitchen break our silence, and I'm reminded that I haven't congratulated him on the news.

"I can't believe you didn't tell me that your mother is pregnant!" I exclaim, thankful for the easy subject change.

"I know, I'm sorry. She just told me, and you've been keeping yourself locked in that room." He smiles, gently teasing me.

"Are you sad that you're leaving now with a baby sibling on the way?" I briefly wonder if Landon likes being an only child. We have only discussed it a few times, but he always avoids talking about his father, so the attention was quickly directed back to me each time.

"A little. I'm just worried how my mom will handle the pregnancy alone. And I'll miss her and Ken, but I'm ready for this." He smiles at me. "I think I am, at least."

I nod with assurance. "We will be fine. Especially you; you've already been accepted. I'm moving there without knowing if I will even get in. I'll just be floating around New York without being enrolled, and I'll have no job and—"

Landon's hand covers my mouth, and he laughs. "I feel that same panic when I think about the change, but I force myself to focus on the positives."

"Which are?" I mumble against his hand.

"Well, it's New York. That's all I've gotten so far," he admits with a deep laugh, and I find myself smiling from ear to ear as Karen joins us in the hallway.

"I'll miss that sound when you two leave," she says, her eyes shining under the lights.

Ken walks up behind her and places a kiss on the back of her head. "We all will."

chapter forty-six

HARDIN

When I answer the knock at my door, I don't bother trying to hide my disappointment when I'm greeted with Ken's awkward smile instead of the girl I want.

He stands there, clearly waiting for permission to enter. "I wanted to talk to you about the baby," he says tentatively.

I knew this was coming, and much to my disappointment, there is no way to avoid this shit. "Come in, then." I move out of his way, sitting down in the chair next to the desk. I have no fucking clue what he's going to say, or what I'm going to say, or how this will end up, but I can't see it going well.

Ken doesn't sit down. He just stands by the dresser with his hands shoved into the pockets of his gray dress slacks. The fact that the gray matches the stripes on his tie and he's wearing a black sweater vest just screams, *I'm the chancellor at an accredited university!* But looking past that, I see the worry in his brown eyes and how his brows are knitted together. He's fumbling with his hands in such a pathetic way that I just want to put him out of his misery.

"I'm fine. I know you probably assumed I'd be breaking shit and throwing a tantrum, but, honestly, I don't care if you're having a baby," I finally say.

He sighs, not looking relieved as I had sort of hoped he would. "It's okay if you are a little upset about it. I know it's unexpected, and I know how you feel about me. I just hope this doesn't make your ill feelings toward me grow." He looks down at the floor, and I find myself wishing Tessa were here next to me, instead of wherever with Karen. I need to see her before she leaves. I promised to give her space, but I didn't expect this father-son moment to be thrown at me.

"You know nothing of how I feel about you." Hell, I don't think *I* even know how I feel about him.

His patience with me is never ending as he says, "I hope this doesn't change or take away from any of the progress we've made. I know I have a lot to make up for, but I really hope you'll allow me to keep trying."

When I hear that, I feel a kinship between us that I hadn't before. We are both fuck-ups; both of us have been led by stupid decisions and addictions, and I'm pissed that I got this trait from being raised by him. If Vance had raised me, I wouldn't be this way. I wouldn't be so fucked-up inside. I wouldn't have been afraid of my dad's coming home drunk, and I wouldn't have sat on the floor with my mum for hours while she wept and bled and struggled to stay conscious after the beating she endured because of his mistakes.

Anger simmers inside me, humming in my veins, and I'm two breaths away from calling for Tessa. I need her at times like this—well, I need her always—but especially now. I need her soft voice to speak encouraging words. I need her light to push against the shadows inside my mind.

"I want you to be a part of the baby's life, Hardin. I think this could be a really good thing for all of us."

"*Us?*" I scoff.

"Yes, *all* of us. You're a part of this family. When I married Karen and took on the role of Landon's father, I know you felt like I was forgetting about you, and I don't want you to feel this way because of the baby."

"*Forgetting* me? You forgot about me long before you married

Karen." But I don't get the same thrill out of throwing shit into his face now that I know the truth about his past with my mum and Christian. I feel for him and the shit those two pulled, but at the same time I'm fucking pissed at him for being such a shitty father up until this last year. Even if he wasn't my biological dad, he was in charge of taking care of us—he accepted that role and then just gave it up to drink.

So I can't help myself. I should, but the anger is buzzing in me, and I need to know. I have to know why he would attempt to make amends with me if he isn't completely positive that he's my father.

"When did you know that my mum was fucking Vance behind your back?" I ask, releasing the words like a grenade.

All the air leaves the room, and Ken looks as if he will pass out any second.

"How . . ." He stops and rubs a hand across the stubble on his chin. "Who told you that?"

"Cut the shit. I know all about them. That's what happened in London. I caught them together. He had her on the kitchen counter."

"Oh God," he says, his voice strangled and his chest heaving. "Before or after the wedding?"

"Before, but she still got married anyway. Why did you stay with her if you knew she wanted him?"

He takes a few breaths and looks around the room. Then he shrugs. "I loved her." He looks me in the eyes, naked honesty seeming to remove any distance between us. "I don't have a reason aside from that. I loved her, and I loved you, and I kept hoping that one day she would stop loving him. That day never came . . . and it was eating me alive. I knew what she was doing and what he—my *best* friend—was doing, but I had so much hope for us, and I thought she would eventually choose me."

"She didn't," I note. She may have chosen to marry him and spend her life with him, but she didn't choose him in any way that mattered.

"Clearly. And I should have given up long before I turned to alcohol." The shame in his eyes is humbling.

"Yeah, you should have." Everything would be so different if he had.

"I know you don't understand it, and I know that my poor choices and false hopes ruined your childhood for you, so I don't expect your forgiveness or understanding." He puts his hands together as if he were praying and covers his mouth with them.

I stay silent because I can't think of anything to say. My mind is reeling with horrid memories and the reality of how fucked all three of my . . . parentlike figures are. I don't even know what to call them.

"I suppose I felt like she would see that he couldn't offer her the stability that I could. I had a good job, and I wasn't as much of a flight risk as Christian was." He pauses, and with his deep breath his vest tightens on his chest and he looks at me. "I reckon if Tessa marries another man, this is how he will feel. He will always be competing with you, and even when you leave her for the hundredth time, he will be competing with the memory of you." He's confident in what he's saying, I can tell by his tone and by the way he's looking me square in the eyes.

"I'm not leaving her again," I say through gritted teeth. My fingers are clenching the edge of the desk.

"He said that, too." He sighs and leans back against the dresser.

"I'm not him."

"I know you aren't. I'm in no way saying that you are Christian or that Tessa is like your mum. Lucky for you, it's only you that Tessa sees. If your mum wouldn't have fought her feelings for him, they could have been happy together; instead they allowed their toxic relationship to ruin the lives of everyone around them." Ken brushes his hand over his facial hair again. An annoying habit.

Catherine and Heathcliff come to my mind, and I want to vomit at the easy comparison. Tessa and I may be a huge fucking disaster like the two characters, but I won't allow us to suffer the same fate.

But none of what Ken is saying makes sense to me. Why would he put up with so much shit from me if he had the slightest inkling that I wasn't his problem to begin with?

"So it's true, then? He's your father, isn't he?" he asks as if losing some vital force that had been animating him. The strong, scary man from my childhood has disappeared and been replaced by a heartbroken man on the verge of tears.

I want to tell him that he's a damn idiot for putting up with this shit from me, that my mum and I can't forget the hell he made my life as a child. It's his fault that I side with the demons and fight against the angels—it's his fault that I have a special place in hell and am not welcomed in heaven. It's his fault that Tessa won't be with me. It's his fault that I hurt her too many times to count, and it's his fault that I'm just now trying to fix twenty-one years of mistakes.

When instead of all that I don't say anything, Ken lets out a breath. "I knew from the first time I saw you that you were his."

His words nearly knock the wind from my chest along with the angry thoughts in my mind.

"I knew it." He's trying not to cry, but failing. I cringe and look away from the tears on his cheeks. "I knew. How could I not have? You looked just like him, and as each year passed, your mum would cry a little harder, she would sneak off with him a little more. I knew. I didn't want to admit it because you were all that I had. I didn't have your mum; I never really did. Since I met her, she was his. You were all I had, and as I allowed my anger to take over, I ruined that, too." He stops to catch his breath, and I sit in confused silence. "You would have been better off with him, I know you would have been, but I loved you—I *still* love you as if you are my own flesh—and I can only hope that you will let me stay in your life."

He's still crying; too many tears roll down his face, and I find myself feeling for him. Some of the weight on my chest has lifted, and I can feel years of anger dissolving inside me. I don't know what this feeling is; it's strong and it's freeing. By the time he looks up at me, I don't even feel like myself. I'm *not* myself—that's the only explanation for why my arms are touching his shoulders and wrapping around his back to comfort him.

As I do so, I feel him shake, and then he really begins sobbing with his whole body.

chapter forty-seven

TESSA

The drive was just about as terrible as I had anticipated. The road never seemed to want to end; each yellow line was one of his smiles, one of his scowls. Every endless line of traffic seemed to be mocking every mistake I've ever made, and each car on the road was yet another stranger, another person with his or her own problems. I felt alone, too alone, in my small car as I drove farther and farther from where I wanted to be.

Am I foolish to even fight this? Could I possibly be strong enough to fight the current this time? Do I even want to?

What are the chances that this one time, out of what feels like hundreds of times, will be so different? Is he just using the words I've always wanted to hear out of desperation because he knows how detached I've become?

My head feels like a two-thousand-page novel full of deep thoughts, mindless chatter, and a bunch of crap questions that I don't know the answers to.

When I'd pulled up in front of Kimberly and Christian's house only minutes ago, the tension in my shoulders was nearly unbearable. I could literally feel the muscles underneath my skin tightening to the point of snapping, and as I stand in the living room now, waiting for Kimberly to come down, that tension only continues to grow.

Smith descends the stairs and crinkles his nose in disgust. "She said she will be down when she's done rubbing my dad's leg."

I can't help but laugh at the dimpled little boy. "Okay. Thank you." He didn't say a word when he opened the door for me minutes ago. He just looked me up and down and waved me inside with a small smile. I was impressed by the smile, small or not.

He sits down on the edge of the couch without a word. He focuses on a gadget in his hand while I focus on him. Hardin's little brother. It's such a weird idea that this adorable little boy who seems to dislike me for some reason has been Hardin's biological brother all along. It makes sense in a way; he was always so curious about Hardin and seemed to enjoy his company when most people don't.

He turns, catching me staring at him. "Where's your Hardin?"

Your Hardin. It feels like every single time he asks that question, *my Hardin* is far away. Farther than ever, this time. "He's—"

Then Kimberly enters the room, barreling toward me with outstretched arms. Of course she would be wearing heels and makeup. I suppose the outside world is still revolving even though mine has stopped.

"Tessa!" she screeches, wrapping her arms around my shoulders and squeezing so tight that I let out a cough. "Gah! It's been too long!" She squeezes one more time before pulling back and dragging me by the arm into the kitchen.

"How is everything?" I ask and climb up on the same stool I always seem to find myself on.

She stands in front of the breakfast bar and runs her hands through her shoulder-length, blond hair, pulling it back and tying it into a messy bun on top of her head. "Well, we all survived that damned trip to London." She grimaces, and I do the same. "Barely, but we did."

"How is Mr. Vance's leg?"

"Mr. Vance?" She laughs. "No, you're not reverting to that because of all that weirdness. I'd say you can go ahead and say Christian, or Vance. His leg is healing; luckily the fire mostly caught his clothes, not skin." A frown takes over her face, and a shiver rakes her shoulders.

"Is he in trouble? Legal trouble?" I ask, trying not to be pushy.

"Not really. He fabricated a story about a group of punks who broke in there and vandalized the house before burning it. It's now an arson case with no leads." She shakes her head and rolls her eyes. She brushes her hands on her dress and looks back to me. "How are you, though, Tessa? I'm really sorry to hear about your dad. I should have called you more—I've just been busy and trying to figure all this out." Kimberly reaches across the granite and places her hand over mine. "Though that's not really a good excuse . . ."

"No, no. Don't apologize. You've had so much going on, and I haven't been the best company anyway. If you had called, I might not have even been able to answer it—I've been going out of my mind, literally." I try to laugh, but even I catch how false and dry the awkward noise comes out.

"I can tell." She eyes me skeptically. "What's with this?" Her hands wave in front of me, and I look down at my sloppy sweatshirt and dirty jeans.

"I don't know; it's been a long two weeks." I shrug and tuck my unbrushed hair behind my ears.

"You're obviously going through a funk again. Hardin did something new, or is it still from London?" Kimberly raises an arched brow, reminding me of how overgrown mine must be. Plucking and waxing have been the farthest thing from my mind, but Kimberly is one of those women that make you want to be pretty all the time to keep up with her.

"Not exactly. Well, he just did what he always does in London, but I finally told him we are done." Seeing the skepticism in her blue eyes, I add, "I mean it. I'm thinking of moving to New York."

"New York? What the hell? With Hardin?" Her mouth falls open. "Oh, never mind—you just told me you broke up." She smacks her hand to her forehead in a dramatic display.

"With Landon, actually. He's going to NYU, and he asked me to come along. I'm going to take the summer and hopefully be able to get into NYU in the fall."

She laughs. "Wow, I need a minute."

"It's a big change. I know. It's just that I . . . well, I need to get away from here, and with Landon already going, it just made sense." It's insane, completely insane, to just move across the country, and Kimberly's reaction proves that.

"You don't have to explain to me. I think it's a really good idea—I'm just surprised." Kim doesn't even try to control her smirk. "You, moving across the country without a schedule or taking a year to plan things out."

"It's stupid, right? Isn't it?" I ask, not sure of what I'm hoping to hear.

"No! Since when are you so unsure about yourself? Girl, I know you've been through a lot of shit, but you need to get it together. You're young, brilliant, and beautiful. Life is not that bad! Hell, try cleaning the burn wounds of your fiancé after he covered for his surprise grown-ass son because he'd just cheated on you with his"—she curls her fingers into air quotes and rolls her eyes—"'long-lost love' and having to nurse him while you really just want to choke him out."

I don't know if she meant to be funny, but I have to bite my tongue to stop from laughing at the picture she's created in my head. But when she chuckles a little, I follow suit.

"Seriously, it's okay to be sad, but if you let sadness control your life, you'll never have one." Her words hit me somewhere between my selfish whining and my nerves over moving to New York without a solid plan.

She's right; I've been through a lot in the last year, but what good will it do to be this way? To feel the sadness and sting of loss with every thought? As much as I loved the ease of feeling nothing, I didn't feel like myself. I felt my being slipping with each negative thought, and I was beginning to fear that I would never be myself again. I'm still not now, but maybe one day?

"I know you're right, Kim. I just don't know how to stop. I'm just so mad all the time." I ball my fists, and she nods. "Or sad. There's a lot of sad, and pain. I don't know how to separate it, and now it's eating away at me, taking over my mind."

"Well, it's not as easy as I just tried to make it sound, but, first of all, you need to get excited. You are moving to New York, girl! Act like it. If you go around moping up the streets of New York City, you'll never make any friends." She smiles, softening her words.

"And what if I can't? Like, what if I just always feel this way?"

"Then you'll always feel that way. That's that, but you can't think that way right now. I've learned in my years"—she grins—"not *too* many years, mind you, but I've learned that shit happens and you move on. It sucks, and trust me, I know this is about Hardin. It's always about Hardin, but you need to accept the fact that he won't give you what you want and need, and try your best to pretend you are moving on. If you can fool him and everyone else, you will eventually believe it, too, and it'll become real."

"Do you think I could? You know, ever really get over him?" I twist my fingers in my lap.

"I'll go ahead and lie to you because it's what you need to hear right now." Kimberly walks over to the cabinet and pulls out two wineglasses. "You need to hear a lot of bullshit and praise at this point. There is always time to face the truth later, but for now . . ." She rummages through the drawer just below the sink and pulls out a corkscrew. "Now, we drink wine and I'll tell you all kinds of breakup stories that will make yours seem like child's play."

"The horror movie?" I ask, knowing she meant the opposite of that creepy redheaded doll.

"No, smart-ass." She smacks my thigh. "I'm talking I know women who were married for years and their husbands banged their sisters. That kind of crazy shit will make you realize you don't have it that bad."

A glass full of white wine is placed in front of me, and just as I am about to object, Kimberly raises it and presses it to my lips.

A bottle and a half later, I am laughing and leaning on the counter for support. Kimberly has gone through an amazing array of crazy relationships, and I've finally stopped checking my phone every ten seconds. Hardin doesn't have my phone number anyway, I keep reminding myself. Of course, this is Hardin we are talking about; if he wants the number, he will find a way to get it.

Some of the stories Kimberly has told in the last hour seem too crazy to be true. I'm convinced that the wine has made her embellish each one just to make them worse.

The woman who came home to find her husband naked in bed with the neighbor . . . and her husband.

The too-detailed story about the woman who tried to put a hit on her husband but gave the wrong picture to the hired gun so he tried to kill her brother. Her husband ended up with a much better life than her.

Then there was the man who left his wife of twenty years for a woman half his age only to find out she was his great-niece. Yuck. (Yes, they stayed together.)

A girl was sleeping with her college professor and bragged about it to her manicurist, who (surprise) was the professor's wife. The girl failed that term.

The man who married the sexy French girl who he met at the grocery store only to find out she wasn't French. She was from Detroit and was a pretty convincing con artist.

The one about the woman who, for over a year, was cheating

on her husband with a man she met online. When she finally met the man, she was surprised when he turned out to be her husband.

There is no way a woman caught her husband sleeping with her sister, then her mother, then her divorce attorney. There is no possible way that she then chased him around the law office, hurling her heels at his head while he ran, pantless, through the halls.

I'm laughing, really laughing now, and Kimberly is holding her stomach, claiming that she saw the man a few days later, with the imprint of his soon-to-be-ex-wife's heel glowing in the middle of his forehead.

"I'm not even joking! It was a mess! The best part of this entire story is that they are remarried now!" She smacks her hand against the counter, and I shake my head at the volume of her voice now that she's drunk. I'm happy to see that Smith has gone upstairs and left the loud, wine-drinking women alone so I don't have to feel bad about confusing him with our laughter at other people's misery.

"Men are assholes. Every single one of them." Kimberly raises her freshly refilled glass to my empty one. "But truth be told, women are assholes, too, so the only way for it to work is if you find an asshole you can deal with. One that makes you a little less of an asshole."

Christian chooses this moment to enter the kitchen. "All this talk about assholes is traveling down the hallway." I'd basically forgotten he was around at all. It takes me a moment to realize that he's in a wheelchair. I hear myself gasp and Kimberly looks at me, a small smile playing on her lips.

"He will be fine," she assures me.

He smiles at his fiancée and she squirms in the way she always does when he looks at her like that. I'm surprised by this. I knew she was forgiving him; I just didn't know it was such a done deal or that she could look so happy doing it.

"Sorry." She smiles down at him and he reaches for her hips, pulling her onto his lap. He winces when her thigh touches his injured leg, and she quickly adjusts herself on the opposite leg.

"It looks worse than it is," he tells me when he notices me staring back and forth between the metal chair and the burned flesh on his leg.

"It's true. He's really milking this whole thing," Kimberly teases, poking the dimple on his left cheek.

I look away.

"You're here alone?" Vance asks, ignoring the glare Kimberly sends him when he bites at her finger. I can't stop watching them even though I know I won't be in their position anytime soon, if ever.

"Yeah. Hardin is back at his"—I stop to correct myself—"at Ken's."

Christian looks disappointed, and Kimberly has stopped her glaring, but I feel like the hole inside me that has been covered for the last hour is starting to show itself at the mention of Hardin's name.

"How is he? I really wish he would answer my calls, the little asshole," Christian mutters.

I blame the wine, but I snap at him, "He has a lot going on right now." The bite in my tone is evident and I instantly feel like a jerk. "I'm sorry. I didn't mean it to sound that way. I just know he is going through a lot right now. I don't mean to be rude."

I choose to ignore the smirk covering Kimberly's face as I defend Hardin.

Christian shakes his head and laughs. "It's fine. I deserve it all. I know he is. I just want to talk to him, but I know he will come around when he's ready. I'll leave you ladies to it; I just wanted to see what all the laughing and screeching was about. Make sure it wasn't too much at my expense."

With that, he kisses Kimberly, swiftly but tenderly, and he

wheels himself out of the room. I hold my glass out, asking for a another refill.

"Wait, so that means you won't be working with me any-more?" Kimberly asks. "You can't leave me with all those bitchy women! You're the only one I can stand, aside from Trevor's new girlfriend."

"Trevor has a girlfriend?" I sip the cool wine. Kimberly was right; the wine and laughter are helping. I can feel myself peering out of this shell, trying to come back to life; with each joke and absurd story, I'm finding it a little easier.

"Yes! The redhead! You know, the one who runs our social media?"

I try to place the woman but I can't see past the wine dancing in my mind. "I don't know her. How long have they been dating?"

"Only a few weeks. Get this, though." Kimberly's eyes light up at her favorite thing: office gossip. "Christian heard them to-gether."

I take another drink of wine, waiting for her to explain.

"As in *together* together. As in, they were banging in his office! And what's even crazier is that the things he heard . . ." She stops to laugh. "They were kinky. I'm talking, Trevor is a total badass in bed. There was spanking, some kinky name-calling, all of that stuff."

I burst into laughter like a giddy schoolgirl. A schoolgirl who has consumed too much wine. "No way!"

I can't imagine sweet Trevor spanking anyone. The image alone makes me laugh harder, and I shake my head trying not to think too much into it. Trevor is handsome, very handsome, but he's just so well mannered and sweet.

"I swear! Christian was convinced he had her like tied to the desk or something, because when he saw him next, he was de-taching something from its corners!" Kimberly waves her hands through the air, and a burst of cold wine shoots up and out my nose.

After this glass, I'm cutting myself off. Where is Hardin, the alcohol authority, when I need him?

Hardin.

My heart begins to race, and my laughter is quickly derailed until Kimberly adds another dirty detail to the story.

"I've heard he keeps a crop in his office."

"Crop?" I ask, lowering my voice.

"Riding crop. Google it." She laughs.

"I can't believe it. He's so sweet and gentle. He couldn't *possibly* tie a woman to his desk and have his way with her!" I just can't picture it. My traitorous and wine-controlled mind starts imagining Hardin and desks and ties and spanking.

"Who has sex in their office, anyway? My god, those walls are paper thin."

I feel my mouth fall open. Real images, memories of Hardin bending me over my desk, flash through my mind, and my already-heated skin flushes and burns.

Kimberly shoots me a knowing smile and tilts her head back. "I guess the same people who have sex in people's home gyms," she accuses with a giggle.

I ignore her despite the burning embarrassment I feel. "Back to Trevor," I say, hiding as much of my face behind my glass as I can manage.

"I knew he would be a freak. Men who wear suits every day are always freaks."

"Only in those smutty novels," I counter, thinking of a book I've been planning to read but haven't gotten around to yet.

"Those stories have to come from somewhere, don't they?" She winks at me. "I keep walking by Trevor's office hoping to hear him nailing her, but no such luck . . . yet."

The ridiculousness of this entire night has made me feel light in a way I haven't felt in so long. I try to grasp this feeling and hold it as tightly to my chest as I can—I don't want it to slip away.

"Who knew Trevor was such a freak, yeah?" She wiggles her eyebrows, and I shake my head.

"Fucking Trevor," I say, and wait in silence as Kimberly bursts into loud laughter.

"*Fucking* Trevor!" she screeches, and I join her, thinking of the source of the nickname as we take turns repeating it in our best impressions of its creator.

chapter forty-eight

HARDIN

This day has been long. Too damn long, and I'm ready to sleep. After the heart-to-heart with Ken, I'm worn-out. That, followed by Sarah, Sonya, S'whocares—whatever the hell her name is—and Landon eye-fucking her across the dinner table, has bored me to death.

Even though I wish Tessa hadn't left without telling me, I can't say that out loud because she doesn't owe me any type of explanation.

I played nice, the way I promised Tessa I could, and ate my dinner in silence as Karen and my dad, or whoever he is, watched me with caution, waiting for me to explode or ruin their dinner somehow.

But I didn't. I stayed quiet and chewed each bite. I even kept my elbows off the ugly-ass table-cover thing that Karen thinks adds a nice pastel spring touch or some shit, but it doesn't. It's hideous, and someone should burn it when she's not looking.

I felt a little better—awkward as fuck—but a little better after talking with my dad. I find it amusing that I keep defaulting to calling Ken my dad now whereas when I was a teen I could barely speak his name without scowling or wishing he hadn't left just so I could punch him. Now that I understand—well, somewhat understand—how he felt and why he did what he did, some of the anger I held inside me for so long has sort of fizzled.

It was weird, though, feeling that slip from my body. I've heard it explained in novels—forgiveness, they call it—but I've never felt it until tonight. I'm not quite convinced that I like the feeling, but I'll admit it helps distract me from the constant ache of missing Tessa. Sort of.

I feel better . . . happier? I don't know, but I can't stop thinking of the future now. A future where Tessa and I shop for carpet and shelves, or whatever married people do. The only married people I know who can tolerate each other are Ken and Karen, and I have no clue what they do together. Aside from making babies in their forties. I immaturely cringe at the thought and pretend that I wasn't just thinking about their sex life.

Truth be told, thinking of the future is much more fun than I ever imagined. I never expected anything from the future, or the present, before. I always knew I would be alone, so I didn't bother entertaining stupid plans or wishes. Up until eight months ago, I didn't know there could be someone like Tessa. I had no clue that this obnoxious blonde was walking around waiting to turn my entire life upside down by driving me absolutely insane and making me love her more than I love breathing.

Hell, if I had known she was out there, I wouldn't have wasted my time fucking every chick that I could. I wasn't running on anything before; no driving force with blue-gray eyes was helping me, guiding me through my fucked-up life, so I made too many mistakes, and now I have to work harder than most at trying to right those wrongs.

If I could take it back, I wouldn't have touched another girl. Not one. And if I had known just how good touching Tessa would be, I would have been preparing myself, counting down the days until she barged into my room at that frat house, touching all my books and things after I explicitly told her not to.

The only thing that's keeping me remotely in control of myself is the hope that she will come around eventually. She will see that this time I'm not going to take my words back. I will marry her ass, even if I have to drag her down the aisle.

This is another of our problems, these pushy thoughts. As much as I'll deny them to her face, I can't help but smile now at the vision of her in a white dress, scowling and yelling at me, as I literally drag her by her feet down a carpeted aisle while some bullshit song is played on a harp or some other instrument that no one uses outside of weddings and funerals.

If I had her number, I would text her just to make sure she's okay. She doesn't want me to have it, though. It took a lot of control not to snatch Landon's phone from his pocket and just steal it after dinner.

I'm lying in this bed when I should be driving to Seattle. Should be, could be, need to be, but can't. I need to give her a little space or she'll pull farther away from me. I hold my phone up in the dark and scroll through the pictures of her. If images of memories are all I will have for a while, I'm going to need more pictures. Seven hundred and twenty-two isn't enough.

Instead of continuing down the path of an obsessive stalker, I climb out of bed and pull on some pants. I don't think Landon or pregnant Karen would appreciate seeing me naked. Well, maybe they would. I smile at my thoughts and take a moment to come up with my plan. Landon will be stubborn, I know it, but he's easy to break. By the second embarrassing joke I crack about his new crush, he'll be shouting Tessa's number and blushing like a kindergartener.

I knock twice, giving the kid fair warning before pushing the door open. He's asleep, lying on his back with a book on his chest. Fucking *Harry Potter*. Should have known . . .

I hear a noise and see a little flash. As if a sign from above, his phone screen lights up, and I grab it from his nightstand. Tessa's name and the beginning of a text: Hey Landon, you up? Because . . .

The preview doesn't show the rest. I need to see the rest.

I circle my neck, trying not to allow the jealousy to take over. *Why is she texting him so late?*

I try to guess his pass code, but he's harder to read than Tessa. Hers was so obvious and comical, really. I knew that, like me, she would be afraid to forget the thing and choose 1234. That's our password for everything. PIN numbers, pay-per-view code on our cable box, anything that requires numbers, that's what we always use.

See, we are practically fucking married anyway. We could be wed together at the same time some hacker steals our identities—ha.

I smack Landon with a pillow from his bed, and he groans. "Wake up, dickhead."

"Go away,"

"I need Tessa's number." Smack.

"No."

Smack. Smack. Harder smack.

"Ugh!" he whines, sitting up. "Fine. I'll give you the number."

He reaches for his phone, which I place in his hand while watching the numbers he presses, just in case. He hands me the phone once it's unlocked. I thank him and type her number in my phone. The relief I feel as I press save is pathetic, but I don't care.

I smack Landon again with the pillow, just for good measure, and leave the room.

I think I hear him cussing at me until I close the door, laughing. I could get used to this feeling, this . . . hope-like feeling as I type in a simple good-night text to my girl and wait anxiously for her to reply. Everything seems to be getting better for me, finally, and the last step is Tessa's forgiveness. I just need a sliver of the hope she has always had for me to return.

Harrrdin? the message reads.

Fuck, I was beginning to think she was going to ignore me.

No, not Harrrdin. Just Hardin. I decide to start the conversation with teasing even though I want to beg her to come back from Seattle, or not to freak out if I show up there in the middle of the night.

Sorry, I can't type on this keyboard. It's too touchy.

I can picture her lying in her bed in Seattle, squinting and frowning as she uses her index finger to tap each letter.

Yeah, iPhones huh? Your old keyboard was massive so I can see why you are having a problem.

She responds with a smiley face, and I'm impressed and amused by her newfound use of the emojis. I fucking hate them and have always refused to use them, but here I am rushing to download the shit so I can respond with a matching smiley face.

You still there? she asks just as I send a matching face.

Yeah, why are you up so late. I saw that you texted Landon. I shouldn't have sent that.

A few seconds pass, and she sends an image of a tiny wineglass. I should have known she was hanging out with Kim after all.

Wine, huh? I send, accompanied by something that looks like a surprised face, I think. *Why are there so many of these damn things? When would anyone ever need to send a picture of a tiger, for fuck's sake?*

Being curious and a little high off the attention she's giving me, I send the damn tiger and laugh to myself when she responds with a camel. I laugh each time she sends me a stupid little image that no one could possibly have a use for.

I love that she caught on, that she knew I sent the tiger because it literally makes no damn sense, and now we are playing a "send the most random emoji" game, and I'm lying here in the dark, alone, laughing so hard that my stomach actually hurts.

I ran out, she says after about five minutes of back-and-forth.

Me too. Are you tired?

Yes, I drank too much wine.

Did you have fun? I'm surprised when I want her to say yes, that she did have a good time, even though I wasn't a part of her night.

Yes, I did. Are you okay? I hope everything went well with your father.

It did, maybe we can talk about it when I get to Seattle? I accompany my pushy message with a heart and the picture of what looks like a skyscraper.

Maybe.

I'm sorry I was such a shitty boyfriend. You deserve better than me but I love you. I send the message before I can stop myself. It's true and I just can't help saying it now. I've made the mistake of keeping my feelings for her inside, and that's why she's so quick to doubt my promises now.

Too much wine in my brain for this conversatoine. Christian heard Trevor having sex in his office.

I roll my eyes at his name on my screen. Fucking Trevor. Fucking Trevor.

That's whatf I said. I otld Kim that sain things.

Too many typos to read. Go to sleep, text me tomorrow, I send, then start a new message. Please. Please text me tomorrow.

A smile creeps across my face when she sends a picture of a cell phone, a sleepy face, and that damn tiger.

chapter forty-nine

HARDIN

The familiar voice of Nate echoes through the narrow hallway: "Scott!"

Fuck. I knew I wouldn't make it through this shit without seeing one of them. I came to campus to talk to my professors. I wanted to make sure my father could drop my last assignments off to them. Having friends, or parents, in high places really does help, and I'm given permission to miss the remainder of classes for this semester. I have been missing so many anyway, there won't be much of a difference.

Nate's blond hair is longer now, pushed up into some sort of messy spike in the front. "Hey, man, I get the feeling you were trying to avoid me just now," he says, looking me straight in the face.

"Perceptive, aren't you?" I shrug, no point in lying.

"I always hated your big words." He laughs.

I could have done without seeing him today, or ever again. It's nothing against him; I always sort of liked him more than any of my other friends, but I'm over this shit.

He takes my silence for another opening to speak. "I haven't seen you on campus in forever. Aren't you graduating soon?"

"Yeah. Middle of next month."

He follows next to me at a slow pace. "Logan is, too. You're going to walk, right?"

"Hell no." I laugh. "Did you really just ask me that?"

Tessa's scowl flashes in my head, and I bite down on my lip to keep a smile away. I know she wants me to walk at my graduation, but there's no way in hell I'm going to.

Maybe I should at least consider it?

"Okay . . ." he says. Then he points to my hand. "What's with the cast?"

I lift it a little and look at it. "Long story." *One that I'm not going to tell you.*

See, Tessa, I have learned some self-control.

Even though I'm talking to you inside of my head and you're not even here.

Okay, so maybe I'm crazy still, but I'm being nice-ish to people . . . You would be proud.

Fuck, I've got it so bad.

Nate shakes his head and holds the door open for me as we walk out of the administration building. "So, how are things?" he asks, always having been the most talkative of the bunch.

"Fine."

"How's she?"

My boots stop moving against the concrete sidewalk, and he takes a step back, holding his hands in the air in defense.

"I'm only asking as a friend. I haven't seen either of you, and you stopped taking our calls a while ago. Zed's the only one that talks to Tessa."

Is he trying to piss me off? "Zed doesn't talk to her," I snap, annoyed that I let Nate and his mention of Zed get under my skin so easily.

Nate lifts his hand to his forehead, a nervous gesture. "I wasn't saying it like that, but he told us about her dad and he said he was at the funeral so . . ."

"So nothing. He's nothing to her. Move on." This conversation is going nowhere and I'm reminded why I don't waste my time hanging out with any of them anymore.

"All right." If I look over at him, I know he will be rolling his eyes. But then I'm surprised when he says with a hint of emotion, "I never did anything to you, you know." When I turn to him, sure enough his expression matches his voice.

"I'm not trying to be a dick," I tell him, feeling a tiny bit guilty. He's a nice guy, nicer than me and most of our friends. His friends, not mine anymore.

He looks a little past me. "Seems like it."

"Well, I'm not. I'm just over the bullshit. You know?" I face him. "I'm over all the shit. The parties, the drinking, the smoking, the hookups—I'm just over all of it. So I'm not trying to be an asshole toward you personally, but I'm just over all that shit."

Nate pulls a cigarette from his pocket, and the only noise between us is the click of his lighter. It feels so long ago that I would walk around campus with him and the rest of our group. It feels so long ago that talking shit about people and nursing hangovers was my morning routine. It feels so long ago that my life revolved around anything other than her.

"I get what you're saying," he says after taking a drag. "I can't believe you're saying it, but I do get it, and I hope you know that I'm sorry for my part in the shit with Steph and Dan. I knew they were up to something, but I had no clue what."

The last thing I want to think about is Steph and Dan and the shit they pulled. "Yeah, well, we could go on and on about it, but the outcome would be the same. They won't ever be close enough to even dare to breathe the same air as Tessa."

"Steph is gone, anyway."

"Gone where?"

"Louisiana."

Good. I want her as far away from Tessa as possible.

I hope Tessa texts me soon; she sort of agreed to today, and I'm holding her to that. If she doesn't soon, I'm sure I'll break down and text her first. I'm trying to give her space, but our emoji conversation last night was the most fun I've had since . . . well, since I was inside her only hours before. I still can't believe what a lucky son of a bitch I am that she allowed me near her.

I was a dick afterward, but that's beside the point.

"Tristan went with her," Nate tells me.

The wind is picking up, and the entire campus just seems like a better fucking place now that I know Steph has left the state.

"He's a dumb-ass," I say.

"No, he's not," Nate says, defending his friend. "He really likes her. Well, loves her, I guess."

I snort. "Like I said, he's a dumb-ass."

"Maybe he knows her in a way that we don't."

His words make me laugh, a quiet and annoyed laugh. "What else is there to know? She's a crazy bitch." I can't believe he's actually defending Steph—well, Tristan, who is dating Steph again, despite that she's a fucking psycho who tried to hurt Tessa.

"I don't know, man, but Tristan's my boy, so I don't judge him," Nate says, then looks at me coolly. "Most people would probably say the same shit about you and Tessa."

"You better be comparing me and Steph, not Tessa and Steph."

"Obviously." He rolls his eyes and ashes his cigarette beside him. "You should come with me to the house. Just for old times' sake. There won't be a lot of people, just a few of us."

"Dan?" My phone vibrates in my pocket, and I pull it out to find Tessa's name on the screen.

"I don't know, but I can make sure he doesn't come around while you're there."

We are standing in the parking lot now. My car is only a few feet away, and his motorcycle is parked in the front row. I still can't believe he hasn't wrecked the damn thing. He dropped the piece of shit at least five times the day he got his permit for it, and I know his ass doesn't wear a helmet while speeding across town.

"I'm good. I have plans, anyway," I lie as I send back a hello to Tessa. I'm hoping my plans could involve talking to Tessa for hours. I almost agreed to go by that damn frat house, but that my old "friends" still hang out with Dan reminds me exactly why I stopped hanging out with them to begin with.

"Are you sure? We could hang one last time before you graduate and knock your girl up. You know that's coming, right?" he teases. His tongue flashes in the sun, and I push his arm back.

"You got your tongue pierced?" I ask, absentmindedly running my finger over the small scar next to my eyebrow.

"Yeah, like a month ago. I still can't believe you took those rings out. And nice save on avoiding the second part of what I said." He laughs, and I try to remember what it was that he said.

Something about my girl . . . and pregnant.

"Oh, hell no. No one will be getting pregnant, asshole. Go to hell for even trying to curse me with that shit." I shove at his shoulder, and he laughs harder.

Marriage is one thing. Babies, a totally fucking other thing.

I glance down at my phone. As nice as it is to play catch-up with Nate, I want to focus on Tessa and her messages, especially since she wrote something about going to the doctor. I type out a quick reply to her.

"There's Logan right there." Nate pulls me from my phone, and I follow his eyes to Logan, walking toward us. "Shit," Nate adds, and my eyes focus on the chick walking next to Logan. She looks familiar, but not quite . . .

Molly. It's Molly, but her hair is black now instead of pink. My luck today is remarkable, really.

"Well, that's my cue. I got shit to do," I say, attempting to avoid the potential disaster walking in my direction. Just as I turn to go, Molly leans into Logan and he wraps his arm around her waist.

What the fuck? "Them?" I gape. "Those two? Fucking?"

I look at Nate; the fucker doesn't even try to hide his amusement. "Yep. For a while now. They didn't tell anyone until about three weeks ago. I caught on early, though. I knew something was up when she stopped being such a bitch all the time."

Molly flips her black hair and smiles at Logan. I don't even remember her smiling, ever. I can't stand her, but I don't hate her the way I used to. She did help Tessa . . .

"Don't even think about leaving until you tell me why you've been avoiding us!" Logan's voice shoots across the lot.

"I had better shit to do!" I yell back, checking my phone again. I want to know why Tessa is at the doctor again. Her last text avoided the question, and I need to know. I'm sure she's okay, I'm just being a nosy asshole.

Molly's lips curl into a smirk. "Better shit? Like fucking Tessa's brains out in Seattle?"

And just like old times I raise my middle finger at her. "Fuck off."

"Don't be such a pussy. We all know you two haven't stopped fucking since you met," she taunts me.

I look at Logan in that "get her to shut her mouth or I will" way, but he shrugs his shoulders.

"You two make a grand couple." I raise a brow at my old friend, and it's his turn to raise a finger to me.

"At least she's leaving you alone now, right?" Logan fires back, and I laugh. He's got a point there.

"Where is she anyway?" Molly asks. "Not that I care; I don't like her."

"We know," Nate says, and Molly rolls her eyes.

"She doesn't like you either. No one does, actually," I remind her mockingly.

"Touché." She grins and leans into Logan' shoulder.

Nate may have been right: she does seem less bitchy. A little.

"Well, nice to see you guys, really," I sarcastically remark and turn to walk away. "I have better shit to do, though, so have fun doing whatever you're doing. And, Logan, you really should keep fucking her. It seems to be doing the trick." I nod at them and climb into my car.

Just as I shut the door, I hear a mixture of "He's in a better mood" and "Pussy-whipped" and "I'm happy for him."

The weirdest part was that the last one came from the Evil Bitch herself.

chapter fifty

TESSA

I'm uncomfortable, nervous, and a little cold, sitting here dressed in only a thin hospital gown, inside a small exam room that mirrors the others lining the hall. They should add some color in the rooms—just a little paint would do, or even a framed photograph like in every other exam room I've ever been inside. Except this one. This one is nothing but white. White walls, white desk, white floor.

I should have taken Kimberly up on her offer to accompany me today. I'm fine on my own, but having a little support today, even just a little of Kimberly's humor, would have helped calm my nerves. I woke up this morning feeling much better than I deserve, no trace of a hangover present. I felt sort of good. I fell asleep with a wine-and-Hardin-influenced smile on my face, and I slept more peacefully than I have in weeks.

I keep going round and round in my head, as usual, when it comes to Hardin. Reading and rereading our playful conversation from last night hasn't failed to make me smile, no matter how many times I look through the messages.

I like this nice, patient, playful Hardin. I would love to get to know that Hardin better, but I'm afraid that he won't be around long enough to do so. I won't be around long enough either. I'm leaving for New York with Landon, and the closer the date comes, the more restless the fluttering inside me becomes. I can't tell if it's a good flutter or bad, but it's out of control today, and in this moment it's multiplied.

My feet are dangling over the edge of this uncomfortable examination bed, and I can't decide whether I want to keep my legs crossed or not. It's a trivial decision, but it does the job at distracting me from the cold temperature and awkward butterflies attacking my stomach.

I pull my phone from my purse and type a message to Hardin—just to keep occupied while I wait, of course.

A simple hey is all I send and wait, while crossing and uncrossing my legs.

I'm glad you text me because I was only going to wait another hour before I text you, he replies.

I smile at the screen; even though I shouldn't like the demand behind his words, I do. He's being so honest lately, and I'm loving it.

I'm at the doctor and I've been waiting a while. How are you today?

He responds quickly. Stop being so formal. Why are you at the doctor? Are you okay? You didn't tell me you were going. I'm okay, don't worry about that, though I am here with Nate, who's trying to get me to hang out later. Like that'll happen.

I hate the way my chest aches at the thought of Hardin's hanging out with his old friends. It's none of my business what he does or who he spends his time with, but I can't shake the sick feeling that comes over me when thinking about the memories associated with them.

Seconds later: Not that you needed to tell me, but you could have. I would have come with you?

It's okay. I'm okay alone. I find myself wishing I would have given him the option.

You've been alone too much since I've met you.

Not really. I don't know what else to say because my head is fuzzy, and I'm feeling sort of happy that he's concerned for me and being so open.

The word Liar is paired with a pair of jeans and a ball of fire. I cover my mouth with my hand to stifle the noise as the doctor enters the exam room.

Doctor is here, I'll text you later.

Let me know if he doesn't keep his hands to himself.

I tuck my phone away and try to wipe the giddy smile from my face as Dr. West pulls a latex glove over each of his hands.

"How have you been?"

How have I been? He doesn't want to know the answer to that, nor does he have the time to listen. He's a medical doctor, not a psychiatrist.

"Good," I reply, cringing at the thought of small talk as he positions himself to examine me.

"I ran the blood work from your last appointment, but there wasn't anything triggering concern there."

I let out a breath of relief.

"However," he says ominously, and pauses.

I should have known there would be a *however.*

"As I looked over the images from your exam, I concluded that your cervix is very narrow, and from what I can see, very short. I'd like to show you what I mean, if that's okay?"

Dr. West adjusts his glasses and I nod in agreement. Short and narrow cervix. I did enough research online to know what that means.

TEN LONG MINUTES LATER, he's shown me in great detail the things I already knew. I've known what he would conclude with. I knew the moment that I left his office two and a half weeks ago. As I get myself dressed, his words play on repeat through my mind:

"Not impossible, but highly unlikely."

"There are other options—adoption is a route many people choose to go."

"You're still really young. As you get older, you and your partner can explore the best options for you."

"I'm sorry, Ms. Young."

Without thinking, I dial Hardin's number on the way to my car. I'm greeted by his voicemail three times before I force myself to put my phone away.

I don't need him, or anyone, right now. I can deal with this on my own. I already knew this. I have already dealt with this in my mind and filed it away.

It doesn't matter that Hardin didn't answer the phone. I'm fine. Who cares if I can't get pregnant? I'm only nineteen, and all of the other plans I've made have fallen through so far anyway. It's only fitting that this last piece of my ultimate plan is blown to pieces, too.

The drive back to Kimberly's is long because of congested traffic again. I hate driving, I've decided. I hate people who have road rage. I hate the way it always rains here. I hate the way young girls blare loud music with their windows rolled down, even in the rain. Just roll your windows up!

I hate the way I'm trying to stay positive and not turn into the pathetic Tessa I was last week. I hate that it's so hard to think of anything except that my body betrayed me in the most final and intimate way.

I was born this way, Dr. West says. Of course I was. Just like my mother, no matter how perfect I try to be, it will never happen. There is a silver lining here, a sick one, in that at least I won't pass any of the traits I got from her to a child. I suppose I can't blame my mother for my faulty cervix, but I want to. I want to blame someone or something, but I can't.

This is the way the world works: if you want something bad enough, it gets stripped away and held out of reach. Just the way

Hardin is. No Hardin and no babies. The two would never have mixed anyway, but it was nice to pretend I could have the luxury of both.

As I walk into Christian's house, I'm relieved to find I'm home alone. Not home, but here. Without checking my phone, I strip down and get into the shower. I don't know how long I stay in there, watching the water circle the drain over and over. The water is cold when I finally climb out and dress myself in the T-shirt of Hardin's that he left for me in my suitcase, when he sent me away in London.

I'm just lying here now, in this empty bed, and by the time I start to wish Kimberly were home, I get a text from her saying she and Christian are staying overnight downtown and Smith will be at the sitter's all night. I have the entire house to myself and nothing to do, no one to talk to. No one now, not even a little baby later to care for and love.

I keep pitying myself and I know it's ridiculous, but I can't seem to stop it.

Have some wine and rent a movie, our treat! Kimberly responds to my text wishing her fun for the night.

My phone starts to ring as soon as I send my thanks to her. Hardin's number flashes on the screen, and I debate whether to answer.

By the time I reach the wine fridge in the kitchen, he's routed to my voicemail, and I've reserved a ticket to Pity Party Central.

A BOTTLE OF WINE LATER, I'm in the living room halfway through a terrible action film that I rented about a marine turned nanny turned mighty alien hunter. It seemed to be the only movie on the list that had nothing to do with love, babies, or anything happy.

When did I become such a downer? I take another drink of wine, straight from the bottle. I gave up on the wineglass five blown-up spaceships ago.

My phone rings again, and this time, as I look at the screen, my drunken thumbs accidently answer for me.

chapter fifty-one

HARDIN

Tess?" I say into the phone, trying to hide my panic. She has been ignoring my calls all night, and I've been going insane wondering what I could have done wrong—what *else* I could have done wrong this time.

"Yeah." Her voice is cloudy, slow, and off. With one word I can tell she's been drinking.

"Wine again?" I chuckle. "Should I lecture you yet?" I tease her but only get silence on the line. "Tess?"

"Yeah?"

"What's wrong?"

"Nothing. I'm just watching a movie."

"With Kimberly?" My stomach twists at the possibility of anyone else being there with her.

"Myself. I'm alone here in this *biiiiiig* house." Her voice is flat, even as she exaggerates her words.

"Where're Kimberly and Vance?" I shouldn't be this worried, but her tone has me on edge.

"Out for the night. Smith, too. I'm just here watching a movie alone. Story of my life, right?" She laughs, but there's nothing behind it. No emotion at all.

"Tessa, what's going on? How much did you drink?"

She sighs into the phone, and I swear I can literally hear her gulping more wine.

"Tessa. Answer me."

"I'm fine. I'm allowed to drink, right, *Dad*?" she tries to joke, but the way she says that last word gives me a chill.

"If you want to get technical, you aren't actually allowed to drink. Not legally, anyway." I'm the last person to lecture her; it's my fault she started drinking so regularly anyway, but this burning paranoia is clawing at the pit of my stomach right now. She's drinking alone, and she sounds sad enough that I jump to my feet.

"Yeah."

"How much did you drink?" I text Vance, hoping he'll respond.

"Not too much. I'm fine. You know what'sss weird?" Tessa slurs.

I grab my keys. Damn Seattle for being so fucking far. "What's that?" I push my feet into my Vans. Boots take too much time, and time is something I can't afford right now.

"It's weird how someone can be a good person but bad things just keep happening to them. You know?"

Fuck. I text Vance again, this time telling him to get his ass home—*now*.

"Yeah, I do know. It's not fair the way that works." I hate that she's feeling this way. She's a good person, the best I've ever met, and she somehow ended up being surrounded by a bunch of fuckups, me included. Who am I kidding? I'm the worst offender.

"Maybe I shouldn't be a g-good person anymore."

What? No. No, no, no. She shouldn't be talking like this, thinking like this.

"No, don't think like that." I wave an impatient hand at Karen, who is standing in the doorway of the kitchen—wondering where I am running off to this late, I'm sure.

"I try not to, but I can't help it. I don't know how to stop."

"What happened today?" It's hard to believe that I'm talking to my Tessa, the same girl who always sees the best in everyone—herself, too. She has always been so positive, so happy, and now she's not.

She sounds so hopeless, so defeated.

She sounds like me.

My blood runs cold in my veins. I knew this would happen; I knew she wouldn't be the same after I got my claws into her. I somehow knew that after me she would be different.

I hoped it wouldn't be true, but tonight it sure as hell seems that way.

"Nothing important," she lies.

Vance still hasn't answered me. He *better* be driving home.

"Tessa, tell me what's wrong. Please."

"Nothing. Just karma catching up to me, I guess," she mumbles, and the sound of a cork's being popped echoes through the silence on the line.

"Karma for what? Are you insane? You've never done anything to deserve any of the shit that's happened to you."

She doesn't say anything.

"Tessa, I think you should stop drinking for the night. I'm on my way to Seattle. I know you need space, but I'm getting worried about you and I . . . well, I can't stay away, I never could."

"Yeah . . ." She isn't even listening.

"I don't like you drinking this much anymore," I say, knowing she won't hear me.

"Yeah . . ."

"I'm on my way. Get a bottle of water. Okay?"

"Yeah . . . a little bottle . . ."

THE DRIVE TO SEATTLE has never seemed this fucking long, and because of the distance between us, I finally see it, this cycle that

Tessa always bitches about. It's a cycle that ends here—this is the last damn time I'll be driving to another city to be close to her. No more endless fucking bullshit. No more running from my problems, and no more fucking excuses. No more long-ass drives across the damn state of Washington because I ran far away.

chapter fifty-two

HARDIN

I've called forty-nine times.

Forty-nine fucking times.

Forty-nine.

Do you know how many rings that is?

A fucking lot.

Too many to count, or at least I can't think clearly enough to count them. But if I could, it would be a *massive* amount of fucking rings.

If I make it through the next three minutes, I plan on ripping the front door off the damn hinges and smashing Tessa's phone—the one she apparently doesn't know how to answer—against the wall.

Okay, so maybe I shouldn't smash her phone against the wall. Maybe I'll accidently step on it a few times until the screen cracks under my weight.

Maybe.

She's going to get a goddamn earful, that's for fucking sure. I haven't heard from her in the last couple hours, and she has no fucking idea how torturous the last few hours of driving have been. I go twenty over the speed limit to make it to Seattle as fast as possible.

When I near the place, it's three in the damn morning, and Tessa, Vance, and Kimberly are all on my shit list. Maybe I should smash all three of their phones, since they obviously have forgotten how to answer the fucking things.

As I reach the gate, I begin to panic, even more than I already have been. *What if they decided to close their security gate? What If they changed the code?*

Do I even remember the fucking code? Of course not. Will they answer when I call to ask the code? Of course not.

What if they aren't answering because something happened to Tessa and they took her to the hospital and she isn't okay and they don't have service and . . .

But then I see the gate is open, and I'm a little annoyed by that, too. *Why wouldn't Tessa turn on the security system when she's here alone?*

As I drive up the winding road, I see that hers is the only car parked in front of the massive house. Good to know that Vance is here when I need him . . . Some fucking friend he is. Father, not friend. Fuck—right now he's neither, really.

When I step out of my car and approach the front door, my anger and anxiety grow. The way she was talking, the way she sounded . . . it was like she wasn't in control of her own actions.

The door is unlocked—of course it is—and I make my way through the living room and down the hall. Hands shaking, I push the door to her bedroom open, and my chest tightens when I find her bed empty. It's not only empty, it's untouched—perfectly made, the corners folded in that way that's impossible to re-create. I've tried it—it's impossible to make a bed like Tessa can.

"Tessa!" I call as I walk into the bathroom across the hall. I keep my eyes closed as I turn the light on. Not hearing anything, I open my eyes.

Nothing.

My breath is released in a heavy pant, and I move to the next room. *Where the fuck is she?*

"Tess!" I yell again, louder this time.

After searching nearly the entire fucking mansion, I can barely breathe. Where is she? The only rooms left are Vance's bedroom and a locked room upstairs. I'm not sure if I want to open that door . . .

I'll check the patio and yard, and if she's not there, I have no fucking clue what I will do.

"Theresa! Where the hell are you? This isn't funny, I swear—" I stop yelling as I take in the curled-up ball on the patio lounge chair.

Approaching, I see that Tessa's knees are tucked up to her stomach and her arms are wrapped around her chest, as if she fell asleep while trying to hold herself together.

All of my anger is dissolved when I kneel down beside her. I push her blond hair away from her face and will myself not to burst into fucking hysterics now that I know she's okay. Fuck, I was so worried about her.

With my pulse racing, I lean into her and run my thumb along her bottom lip. I don't know why I did that, actually; it just sort of happened, but I sure as hell don't regret it when her eyes flutter open and she groans.

"Why are you outside?" I ask, my voice loud and strained.

She winces, clearly put off by the volume of my words.

Why aren't you inside? I've been worried fucking sick for you, going over every possible scenario in my head for hours now, I want to say.

"Thank God you were asleep" comes out instead. "I've been calling you, I was worried about you."

She sits up, holding her neck as if her head might fall off. "Hardin?"

"Yes, Hardin."

She squints in the dark and rubs her neck. When she moves to stand, an empty bottle of wine falls to the concrete patio and cracks in half.

"Sorry," she apologizes, bending down to try to pick up the broken glass.

I gently push her hand away and wrap my fingers around hers. "Don't touch that. I'll get it later. Let's get inside." I help her stand.

"How'd . . . you get . . . here?" Her speech is stunted, and I don't even want to know how much wine she drank after the line went dead. I saw at least four empty bottles in the kitchen.

"I drove, how else?"

"All the way here? What time is it?"

My eyes follow down her body, her body that's covered in only a T-shirt. My T-shirt.

She notices my stare and begins to tug at the ends of the shirt to cover her bare thighs. "I only w-wear it . . ." She trails off, stuttering. "I'm only wearing it now, just once," she says, making little to no sense at all.

"It's fine, I want you to wear it. Let's get inside."

"I like it out here," she quietly says, staring off into the darkness.

"It's too cold. We're going inside." I reach for her hand, but she pulls away. "Okay, okay, if you want to stay out here, that's okay. But I'm staying with you," I say, redirecting my demand.

She nods and leans against the railing; her knees are shaking and her face is colorless.

"What happened tonight?"

She stays silent, still staring.

After a moment she turns to me. "Don't you ever feel like your life has turned into one big joke?"

"Daily." I shrug, unsure where the hell this conversation is going, but hating the sadness behind her eyes. Even in the dark the sadness burns low, blue and deep, haunting those bright eyes that I love so much.

"Well, me, too."

"No, you are the positive one here. The happy one. I'm the cynical asshole, not you."

"It's exhausting being happy, you know?"

"Not really." I take a step closer to her. "I'm not really the poster child for sunshine and happiness, in case you haven't noticed," I say, trying to lighten the mood, and I'm granted a half-drunk, half-amused smile.

I wish she would just tell me what is going on with her lately. I don't know how much I can do for her, but this is my fault—all of this is my fault. The unhappiness inside her is my burden to bear, not hers.

She lifts her arm to rest it on the wooden plank in front of her but misses and stumbles, nearly smacking face-first into the umbrella attached to a patio table.

I wrap my hand around her elbow to steady her, and she begins to lean into me. "Could we go inside now? You need to sleep off all the wine you've had."

"I don't remember falling asleep."

"That's probably because it's more like you passed out than fell asleep." I point to the broken wine bottle a few feet away.

"Don't try and scold me," she snaps, and backs away.

"I'm not." My hands rise in innocence, and I want to scream because of the irony of this whole fucking situation. Tessa's the drunk one, and I'm the sober voice of reason.

"I'm sorry." She sighs. "I can't think." I watch as she lowers herself to the ground and brings her knees to her chest again. She raises her head to look up at me. "Can I talk to you about something?"

"Of course."

"And you'll be completely honest?"

"I'll try."

She seems to be okay with that, and I sit down on the edge of the chair closest to where she is on the ground. I'm slightly afraid of what she wants to talk about, but I need to know what's going on with her, so I wait with my mouth shut for her to speak.

"Sometimes I feel like everyone else gets what I want," she mumbles, embarrassed.

Tessa *would* feel guilty for saying the way she feels . . .

I can barely make out her words when she says, "It's not that I'm not happy for them . . ." But I can all-too-clearly see the tears gathering in her eyes.

For the life of me, I can't figure out what the hell she's talking about, though Kimberly and Vance's engagement pops into my mind. "Is this about Kimberly and Vance? Because if it is, you shouldn't want what they have. He's a liar and a cheater and . . ." I stop before finishing the sentence with something horrible.

"He loves her. So much, though," Tessa murmurs. Her fingers trace patterns against the concrete under her.

"I love you more," I say without thinking.

My words have the opposite effect from what I hoped, and Tessa whimpers. Literally whimpers, and wraps her arms around her knees.

"It's true. I do."

"You only love me sometimes," she says, as if that is the one thing she knows for sure in this world.

"Bullshit. You know that's not true."

"It *feels* that way," she whispers, looking out toward the sea. I wish it were daylight so the view could possibly help soothe her, since I'm obviously not doing a good job at that.

"I know. I know it might feel that way." I can admit that's how she probably experiences it now.

"You'll love someone all the time, later."

What? "What are you talking about?"

"The next time, you'll love her all the time."

In this moment, I have a strange vision of me thinking back to this exact moment fifty years from now, reliving all over again the sharp pain that accompanies her words. The feeling is overwhelming, and it's so obvious—it's never been more obvious.

She has given up on me. On us.

"There isn't a next time!" I can't help the way my voice is rising, the way my blood is burning just beneath the surface, threatening to rip me open right here on this damn patio.

"There is. I'm your Trish."

What is she going on about? I know she's drunk, but what does my mum have to do with this?

"Your Trish. It's me. You'll have a Karen, too, and she can give you a baby." Tessa wipes under her eyes, and I slide off the chair to kneel next to her on the ground.

"I don't know what you're saying, but you're wrong." My arms wrap around her shoulders just as she begins to sob.

I can't make out her words but I hear ". . . baby . . . Karen . . . Trish . . . Ken."

Damn Kimberly for keeping so much wine in the house.

"I don't know what Karen or Trish or any other name you'll throw out there has to do with us."

She pushes against my shoulders, but I tighten my grip on her. She may not want me, but right now she needs me. "You're Tessa, and I'm Hardin. End of—"

"Karen's pregnant." Tessa sobs into my chest. "She's having a baby."

"So?" I move my cast-covered hand up and down her back, unsure what to say or do with this version of Tessa.

"I went to the doctor," she cries, and I freeze.

Holy fucking shit.

"And?" I try not to panic.

She doesn't answer in an actual language. Her response comes out in some form of a drunken cry, and I take a moment to try to think clearly. She's obviously not pregnant; if she were, she wouldn't be drinking. I know Tessa, and I know she would never, ever, do something like that. She's obsessed with the idea of being a mother one day; she wouldn't endanger her unborn child.

She lets me hold her while she calms herself down.

"Would you want to?" Tessa asks, minutes later. Her body is still heaving in my arms, but the tears have stopped.

"What?"

"Have a baby?" She rubs at her eyes and I flinch.

"Uhm, no." I shake my head. "I don't want a baby with you."

Her eyes close, and she whimpers again. I replay the words in my head and realize how they sounded. "I didn't mean it like that. I just don't want kids—you know that."

She sniffles and nods, still quiet. "Your Karen can give you a baby," she says, her eyes still closed, and leans her head against my chest.

I'm still as confused as ever. I draw a connection to Karen and my father, but I don't want to entertain the idea that Tessa thinks she's my beginning, not my ending.

I wrap my arms around her waist and lift her from the ground, saying, "All right, it's time for you to go to bed."

She doesn't fight me this time. "It's true. You said it once," she mumbles and wraps her thighs around my waist, making it easier to carry her through the sliding door and down the hallway.

"Said what?"

" 'There can be no happy end to it,' " she quotes my previous words.

Fucking Hemingway and his shitty outlook on life. "That was a stupid thing for me to say. I didn't mean it," I promise her.

" 'I love you enough now. What do you want to do? Ruin me?' " she quotes the bastard again. Leave it to Tessa to have perfect recall while she's too drunk to even stand.

"Shh, we can quote Hemingway when you're sober."

" 'All things truly wicked start from innocence,' " she says against my neck, arms tightening across my back as I push her bedroom door open.

I used to love that line, as I never understood the meaning. I thought I did, but it's not until now, when I'm living the fucking meaning, that I actually get it.

My mind growing heavy with guilt, I gently lay her on the bed and toss the pillows to the floor, leaving one for her head. "Scoot up," I softly command.

She doesn't have her eyes open and I can tell she's close to sleep, finally. I leave the light off, hoping she will sleep the rest of the night.

"Stayinggg?" she says, drawing the word out.

"Do you want me to stay? I can sleep in another room," I offer, even though I don't want to. She's so off, so detached from herself, that I'm almost afraid to leave her alone.

"Mhmm," she mumbles, reaching for the blanket. She tugs at the corner and huffs in frustration when she can't get the fabric loose enough to cover herself.

After I help cover her, I take my shoes off and climb into the bed with her. While I'm debating how much space to leave between our bodies, she wraps a bare thigh around my waist, pulling me closer.

I can breathe. Finally, I can fucking breathe.

"I was scared you weren't going to be okay," I admit into the silence of the dark room.

"Me, too," she agrees in a broken voice.

I push my arm under her head, and she shifts her hips, turning into me and tightening her leg around my body.

I don't know where to go from here; I don't know what I did to her that made her this way.

Yes—yes, I do. I treated her like shit and took advantage of her kindness. I used up chance after chance, like the supply would never end. I took the trust she gave me and ripped it up like it meant nothing and threw it in her face every time I felt like I wasn't good enough for her.

If I would have just accepted her love from the beginning,

accepted her trust and cherished the life she tried to breathe into me, she wouldn't be this way now. She wouldn't be lying next to me drunk and upset, defeated and destroyed by me.

She fixed me; she glued the tiny fragments of my fucked-up soul into something impossible, something almost attractive even. She made me into something—she made me normal almost—but with each drop of glue she used on me, she lost that drop of herself, and me being the piece of shit I am, didn't have anything to offer her.

Everything that I feared would happen has happened, and no matter how much I tried to prevent it, I see now that I made it worse. I changed her and ruined her, just the way I promised I would all those months ago.

It seems insane.

"I'm truly sorry that I ruined you," I whisper into her hair as her breathing begins to show signs of sleep.

"Me, too," she breathes, and regret fills in the little spaces between us as she drifts off.

chapter fifty-three

TESSA

Buzzing. All I can hear is constant buzzing, and my head feels as if it will explode at any moment. And it's hot. Too hot. Hardin's weight is heavy; his cast is pressing down on my stomach, and I have to pee.

Hardin.

I lift his arm and wiggle, literally, out from under his body. The first thing I do is grab his phone off the nightstand to stop the buzzing. Text messages and calls from Christian fill the screen. I reply with a simple We are fine and turn his phone to silent before walking to the bathroom.

My heart is heavy in my chest, and the remnants of last night's alcohol abuse are swimming through my veins. I shouldn't have had that much wine; I should have stopped after the first bottle. Or second. Or third.

I don't remember falling asleep, and I can't remember how Hardin came to be here. A muddled memory of his voice through the phone surfaces, but it's hard to make out, and I'm not fully convinced it actually happened. But he's here now, asleep in my bed, so I suppose the details don't really matter.

I lean my hip against the sink and turn on the cold water. I splash some across my face, like they do in the movies, but it doesn't work. It doesn't wake me up or clear my thoughts; it only makes yesterday's mascara bleed even farther down my face.

"Tessa?" Hardin's voice calls.

I shut the faucet off and meet him in the hallway.

"Hey," I say, avoiding his eyes.

"Why are you up? You just fell asleep two hours ago."

"I couldn't sleep, I guess." I shrug my shoulders, hating the awkward tension I feel in his presence.

"How are you feeling? You drank a lot last night."

I follow him back into the bedroom and close the door behind me. He sits on the edge of the bed, and I climb back under the covers. I don't feel like facing the day right now; that's okay, though, since the sun hasn't even decided to come out yet.

"I have a headache," I admit.

"I'm sure—you were throwing up half the night, baby."

I cringe while remembering Hardin holding my hair back, rubbing his hand across my shoulders to comfort me while I emptied my stomach into the toilet.

Dr. West's voice delivering bad news, the worst news, pushes through my aching head. Did I drunkenly share the news with Hardin? *Oh no.* I hope not.

"What . . . what did I say last night?" I ask, treading lightly.

He exhales and runs his hand through his hair. "You were going on about Karen and my mum. I don't even want to know what that meant." He grimaces, and I assume it matches my own expression.

"Is that all?" I hope it is.

"Basically. Oh, and you were quoting Hemingway." He smiles a little, and I'm reminded just how charming he can be.

"I *wasn't.*" I cover my face with my hands in embarrassment.

"You were." A soft laugh falls from his lips, and I peek through my hands to look at him as he adds, "You were also saying that you accept my apology and you will give me another chance."

His eyes meet mine through my fingers, and I can't seem to look away. *He's good. Really good.*

"Liar." I'm not sure if I want to laugh or cry. Here we are again, in the middle of our same old back-and-forth, push-and-pull. I can't ignore that it feels different this time, but I also know that I can't be trusted to judge this. It always seemed to feel different each time he made a promise that he couldn't keep.

"Do you want to talk about what happened last night? Because I hated seeing you that way. You weren't yourself. It really scared me when I was on the phone with you."

"I'm fine."

"You were plastered. You drank yourself to sleep outside on the patio, and there are empty bottles across the entire house."

"It's not fun finding someone that way, huh?" I feel like a jerk as soon as the words are out.

His shoulders drop. "No. It's really not."

I'm reminded of the nights (and sometimes even the days) when I found Hardin drunk. Drunk Hardin always brought along with him broken lamps, holes in walls, and nasty words that were sure to cut deep.

"That won't ever happen again," he says, answering my thoughts.

"I wasn't—" I begin to lie, but he knows me too well.

"Yes, you were. It's okay, I deserve it."

"Either way, it wasn't fair of me to throw it in your face." I need to learn to forgive Hardin or neither of us will ever have peace in our lives after this.

I didn't realize it had been vibrating, but he lifts his phone from the nightstand and presses it to his ear. I close my eyes to relieve some of the throbbing as he curses Christian out. I wave my hand, trying to get him to stop, but he ignores me, rushing to tell Christian what an asshole he is.

"Well, you should have fucking answered. If something would have happened to her, I would have held you fucking responsible," Hardin growls into the phone, and I try to block his voice out.

I'm fine, I drank a little too much because I had a bad day, but I'm fine now. What's the harm in that?

When he hangs up, I feel the mattress dip next to me, and he pushes my hand away from my eyes. "He says he's sorry for not coming home to check on you," Hardin says, inches from my face.

I can see the stubble across his jaw and chin. I don't know if it's because I'm still a little intoxicated, or just plain crazy, but I reach up and run my finger across the line of his jaw. My action surprises him, and his eyes glaze over, almost crossing, as I caress his skin.

"What are we doing?" He leans even closer.

"I don't know." I answer with the only truth that I know. I have no clue what we are doing, what I am doing, when it comes to Hardin. I never have.

Inside, I'm sad and hurt, and I feel betrayed by my own body and the essential nature of karma and life in general, but on the surface, I know that Hardin can make it all go away. Even if only temporarily, he can make me forget all of the worries; he can clear all of the chaos from my mind, the way I used to do for him.

Now I get it. I get what he meant when he said he needed me all of those times. I get why he used me the way he did.

"I don't want to use you."

"What?" he asks, confused.

"I want you to make me forget everything, but I don't want to use you. I want to be close to you right now, but I haven't changed my mind about the rest," I ramble out, hoping he will understand what I don't know how to say.

He leans up on one elbow and looks down at me. "I don't care how or why, but if you want me in any way, you don't need to explain. I'm already yours."

His lips are so close to mine, and I could so easily just lift my head slightly to touch them.

"I'm sorry." I turn my head. I can't use him this way, but mostly I can't pretend that that's all it would be. It wouldn't just be a physical distraction from my problems—it would be more, much more. I love him still, even though I sometimes wish I didn't. I wish I were stronger, that I could brush this off as a simple distraction, no feelings, no wanting more, only sex.

But my heart and conscience won't allow it. As hurt as I am by my ideal future's being ripped away from me, I can't use him this way, especially now that he seems to be making such an effort. It would hurt him so bad.

While I'm battling myself, he rolls his body onto mine and collects both of my wrists into one of his hands. "What are you—"

He lifts my hands above my head. "I know what you are thinking." He presses his lips to my neck, and my body takes over. My neck rolls to the side, giving him easier access to the sensitive skin there.

"It's not fair to you," I gasp when his teeth pull at the skin just under my ear. He releases his grip on my wrists—only long enough to pull my T-shirt over my head and toss it onto the floor.

"This isn't fair. Your even allowing me to touch you after all I've done isn't fair to you, but I want it. I want you, I always want you, and I know you're fighting it, but you want me to distract you. Let me." He pushes his weight onto me, his hips pinning me to the mattress in a dominating and demanding way that has my head swimming faster than last night's wine.

His knee slides between my thighs, and he opens them. "Don't think about me. Only think about you and what you want."

"Okay." I nod, moaning when his knee rubs between my legs.

"I love you—don't ever feel bad about letting me show you that." He speaks such soft words, but his hands are rough as one of them keeps both of my hands pinned to the bed and the other pushes into my panties. "So wet," he groans, moving his finger up and down the moisture there. I try to hold still as he brings his finger to my mouth, pushing it past my lips. "So sweet, isn't it?"

He doesn't allow me to respond before he frees my hands and

positions his head between my legs. His tongue swipes across me, and I push my fingers into his hair. With each stroke of his tongue across my clit, I am lost in this place with him. I'm no longer clouded by darkness, I'm no longer pissed off—I'm not focusing on regrets and mistakes.

I'm only focused on my body and his. I'm focused on the way he groans against me when I pull his hair. I'm focused on the way my nails leave angry little lines across his shoulder blades as he pushes two fingers inside me. I can only focus on his touching me, every part of me, inside and out, in a way that no one else ever could.

I focus on the sharp intake of his breath as I beg him to turn around and let me please him while he pleases me, the way he pushes his jeans to the floor and nearly rips his shirt off in his hurry to touch me again. I focus on the way he lifts me on top of him, my face opposite his cock. I focus on the way we've never done this before, but I love the way he moans my name when I take him into my mouth. I focus on the way his fingers dig into my hips as he licks me and I suck him. I focus on the way I can feel the pressure building inside me, and I focus on the dirty things he's saying to bring me over the edge.

I come first, followed by him filling my mouth, and I nearly collapse from the relief that my body feels after my release. I try not to focus on the way I don't feel guilty for allowing his touch as a distraction from my pain.

"Thank you," I breathe into his chest when he pulls me to lie across him.

"No, thank *you*." He smiles down at me and presses a kiss to my bare shoulder. "Are you going to tell me what's been bothering you?"

"No." I trace my fingertip over the black ink of the tree on his chest.

"Fine. Will you marry me?" His body moves with soft laughter underneath me.

"No." I swat at him, hoping he's only teasing.

"Fine. Will you move in with me?"

"No." I move my finger to another group of tattoos, tracing the heart-shaped end of the infinity symbol drawn there.

"I'll take that as a maybe." He chuckles, wrapping his arm around my back. "Will you let me take you to dinner tonight?"

"No," I answer too quickly.

He laughs. "I'll take that as a yes." His laughter is cut short when the sound of the front door opening echoes through the house and voices fill the hall.

"Shit," we both say at the same time.

He looks up at me, puzzled by my language, and I shrug at him before digging through my drawers to get dressed.

chapter fifty-four

TESSA

The tension in the air is so thick that I swear Kimberly opened the window for that reason alone. Across the living room we exchange sympathetic looks.

"It's not that hard to answer the phone or at least respond with a text. I drove all the way here, and you just got back to me an hour ago," Hardin says furiously, scolding Christian.

I sigh, as does Kimberly. I'm sure she's also wondering just how many times Hardin is going to repeat that "I drove all the way here" sentence.

"I said I was sorry. We were downtown and apparently my phone decided not to have service." Christian wheels his chair past Hardin. "These things do happen, Hardin. 'The best-laid plans of mice and men,' and all that . . ."

Hardin gives Christian one of his patented glares before rounding the island and standing next to me.

"I think he gets it," I whisper to him.

"Yeah, well, he better." Hardin continues glowering, earning an annoyed grimace from his biological father.

"You're in a mood today, considering what we just did," I tease Hardin, hoping to ease his anger.

He leans into me, hope taking the place of the anger in his eyes. "What time do you want to leave for dinner?"

"Dinner?" Kimberly interrupts.

I turn to her, knowing exactly what she's thinking. "It's not like that."

"Yes, it is," Hardin says.

Between her nosiness and his smug grin, I want to slap the both of them. Of course I want to go to dinner with Hardin. Since the day I met him, I have wanted to be near him.

But I'm not giving in to Hardin; I'm not throwing myself back into the cycle of our destructive relationship. We need to talk, really talk, about everything that has happened and my plans for the future. The future as in New York in three weeks with Landon.

There have been too many secrets between us, too many avoidable blowouts when said secrets were revealed in the worst way, and I don't want this to be one of those situations. It's time to be mature, get a backbone, and tell Hardin what I plan to do.

It's my life, my choice. He doesn't have to approve—no one does. But I owe it to him to at least tell him the truth before he finds out from someone else.

"We can go whenever you want," I quietly respond, ignoring Kimberly's smirk.

He smiles down at my wrinkled T-shirt and loose sweats. "You're wearing that, right?"

I didn't have time to pay attention to what I was covering myself with; I was too occupied with the idea of Kimberly's knocking on my door and catching us with no clothes on.

"Hush." I roll my eyes and walk away from him. I can hear him following me, but I close the bathroom door behind me, locking it. He tries the handle and I hear him laugh before a quiet thud sounds against the wood. The image of him hitting his head against the door makes me smile.

Without a word to him from the other side of the door, I turn the shower on and remove my clothes and step in before the water has a chance to heat.

chapter fifty-five

HARDIN

Kimberly is standing in the kitchen with her hand on her hip. How charming. "Dinner, eh?"

"Eh?" I mock her, walking past her like it's my house instead of hers. "Don't look at me like that."

Her heels click behind me. "I should have put money on how fast you would be here." She pulls the refrigerator open. "I told Christian on the way home that your car would be in our driveway."

"Yeah, yeah. I get it." I glance down the hall, hoping that Tessa makes it a quick shower, and wishing I were in the shower with her. Hell, I would be happy if she just let me sit in the bathroom, on the floor even, and listen to her talk while she bathes. I miss showering with her, I miss the way she pinches her eyes closed, too tight, and keeps them screwed shut the entire time she washes her hair—you know, "just in case" shampoo gets into her eyes.

I teased her over it once, and she opened her eyes, only to get a big puff of soap in them. I didn't hear the end of it until hours later when her eyes were finally rid of the red rings.

"What's so funny?" Kimberly places a carton of eggs on the island in front of me.

I didn't realize I was laughing; I was so consumed by the memory of Tessa's glaring and scowling at me—puffy, red eyes and all.

"Nothing." I wave Kimberly off.

The counter is being filled with every type of food imaginable, and Kimberly even slides a cup of coffee, black, in front of me.

"What's with you? You being nice to me so I won't keep re-minding your fiancé what a prick he is?" I raise the suspicious coffee cup into the air.

She laughs. "No. I'm always nice to you. I just don't take your shit like everyone else, but I'm always nice to you."

I nod, not knowing what to say next in the conversation. *Is that what's happening here? I'm having a conversation with Tessa's most obnoxious friend? The same woman who happens to be marry-ing my fuckup of a sperm donor?*

She cracks an egg on the side of a glass bowl. "I'm not so bad once you get past that whole hating-the-world thing you have going on."

I look up at her. She's annoying but she's loyal as hell, I'll give her that. Loyalty is hard to come by, even more so lately, and oddly enough I find myself thinking about Landon and how he seems to be the only person besides Tessa who's loyal to me. He's been here for me in a way that I didn't expect, and I definitely didn't expect to somewhat like it—rely on it, even.

With all this shit going on in my life and the struggle to keep myself on the right path, the path lined with fucking rainbows and flowers and all the shit that leads to a life with Tessa, it's nice to know Landon is there if I need him. He's leaving soon and that fucking sucks, but I know that even from New York City he will be loyal. He may take Tessa's side most of the time, but he's al-ways honest with me. He doesn't keep shit from me the way everyone else does.

"Plus," Kimberly starts, but bites down on her lip to stop her-self from laughing, "we're family!"

And just like that, she's back on my damn nerves.

"Funny." I roll my eyes. If I had been the one to say it, it would have been, but she just had to ruin the silence.

She turns away from me to pour the egg-batter shit into a pan on the stove. "I'm known for my humor."

Actually, you're known for your big-ass mouth, but if thinking you're funny works, fine.

"All joking aside"—she looks at me over her shoulder—"I do hope you will consider talking to Christian before you leave. He's been really upset and worried that your relationship with him is ruined permanently. I wouldn't blame you if it was; I'm just letting you know." Her eyes leave mine, and she continues cooking, allowing me time to gather a response.

Should I even give her one? "I'm not ready to talk . . . yet," I eventually say. For a second, I'm not sure if she heard me, but then she nods her head and I can see the edges of a smile when she turns to grab another ingredient.

What feels like three hours later, Tessa finally emerges from the bathroom. Her hair is dry and pulled away from her face with a thin headband. It doesn't take long to notice that she put makeup on. She could have done without the makeup, but I guess it's a good sign that she's trying to return to normalcy.

I stare at her for too long, and she shifts back and forth under my stare. I love the way she's dressed today—flat shoes, a pink tank top, and a skirt covered in flowers. Fucking beautiful, that's what she is.

"Lunch instead?" I ask, not wanting to be away from her at all today.

"Kimberly made breakfast?" she whispers to me.

"So? It's probably shitty anyway." I wave at the food covering the counter. It doesn't look bad, I guess. But she's no Karen.

"Don't say that." Tessa smiles, and I almost repeat the sentence to earn another smile.

"Fine. We will take a plate to go and then can toss it when we get outside?" I suggest.

She ignores me, but I hear her telling Kimberly to save some leftovers for us to eat later.

Hardin, 1.

Kimberly and her shitty food and annoying questions, 0.

THE DRIVE through downtown Seattle isn't as bad as usual. Tessa is quiet, like I knew she would be. I feel her eyes on me every few minutes, but every time I look at her, she quickly turns away.

For lunch, I choose a small, modern-style restaurant, and when we pull into a nearly empty lot, I know this means one of two things: either they just opened minutes ago and the crowd hasn't started yet, or the food is shit so no one eats here. Hoping for the first, we go through the glass doors and Tessa's eyes study the place. The decor is nice, whimsical, and she seems to like it, which reminds me just how much I love her reaction to the simplest things.

Hardin, 2.

Not that I'm keeping score or anything . . .

But if I were . . . I'd be winning.

We sit in silence while we wait to place our orders. The waiter is a young college kid who's nervous and has some sort of eye-contact issue. He doesn't seem to want to look into my eyes, the asshole.

Tessa orders something that I've never heard of, and I order the first thing I see on the menu that I have. A pregnant woman is seated at the table next to us, and I watch Tessa stare at the woman for just a beat too long.

"Hey." I clear my throat to get her attention. "I don't know if you even remember what I said last night, but if you do, I'm sorry. When I said I didn't want a baby with you, I just meant I don't want kids at all. But who knows"—my heart begins to pound against my ribs—"maybe one day or something."

I can't believe I just said that, and by Tessa's expression, she can't either. Her mouth is wide-open and her hand is in the air, holding her glass of water.

"What?" She blinks. "What did you just say?"

Why did I say that? I mean, I meant it. I think. I could maybe think about it. I don't like kids or babies or teenagers, but then again, I don't like adults either. I pretty much only like Tessa, so maybe a little version of her wouldn't be so bad?

"I'm just saying, maybe it wouldn't be so bad?" I shrug, hiding the panic inside me.

Her mouth is still open. I'm beginning to think that I should lean across and hold her jaw for her.

"Obviously not anytime soon. I'm no idiot. I know you have to finish college and all that shit."

"But you . . ." I've shocked her out of words apparently.

"I know what I said before, but I also never dated anyone, never loved anyone, never gave a shit about anyone, so I think this could be like that. I think after some time, I could change my mind. If you'll give me the chance?"

I allow her a few seconds to collect herself, but she just sits there, mouth open, eyes wide.

"I still have work to do; you still don't trust me, I know that. We have college to finish, and I still have to convince you to marry me first." I'm rambling, searching for something that will catch her and make her mine in this moment. "Not that we have to be married first; I'm no gentleman." A nervous laugh leaves my mouth, which finally seems to snap Tessa back into reality.

"We couldn't," she says, all color drained from her face.

"We could."

"No—"

I hold my hand up to keep her quiet. "We *could*, though. I love you and I want a life with you. I don't give a shit if you're young and I'm young, and if I'm too wrong for you and you're too right for me—I fucking love you. I know I've made mistakes . . ." I run my hand over my hair.

I glance around the small restaurant, and I'm fully aware that the pregnant lady is staring at me. *Doesn't she have a baby thing to do? Eat for two? Pump some milk?* I don't have a clue, but she's making me nervous for some reason, like she's judging me and she's pregnant and it's just plain fucking weird. Why did I choose a public place to spill this shit?

"And I also know that I've said this same speech probably . . . thirty times, but you have to know I'm not fucking around anymore. I want you, always. Fights, makeups, hell, you can even break up with me and move out of our place once a week; just promise me you'll come back, and I won't even complain about it." I take a few breaths and look across the table at her. "Well, I won't complain *much.*"

"Hardin, I can't believe you're saying all of this." She leans in, her voice a whisper. "I . . . it's everything I wanted." Her eyes fill with tears. Happy tears, I hope. "But we can't have children together. We aren't even—"

"I know." I can't help but interrupt her. "I know you haven't forgiven me yet, and I'll be patient. I swear it—I won't be too pushy. I just want you to know that I can be who you need, I can give you what you want, and not only because you want it, but because I want it, too."

She opens her mouth to respond, but the goddamn waiter returns with our food. He sits the steaming plate of whatever the hell Tessa ordered and my burger in front of us and lingers there awkwardly.

"Do you need something?" I snap at him. It's not his fault that I'm pouring out my hopes of a future to this woman and he's interrupting, but he's here and he's wasting my time with her by standing here.

"No, sir. Do you need anything else?" he asks, cheeks red.

"No, thank you so much for asking." Tessa smiles up at him, easing his embarrassment and making up for my asshole tendencies. He returns a smile to her and finally disappears.

"Anyway, I was basically just saying everything that I should have said a long time ago. Sometimes I forget that you can't hear my thoughts, you don't know all the things I think about you. I wish you did; you would love me more if you did."

"I don't think it would be possible for me to love you more than I do." She twists her fingers in her hands.

"Really?" I smile at her, and she nods.

"But I need to tell you something. I don't know how you'll take it." Her voice catches at the end, making me panic. I know she's given up on us, but I can change her mind; I know I can. I feel a determination that I never felt before, never knew existed.

"Go on," I force myself to say as neutrally as possible, then take a bite of the burger. It's the only way to keep my damn mouth shut.

"You know I went to the doctor."

Images of her crying while mumbling about her doctor fill my head.

"Is everything still okay over here?" the fucking waiter asks, popping over. "How's everything taste? Would you like more water, miss?"

Is he fucking serious?

"We are fine," I growl at him—literally growl, like a rabid fucking dog. He pisses off, and Tessa lifts her finger to her empty glass.

"Shit. Here." I slide mine over to her, and she smiles, then gulps the water down. "You were saying?"

"We can talk about it later." She takes the first bite of her food since it arrived in front of her.

"Oh, no you don't. I know this trick, I invented this trick. After you get some food into your belly, you'll tell me. Please."

She takes another bite, trying to distract me, but, nope, it's not going to work. I want to know what her doctor said and why it's making her act so strange. If we weren't in public, it would be much easier to get her to talk. I don't give a shit about making a scene, but I know she will be embarrassed, so I'll play nice. I can do this. I can balance being nice and cooperative and not feel like a total fucking tool.

I let her get away with another five minutes of silence, and soon she's picking at her food aimlessly.

"Are you finished?"

"It's . . ." She glances down at the plate full of food.

"What?"

"It's not very good," she whispers, looking around to be sure no one can hear.

I laugh. "Is that what has you all flushed and whispering?"

"Hush." She swats at the air between us. "I'm so hungry, but the food's so *bad*. I don't even know what it is. I just pointed at something because I was nervous."

"I'll tell them you want something else."

I get to my feet, and she reaches across to grab my arm. "No, it's okay. I'm ready to go."

"Cool. We'll just hit a drive-through and get something for you, and you can tell me what the hell is going on in that head of yours. It's driving me insane guessing."

She nods, looking a little insane herself.

chapter fifty-six

HARDIN

One drive-through taco joint later, Tessa is full and my patience is withering with each silent moment between us.

"I freaked you out talking about kids, didn't I? I know I'm laying a lot of shit on you at once, but I've spent the last eight months keeping shit in, and I don't want to do that anymore."

I want to tell her the crazy shit inside my head—I want to tell her that I want to stare at the cheesy way the sun hits her hair in the passenger seat until I can't see anymore. I want to listen to her moan and close her eyes when she takes a bite of a taco—that I swear tastes like cardboard but she loves—until I can't hear anymore. I want to tease her about the spot just below her knee—that she always misses when she shaves her legs—until I lose my voice.

"It's not that," she interrupts me, and I look up from staring at her legs.

"Then what is it? Let me guess: you are already questioning marriage; now you don't want kids either?"

"No, that's not it."

"I fucking hope not, because you know damn well you'll make the best mum ever."

She whimpers, holding her hands over her stomach. "I can't."

"We can."

"No, Hardin, I *can't*." The way her eyes look down at her belly and her hands makes me thankful we are parked; I would have swerved off the damn road.

The doctor, the crying, the wine, the freaking out about Karen and her baby, the constant "can't" from today.

"You can't . . ." I understand exactly what she means. "It's because of me, isn't it? I did something to you, didn't I?" I don't know what I could have done, but that's the way this works: something bad happens to Tessa because of something I did, always.

"No, no. You didn't do anything. It's something inside of me that isn't right." Her lips tremble.

"Oh." I wish I could say something else, something better, anything, really.

"Yeah." She rubs her hand over the bottom of her stomach, and I can feel the air disappearing from the small space of my car.

As fucked-up as it is, as fucked-up as I am, my chest feels like it's caving in, and little brown-haired girls with blue-gray eyes, little blond boys with green eyes, little bonnet things and tiny socks with little animals—all kinds of shit that used to make me want to vomit repeatedly—swirl through my mind, and I feel dizzy as they are torn away, tossed into the air, and carried off to wherever ruined futures go to die.

"It's possible, I mean, there's a very slim chance. And there would be a high risk for miscarriage, and my hormone levels are all messed up, so I don't think I could ever torture myself by trying. I wouldn't be able to handle losing a baby, or trying for years with no result. It's just not in the cards for me to be a mother, I guess." She's spitting this shit out, trying to make me feel better, but it's not convincing me, not making her seem like she has it under control when it's obvious that she doesn't.

She's looking at me, expecting me to say something, but I can't. I don't know what to say to her, and I can't help the anger I feel toward her. It's fucking stupid and selfish and absolutely fucking wrong, but it's there, and I'm terrified that if I open my mouth, I will say something I shouldn't.

If I weren't such an asshole, I would comfort her. I would hold her and tell her it will be okay, that we don't need to have kids, we can adopt or something, anything.

But this is how reality works: men aren't literary heroes, they don't change overnight, and no one does anything right here in the real world. I'm no Darcy and she's no Elizabeth.

She's on the verge of tears when she squeaks out, "Say something?"

"I don't know what to say." My voice is barely audible, and my throat is closing. I feel like I've swallowed a handful of bees.

"You didn't want kids anyway, right? I didn't think it would make such a difference . . ." If I look over, I will find her crying.

"I didn't think so, but now that it's been taken away—"

"*Oh.*"

I'm thankful for that, because who knows what the fuck would have come out next.

"You can just take me back to the . . ."

I nod and put the car into drive. It's fucked-up how something you never wanted can hurt this way.

"I'm sorry, I just . . ." I stop; neither of us seems to be able to finish a sentence.

"It's okay, I understand." She leans into the window. I suspect that she's trying to get as far away from me as she can.

My emotions are telling me to comfort her, to think of her and how this is affecting her and how she feels about it.

But my head is strong, so fucking strong, and I'm pissed. Not at her, but her body and her mum for whatever she was born with that doesn't work right. I'm pissed at the world for slapping me in the damn face again, and I'm pissed at myself for not being able to say anything to her as we drive through the city.

* * *

A FEW MINUTES LATER, I realize that the silence is so loud it hurts. Tessa's trying to stay quiet on her side of the car, but I can hear her breathing, the way she's trying to control it, to control her emotions.

My chest is so fucking tight, and she's just sitting there, letting my words stew in her mind. Why do I always do this shit to her? I always say the wrong thing no matter how many times I promise that I won't. No matter how many times I promise that I will change, I always do this. I pull away and leave her to deal with the shit herself.

Not again. I can't do it again; she needs me more than ever, and this is my chance to show her that I can be here the way she needs.

Tessa doesn't look at me as I turn the wheel and pull over to the side of the highway. I turn my hazard lights on and hope that a damn cop doesn't come and start shit.

"Tess." I attempt to get her attention while I scramble through my thoughts. She doesn't look up from her hands in her lap. "Tessa, please look at me." I reach my hand across the console to touch her, but she jerks away and her hand smacks against the door loudly.

"Hey." I take off my seat belt and turn toward her, taking both of her wrists into one of my hands, the way I do so often.

"I'm fine." She raises her chin slightly to prove her point, but the moisture in her eyes tells another story. "You shouldn't be parked here; this is a busy highway."

"I don't give a shit about where I am parked. I'm fucked-up, my head isn't right." I stumble for the words to make sense. "I am so sorry. I shouldn't have reacted like that."

After a few beats she lowers her eyes to me, staring at my face but avoiding my eyes.

"Tess, don't shut down again, please. I'm so sorry, I don't

know what I was thinking. I never even considered having kids anyway, and here I am, making you feel bad for this shit." The confession sounds even worse as the words fall between us.

"You're allowed to be upset, too," she quietly responds. "I just needed you to say something, *anything* . . ." The last word is so low that it's barely audible.

"I don't care that you can't have kids," I blurt. *Fucking hell.* "I mean, I don't care about our kids that we can't have."

I'm trying to rub salve onto the wound I've created, but her expression lets me know I'm doing the opposite.

"What I'm trying—and utterly fucking failing to accomplish—to say is that I love you, and I'm an insensitive prick for not being present for you just now. I put myself first, as always, and I'm sorry." My words seem to pull her out of herself, and she brings her eyes to mine.

"Thank you." She pulls one of her wrists from my hand, and I hesitate to let it go, but I'm relieved when she raises her hand to wipe her eyes. "I'm sorry that you feel like I took something from you."

But I can tell she has more to say. "Don't hold back. I know you; say what you need to say."

"I hate the way you reacted," she huffs.

"I know I'm—"

She puts a hand in the air. "I wasn't finished." Tessa clears her throat. "I have wanted to be a mother since I can remember. I was just like every other girl with her dolls, maybe more so. Being a mother was so important to me. I never, ever questioned or worried that I may not be able to be one."

"I know, I—"

"Please, let me *talk*." She grinds her teeth.

I really should shut up, for once. Instead of responding, I nod and stay silent.

"I'm feeling this incredible loss right now. And I don't have the energy to worry about you blaming me. It's okay for you to feel the loss, too; I want you to always be open with how you feel, but you haven't had any of *your* dreams crushed here. You didn't want children until ten minutes ago, and so I don't find it fair for you to be this way."

I wait a few seconds and raise a brow at her, seeking her permission to speak. She nods, but then the loud horn of a semi blares through the air, making her nearly jump out of the car.

"I'm going to drive back to Vance's," I say. "But I would like to come in and be with you."

Tessa looks out of the window but gives me a small nod.

"I mean, in a comforting way, like I should have been."

With a gesture just as slight as her nod, I catch her rolling her eyes.

chapter fifty-seven

TESSA

Hardin shares an awkward glance with Vance as we pass him in the hallway. It's strange, having Hardin here with me after everything that has happened. I can't ignore the effort and restraint he's showing by coming to this house, Vance's house.

It's hard to focus on just one of the many problems that have cropped up of late: Hardin's behavior in London, Vance and Trish, my father's death, my fertility issues.

It's too much, and it seems never ending.

In a way, the relief I feel after telling Hardin about the infertility is huge, massive.

But there's always something else waiting to be revealed or thrown at one of us.

And New York is that next thing.

I don't know if I should just say it now, now that we already have an issue between us. I hate the way Hardin reacted, but I'm thankful for the remorse he showed after his callous dismissal of my feelings. If he wouldn't have pulled the car over and apologized, I don't think I could have found it in myself to speak to him again.

I can't count the times that I've said, thought, sworn, those words since I met him. I owe it to myself to think that I meant them this time.

"What are you thinking?" he asks, closing my bedroom door behind him.

Without hesitation, I answer honestly, "That I wouldn't speak to you again."

"What?" He steps toward me, and I back away from him.

"If you wouldn't have apologized, I wouldn't have anything to say to you."

He sighs, running his hand over his hair. "I know."

I can't stop thinking of what he said: *"I didn't think so, but now that it's been taken away . . ."*

I'm still in shock from it; I'm sure of it. I never expected to hear those words from him. It didn't seem possible that he would change his mind; then again, true to the dysfunction of our relationship, his mind was only changed after tragedy.

"Come here." Hardin's arms open to me, and I hesitate. "Please, let me comfort you the way I should have. Let me talk to you and listen to you. I'm sorry."

Per usual, I'm stepping into his arms. They feel different now, more solid, more real than before. He tightens his embrace around my body, resting his cheek against the top of my head. His hair, too long on the sides now, tickles my skin, and I feel him place a kiss onto my hair.

"Tell me how you feel about all of this. Tell me everything you haven't told me about it," he says, pulling me to sit next to him on the bed. I cross my legs, and he leans his back against the headboard.

I tell him everything. I tell him about my first appointment to get on birth control. I tell him that I have known about the possibility of a problem since before we left for London. His jaw tenses when I tell him that I didn't want him to know, and his fists clench when I tell him that I was afraid he would be happy. He stays quiet and nods along until I tell him that I was going to keep it from him permanently.

He pulls himself up on his elbows to move closer to me. "Why? Why would you that?"

"I thought you would be happy, and I didn't want to hear that." I shrug. "I would have rather kept it to myself than hear how relieved you were about it."

"If you would have told me before London, things could have gone differently."

I snap eyes to him. "Yeah—worse, I'm sure." I hope he isn't taking this where I think he will; he better not be attempting to blame the mess in London on me.

He seems to be thinking it over before speaking—another improvement on his part. "You're right. You know you are right."

"I'm glad I kept it to myself, especially before I knew for sure."

"I'm glad you told me before anyone else." His eyes are on mine.

"I told Kim." I feel slightly guilty that he had assumed he was the first person that I told, but he wasn't there for me.

Hardin's brows knit together. "What do you mean, you told Kim? When?"

"I told her it was a possibility a while ago."

"So Kim knew and I didn't?"

"Yes." I nod.

"What about Landon? Does Landon know, too? Karen? Vance?"

"Why would Vance know?" I snap at him. He's back to being ridiculous.

"Kimberly probably told him. Did you tell Landon, too?"

"No, Hardin. Only Kimberly. I had to tell someone, and I couldn't depend on you enough to tell you."

"Ouch." His tone is harsh and his frown overwhelming.

"It's true," I quietly say. "I know you don't want to hear it, but it's true. You seem to forget that you didn't want anything to do with me until my father died."

chapter fifty-eight

HARDIN

Didn't want anything to do with her? I've loved this girl with every ounce of me for so long. I hate that she feels this way, that she has forgotten how deep my love for her is and has reduced it to this one fuckup of mine. Not that I can blame her. It is my fault that she feels this way. "I always wanted you; you know that. I just couldn't stop trying to ruin the only good thing in my life, and I'm sorry for that. I know it's fucked-up that it took me so long, and I hate that it took your dad dying to get my ass in shape, but I'm here now—and I love you more than ever, and I don't care if we can't have babies." Desperate, not liking the look in her eyes, I impulsively add, "Marry me."

She glares at me. "Hardin, you can't just throw that around like that—stop saying that!" Her arms cover her chest as if she's protecting herself from my words.

"Fine, I'll buy you a ring firs—"

"Hardin," she warns, lips pressed together in a tight line.

"Fine." I roll my eyes at her, and I think she wants to slap me. "I am so in love with you," I promise, and reach for her.

"Yeah, now you are." She backs away, challenging me.

"I've been in love with you for a long time."

"Sure you have," Tessa mumbles. How can she be so fucking cute and obnoxious at the same time?

"I loved you even when I was being a dumb-ass in London."

"You didn't show it, and it doesn't matter how much you say

it if you don't remotely show it or make me feel the truth in your words."

"I know, I was high out of my mind." I pick at the annoying fraying fabric on my cast. *How many more weeks until this thing is off?*

"You let her wear your shirt after you had sex with her." Tessa looks away from me, focusing her eyes on the wall behind me.

What? "What are you talking about?" I gently press my thumb under her chin to force her to look at me.

"That girl, Mark's sister. Janine, I think I heard someone say?"

I gape. "You think I fucked her? I *told* you I didn't. I didn't touch anyone in London."

"You say that, and yet you practically waved the condom in front of my face."

"I didn't fuck her, Tessa. Look at me." I try to convince her, but she turns away again. "I know what it looked like . . ."

"It looked like she was *wearing your shirt.*"

I hate the way Janine looked in my shirt, but she simply wouldn't shut her damn mouth until I gave it to her.

"I know she was, but I didn't fuck her. Are you that deluded that you think I would do that?" My heart is racing at the idea that I've let her walk around for the last few weeks with this bull-shit in her head. I should have realized our previous conversation didn't end it.

"She was all over you, Hardin—in front of me!"

"She kissed me and tried to blow me, but that's it."

Tessa makes a small noise and closes her eyes.

"I didn't even get hard for her, only for you," I say to try and explain better, but she shakes her head and holds her hand up for me to stop.

"Stop talking about her, I'll get sick." I know she means it.

"I got sick, too. I threw up all over the place after she touched me."

"You *what*?" Tessa stares at me.

"I literally vomited, as in I had to run to the bathroom because I got sick from her touching me. I couldn't bear it."

"You did?" I wonder if I should be worried about the small smile tugging at the corners of her lips as I tell her about my vomit experience.

"Yes, I did." I smile at her, trying to lighten the mood. "Don't look so happy about it," I say, but if it shifts her mood, I'm all for it.

"Good. I hope you were *really* sick." Her smile is full now.

We are the most fucked-up couple.

Fucked-up but perfect, that is.

"I was!" I say, seizing the moment. "So fucking sick. I'm sorry that you thought that this whole time. No wonder you were pissed at me." It sort of makes sense now; then again, she's always pissed at me lately. "Now that you know I didn't fuck around on you"—I raise a sarcastic brow—"will you take me back and let me make an honest woman out of you?"

She cocks her head at me. "You promised you would stop throwing that at me."

"I didn't promise. The word *promise* was never used."

She's going to slap me any minute.

"Are you going to tell anyone else about the baby shit?" I say to change the subject, sort of.

"No." She pulls her lip between her teeth. "I don't think so. Not anytime soon."

"No one has to know until we adopt in a few years. I'm sure there are loads of damn babies waiting for parents to buy them. We will be fine."

I know she hasn't accepted my offer of marriage, or even being in a relationship with me, but I hope she doesn't use this opportunity to remind me of that.

She laughs softly. "Damn babies? Please tell me you don't

think there is a store somewhere downtown where you walk in and purchase a baby?" She lifts her hand to her mouth to stop herself from laughing at me.

"There isn't?" I joke. "What's Babies 'R' Us, then?"

"Oh my goodness!" She tilts her head back in laughter.

I reach across the small space between us and grab hold of her hand. "If that damn store isn't full of babies, lined up, ready for purchase, than I'm suing for false advertisement."

I pull my best smirk out at her, and she sighs, relieved to be laughing. I know this somehow. I know exactly what she's thinking.

"You need help." She pulls her hand out of mine and stands.

"Yeah." I watch her smile fade. "Yeah, I do."

chapter fifty-nine

HARDIN

"You two travel across the state of Washington more than anyone else I know," Landon says, looking up from the couch in my father's living room.

After our laughter broke back down into silence, I'd convinced Tessa that we should come back east and hang out with Landon before he leaves for good. I had thought she would immediately be ready for that—she loves hanging out with Landon, after all—but she sat quietly for a few uncomfortable moments before agreeing. I waited on her bed while, for some reason, she packed up basically everything she had, and then I waited in the car as she engaged in far too long of a goodbye to Kimberly and Vance.

I give Landon a flat-eyed stare. "You don't know many people, so I don't know how relevant that is," I tease.

He glances at his mum, sitting on the chair, and I know he wants to say some smart-ass comment to me, and if she weren't sitting there, he sure as hell would. He's gotten better at the comebacks lately.

Instead he just rolls his eyes, says, "Ha-ha," and goes back to the book on his lap.

"I'm glad you guys made it safe. The rain is heavy and only supposed to get worse by the end of the night." Karen's voice is soft as she smiles at me, causing me to look away. "Dinner is already in the oven; it will be ready soon."

"I'm going to change," Tessa says from behind me. "Thank you for letting me stay here again." She disappears up the stairs.

I stand at the bottom of the staircase for a few seconds before following her like a puppy. When I enter her room, she's dressed in only a bra and panties.

"Good timing, self," I mumble when she looks up at me in the doorway.

She uses her hands to cover her chest, then moves them down to her hips, and I can't help but smile. "It's a little late for that, don't you think?"

"Hush," she scolds me, and pulls a dry shirt down over her rain-damp hair.

"You know hushing isn't my strong point."

"And what is, exactly?" she taunts me, shaking her hips as she pulls a pair of pants up to her stomach. *Those* pants.

"You haven't worn those yoga things in a while . . ." I rub the stubble on my jaw and stare at the tight, black material that she seems to be poured into.

"Do not start on these pants." She waves a sassy finger at me. "You hid them from me; that's why I haven't worn them." She smiles but seems surprised by her easy humor with me. She hardens her stare at me and straightens her back.

"Did not," I lie, wondering when she found them in our closet at that damn apartment. Looking at her ass in them, I remember why I hid them. "They were in the closet."

As soon as I say that, images of Tessa scrambling through that closet looking for her pants make me laugh, until I remember something else in there that I didn't want her to find.

I look at her, searching her face for any indication that my mention of the closet reminds her that she found that damn box.

"What?" she asks, pushing her feet into a pair of pink socks. Hideous, fuzzy things with polka dots covering the top of her feet.

"Nothing," I lie, shrugging my paranoia off.

"Okay . . ." She wanders off.

I follow her downstairs, again like a puppy, and sit next to her at the massive dining-room table. That S-girl is here again, staring at Landon like he's some kind of brilliant jewel or something. This clearly qualifies her as a weirdo.

Tessa beams at the woman. "Hey, Sophia."

Sophia takes her eyes away from Landon only long enough to smile back at Tessa and wave to me.

"Sophia helped with the ham," Karen exclaims proudly. The large dining table is set with a massive feast, with lit candles and flower arrangements. We make small talk while we wait for Karen and Sophia to cut the ham.

"Mhm, it's so good. The sauce is really good," Tessa moans around her fork.

These women and their damn food. "You would think you guys are talking about porn," I say, much too loud.

Tessa kicks my foot under the table, and Karen covers her mouth and coughs around her mouthful of food. Everyone's surprised when Sophia laughs. Landon looks uncomfortable, but his expression softens when he notices how hard she's laughing.

"Who *says* that?" she giggles.

Landon is pathetically staring at her, and Tessa is smiling now.

"Hardin. Hardin says stuff like that." Karen smiles, humor in her eyes.

Okay, this is weird.

"You'll get used to him." Landon briefly looks at me before focusing back on his new infatuation. "I mean, if you're around a lot. Not that you will be around a lot." His cheeks are bright red. "If you wanted to be, I mean. Not that you would want to be."

"She gets it." I put him out of his misery, and he looks like he's going to piss himself.

"I do." She smiles at Landon, and I swear his face turns from red to purple. Poor thing.

"Sophia, how long are you in town for?" Tessa chimes in, changing the subject in a sweet way to help her friend.

"Only a few more days. I leave to go back to New York this coming Monday. My roommates are dying for me to get back."

"How many roommates do you have?" Tessa asks.

"Three, all dancers."

I laugh.

Tessa smiles a forced smile. "Oh, wow."

"Oh gosh! Ballet dancers, not strippers." Sarah bursts into laughter, and I join her, only to laugh at Tessa's relief and embarrassed expression.

Tessa carries most of the conversation, asking random shit about the woman, and I zone them both out, only focusing on the curve of Tessa's lips as she talks. I love the way she stops every few bites and primly rubs a napkin against her lips, just in case she's got something on her.

Dinner continues this way until I'm bored, nearly to death, and Landon's face is only a little red.

"Hardin, have you decided on graduation? I know you declined to walk, but have you given it further thought?" Ken asks while Karen, Tessa, and Sarah clear the table.

"Nope, haven't changed my mind." I pick at my teeth with my fingernail. He keeps doing this, bringing this shit up in front of Tessa to bully me into walking across the stuffy auditorium where thousands of people will be crammed into bleachers, sweating profusely and howling like wild animals.

"You haven't?" Tessa asks. I look back and forth between her and my father. "I thought maybe you would reconsider?" She knows exactly what she's doing.

Landon is grinning like the asshole he is, and Karen and the S-girl are chatting away in the kitchen.

"I . . ." I begin. *Fucking hell.* Tessa's eyes are hopeful yet edgy, almost daring me to deny the idea. "Yeah, sure, fine. I'll fucking walk for graduation," I huff. This is such bullshit.

"Thank you," Ken says. As I'm about to tell him that he's fucking welcome, I realize that he's thanking Tessa, not me.

"You two are so . . ." I begin, but am silenced by the warning in Tessa's expression. "You two are so wonderful," I say instead.

You two are conniving little shits, I repeat in my head, over and over, as they share a smug grin.

chapter sixty

TESSA

Every single time Sophia talked about New York during dinner, I began to panic. I'm the one who brought it up, I know. But I was only trying to take the attention away from Landon. I knew he was embarrassed, and I said the first thing that came to my mind. It just so happened to be the one topic that I shouldn't have mentioned in front of Hardin.

I need to tell him tonight. I'm being a ridiculous, immature coward by keeping this from him. The progress he has made within himself will either help him handle the news well, or he will explode. I never know what to expect from him; it could go either way. But I do know both that I'm not personally responsible for his emotional reactions to things and that I owe it to him to tell him myself.

Leaning against the doorway of the dining room, standing in the hallway, I watch Karen wipe the top of the stove with a wet cloth. Ken has moved to the chair in the living room and is now asleep. Landon and Sophia are sitting at the dining-room table in silence. Landon attempts to sneak a glance at the woman, and when she looks up at him, she catches his eyes on hers and shows him her beautiful smile.

I'm not sure how I feel about this, with him so fresh out of a long-term relationship and already on to someone else. Then again, who am I to have any opinions on the relationships of others? I clearly have no freaking clue how to navigate my own.

From my vantage point here in the passway that connects the living room, dining room, and kitchen, I have the most perfect picture of the people who mean the most to me in the world. This includes the most important, Hardin, who sits quietly on the couch in the living room, staring blankly at the wall.

I smile at the idea of his walking during his graduation in June. I can't imagine him in a cap and gown, but it's certainly something that I am looking forward to seeing, and I know that it meant so much to Ken that he agreed to do it. Ken has made it clear on multiple occasions that he never expected Hardin to graduate from college, and now that the truth of their past is out in the open, I'm sure that Ken never expected Hardin to change his mind and go along with the typical graduation ritual. Hardin Scott is anything but typical.

I press my fingers to my forehead, willing my brain to function properly. *How should I bring it up now? What if he offers to come along to New York? Would he do that? If he does offer, should I agree?*

Suddenly I can feel his eyes on me from where he sits in the living room, and sure enough, when I look over at him, he's studying me, his green eyes curious, his soft mouth pressed into a soft line. I give him my best "I'm okay, just thinking" smile and watch as he frowns and gets up. In a few long strides, he's across the room and leaning with one of his palms pressed against the wall for support while he hovers over me.

"What is it?" he asks.

Landon's head lifts from his focus on Sophia at the sound of Hardin's loud voice.

"I need to talk to you about something," I quietly admit. He doesn't look concerned—not as concerned as he should be.

"Okay, what is it?" He leans closer, too close, and I try to step away, only to be reminded that he has me cornered against the wall. Hardin raises his other arm to completely block me in, and when my eyes meet his, an obvious smirk covers his face. "Well?" he presses.

I stare at him in silence. My mouth is dry now, and when I open it to speak, I begin to cough. It's always that way it seems, in a quiet movie theater, in church, or while having a conversation with someone important. Basically in situations where coughs don't fit in. Like right now for example, I'm having an inner rambling session about coughing, while coughing, and while Hardin stares at me like I'm dying in front of him.

He pulls back and walks into the kitchen with purpose. He moves around Karen and returns to me with a glass of water for what feels like the thirtieth time in the last two weeks. I take it, and I'm relieved when the cool water calms my itchy throat.

I'm aware that even my body is trying to back out of breaking this news to Hardin, and I want to pat myself on the back and kick myself in the chin at the same time. If I did that, I assume Hardin would feel a little sorry for me due to my insane behavior and possibly change the subject.

"What is going on? Your mind is moving a mile a minute." He looks down at me, holding his hand out for the empty glass. When I begin to shake my head, he insists, "No, no, I can tell."

"Can we go outside?" I turn toward the patio door, trying to make it clear that we shouldn't talk in front of an audience. Heck, we should probably drive back to Seattle to discuss this mess. Or farther. Farther is good.

"Outside? Why?"

"I want to talk to you about something. In private."

"Fine, sure."

I take a step in front of him to keep the balance. If I lead the way outside, then I may have a better chance to lead the conversation. If I lead the conversation, then I may have a better chance of not allowing Hardin to steamroll the entire thing. Maybe.

I don't pull my hand from Hardin's when I feel his fingers lace into mine. It's so quiet—only the soft sound of the voices from the crime show Ken fell asleep watching, and the low rumbling of the dishwasher in the kitchen.

When we step onto the deck, those sounds dissolve, and I'm left alone with the sound of my chaotic thoughts and Hardin's low humming. I'm grateful for whatever song he's quietly filling the air with, but it's distracting and helps me focus on something outside of the blowup that is sure to come. If I'm lucky, I will have a few minutes to explain myself and my decision before he goes nova.

"Spill," Hardin says as he drags one of the patio chairs across the wood of the deck.

There goes my chance at having him calm for a few minutes; he's not in a waiting mood. He sits down and rests his elbows on the table between us. I scramble to sit across from him and struggle with where to place my hands. I move them from the top of the table to my lap, to my knees, and back to the table before he reaches across and flattens his palm across my fidgeting fingers.

"Relax," he softly says. His hand is warm, and it completely covers mine, giving me a sliver of clarity, if only for a moment.

"I have been keeping something from you, and it's driving me insane. I need to tell you now, and I know this isn't the time, but you have to know before you find out another way."

He lifts his hand from mine and leans against the back of the chair. "What did you do?" I can hear the anxiety in his tone, the suspicion in his controlled breath.

"Nothing," I hastily remark. "Nothing like what you are assuming."

"You haven't . . ." He blinks a few times. "You weren't . . . with anyone else, were you?"

"No!" My voice squeaks, and I shake my head to prove my point. "No, nothing like that. I've just made a decision about something and have kept it from you. It doesn't involve me being with anyone else."

I'm not sure if I am relieved or offended that this was his first thought. In a way, I'm relieved, because moving to New York couldn't possibly be as painful for him as my being with another man, but I'm slightly offended, because he should know me better than that by now. I've done my share of irresponsible, hurtful things to him, involving Zed mostly, but I would never sleep with someone else.

"Okay." He rubs his hand over his hair and rests his curved palm over the back of his neck, massaging the muscles there. "It couldn't be that bad, then."

I take a breath, deciding to just throw it onto the table, no more dancing around the subject. "Well—"

He holds a hand up to stop me. "Wait. How about before you tell me what it is, you tell me why."

"Why what?" I tilt my head in confusion.

He raises a brow to me. "Why you made whatever choice you're pissing yourself over about."

"Okay." I nod. I sift through my thoughts while he watches me with patient eyes. Where should I begin? This is much harder than simply telling him that I'm moving, but it's a much better way to communicate the news to him.

Now that I think about it, I don't think we've ever done this. Anytime some big, dramatic thing was happening, we always found out from other sources in that same big, dramatic way.

I glance at him one last time before I begin to speak. I want to take in every inch of his face, remember and study the way his green eyes can appear so patient at times. I notice the way the soft pink of his lips appears so inviting now, but I also remember the times when they were split open on one side, straight down the middle, blood pouring from the gashes from fighting. I remember his piercing there, and how it grew on me so quickly.

I relive the way it felt when the cool metal would brush across my lip. I focus on thinking back to the way he would pull it between his own lips whenever he was deep in thought, and how it just looked so tempting.

I think back to the night when he took me ice-skating in his attempt to prove that he could be a "normal" boyfriend to me. He was nervous and playful and had taken out both of his piercings. He claimed that he did it because he wanted to, but still, to this day, I think he removed them to prove something to himself and to me. I missed them for a while—I still do sometimes—but I sort of loved what their absence represented, no matter how undeniably sexy they looked on him.

"Hardin to Tessa: Care to share?" he teases, and leans up and rests his chin in the palm of one hand.

"Yes." I smile nervously. "Well, I made the decision because we need time apart, and it seemed like the only way to be sure that actually happens."

"Time apart, huh? Still?" His eyes set on mine, pressuring me to back down.

"Yes, time apart. Everything is such a mess between us, and I needed to put distance between us—really this time. I know we say that all the time, we do this little song and dance around everything, and we drive back and forth from Seattle to here, and then London got thrown into the mix; we are basically spreading our mess of a relationship across the globe." I pause for his reaction, and receiving only an indecipherable expression, I finally tear my eyes from his.

"Is it really that much of a mess?" Hardin's voice is soft.

"We fight more than we get along."

"That isn't true." He tugs at the collar of his black T-shirt. "Technically and literally, that isn't true, Tess. It may feel that way, but when you think back over all the bullshit we've gone through, we've spent more time laughing and talking, reading, teasing, and in bed, of course. I mean, I take a *long* time in bed." He smiles a small smile, and I can feel my resolve weakening.

"We solve everything with sex, and that's not healthy," I say, pushing my next point.

"Sex isn't healthy?" he scoffs. "We are having consensual sex, full of love and full of fucking trust." He looks at me with intensity. "Yeah, it also doubles as amazing, mind-blowing fucking sex, but don't forget why we do it. I don't fuck you just to get off. I do it because I love you, and I love the trust you place in me when you allow me to touch you in that way."

Everything he is saying is making sense, despite that it shouldn't. I agree with him, no matter how cautious I try to be.

I feel New York City slipping farther and farther away, so I decide to drop the bomb sooner rather than later: "Have you ever looked into the signs of an abusive relationship?"

"Abusive?" He sounds as if he's gasping for air. "You find me *abusive*? I've never laid a hand on you, and I never would!"

I stare down at my hands and press forward with the honesty. "No, that's not what I meant. I was referring to both of us and the way we do things to purposely hurt each other. I wasn't accusing you of being physically abusive."

He sighs and runs both hands over his hair, a sure sign he's starting to panic. "Okay, so this is obviously much more than some stupid decision to not live with me in Seattle or something." Then he stops and looks at me with a deathly seriousness. "Tessa, I'm going to ask you something, and I want your real honest answer—no bullshit, no thinking about it. Just say what comes to your mind when I ask, okay?"

I nod, unsure where he is going with this.

"What's the worst thing I've done to you? What's the most disgusting, terrible thing that I've put you through since we met?"

I begin to think through the last eight months, but he clears his throat, reminding me that he wanted me to say the first thing that came to mind.

I fidget in the chair, not wanting to open that vault right now, or anytime in the future, really. But finally I spit it out. "The bet. The fact that you had me completely fooled when I was falling in love with you."

Hardin appears thoughtful, lost for a moment. "Would you take it back? Would you change that mistake of mine if you could?"

I take my time to think this through, really think this through before answering. I've answered this question before, many times, and I've changed my mind even more than that, but now the answer feels so . . . final. It feels so final and certain, and it just feels like it matters more now than ever before.

The sun is moving lower in the sky, hiding behind the thick trees lining the Scotts' property, activating the automatic patio lights.

"No. I wouldn't take it back," I say, mostly to myself.

Hardin nods as if he knew exactly what my response would be. "Okay, so next to that, what is the worst thing I've done?"

"When you ruined that apartment for me in Seattle," I answer easily.

"Really?" He sounds surprised by my response.

"Yes."

"Why that? What was it about me doing that that pissed you off so bad?"

"The fact that you completely took control of a decision that was mine and you hid it from me."

He nods, then shrugs. "I won't try to justify that shit, because I know it was fucked-up."

"Okay?" I hope he has more to say on that.

"I do understand where you are coming from with that. I shouldn't have done that; I should have talked to you instead of trying to keep you from going to Seattle. I was fucked in the head at the time, still am, but I'm trying, and that's something different than before."

I'm unsure how to respond to that. I agree that he shouldn't have done it, and I agree that he is trying now. I look into his very earnest, very brilliant green eyes, and it's hard to remember what my point behind this entire conversation is supposed to be.

"You have this idea in your head, baby, an idea that someone planted there, or maybe you saw it on some shitty television show, or maybe in one of your books, I don't know. But real life is fucking hard. No relationship is perfect, and no man is ever going to treat a woman exactly how he should." He lifts a hand in the air to stop me from interrupting. "I'm not saying it's right, okay? So hear me out: I'm only saying that I think if you and maybe some other people in this fucked-up, criticizing world would just pay closer attention to the shit behind the scenes, you would see things differently. We aren't perfect, Tessa. I'm not fucking perfect, and I love you, but you are far from perfect, too." He winces at that, letting me know that he means that in the least terrible way possible. "I have done a lot of shit to you, and, fuck, I've made this speech one thousand damn times, but something inside of me has changed—you *know* it's true."

When Hardin stops speaking, I stare into the sky behind him for a few seconds. The sun is setting just below the trees, and I wait for it to disappear before responding. "I'm afraid we are too far gone. We have both made so many mistakes."

"It would be a waste to give up instead of fixing those mistakes, and you fucking know it."

"A waste of what? *Time?* We don't have much time to waste now," I say, inching into the inevitable train wreck.

"We have all the time in the world. We're still young! I'm about to graduate, and we'll live in Seattle. I know you are sick of my bullshit, but I'm selfishly counting on your love for me to convince you that I should have one last chance."

"What about all the things I've done to you? I've called you names, all the stuff with Zed?" I bite my lip and look away at the mention of Zed.

Hardin's fingers tap against the glass countertop of the table. "First off, Zed doesn't have a place here, in this conversation. You've done stupid shit; so have I. Neither of us had any damn clue how to be in a relationship. You may have thought you did because you were with Noah for so long, but let's be real here: the two of you were basically kissing cousins. That shit wasn't real."

I glare at Hardin, waiting for him to continue digging this hole he's working on.

"And as far as you calling me names, which is hardly ever"—he smiles, and I begin to wonder who this man sitting across from me actually is—"everyone calls each other names. I'm sorry, but even your mum's pastor's wife is calling her husband an asshole sometimes. She probably doesn't say it to his face, but it's the same shit." He shrugs his shoulders. "And I would much rather you call me an asshole to my face."

"You have an explanation for everything, don't you."

"No, not everything. Not much, really, but I know you're sitting across from me looking for a way out of this, and I'm going to do my damn best to make sure you know what you're saying."

"Since when do we communicate this way?" I can't help but be astonished at the lack of yelling and screaming coming from both of us.

Hardin crosses his arms in front of his chest, picks at the frayed edges of his cast, and shrugs. "Since now. Since, I don't know, since the other shit didn't seem to work for us. So why not try this way?"

I feel my mouth fall open in surprise at the nonchalance of

his statement. "Why do you make it sound so easy? If it was this easy, we could have done it before."

"No; I wasn't the same before, and neither were you." He stares at me, waiting for me to speak again.

"It's not that simple; the time it took for us to get here *matters*, Hardin. It matters that we went through that, and I need time to myself now. I need time to find out who I am and what I want to do with my life, and how I'm going to get there, and I need to do that on my own." I say the words with full bravado, but they taste like acid as they leave my mouth.

"You've made your mind up, then? You don't want to live with me in Seattle? Is that why you're so closed off and unwilling to actually listen to what I'm saying?"

"I am listening, but I've already made up my mind . . . I can't keep doing this back-and-forth, back-and-forth. Not just with you, but with myself."

"I don't believe you, especially since it doesn't sound like you believe yourself." He leans back against the cushion on the chair and lifts his legs onto the table. "Where's your place at, then? Which neighborhood in Seattle?"

"It's not in Seattle," I say curtly. My tongue is suddenly made of lead, and I can't get a word out.

"Oh, where, then? Which suburb?" he asks snidely.

"It's New York, Hardin. I want to go—"

That gets him believing. *"New York?"* He removes his feet from the table and stands up. "You're talking about *actual* New York? Or is that some little hipster neighborhood in Seattle that I haven't come across yet?"

"Actual New York," I clarify as he paces across the deck. "In a week."

Hardin is silent except for his feet hitting the wood as he walks up and down the length of the deck. "When did you decide this?" he finally asks.

"After London and after my father passed away." I stand.

"So me being an asshole to you made you want to pack your shit and go to New York City? You've never even left the state of Washington—what makes you think you could live in a place like that?"

His response stirs my defensive side. "I could live anywhere that I want! Don't try to belittle me."

"Belittle you? Tessa, you're one thousand times better at everything than I am—I am not trying to belittle you. I'm only asking, what makes you think that you can live in New York? Where would you even live?"

"With Landon."

Hardin's eyes widen. *"Landon?"*

This is the look I've been waiting for, wishing wouldn't come, but now that it's here, sadly, I feel slightly at ease. Hardin was taking everything so well; he was being more understanding, calm, and cautious with his words than ever before. It was throwing me off.

This look I know. This is Hardin trying to control his temper.

"Landon. You and Landon are moving to New York."

"Yes, he was already going, and I—"

"Whose idea was this—yours or his?" Hardin's voice is low, and I realize that it's much less angry than I expected. There is something worse than anger, though, and it's hurt. Hardin is hurt, and I can feel my stomach and chest tightening at the surprised, betrayed, guarded energy taking over him.

I don't want to tell Hardin that Landon asked me to move to New York. I don't want to tell Hardin that Landon and Ken have been helping me with recommendation letters and transcripts, admission packets and applications.

"I'm going to take a semester off when I get there," I tell him, in hopes of distracting him from his question.

He turns to me, cheeks red under the patio light, eyes wild, and hands clenched at his sides. "It was his idea, wasn't it? He knew this all along, and while he had me convinced that we were—I don't know—friends . . . *brothers* even, he was going behind my back."

"Hardin, it isn't like that," I say to defend Landon.

"Like hell it isn't. You two are *something fucking else,*" he shouts, waving his hands frantically in front of his body. "You sat there and let me make a fool out of myself offering you marriage and adoption and all kinds of shit, and you knew—*you fucking knew*—you were leaving anyway?" He tugs at his hair and changes the direction of his moving feet. He's walking toward the door now, and I try to stop him.

"Don't go in there like this, please. Stay out here with me and we can finish talking about this. We have so much more to talk about."

"Stop! Just fucking stop!" He shrugs my hand off his shoulder when I try to touch him.

Hardin yanks on the handle of the screen door, and I am sure that the noise I hear is its hinges loosening. I follow closely behind him, hoping that he isn't going to do exactly what I think he will, exactly what he always does when anything bad happens in his life, in our life.

"Landon!" Hardin yells the moment he steps into the kitchen. I'm thankful that Ken and Karen seem to have gone upstairs for the night.

"What?" Landon shouts back.

I follow Hardin into the dining room, where Landon and Sophia are still seated at the table, a nearly empty plate of desserts between them.

As Hardin barrels into the room, jaw clenched, fists tight, Landon's expression changes. "What's going on?" he asks, eyeing his stepbrother carefully before looking to me.

"Don't look at her, look at *me*," Hardin snaps.

Sophia jumps in her seat, but quickly recovers and turns her focus to me as I stand behind Hardin.

"Hardin, he didn't do anything wrong. He is my best friend, and he was only trying to help," I say. I know what Hardin's capable of, and the thought of Landon being on the receiving end of that makes me sick to my stomach.

Hardin doesn't turn around, but just says, "Stay out of this, Tessa."

"What are you talking about?" Landon asks, though I know that he is fully aware of what it is that made Hardin so angry. "Wait, this is about New York, isn't it?"

"*Fuck yes, it's about New York!*" Hardin yells at him.

Landon stands up, and Sophia sends Hardin a murderous warning glare. Right then I decide that I'm okay with her and Landon becoming more than friendly neighbors.

"I was only looking out for Tessa when I invited her to come with me! You broke up with her and she was broken, absolutely broken. New York is what is best for her," Landon calmly explains.

"You know how fucked-up you are? You pretended to by my fucking friend, and then you go and pull *this* shit?" Hardin begins pacing again, this time in a smaller circle across the empty space in the dining room.

"I wasn't pretending! You messed up again, and I was trying to help her!" Landon yells back at Hardin. "I'm *both* of your friends!"

My heart is racing as Hardin crosses the room and wraps his fists around Landon's shirt.

"Help her by taking her away from me!" Hardin pushes Landon against the wall.

"You were too high to care!" Landon screams into Hardin's face.

Sophia and I are both watching, frozen. I know Hardin and Landon much better than she does, and even I don't know what to say or do. It's pure chaos: the two men yelling in each other's face, the noise from Ken and Karen rushing down the stairs, the rattling and shattering glasses and plates from how Hardin grabbed and dragged Landon to the wall.

"You knew what you were fucking doing! I trusted you, you piece of shit!"

"Go on, then! Hit me!" Landon exclaims.

Hardin's fist rises, but Landon doesn't blink. I yell Hardin's name, and I think I hear Ken doing the same. Out of the corner of my eye, I see Karen tug at Ken's shirt, holding him back from stepping between the two men.

"Hit me, Hardin! You're so tough and violent—go on and fucking hit me!" Landon goads again.

"I will! I'll—" Hardin's hand lowers, only to rise again.

Landon's cheeks are red with anger and his chest is heaving, but he doesn't look the least bit afraid of Hardin. He looks pissed off and very collected at once. I feel the opposite; I feel like if the two people I care about the most get into a fight right now, I don't know what I would do.

I look at Karen and Ken again. They don't seem concerned for Landon's health. They are too calm right now while Hardin and Landon are screaming back and forth.

"You won't do it," Landon says.

"Yes, I fucking will! I will smash this stupid fucking cast . . ." But Hardin trails off. He stares at Landon and turns back to look at me before focusing on Landon once more. "Fuck you!" he shouts.

He lowers his fist and turns on his heel to leave the room. Landon is still against the wall, looking as if he might punch something himself. Sophia is on her feet now, moving to comfort him. Karen and Ken are talking quietly between themselves, walking toward Landon, and I . . . well, I'm standing in the middle of the dining room, trying to understand what just happened.

Landon demanded that Hardin hit him. Hardin's temper was already shot; he felt betrayed and screwed over again, and yet he didn't do it. Hardin Scott walked away from violence, even in the heat of the moment.

chapter sixty-one

HARDIN

keep walking until I'm outside, and only then do I realize that Ken and Karen had been in the room. Why didn't they try to stop me? Did they somehow know that I wouldn't hit him?

I'm not sure how I feel about that.

The spring air isn't fucking crisp or fresh or flowery or anything that could help me snap out of this shit. I'm getting back there; I'm seeing red around the corners of my vision, and I don't want to. I don't want to slip and fucking lose everything that I've been working toward. I don't want to lose this new and much easier version of myself. If I had hit him, if I had knocked Landon's goddamn teeth down his throat, I would have lost. I would have lost everything, including Tessa.

Then again, I don't really have her. I haven't had her since I sent her packing in London. She's been planning this little getaway the entire time. Right alongside Landon. Both of them have been plotting behind my fucking back, planning to leave me behind in the shitty state of Washington while they travel the country together. She sat there in silence as I poured myself out to her and let me make a fucking fool of myself.

Landon had me fooled this entire time, thinking that he actually gave a fuck about me. Everyone around me keeps fucking me over and lying, and I'm sick of it. Hardin, stupid fucking Hardin, the guy who no one gives a fuck about, always the last to know every fucking thing. That's me—always has been, always will be.

Tessa is the only person in my entire life that ever took the time to care about me, care for me, and make me feel like I'm actually worth someone's time.

I agree we haven't had the easiest relationship. I've made mistake after mistake, and I could have done a lot of shit differently—but I would never abuse her. If she sees me or our relationship like that, then there really is no hope for us.

I think the hardest thing to explain is that there is a big difference between our relationship being unhealthy and being abusive. I think that a lot of people are quick to judge without putting themselves in the shoes of people who deal with this shit.

My shoes track across the grass and toward the line of trees at the end of the property. I don't know where the hell I'm going or what I'm going to do back here, but I need to calm my breathing and concentrate before I snap.

Fucking Landon had to push me; he just had to push my fucking buttons and try to make me hit him. But I didn't have the raging rush of adrenaline, my blood wasn't singing in my veins—my mouth wasn't watering at the idea of a fight, for once.

Why the hell would he tell me to hit him? He's an idiot, that's why.

Motherfucker is what he is.

Bastard.

Asshole.

Fucking idiot asshole motherfucker.

"Hardin?" Tessa's voice travels through the dark silence, and I try to make a quick decision whether to talk to her. I'm just too fucking mad to deal with her shit and be scolded for picking on Landon.

"He started this shit," I say, stepping out into the open space between two large trees.

So much for hiding. *See, I can't even fucking do that correctly.*

"Are you okay?" she asks, her voice light and nervous.

"What do you think?" I snap, looking past her and into the darkness.

"I'm—"

"Save it. Please, I know you're going to say you're right and I'm wrong, and I shouldn't have slammed Landon against the wall."

She steps toward me, and I can't help but notice the way I take a step closer to her at the same time. As angry as I am, I am fucking drawn to her—always have been, always fucking will be.

"Actually, I was going to apologize. I know how wrong it was to keep that from you. I want to take ownership for my mistake, not blame you," she says softly.

What? "Since when?"

I remind myself yet again that I'm pissed off. But it's hard to remember how pissed off I am when I just want her to hug me, to remind me that I'm not as big of a fuckup as I think I am.

"Can we talk again? You know, how we did on the patio?" Her eyes are wide and hopeful even in the dark, even after my blowup.

I want to tell her no, that she had her damn chance to talk every day since she decided to move across the fucking country to "put some space between us." Instead, I huff and nod in agreement. I don't give her the satisfaction of answering, but I nod again and lean against the trunk of the tree behind me.

I can tell by the look on her face that she didn't expect me to acquiesce so easily. The childish little shit inside me smiles at my having caught her off guard.

She kneels down and sits cross-legged on the grass. She rests her hands on her bare feet. "I'm proud of you," she says, looking up at me. The lights from the patio cast only enough light to make out her small smile, the soft praise in her eyes.

"For what?" I pick at the bark on the tree, waiting for her answer.

"For walking away like that. I know Landon was pushing and

pushing, but you walked away, Hardin. That was a huge step for you. I hope you know how much that means to him, that you chose not to hit him."

Like he fucking cares. He's been going behind my back for the last three weeks.

"It doesn't mean shit."

"Yes, it does. It means a lot to him."

I pull off a particularly large piece of bark and toss it to the ground at my feet. "And what does it mean to you?" I ask, eyes focused on the tree.

"Even more." She runs her palm across the grass. "It means even more to me."

"Enough to keep you from moving? Or 'even more' as in you're really proud of me, I'm a good boy, but you're still leaving?" I can't disguise the pathetic whine in my voice.

"Hardin . . ." She shakes her head—trying to think of an excuse, I'm sure.

"Landon out of all people knows exactly what you mean to me. He knows that you are my fucking lifeline, and he didn't care. He's going to take you across the country, pulling the cord on me, and that hurts, okay?"

She sighs, biting on her bottom lip. "When you say things like that, it makes me forget why I'm fighting against you."

"What?" I push my hair back and sit down on the ground, my back resting against the tree.

"When you say things like I'm your lifeline, and when you admit that something hurts you, it reminds me why I love you so much."

I look at her and notice the way she sounds so sure, despite her claim to be uncertain of our relationship. "You know damn well you are, you know that I'm not shit without you." Maybe I should have said, *I'm nothing without you, love me,* but I already blurted out my own version.

"You are, though." She smiles hesitantly. "You are a good person, even at your worst. I have a really bad habit of reminding you of your mistakes and holding them over you when, in reality, I'm just as bad at this relationship as you are. I had an equal share in dooming it."

"Dooming it?" I've heard this way too many damn times.

"Ruining us, I mean. It was just as much my fault as it was yours."

"Why is it ruined? Why can't we just fix our issues?"

She takes another breath and tilts her head back slightly to look at the sky. "I don't know?" she says, sounding as surprised as I am.

"You 'don't know'?" I repeat, a smile on my lips. *Fuck, we are insane.*

"I don't know. I just had my mind set, and now I'm confused because you are truly, honestly trying, and I see that."

"You do?" I try not to sound too interested, but of course my fucking voice breaks and I sound like a damn mouse.

"Yes, Hardin, I do. I'm just not sure what to do about it."

"New York won't help us. New York isn't going to be this new start at life or whatever you think. You and I both know that you're using that city as an easy way out of this," I say, waving my hand back and forth between us.

"I know." She pulls a handful of grass from its roots, and I can't help but love the way I've been with her so long that I know she does this every time she sits on grass.

"How much time?"

"I don't know. I really do want to go to New York now. Washington hasn't been good to me so far." She frowns, and I watch as she leaves me and disappears into her own mind.

"You've been here your whole life."

She blinks once, takes a deep breath, and tosses her little stray pieces of grass onto her foot. "Exactly."

chapter sixty-two

TESSA

"A re you ready to go inside?" My voice is a whisper, breaking the silence between us. Hardin hasn't spoken, and I haven't been able to come up with anything worth saying in the last twenty minutes.

"Are you?" He lifts himself up using the tree and brushes the dirt off his black jeans.

"If you are."

"I am." He smiles a sarcastic smile. "But if you would like for us to keep *talking* about going inside, we could do that, too."

"Ha-ha." I roll my eyes, and he reaches his hand out to help me to my feet. His hand gently wraps around my wrist, and he pulls me up. He doesn't let go; he only slides his hand down to cup mine. I don't comment on his gentle touch, or that he's looking at me in that familiar way, the way that he looks when his anger is masked, overpowered even, by his love for me. This raw and unplanned look on his face reminds me that a part of me needs and loves this man more than I am willing to admit.

There is no plan behind this touch; it's not a calculated gesture when his arm moves around my waist and he draws me to him as we walk up the grass to the deck.

Once we're inside, not a word is spoken—we get only a worried glance, from Karen. Her hand is resting on her husband's arm, and he's leaning down, talking quietly to Landon, who has now taken a seat back at the dining-room table. Sophia's no longer around, and I assume she left after the chaos. Who could blame her?

"Are you okay?" Karen turns her attention to Hardin as he walks near.

Landon looks up at the same time as Ken, and I gently nudge Hardin.

"Who, me?" he asks, confused. He stops in front of the staircase, and I bump into him.

"Yes, dear, are you okay?" Karen clarifies. She pushes her brown hair behind her ears and takes a step toward us, her hand moving to her belly.

"You mean"—Hardin clears his throat—"am I going to go on a rampage and bash Landon's face in? No, I'm not," he huffs.

Karen shakes her head, patience clear in her soft features. "No, what I meant was, are you *okay*? Is there anything I can do for you? That's what I meant."

He blinks once, composing himself. "Yeah, I'm fine."

"If the answer to that question changes, be sure to let me know. Okay?"

He nods once and leads me upstairs. I look back down for Landon to follow, but he closes his eyes, turning his face away.

"I need to talk to Landon," I tell Hardin as he opens the door to his room.

He switches the light on and lets go of my arm. "Now?"

"Yes, now."

"Right now?"

"Yes."

The moment I say the word, Hardin has me against the wall. "This second?" He leans into me, his breath warm against my neck. "You're sure?"

I'm not sure, of anything, really.

"What?" My voice is thick, my head cloudy.

"I think you were going to kiss me." He presses his lips to mine, and I can't help but smile into it, into the madness, into the relief of his affection. His lips aren't soft; they are dry and cracked, but so perfect, and I love the way his tongue laps around mine, pushing into my mouth, not giving me the option to overthink or pull away.

His hands are at my waist, fingers pressing deliciously into the skin there as his knee pushes between my thighs to separate them.

"I can't believe you are moving so far from me." He drags his mouth across my jaw to the skin just below my ear. "So far away from me."

"I'm sorry," I breathe, unable to say more than that when his hands move from my hips to my stomach, pushing the fabric of my T-shirt along with the heavy drag of his hands.

"Between the two of us, we keep running." His voice is calm, despite his hands moving quickly to cup my chest. My back is pressed against the wall, and my shirt is lying on the floor at our feet.

"We do."

"One Hemingway quote, and then I'll keep my mouth busy elsewhere." He smiles against my mouth, his hands rubbing, teasing, just above the waist of my pants.

I nod, wanting him to follow through on that promise.

" 'You can't get away from yourself by moving from one place to another.' " He pushes his hand into my pants.

I groan, equally overwhelmed by his words and his touch. His words play on an endless stream inside my mind as he touches me, and I reach for him. He's clearly straining against his zipper, and he moans my name under his breath as I fumble with the button of his jeans.

"Don't go to New York with Landon, stay with me in Seattle."

Landon. I turn my head and remove my hand from Hardin's zipper. "I need to talk to Landon, this is important. He seemed upset."

"So? I'm upset, too."

"I know." I sigh. "But you clearly aren't that upset." I glance down at his cock, boxers barely covering it.

"Well, that's because I'm distracted from being angry at you—and Landon," he adds weakly, as an afterthought.

"I won't be long." I pull away from him and lift my shirt from the floor, tugging it down over my stomach.

"Okay, I need a few minutes anyway." Hardin pulls his hair back and drops the messy fringe onto his neck. This is the longest his hair has been since I met him. I like it this way, but sort of miss being able to see the traces of ink that peek up from the neckline of his shirt.

"A few minutes away from me?" I ask before considering how desperate the question sounds.

"Yes. You did just tell me that you are moving across the country and I lost my temper with Landon. I need a few minutes to sort through the shit going on in my head."

"Okay, I understand." I do understand. He's handling this much better than I expected, and the last thing I should do is jump into bed with Hardin and neglect settling things with Landon.

"I'm going to take a shower," he tells me as I walk into the hallway.

My mind is still in the bedroom with Hardin, pressed against the wall, living in the distraction as I go downstairs. With each step, the ghost of his touch lessens, and when I walk into the dining room, Karen moves from Landon's side and Ken gestures for her to leave the room with him. She offers me a small smile and a gentle squeeze of my hand as she passes.

"Hey." I pull a chair out and sit down next to Landon, but he stands just as I take my seat.

"Not now, Tessa," he snaps, and goes into the living room.

Confused by his harsh tone, I miss a beat. Apparently I'm missing more than that, though.

"Landon . . ." I stand up and follow him into the living room. "Wait!" I shout at his back.

He stops walking. "I'm sorry, but this isn't working anymore."

"What's not working?" I tug at his long-sleeved shirt to stop him from walking away from me.

Without turning around, he says, "This thing between you and Hardin. It was okay when it was only affecting the two of you, but now you're dragging everyone else into it, and that's not fair."

The anger in his voice cuts deep, and it takes me a moment to remember that he's talking to me. Landon has always been supportive and kind, and I never expected to hear this from him.

"I'm sorry, Tessa, but you know I'm right. You guys can't keep bringing all this here. My mom is pregnant now, and that scene could have done real damage to her nerves. You guys go back and forth between Seattle and here, fighting in both cities and every-where in between."

Ouch.

I struggle for words, not that any great ones come to mind. "I know, I'm so sorry for what just happened—I didn't mean for any of that to happen, Landon. I had to tell him about New York, I couldn't keep it from him. I thought he handled it really well." I stop when my voice breaks. I'm confused and panicked because Landon is upset with me. I knew he wasn't happy with Hardin's putting his hands on him, but I didn't expect *this*.

Landon spins to look at me. "He 'handled it well'? He *slammed me against the wall* . . ." Landon sighs and pushes the sleeves of his shirt up his elbows, taking a couple of breaths. "He did, I guess. But that doesn't mean this isn't becoming more and more of a problem. You guys can't travel the world breaking up and getting back together. If it doesn't work in one city, why would you think it would work in another?"

"I know that; that's why I'm coming to New York with you. I

needed to figure myself out, alone. Well, without Hardin. That was the whole point behind it."

Landon shakes his head. "Without Hardin? You think he's going to let you go to New York without him? He will either come with you, or you'll stay here, fighting like this."

Those words, and the ones he rattles off next, make my heart sink in my chest.

Everyone always says the same things about my relationship with Hardin. Hell, I make the same points. I've heard it all before, many times, but as Landon throws them at me, one after another, it's different. It's different, and it means more and hurts more and makes me doubt everything, more.

"I really am sorry, Landon." I feel like I could cry. "I know I drag everyone into our mess, and I'm so sorry for that. I don't mean to—I don't mean for it to be this way, especially with you. You're my best friend. I never want you to feel like that."

"Yeah, well, I do. And a lot of other people do, too, Tessa." His words are sharp and puncture me in that one place I had left, the only untouched, clean place inside me, which was re-served for Landon and his loving friendship. That sacred little place was essentially all I had left when it came to the people around me. It was my safety spot, and now it's dark, like its surroundings.

"I'm sorry." My voice comes out as a broken whine, and I'm convinced that my mind hasn't caught up with the fact that Landon is the person saying these things to me.

"I just . . . I thought you were on our side?" I ask, simply because I have to. I have to know if it's truly as hopeless as it seems.

He takes a deep breath and releases it. "I'm sorry, too, but tonight was too much. My mom being pregnant and Ken trying to fix things with Hardin, me moving, it's too much. This is our family, and it needs to come together. You aren't helping that."

"I'm sorry," I repeat, because I don't know what else to say. I can't argue with him, I can't even disagree with him, because he's right. This is their family, not mine. No matter how much I try to pretend that it's my family, I'm disposable here. I've been disposable in every place that I've tried to settle since I left my mother's house.

He stares down at his feet, and I can't seem to look away from his face as he says, "I know you are. I'm sorry for being a jerk, but I had to say it."

"Yeah, I understand." He still doesn't look at me. "It won't be like this in New York, I promise. I just need some time. I'm so confused about everything in my life, and I can't seem to make sense of anything."

The feeling of not being wanted somewhere when you aren't sure how to leave is one of the worst feelings. It's so incredibly awkward, and you take a few seconds to try to assess the situation to make sure you aren't just being paranoid. But when my best friend won't look at me after telling me that I'm causing problems with his family, the only family I have, I know it's true. Landon doesn't want to talk to me right now, but he's too nice to say it.

"New York." I swallow the lump in my throat. "You don't want me to come anymore, do you?"

"It's not that. I just thought New York was going to be a fresh start for both of us, Tessa. Not just another place for you and Hardin to fight."

"I get it." I shrug and dig my fingernails into my palms to stop myself from crying. I do get it. I understand completely.

Landon doesn't want me to go to New York with him. I didn't have a solid plan anyway. I don't have much money, or an acceptance letter to NYU yet, if ever. Until now I didn't realize how ready I was to move to New York. I needed this, I needed to at least try to do something spontaneous and different, and I needed to jump out into the world and land on my own two feet.

"I'm sorry," he says, lightly kicking at the leg of the chair to shift the focus from his words.

"It's okay, I understand." I force a smile at my best friend and manage to make it up the stairs before the tears flow freely down my cheeks.

In the guest room, the bed feels solid underneath me, holding me in place while my mistakes are laid out in front of my eyes.

I have been so selfish, and I haven't even realized it until now. I have ruined so many relationships in the past eight months. I started college in love with my Noah, my childhood boyfriend, only to cheat on him, more than once, with Hardin.

I made friends with Steph, who betrayed me and tried to hurt me. I judged Molly when she wasn't even the one I should have been worried about. I forced myself to believe that I could fit in at college—that this group of people were actually my friends, when in reality I was a joke to them.

I fought and fought to keep Hardin; I fought for his acceptance from the start. When he didn't want me, I only wanted him more. I fought with my mother to defend Hardin; I fought with myself to defend Hardin; I fought with Hardin to defend Hardin.

I gave my virginity to him as part of a bet. I loved him and cherished that moment, and he was hiding his motives from me all along. Even after what he did, I stayed, and he always came back with an apology even bigger than the last. It wasn't always him, though; while his mistakes held more depth, more pain, mine were just as frequent.

Out of pure selfishness, I used Zed to fill the void nearly every time Hardin left me. I kissed him, I spent time with him, I led him on. I held my friendship with him over Hardin's head, knowingly continuing the game that the two of them had started all those months ago.

I have forgiven Hardin so many times, only to throw his mistakes back in his face. I always expected too much from him, and I never let him forget it. Hardin is a good man, despite his flaws—he's such a good man and he deserves to be happy. He deserves everything. He deserves quiet days with a loving wife who doesn't have to struggle to give him children. He doesn't deserve games and bad memories. He shouldn't have to try to live up to some ridiculous expectation I've set for him that is nearly impossible to meet.

I have been through hell and back in the last eight months, and now here I sit, on this bed, alone. I've spent my entire life planning and scheduling, organizing and anticipating, yet here I am with nothing but mascara-stained cheeks and broken plans. Not even broken—none of them ever had enough backing in the first place to end up broken. I don't have a clue where my life is headed. I don't have a college to be in, a place to belong in, or even the romantic notion of love from the books I've always loved and used to believe in. I have no idea what the hell I'm doing with my life.

So many breakups, so many losses. I had my father come back into my life, only to be slain by his own demons. I've watched as Hardin's entire life was revealed as a lie, and his mentor revealed as his biological father, whose long history with his mother drove the man who raised him to drink. His childhood was torment for nothing; he went through years of dealing with an alcoholic for a father, and he witnessed things as a child that no one should ever have to. I have watched from the beginning Hardin's attempts to reconnect with Ken, from my first meeting the man outside a yogurt shop to becoming part of this family and watching as Hardin struggled to forgive him his mistakes. He's learning to accept his past and forgive Ken, and it's incredible to see. He has been so angry his entire life, and now that he's finally getting some peace in his life, I can see this for what it is. Hardin needs this peace. He needs resolve. He doesn't need constant backtracking and constant turmoil. He doesn't need doubts and arguments; he needs family.

He needs his friendship with Landon and his relationship with his father. He needs to accept his place in his family and be able to enjoy the thrill of watching his family expand. He needs Christmas dinners full of love and laughter, not tears and tension. I've watched him change so much since the day I met the rude, tattooed boy with the piercings and the messiest hair I had ever seen. He's not that boy anymore; he's a man now, a man recovering. He doesn't drink the way he used to. He doesn't break things as often. And he stopped *himself* from hurting Landon.

He's managed to build this life around him, full of people who love and cherish him, while I've managed to destroy every relationship I thought I had. We fought and we battled, we won and we lost, and now my friendship with Landon has become just another casualty of Hardin and Tessa.

As soon as I've thought his name, like he's some kind of genie I can summon, Hardin opens the door, strolling in calmly while he rubs a towel over his wet hair.

"What's going on?" he asks. But as soon as he sees my state, the towel is quickly discarded, and he darts across the room to kneel before me.

I don't try to mask my tears; I don't see the point. "We are Catherine and Heathcliff," I proclaim, devastated by the truth.

Hardin frowns. "What? What the hell happened?"

"We have made everyone around us miserable, and I don't know if I just didn't notice or I was too selfish to care, but it happened. Even Landon—even Landon has been affected by us."

"Where is this coming from?" Hardin stands. "Did he fucking say something to you?"

"No." I pull Hardin by the arm, begging him not to go downstairs. "He only said the truth. I see it now, I was just trying to force myself to see it, but now I get it." I wipe my fingers under my eyes and take a breath to continue. "You aren't the one who was ruining me; I did it myself. I changed, and you changed. But you changed for the better. I did not."

Saying it out loud makes it easier to accept. I'm not perfect. I never will be. And that's okay, but I can't drag Hardin down with me. I have to fix what is wrong inside me—it isn't fair to want that from Hardin without doing it myself.

He shakes his head, staring at me with those beautiful emerald eyes. "You're talking crazy. None of this makes any sense."

"Yes." I stand and tuck my hair behind my ears. "It's completely clear to me."

I am trying to stay as calm as I can, but it's hard, because he doesn't get it and it's so clear—*how does he not get it?*

"I need you to do something for me. I need you to promise me something right now," I beg.

"What? Hell no, I'm not promising anything, Tessa—what the fuck are you going on about?" He reaches under my chin and gently lifts my head to him. His other hand wipes at the moisture covering my face.

"Please, promise me something. If we could ever have a chance of a future together, you have to do something for me."

"Fine, fine," he quickly agrees.

"I mean it, I am begging you, if you love me, you will listen to me and do this for me. If you can't, we will never have a future, Hardin."

I don't mean the words as a threat. They are a plea. I need this from him. I need him to understand and to heal and to live his life while I try to fix mine.

He swallows; his eyes meet mine, and I know he doesn't want to agree, but he says anyway, "Okay, I promise."

"Don't follow me this time, Hardin. Stay here and be with your family and—"

"Tessa"—he cups my face with his hands resting under my

jaw—"no, stop this. We will figure this New York shit out, don't overreact."

I shake my head. "I'm not going to New York, and I promise you that I'm not overreacting. I know this seems dramatic and impulsive, but I promise it's not. We have both been through so much in the last year, and if we don't take a little time to make sure this is what we want, we will end up taking everyone down with us, even more so than we already have." I try to make him understand; he has to understand.

"How long?" His shoulders slump and his fingers brush his hair back.

"Until we know that we're ready." I feel more resolute than I have in the last eight months.

"Know what? I already know what I want with you."

"I need this, Hardin. If I can't get myself together, I would resent you and myself. I need this."

"Fine, you can have it. I'm giving this to you, not because I want to, but because this will be the last doubt I will ever entertain from you. After I give you this time and you come back to me, that's it. You aren't leaving again, and you will marry me. This is what I want in return for this time you need."

"Okay." If we make it through this, I will marry this man.

chapter sixty-three

TESSA

Hardin kisses my forehead and closes the passenger door of my car. My bags have been packed for the thousandth and last time, and Hardin is leaning against the car now, bringing me to his chest.

"I love you; please remember that," he says. "And call me the second you get there."

He isn't happy about this, but he will be. I know this is right; we need this time for ourselves. We are so young, so confused, and we need this time to repair some of the damage that has been done in the people's lives around us.

"I will. Tell them bye for me, remember?" I lean into his chest and close my eyes. I'm not sure how this will end, but I know it's necessary.

"I will. But get in the car, please. I can't draw this out and pretend that I'm happy about it. I'm a different person now, and I can cooperate, but much longer, and I'll want to drag you back into that bedroom for all time."

I wrap my arms around Hardin's torso, and he rests his arms around my shoulders. "I know you are—thank you."

"I love you, Tessa, so fucking much. Remember that, okay?" he says into my hair. I can hear his voice breaking, and the need to protect him starts to claw its way into my heart again.

"I love you, Hardin. Always." I press my palms against his chest and lean up to kiss him. I close my eyes, wishing, wanting, hoping that this won't be last time I feel his lips against mine, that this won't be the last time I ever feel this way. Even now, through the sadness and pain of leaving him here, I feel the constant pulse of electricity between us. I feel the soft curve of his lips and the burn of need for him, then the desire to change my mind about this and continue living in the cycle. I feel the compulsion that he holds over me, and I over him.

I pull away first, memorizing the low groan he makes when I do, and kiss his cheek. "I'll call you when I get there." I kiss him once more, just a small, quick goodbye kiss, and he runs his hands over his hair when he steps away from my car.

"Be safe, Tess," Hardin says as I climb into the car and close the door.

I don't trust myself enough to speak, but finally, as my car pulls away form the house, I whisper, "Bye, Hardin."

chapter sixty-four

TESSA

June

A m I okay?" I turn around before the full-length mirror, tugging at my dress, which hits right at the knees. The maroon silk has a nostalgic feel to it underneath my fingers. The moment I tried the dress on, I fell in love with the way the material and color reminded me of my past, of a time when I was someone else. "Do I look okay?"

This dress is different from its earlier version. That dress was loose fitting and high collared, with three-quarter-length sleeves. This dress is formfitting and has a slightly lower collar with a cut-out pattern across the neckline and lacks sleeves. I will always love that old dress, but I'm happy with the way this dress fits me now.

"Of course you do, Theresa." My mother leans against the doorway with a smile.

I've tried to calm my nerves in preparation for today, but I've drunk four cups of coffee, eaten half a bag of popcorn, and paced around my mother's house like a madwoman.

Hardin's graduation. I'm slightly paranoid that my company will be unwelcome, that the invitation was made out of politeness, only to be silently taken back in the time we've been separated. The minutes and hours have ticked by somehow, in the same way they always have and always will, but this time I'm not trying to forget him. This time, I'm remembering and healing and thinking back on my time with Hardin with a smile.

That night in April, the night that Landon handed me a reality check on a silver platter, I drove straight to my mother's house. I called Kimberly and cried into the phone until she told me to suck it up, stop crying, and do something about the direction my life was headed in.

I hadn't realized just how dark my life had become until I started to see light again. I spent the first week in complete solitude, barely leaving my childhood bedroom and forcing myself to eat. Every single thought I had revolved around Hardin and how much I missed him, needed him, loved him.

The next week was less painful, as it was in the past during our breakups, but this time was different. This time, I had to remind myself that Hardin was in a better place with his family, and I wasn't leaving him to fend for himself. He had his family, if he needed anything. The daily calls from Karen were the only thing that kept me from driving back there to check on him one hundred times. I needed to get my life together, but I also needed to be sure I wasn't doing more damage to Hardin's life, or anyone else's around me.

I had become that girl, the one that burdens everyone around her, and I didn't realize it, because Hardin was all I could see. His opinion of me was the only thing that seemed to matter, and I spent my days and nights trying to fix him, fix us, while breaking everything else, including myself.

Hardin was persistent the first three weeks, but just like Karen's daily calls, his lessened and lessened in frequency until I was only getting two calls a week, between the two of them. Karen assures me that Hardin is happy, so I can't find it in myself to be upset that he doesn't keep in touch as much as I wanted or hoped that he would.

I keep in touch with Landon the most. He felt terrible the morning after saying all those things to me. He came to Hardin's room to apologize to me, only to find Hardin alone and pissed off.

Landon immediately called me, begging me to come back and let him explain, but I assured him that he was right and I needed to stay away for a while. As much as I wanted to go to New York with him, I needed to go back to where the destruction of my life began and start over, alone.

Landon's reminder that I wasn't a part of their family hurt me the most. It made me feel unwelcomed, unloved, and unattached to anything or anyone. I felt like it was just me, untethered, floating around trying to latch myself onto anyone who would take me. I had become too dependent on others and was lost inside the cycle of wanting to be wanted. I hated that feeling. I hated it more than anything else, and I understand that Landon made that statement out of anger alone, but he wasn't wrong. Sometimes anger breaks through to things we're really feeling.

"Daydreaming won't help you get out of the door any faster." My mother walks toward me and pulls open the top drawer of my jewelry box. Dropping a pair of small diamond studs in my palm, she closes her hand around mine. "Wear these. It won't be as bad as you think. Just keep yourself composed and don't show any weakness."

I laugh at her attempt to comfort me and push the back onto the second earring. "Thank you." I smile at her reflection in the mirror.

And she, being Carol Young, suggests that I pull my hair back away from my face, add more lipstick, wear higher heels. I kindly thank her for her advice, though I don't follow it, and silently thank her again when she doesn't push her suggestions further.

My mother and I are on the path to the relationship I always dreamed we would have. She's learning that I am a woman, young but capable of making my own decisions. And I'm learning that she never intended to become the woman she is now. She was broken by my father all those years ago, and she never recovered. She's working on that now, sort of in a parallel way to how I am.

I was surprised when she told me she had met someone and has been dating for a few weeks now. The biggest surprise of all was that the man, named David, is not a lawyer, not a doctor, and doesn't drive a luxury car. He owns a bakery in town, and he laughs more than anyone else I've ever met. He has a ten-year-old daughter, who has taken a strong liking to trying on my clothes, which are far too big on her small frame, and to letting me practice my slowly developing makeup and hairdressing skills on her. She's a sweet girl, named Heather, and her mother passed away when she was seven. The biggest surprise of all is how sweet my mother is to that girl. David brings something out in my mother that I have never before seen, and I adore the way she laughs and smiles when he is around.

"How much time do I have?" I turn to my mother and step into my shoes, ignoring the way she rolls her eyes when I choose the lowest-heeled ones in my closet. I am already a nervous wreck; the last thing I need to add to my anxiety is walking in heels.

"Five minutes, if you want to arrive early, which I know you do." She shakes her head and pulls her long blond hair to one shoulder. It's been an amazing and emotional experience to watch the shift in my mother, to watch some of the stone crack, and to watch her become a better version of herself. It's nice to have her support today—especially today—and I am thankful that she has kept her opinion of my going to the ceremony to herself.

"I hope traffic isn't bad. What if there's a wreck? The two-hour drive could easily turn into four hours, and my dress will be wrinkled and my hair will be flat and—"

My mother cocks her head to one side. "You will be *fine*. You're overthinking things. Now, apply some lipstick and get on the road."

I sigh and do exactly what she says, hoping that everything will go as planned. For once.

chapter sixty-five

HARDIN

I groan, staring at the hideous black gown in the mirror. I'll never understand why I'm being forced to wear this shit. What's wrong with wearing normal clothes during the ceremony? My street clothes would already be color coordinated with the mass of black anyway.

"The dumbest fucking shit I've ever worn in my life, hands down."

Karen rolls her eyes at me. "Oh, come on. Just wear it."

"Pregnancy is making you a lot less tolerable," I tease her, and move out of the way before she can smack my arm.

"Ken has already been at the Coliseum since nine this morning. He will be so proud to see you dressed in this gown and walking across the stage." She smiles as her eyes gloss over. If she cries, I'm going to need an exit. I'll just slowly walk out of the room and hope her vision is too blurry for her to follow.

"You make it sound like I am going to prom," I grumble, adjusting the stupid material that is swallowing my entire body.

My shoulders are tense, my head is throbbing, my chest is burning in anticipation. Not because of the ceremony or the diploma—I couldn't give a shit less about either of those. The overwhelming anxiety stems from the possibility that *she* might be there. Tessa is the only reason behind my putting on this show for everyone; she is the one who convinced (well, *conned*) me into going in the first place. And if I know her as well as I know I do, she'll be there to witness her triumph.

Though her calls have become less and less frequent, and her texts have become practically nonexistent, she will come today.

An hour later, we are pulling into the parking lot of the Coliseum, where the graduation is being held. I agreed to ride with Karen after the ninetieth time she asked me. I would have preferred to drive myself, but she's been clingy lately. I know she's trying to compensate for Tessa's departure from my life, but nothing will fill that gap.

Nothing and no one would ever provide what Tessa has provided for me; I will always need her. Everything I do, every single day since she left me, is only to be better for her. I've made some new friends—okay, two friends. Luke and his girlfriend, Kaci, are the closest things I have to friends, and they are okay company. Neither of them drinks much, and they definitely don't come close to spending their time at shitty parties or making bets. I met Luke, who is a few years older than me and being dragged to couple's therapy once a week, during my weekly session with Dr. Tran, mental health professional extraordinaire.

Okay, not really; he's a scam artist I pay $100 an hour to, to listen to me talk about Tessa for two hours a week . . . but it does make me feel better talking to someone about all the shit inside my head, and he's decent at listening to me.

"Landon said to remind you that he's really sorry that he couldn't make it. He's so busy in New York," Karen tells me as she pulls into the parking space. "I promised him that I would take a lot of pictures for him today."

"Yay." I smile at Karen and climb out of the car.

The building is packed, the stadium-style seats filled with proud parents, relatives, and friends. I nod at Karen when she waves to me from her seat in the front. Being the wife of the chancellor gives some advantages, I guess. Like front-row seats to a fun-filled graduation.

I can't help but attempt to find Tessa in the crowd. It's impossible to see half the faces because the damn lights are so bright and blinding and excessive. I would hate to see how much this extravagant ceremony is costing the university. Finding my name on the seating chart, I smile at the grumpy woman who is in charge of seating. She's annoyed, I'm guessing, because I missed the rehearsal. But, really, how complicated could this shit possibly be? Sit. Name called. Walk. Take worthless piece of paper. Walk. Sit back down.

Of course, when I do sit down in my place, the plastic seat is uncomfortable and the guy next to me is sweating like a damn whore in church. He's fidgeting, humming to himself, and shaking his knee. I almost want to say something until I realize I'm doing the exact same thing, minus the disgusting sweat.

I'm not sure how many hours have passed—it feels like four—when my name is finally called. It's awkward and vomit inducing, the way everyone is staring at me, and I rush off the stage as soon as I notice Ken's eyes starting to tear up.

I just have to make it through the rest of the alphabet until I can go and find her. By the letter V, I think I may just stand from my seat and interrupt the entire thing. How many people can possibly have a last name starting with V?

Apparently a lot, that's how many.

At last, after I've traveled through multiple states of boredom and the climactic cheering has gone down, we are able to leave our seats. I practically jump from mine, but Karen rushes to me for a hug. After what feels like an appropriate amount of my tolerance expended, I excuse myself from Karen's weeping congratulation speech and rush off to find *her*.

I know she's here, I can feel it somehow.

I haven't seen her in two months—two fucking long-ass months—and I am buzzing, high on adrenaline, when I finally spot her near the exit. I had a feeling she would do this, come here and try to sneak off before I could find her, but I won't allow it. I'll chase her car down the street if need be.

"Tessa!" I push through the huddled families in my way to get to her, and she turns around just as I sort of shove a young boy out of the way.

It's been so long since I've seen her that the relief is overwhelming. So fucking overwhelming. She looks as beautiful as ever. Her skin has a tan glow that it didn't have before, and her eyes are brighter, happier, and the shell that she had become has been replaced by life. I can tell all of this just by looking at her.

"Hey." She smiles and does that thing where she tucks her hair behind her ear when she's nervous.

"Hey," I repeat her greeting and take a few moments to just take her in. She's even more angelic than my memory of her.

She seems to be doing the same thing I am, and I watch as she looks me up and down. I wish I weren't wearing this stupid cloak thing. Then she could see how much I've been working out.

She speaks first. "Your hair is so long."

I laugh softly and push my fingers through the mess. It's probably all fucked-up from that cap. Right then I realize I don't know where the damn thing went. But who knows, and who cares?

"Yeah, yours is, too," I say without thinking. She laughs and brings her fingers to her mouth. "I mean, your hair is long. It's always been long though," I try to recover, but it only makes her laugh again.

Smooth, Scott. Really fucking smooth.

"So, was the ceremony as bad as you expected?" she asks.

She's standing less than four feet away from me, and I wish we were sitting down or something. I feel like I need to sit down. *Why am I so fucking anxious?*

"Worse. Did you see how long it was? The man reading off the names was ancient." I hope that she smiles again. When she does, I smile back at her and push my hair away from my face. I do need a haircut, but I think I may keep it this way for a while.

"I'm really proud of you for walking. I'm sure Ken is so happy."

"Are you happy?"

She crinkles her brow. "For you? Yes, of course. I'm very happy that you walked. It's okay that I came, isn't it?" She looks down at her feet for only a second before focusing her eyes on mine.

Something about her is different, more confident, more . . . I don't know, *strong*? She's standing up straight, her eyes are sharp and focused, and even though I can tell she's nervous, she's not intimidated like she used to be.

"Of course it is. I would have been quite pissed if I walked for nothing." I smile at her, then again at how the two of us seem to be doing nothing but smiling and fidgeting with our hands. "How are you? I'm sorry that I haven't called much. I've been really busy . . ."

She shakes her head at me. "It's okay, I know you have a lot going on with graduation and preparing your future, all of that." She smiles a barely there smile. "I've been well. I applied to every college within a fifty-mile radius of New York City."

"You're still wanting to go there? Landon said you weren't sure yesterday."

"I'm not yet. I'm waiting to hear back from at least one college before I relocate. Transferring to the Seattle campus hurt my record. The admissions department at NYU said that it made me seem flaky and unprepared, so I'm hoping that at least one of the colleges there will disagree. Otherwise, I am going to take classes at a community college until I can transfer back into a four-year." She takes a deep breath. "*Wow*, that was a long explanation to a short question." She laughs and steps out of the way of a sobbing mother walking hand in hand with her gown-clad daughter. "Did you decide what you want to do next?"

"Well, I have some interviews set up over the next few weeks."

"That's good. I'm really happy for you."

"None of them are here, though." I watch her face closely as she takes in my words.

"Here, as in this town?"

"No, as in Washington."

"Where are they? If you don't mind me asking?" She's composed and polite, and her voice is so soft and sweet that I have to take a step closer to her.

"One in Chicago, three in London."

"London?" She tries to hide the surprise in her voice, and I nod.

I didn't want to have to tell her this, but I was just taking advantage of every opportunity that came my way. I probably wouldn't move back there anyway—I'm just exploring my options. "I wasn't sure what was going to happen, you know, with us," I try to explain.

"No, I understand. I'm just surprised, that's all."

I know what she's thinking just by looking at her. I can practically hear her exact thoughts.

"I've been talking to my mum a little lately." It sounds weird coming from my mouth, and it was even weirder to have finally picked up the phone when my mum called. I had been avoiding her up until two weeks ago. I haven't exactly forgiven her, but I'm sort of working on trying not to be so angry about the whole mess. It doesn't get me anywhere.

"You have? Hardin, that is so great to hear." Her frown is gone, and she's smiling so brightly at me that my chest literally fucking aches from the beauty of it.

"Yeah, a little." I shrug my shoulders.

She is still smiling at me like I've just told her she won the damn lottery. "I'm so happy that everything is working out for you. You deserve everything good in your life."

I'm not sure what to say to that, but I've missed her kindness so much that I can't stop myself from reaching for her arm and pulling her into a hug. Her arms move to my shoulders, and her head drops down to my chest. I swear that a sigh escapes her lips. If I'm wrong, I'll just pretend it was so.

"Hardin!" someone calls, and Tessa pulls away to stand next to me. Her cheeks are flushed, and she looks nervous again. Luke approaches with Kaci, a bouquet of flowers in his hand.

"I *know* you didn't bring me fucking flowers," I groan, knowing that it must have been his woman's idea.

Tessa stands at my side, staring wide-eyed at Luke and the short brunette at his side.

"You know it. And I know how much you love lilies," Luke says, shit-talking while Kaci waves to Tessa.

Tessa turns to me, confused, but smiling the most beautiful smile I've seen in the last two months.

"It's so nice to finally meet you." Kaci wraps her arms around Tessa's body, and Luke tries to shove the hideous bouquet into my chest. I let the flowers fall to the floor, and he curses at me as we watch a horde of way-too-proud parents trample over them in passing.

"I'm Kaci, Hardin's friend. I've heard so much about you, Tessa." The woman withdraws a little to tuck one arm into Tessa's, and I'm a little surprised when Tessa smiles back and, instead of looking to me for help, jumps into a conversation about wasted flowers.

"Hardin seems like a flower type of guy, right?" Kaci says, laughing, and Tessa giggles along. "That's why he got those ridiculous leaves tattooed on him."

Tessa raises a questioning brow. "Leaves?"

"They aren't exactly leaves; she's just giving me shit, but I did get a few new tattoos since I've seen you." I'm not sure why I feel slightly guilty about that, but I do.

"Oh." Tessa tries to smile, but I can tell it's not authentic. "That's good."

The mood has shifted into slightly awkward territory, and as Luke tells Tessa about the new tattoos across the bottom of my stomach, he makes a big mistake: "I told him not to get them. The four of us were out, and Kaci got curious about Hardin's tattoos and decided she wanted one."

"Four?" Tessa blurts the word, and I can see the regret in her eyes when she asks.

I glare at Luke at the same time that Kaci digs her elbow into his side.

"Kaci's sister," Luke tells Tessa, trying to fix his fuckup, but making it worse.

The first time I hung out with Luke, we met Kaci for dinner. That weekend, we went to a movie, and Kaci brought her sister along. A few hangouts later, I realized that the woman was sporting a little infatuation and told them to call her off. I didn't and still don't want or need a distraction while waiting for Tessa to come back to me.

"Oh." Tessa gives Luke her fake smile and stares off into the crowd.

Fuck, I hate the look on her face right now.

Before I can tell Luke and Kaci to fuck off and explain this shit to Tessa, Ken approaches and says, "Hardin, I have someone I would like you to meet."

Luke and Kaci excuse themselves, and Tessa steps to the side. I reach for her, but she brushes me off.

"I need to find a restroom anyway." She smiles and walks away after a quick hello to my father.

"This is Chris, the man I was telling you about. He's head of publishing out at Gabber in Chicago, and he came all the way here to talk to you." Ken smiles wide and grips this guy's shoulder, but I can't help but look for Tessa in the crowd.

"Yeah, thanks." I shake the short man's hand, and he launches into conversation. Between wondering what kind of shit Ken had to pull to get this guy here and worrying that Tessa won't find the bathroom, I barely catch half of his offer.

Afterward, wandering around to every bathroom and calling her phone twice, I realize that Tessa has left without saying goodbye.

chapter sixty-six

September

Landon's apartment is small, and the closet space almost non-existent, but it works for him. Well, us. Every time I remind Landon that this is his apartment, not mine, he reminds me that I am living here now, in this apartment, in New York City.

"You're sure you're okay, right? Remember, Sophia said you could stay with her for the weekend if you aren't comfortable," he says, placing a stack of clean, folded towels into the cubbyhole he calls a closet.

I nod at him, disguising my burning anxiety at the weekend ahead. "It's okay, really. I have to work most of the weekend anyway."

It's the second Friday in September, and Hardin's flight will be landing any minute. I didn't ask why he was coming—I couldn't bring myself to—and when Landon awkwardly brought up his wanting to stay here, I just nodded and forced a smile.

"He's taking a cab from Newark, so he'll be here in about an hour, given the traffic." Landon runs his hand over his chin, before burying his face in his hands. "I feel like this isn't going to go well. I shouldn't have agreed to it."

I reach up and pull his hands away from his face. "It's fine. I'm a big girl; I can handle a little Hardin Scott," I tease. I'm nervous as heck, but the comfort of work and knowing that Sophia is just down the block will get me through the weekend.

"Will you-know-who be around this weekend? I don't know how that will go over . . ." Landon looks panicked, like he is going to cry or scream at any moment.

"No, he works all weekend, too." I walk over to the couch and lift my apron from the pile of clean clothes. Living with Landon is easy, despite his recent relationship problems, and he loves to clean, so we get along well that way.

Our friendship bounced back quickly, and we haven't had an awkward moment since I arrived four weeks ago. I spent the summer with my mother, her boyfriend, David, and his daughter, Heather. I even learned to Skype with Landon and spent my days planning for the move. It was one of those summers where you fall asleep on a June night and wake up to an August morning. It went too quickly, and a lot of my time was spent being reminded of Hardin. David rented a cabin for a week during July, and we ended up less than five miles away from the Scott cabin, and I saw that little bar we got far too drunk in when we were driving around.

I walked down the same streets, this time with David's daughter, and she stopped at every block to pick a flower for me. We ate at the same restaurant where I had one of the most tense nights of my life, and we even had the same server, Robert. I was surprised when he told me that he, too, was moving to New York, for medical school. He was offered a significantly larger grant to attend New York University than his previous choice in Seattle, so he was going with that. We exchanged phone numbers and text-messaged during the summer, and we both moved to the city around the same time. He arrived a week before me, and now he works at the same place that I do. He also works almost as much as me for the next two weeks until he starts school full-time. I would be doing the same, but, unfortunately, I was too late to get into the fall semester at NYU.

Ken advised me to wait it out, at least until the spring semester, before attending another college. He said that I shouldn't bounce back and forth again; it would only muddy my transcripts, and New York University is picky as it is. I'm okay with taking a break, despite that I will have to work harder to catch up, because I am going to use the time working and experiencing this sprawling and bizarre city.

Hardin and I have only spoken a few times since he left his graduation without saying goodbye to me. He texted me a few times here and there and has sent some emails, which were stiff, awkward, and formal, so I only responded to a few of them.

"Do you guys have any plans for the weekend?" I ask Landon while tying the strings of my apron around my waist.

"Not that I know of. I think he's just sleeping here and leaving Monday afternoon."

"Okay. I am working a double shift today, so don't wait up for me. I won't be home until at least two."

Landon sighs. "I really wish you wouldn't work so much. You don't have to help pay anything, I got enough money from grants, and you know Ken refuses to let me pay for much anyway."

I give Landon my sweetest smile and pull my hair back into a low ponytail, resting just above the collar of my black button-up shirt. "I won't go over this with you again." I shake my head and tuck my shirt into my work pants.

My work uniform isn't too bad, a black button-up, black pants, and black shoes. The only part of the ensemble that bothers me is the neon-green tie I have to wear. It took me two weeks to get used to the look, but I was so grateful that Sophia got me a waitressing job at such an upscale restaurant that the color of the tie didn't matter. She's the head pastry chef at Lookout, a newly opened and highly over-priced modern restaurant in Manhattan. I stay out of her and Landon's . . . *friendship?* Especially after meeting her roommates, one of whom I had already met back in

Washington. Landon and I seem to have the same sort of "it's a really, really small world" luck.

"Text me when you're off, then?" Landon reaches for my keys on the hook and places them into my hand. I agree, assuring him that Hardin's arrival isn't going to upset me, and with that, I leave for work.

I don't mind the twenty-minute walk each way. I am still learning my way through this massive city, and each time I get lost in the crowds of busy people, somehow I feel more connected to its vibe. The noise of the streets, the constant voices, sirens, and blaring horns only kept me up for the first week. Now it's almost calming the way I just sort of blend into the masses.

People-watching in New York is unlike anything else I've ever experienced. Everyone seems so important, so official, and I love guessing at people's life stories, where they came from, why they are here. I don't know how long I plan to stay here; not permanently, but I like it here for now. I miss him, though, so much.

Stop this. I need to stop thinking this way; I'm happy now, and he has clearly made a life for himself that doesn't involve me. I'm okay with that. I just want him to be happy, that's all. I loved seeing him with his new friends at his graduation; I loved the way he was so collected, so . . . happy.

I just hated the way he walked off when I took too long coming back from the restroom. I'd left my phone on the counter by the sink, but when I remembered it and returned, it was already gone. Then I'd spent a half hour trying to find the lost and found, or a guard to help me find it. Eventually I saw it sitting on a trash can, like someone realized it wasn't theirs, but didn't bother to put it back where they found it. In any event, the battery was already dead. I tried to find Hardin at the spot where I'd left him, but he was gone. Ken said he'd left with his friends, and something clicked then—that this was over. It was really over.

Do I wish he would have come back for me? Of course. But he didn't, and I can't live my life wishing that he did.

I purposely picked up extra shifts this weekend, wanting to keep myself as busy as possible and keep my time at the apartment to a minimum. Due to the tension and bickering between Sophia and her roommates, I am going to try my hardest to avoid staying there, but I certainly will if things are too awkward with Hardin. Sophia and I have become closer, but I try not to pry too much. I am too biased due to my friendship with Landon, and I don't think I want to hear the details. Especially if she started to feel comfortable talking to me about sex with him. I shudder thinking about Kimberly's revelations about sweet, reserved Trevor's escapades in the office.

Two blocks from Lookout, I look down at my phone to check the time and nearly walk straight into Robert. His hands reach out and stop me before I collide with him.

"*Lookout!*" he says lamely, and chuckles while I groan. "See, it's hilarious, because we work at Lookout and, and . . ." He smiles and adjusts his own lime-green tie comically.

The tie looks much better on him than it does on me, with his blond hair messy and sticking straight up in some places. I debate whether to remind him about Hardin, but stay silent while we cross the street with a group of teenage girls, all giggling and smiling at him. I don't blame them—he's handsome.

"Just a little distracted," I finally admit as we turn the corner.

"He's coming today, right?" Robert holds the door open for me, and I step into the darkly lit restaurant. The inside of Lookout is so dark that it takes a few seconds for my eyes to adjust to the difference whenever I walk inside from a sunny afternoon, and even now though it's barely noon. I follow him back to the break room, where I store my purse in a small locker and he slides his cell phone onto the top shelf.

"Yes." I close the door to the locker and lean my back against it.

Robert reaches his hand out to touch my elbow. "You know I'm okay with you talking about him to me. I don't exactly love the guy, but you can talk to me about anything."

"I know." I sigh. "I appreciate that so much. I just don't think it's a good idea to open that drawer. I've had it closed too long." I laugh and hope that it comes out more authentic than it feels. I lead the way out of the break room, and Robert follows close behind.

He smiles and looks up at the clock on the wall. If it weren't glowing red with deep blue numbers, I don't think I would be able to read the time in the hallway. The hallways are the darkest part of the restaurant, and the kitchen and the break room are the only areas that have standard lighting.

My shift begins normally, and the hours tick by quickly as the lunch crowd leaves and the dinner crowd begins to pour in. I've gotten myself to the point where I had almost been able to forget about Hardin's arrival for five minutes straight, when Robert walks over with a worried look on his face.

"They're here. Landon and Hardin." Robert's hands grab the hem of his apron, and he wipes the cloth across his forehead. "They're requesting your section."

I don't panic the way I had assumed that I would. Instead, I simply nod and work my way toward the entrance and search for Landon. I force my eyes to only search for Landon and his plaid shirt, not Hardin. Nervously, I glance around the area, looking over face after face, none of them Landon's.

"Tess." A hand touches my arm and I jump back.

It's that voice, that deep, beautiful, accented voice that I have played in my head for months and months.

"Tessa?" Hardin touches me again; this time his hand wraps around my wrist, the way it always used to.

I don't want to turn and face him—well, I do, but I'm terrified. I'm terrified to see him, to see the face that has been permanently branded into my mind, never to be altered or diluted by time the way that I had assumed it would be. His face, grumpy and ever frowning, will always be as vivid as the first time I saw him.

I quickly snap out of my trance and turn around. In the mere seconds that I have to plan, I try to focus on finding Landon's eyes before Hardin's, but what's the use?

It's impossible to miss those eyes, those gorgeous green eyes that could never be duplicated.

Hardin smiles at me, and I stand there, unable to speak for a few seconds. I need to get it together. "Hi," he says.

"Hi."

"Hardin wanted to come here." I hear Landon's voice, but my eyes don't seem to want to cooperate with my mind. Hardin is staring at me just the same, his fingers still pressing against the skin on my wrist. I should pull away before the pounding of my pulse betrays my reaction to seeing him after three months.

"We don't have to stay and eat here if you are busy," Landon adds.

"No, it's okay. Really," I assure my best friend. I know what he's thinking; I know he feels guilty and worried that bringing Hardin here will ruin the new Tessa. The Tessa who laughs and makes jokes, the Tessa who has become her own person, maybe even stubbornly so. That won't happen, though. I have myself in check, under control, totally cool and collected. Totally.

I gently pull my wrist from Hardin's soft grip and grab two menus from the board. I nod to the confused hostess, Kelsey, letting her know I'll be taking these two to their table.

"How long have you worked here?" Hardin asks, walking with me. He's dressed the same way he always was, same black T-shirt, same pair of boots, same tight, black jeans, though this pair has a small tear at the knee. I have to keep reminding myself that it has only been a few months since I left for my mother's house. It feels like so much more time has passed—years, even.

"Only three weeks," I say.

"Landon said you've been here since noon today?"

I nod. I gesture to a small booth against the back wall, and Hardin slides in on one side and Landon on the other.

"When will you get off?"

Get off? Is he making an innuendo? I can't tell after all this time. *Do I want him to?* I can't tell that, either.

"We close at one, so I usually get home around two when I work a closing shift."

"Two in the morning?" His mouth drops open dramatically.

I set the menus in front of the two men, and Hardin reaches for my wrist again. I pull back this time, pretending not to notice his intentions.

"Yes, in the morning. She works like this every day almost," Landon says.

I shoot him a glare, wishing he would have kept that to himself, then wonder why I feel that way. It shouldn't matter to Hardin how many hours I spend here.

Hardin doesn't say much after that; he just stares at the menu, points to the lamb ravioli, and orders a water. Landon orders his usual, asking if Sophia is busy in the kitchen, and gives me more "I'm sorry" smiles than necessary.

My next table keeps me busy. The woman is drunk and can't decide what she wants to eat; her husband is too busy on his phone to pay attention. I'm actually grateful for the drunk wife sending her food back three times; it makes it easier to only stop by Landon and Hardin's table once to fill their drinks and once to clear their plates.

Sophia being Sophia, she wrote off their tab. Hardin being Hardin, he left me a ridiculous tip. And me being me, I forced Landon to take it and return it to Hardin when they got back to the apartment.

chapter sixty-seven

HARDIN

I curse when I step on something plastic, but not too loudly, since I'm sure you can hear everything in this apartment—an apartment that, having few windows, is entirely too dark to see shit. And here I am, trying to remember the way back to the couch from the minuscule bathroom. This is what I get for drinking all that water at the restaurant in the hopes that Tessa would have to stop by more often. It didn't work, and another server ended up filling up my glass several times. It did, however, make me have to piss all night long.

Sleeping on the couch while knowing Tessa's closetlike room is empty drives me fucking crazy. I hate the idea of her walking through the city alone in the middle of the damn night. I scolded Landon for giving her the tiniest of the two "bedrooms," but he swears that Tessa won't allow him to change the arrangement.

Go figure. It doesn't surprise me that she's still as stubborn as she has always been. Another example of this: she works until two in the morning and walks home alone.

I should have thought about this sooner. I should have been waiting outside that ridiculous establishment to walk her home. Grabbing my phone from the couch, I check the time. It's only one now. I can take a cab and get there in less than five minutes.

Fifteen minutes later, thanks to the near impossibility of catching a cab on a Friday night, I guess, I'm standing outside

Tessa's workplace, waiting for her. I should text her, but I don't want to give her the chance to tell me no—especially since I'm already here.

People pass on the streets—mostly men, which only increases my anxiety about her leaving work alone at such a late hour. While analyzing her safety, I hear laughter. Her laughter.

The doors to the restaurant open and she walks out, laughing and covering her mouth with her hand. A man is next to her, holding the door for her. He looks familiar, too familiar . . . *Who the hell is this guy?* I swear I've seen him before but I can't remember . . .

The server. The server from that place up by the cabin.

How the hell is that possible? What the hell is this guy doing in New York?

Tessa leans into him, still laughing, and as I take a step forward out of the dark, her eyes meet mine immediately.

"Hardin? What are you doing?" she exclaims loudly. "You scared the crap out of me!"

I look at him, then at her. Months of working out to relieve anger, months of talking shit with Dr. Tran to control my emotions, haven't prepared me, and never could, for this. I have had small thoughts about Tessa's having a boyfriend, but I wasn't expecting or prepared to actually have to deal with it.

As nonchalantly as I can manage, I shrug and say, "I came to make sure you got home okay."

Tessa and the guy share a look before he nods and shrugs his shoulders. "Text me when you get home," he says, brushing his hand across hers as he departs.

Tessa watches him go, then turns to me with a not-unpleasant smile.

"I'll hail a cab," I say, still talking myself down internally. What did I think? That she would still be figuring shit out?

Yeah, I guess I did.

"I usually walk."

"You walk? Alone?" I regret asking the second part of that question the moment it leaves my fucking mouth. After a beat, I conclude, "He walks you home."

She winces. "Only the shifts we work together."

"How long have you been dating him?"

"What?" She stops us before we even make it around the corner. "We aren't dating." She creases her brows.

"Seems like it." I shrug, trying my fucking hardest to not be a sulking asshole about it.

"We aren't. We spend time together, but I'm not dating at all."

Looking at her, I try to determine if she's telling the truth. "He wants to. The way he touched your hand."

"Well, I don't. Not yet." She stares down at her feet while we cross the street. There aren't nearly as many people out as earlier today, but the streets are still far from empty.

"Not yet? You haven't dated anyone?" I watch a fruit vendor pack up for the night while praying for the answer that I want to hear.

"No, I don't intend to date for a while." I feel her eyes on me when she adds, "Are you? Dating anyone, I mean?"

The relief I feel to find out that she hasn't been dating is beyond words. I turn and smile at her. "No. I don't date." I hope she catches my joke.

And she does smile. "I've heard that before."

"I'm a conservative guy, remember?"

She laughs but doesn't add any commentary as we stroll block after block. I need to talk to her about walking home this late. I have spent night after night, week after week, trying to imagine how she's living her life here. Her working long days as a waitress and wandering home in the darkness of New York City was not something that crossed my mind.

"Why are you working in a restaurant?"

"Sophia got me the job. It's a really nice place, and I make more money than you would think."

"More money than you would at Vance?" I ask her, knowing the answer.

"I don't mind it. It keeps me busy."

"Vance told me you didn't even ask for a recommendation, and you know he's planning on opening something here, too."

She is staring down the street now, mindlessly gazing into traffic. "I know, but I want to do something on my own. I like my job, for now, until I can get into NYU."

"You haven't gotten into NYU yet?" I exclaim, unable to hide my surprise. *Why hasn't anyone told me any of this?* I force Landon to give me updates on Tessa's life, but apparently he likes to leave out the important shit.

"No, but I am hoping for the spring semester." She reaches her hand into her bag and pulls out a set of keys. "The deadlines had all passed."

"You're okay with that?" I'm surprised by the calm in her voice.

"Yeah, I'm only nineteen. It will be fine." She shrugs, and I think my heart stops. "It's not ideal, but I have time to make up for it. I could always take double courses and maybe even graduate early like you did."

I don't know what to say about this . . . calm and nonpanicked Tessa, Tessa without a rock-solid plan, but I'm more than happy to be around her.

"Yeah, I suppose you could—"

Before I can finish, a man steps out in front of us. His face is covered in dirt and overgrown whiskers. Instinctively, I step in front of Tessa.

"Hey, girly," the man says.

My stance shifts from paranoid to protective, and I stand up straight, waiting for this asshole to try something.

"Hey, Joe. How are you tonight?" Tessa gently nudges me out of the way and pulls a small bag from her purse.

"I'm good, darling." The man smiles and reaches his hand out for the bag. "What did you bring this time?"

I force myself to stay back, but not too far.

"Some fries and those sliders that you love." She smiles, and the man grins back before unfolding the paper bag and lifting it to his face to smell the contents.

"You're too good to me." He pushes a dirt-stained hand into the bag and pulls out a handful of fries to shove into his mouth. "Want some?" He looks at each of us with one fry hanging from his mouth.

"No." Tessa giggles, waving her hand in front of her. "You enjoy your dinner, Joe. I'll see you tomorrow." She waves for me to follow her around the corner, where she punches in her code to Landon's apartment building.

"How do you know that guy?"

She stops in front of a row of mailboxes lining the lobby and opens one with her key while I wait for her response.

"He lives there, on that corner. He's there each night, and so when we have leftovers in the kitchen, I try and bring them to him."

"Is that safe?" I look behind us as we walk down the empty hall.

"Giving someone food? Yes." She laughs. "I'm not as fragile as I used to be." Her smile is genuine, not at all offended, and I don't know what to say.

Inside the apartment, Tessa steps out of her shoes and pulls the tie from her neck. I haven't allowed myself too many glances at her body. I have tried to keep my eyes on her face, her hair, hell, even her ears, but now, as she unbuttons the black shirt, revealing only a tank top underneath, I am distracted and I can't seem to remember why I was avoiding admiring such a beautiful thing. Her fucking body is the most perfect, most fucking mouth-watering body, and the curve of her hips is something I fantasize about daily.

She goes to the kitchen and calls over her shoulder, "I'm going to get to bed. I have an early shift tomorrow."

I walk toward her and wait until she finishes her glass of water. "You work tomorrow, too?"

"Yeah, I work all day."

"Why?"

She sighs. "Well, I have bills to pay."

She's lying. "And?" I press.

She wipes at the counter with her hand for a minute. "And maybe I was trying to avoid you."

"You've been avoiding me long enough, don't you think?" I raise a brow at her.

She swallows. "I wasn't avoiding you. You barely reach out to me anymore."

"That's because you avoid me."

She walks past me, pulling her hair from its ponytail as she does. "I didn't know what to say. I was pretty hurt by you leaving the graduation and—"

"*You* left. Not me."

"What?" She stops and turns around.

"You left the graduation. I only left after looking for you for thirty minutes."

She looks offended. "I looked for *you*. I did. I never would have just left your graduation."

"Okay, well, I seem to remember a different story there, but there's no real point in arguing over it now."

Her eyes lower and she seems to agree with me. "You're right." She refills her empty glass. And takes a small sip.

"Look at us, not fighting and shit," I tease her.

She leans her elbow onto the counter and shuts the faucet off. " 'And shit,' " she repeats with a smile.

"And shit."

We both laugh and continue to stare at each other.

"This isn't as awkward as I thought it would be," Tessa says. Untying her apron, her fingers get stuck on the knot.

"Need help?"

"No." Her answer comes too quickly and she tugs at the strings again.

"You sure about that?"

After a few more minutes of struggling, she finally scowls and turns around to give me access to her back. Within a few seconds I've untangled the strings and she's counting her tip money on the counter.

"Why won't you get another internship? You're more than a waitress."

"There is nothing wrong with being a server, and this isn't the end goal for me. I don't mind it and—"

"And because you don't want to ask Vance for help." Her eyes widen. I shake my head, pushing my hair back. "You act like I don't know you, Tess."

"It's not only that; I just like that this job is *mine*. He would have to pull some serious strings to get me an internship out here—I'm not even actively enrolled in college for a few months."

"Sophia helped you get your job," I point out. Not to be cruel, but I just want to hear her say the truth. "What you really wanted was something that wasn't tied to me. Am I correct?"

She takes a few breaths, looking everywhere in the room except at me. "Yes, that's true."

We stand there quietly, too near each other and too far away in the tiny kitchen. After a few seconds, she stands up straight and gathers her apron and water glass. "I need to go to bed. I have to work all day tomorrow and it's late."

"Call in," I casually suggest, even though I want to demand it.

"I can't just call in," she lies.

"Yes, you can."

"I've never missed a day."

"You've only been there three weeks. You haven't had time to miss a day, and really, it's what people do on a Saturday in New York. They call in to work and spend time with better company."

A playful smile tugs at the corners of her full lips. "And you are this said better company?"

"Of course." I wave my hands over my torso to prove my point.

She regards me for a moment, and I can tell she's actually considering taking the day off. But at last she says, "No, I can't. I'm sorry, I just can't. I can't risk the shift not being covered. It will make me look bad, and I need this job." She frowns, all playfulness gone now, replaced by overthinking.

I almost tell her that she doesn't actually need the job, that what she needs to do is pack her shit and come back to Seattle with me, but I bite my tongue. Dr. Tran says control is a negative factor in our relationship, and I "need to find the balance between control and guidance."

Dr. Tran really pisses me off.

"I get it." I shrug, mentally cursing the good doctor out for a few beats before smiling at Tessa. "I'll let you go to bed, then."

With that, she turns on her heel and retreats to her closet-room, leaving me alone in the kitchen, then alone on the sofa, and then alone in the dreams that come.

chapter sixty-eight

TESSA

In my dreams, Hardin's voice rings through loud and clear, begging me to stop.

Begging me to stop? What is that . . .

My eyes open, and I sit up in bed.

"Stop," he strains out again.

It takes me a moment to realize this isn't one of my dreams, it's Hardin's actual voice.

I rush out of my room and into the living room, where Hardin is sleeping on the couch. He's not yelling or thrashing the way he used to, but his voice is pleading, and when he says, "Please, stop," my heart sinks.

"Hardin, wake up. Please, wake up," I calmly say, running my fingers over the clammy skin on his shoulder.

His eyes pop open, and his hands lift to touch my face. He's disoriented when he sits up and pulls me onto his lap. I don't fight it. I couldn't possibly.

Silent seconds pass by before he rests his head against my chest.

"How often?" My heart is twisted and aching for him.

"Only about once a week or so. I take pills for them now, but on nights like tonight, it was too late to take them."

"I'm sorry." I force myself to forget that we haven't seen each other in months. I don't think about the way we have already slipped back into touching one another. I don't care, though; I would never turn away from comforting him, no matter the circumstance.

"Don't be. I'm fine." He nuzzles further into my neck and wraps both arms around my waist. "I'm sorry that I woke you."

"Don't be." I lean into the back of the couch.

"I've missed you." He yawns, drawing my body into his chest. He lies back, bringing me with him, and I let him.

"Me, too."

I feel his lips press against my forehead and I shiver, basking in the warmth and familiarity of his lips on my skin. It doesn't make sense to me how it could be this easy, this natural, to find myself in Hardin's arms again.

"I love how real this is," he whispers. "It's never going to go away, you know that, don't you?"

Grasping for a sliver of logic, I say, "We have different lives now."

"I'm still waiting for you to see it, that's all."

"See what?" When he doesn't respond, I look up at him to find his eyes closed, his lips slightly parted in sleep.

I WAKE TO THE SOUND of the coffeepot beeping in the kitchen. Hardin's face is the first thing I see when my eyes open, and I'm not sure how to feel about it.

I detach my body from his, lifting his arms off my waist, and scramble to my feet. Landon walks out from the kitchen, holding a cup of coffee between his hands. An unmistakable smile is painted across his face.

"What?" I ask, stretching my arms. I haven't shared a bed, or couch, with anyone since Hardin. One night Robert stayed over because he locked himself out of his apartment, but he slept on the couch and I slept in my bed.

"Noooooo-thing." Landon's smile grows, and he tries to hide it by taking a drink of steaming coffee.

I roll my eyes at him, fighting a smile, and walk to my room to grab my phone. I panic when the time reads eleven thirty. I haven't slept this late since I moved here, and now I don't have time to take a shower before I leave for work.

I pour a cup of coffee and place it inside the freezer to cool while I brush my teeth, wash my face, and get dressed. I've become a huge fan of iced coffee, but I hate paying the overpriced fee at the coffee shops for them to only dump ice into the cup. Mine tastes just about the same. Landon agrees.

Hardin is still asleep when I leave, and I find myself leaning over him, ready to kiss him goodbye. Fortunately, Landon walks into the room at the right time, stopping my insane behavior. *What is wrong with me?*

The walk to work is filled with thoughts of Hardin: how it felt to sleep in his arms, how comforting it was to wake up on his chest. I'm confused, as I always am when encountering him, and feel rushed to make it to work on time.

When I get to the break room, Robert is already there and opens my locker for me when he sees me coming.

"I'm late, did they notice?" I rush to throw my purse in and close the locker.

"No, you're only five minutes late. How was your night?" His blue eyes shine with a barely veiled curiosity.

I shrug. "It was okay." I know how Robert feels about me, and it's not fair of me to talk about Hardin with him, whether he encourages it or not.

"Okay, huh?" He smiles.

"Better than I thought." I stick with short answers.

"It's okay, Tessa. I know how you feel about him." He touches my shoulder with his hand. "I've known since that first time I met you."

I am getting emotional now, wishing Robert weren't so kind, wishing Hardin weren't in New York for the weekend, then taking that back and wishing he would stay longer. Robert doesn't ask any more questions, and we're so busy at work that I don't have time to think about anything else except serving food and drinks until one in the morning. Even my breaks go too quickly, allowing me just enough time to shovel down a plate of meatballs and queso.

When closing comes, I'm the last one out. I assured Robert that I would be fine if he left early to get drinks with the other servers. I have a feeling that when I walk out of the restaurant, Hardin will be waiting anyway.

chapter sixty-nine

TESSA

And I'm right. There, leaning against the wall with the fake Banksy graffiti, is Hardin.

"You didn't tell me that Delilah and Samantha are roommates" is the first sentence out of his mouth. He's smiling, that smile where his nose turns up at the end because his smile is so big.

"Yeah, it's a mess." I shake my head, rolling my eyes. "Especially since those aren't their names, and you know it."

Hardin laughs. "That is some good shit, though. What are the fucking odds of that?" He lifts his hand to his chest, and his laughter shakes his body. "This is some straight-up soap-opera shit."

"Who are you telling? *I* have to deal with it. Poor Landon, though, you should have seen his face when we met Sophia and her friends for drinks the night he found out. He almost fell out of the chair."

"This is too much." Hardin chuckles.

"Don't laugh about it in front of Landon; he's having a hard time dealing with the two of them."

"Yeah, yeah. I know." Hardin rolls his eyes.

Just then the wind picks up, and Hardin's long hair starts blowing around his head. I can't help but point up at it and laugh. It's safer than the alternative: asking Hardin why he's in the city to begin with.

"My hair looks better like this and gives women more to pull," he teases, but the words drive straight through me.

"Oh," I say, but laugh along, not wanting him to know that my head is spinning and my chest is aching at the thought of anyone else touching him.

"Hey." He reaches for me, turns me around to look at him as if we were alone on the sidewalk. "I was joking, a shitty, stupid, really fucking dumb joke."

"It's okay, I'm okay." I smile up at him, tucking my blowing hair behind my ear.

"You may be all independent and fearless enough to hang out with homeless men, but you're still a shit liar," he says, calling me out.

I try to keep the mood light. "Hey, don't go talking about Joe. He's my friend." I stick my tongue out at Hardin as we pass a couple making out on a bench.

Loud enough for them to hear, Hardin says, "Five bucks says he has his hand up her skirt in less than two minutes."

I playfully shove at his shoulder, and he wraps an arm around my waist. "Don't get too touchy—Joe will ask questions!" I wiggle my brows at Hardin, and he bursts into laughter.

"What is it with you and homeless men?"

Thoughts of my father fill my mind, and I stop laughing for a beat.

"Shit, I didn't mean it like that."

I hold my hand up and smile. "No, it's okay. Really, let's just hope Joe doesn't turn out to be my uncle." Hardin stares at me as if I've grown another set of eyes, and I laugh at him. "I'm fine! I can take a joke now. I have learned not to take myself so seriously."

He seems pleased with that, and he even smiles at Joe when I hand him his bag of catfish and hush puppies.

THE APARTMENT IS DARK when we get back. Landon has most likely been asleep for a few hours.

"Have you eaten?" I ask Hardin when he follows me into the kitchen.

Hardin sits down at the two-person table and lifts his elbows onto the surface. "No, actually, I haven't. I was going to steal that bag of food, but Joe beat me to it."

"I can make you something? I'm hungry, too."

Twenty minutes later, I'm dipping my finger into the vodka sauce, testing the flavor.

"You going to share that?" Hardin asks from behind me. "It wouldn't be the first time I've eaten something off of your finger," he teases with a smirk. "The icing was one of my favorite flavors of Tessa."

"You remember that?" I offer him some sauce on a spoon.

"I remember everything, Tessa. Well, everything that I wasn't too drunk or high during." A frown takes over his teasing smile, and I dip my finger into the spoon and offer it to him. It does the job, and his smile returns.

His tongue is warm on my finger, and his eyes are pouring into mine when he licks the sauce from the tip. Pulling my finger between his lips, he sucks again and continues long after the sauce is gone.

My finger on his lips, he says, "I was going to talk to you about something. It involves what you said about me remembering things."

But the way his soft lips are moving on my skin distracts me. "Right now?"

"Soon, doesn't have to be tonight," he whispers, his tongue darting out to wet the tip of my middle finger, too.

"What are we doing?"

"You've asked me that too many times." He smiles, getting up.

"We haven't seen each other in so long. This isn't a good idea," I say, not meaning a damn word of it.

"I've missed you, and I've been waiting for *you* to miss you, too." His hand is on my hip, resting there, pressing against the fabric of my work shirt. "I don't like seeing you in all black. It doesn't suit you." He leans his head down and nudges my jaw with his nose.

My fingers fumble with the buttons on my shirt, clumsily slipping over the small plastic beads. "I'm happy that *you* didn't show up in another color."

He smiles against my cheek. "I haven't changed much, Tess. Just got a few doctors, hit the gym more."

"You still don't drink?" I drop my shirt to the floor behind us, and he backs me into the counter.

"A little, yes. Usually only wine or a light beer. But, no, I'm never going to chug a bottle of vodka again."

My skin is on fire, and my brain is slowly trying to make sense of how we got here, all these months later, with my hands waiting for permission to remove his shirt. He seems to read my thoughts and lifts my hands in his and pushes them into the thin material.

"It's our anniversary month, you know?" he says as I pull his shirt over his head and take in the sight of his bare chest.

My eyes scan over the area, looking for new designs, and I'm happy to find only the leaves—*ferns,* I believe Hardin called them. They look like odd-shaped leaves to me, with thick sides and a long stem coming out of the bottom. "We don't have an anniversary month, you insane man." I find myself trying to get a glimpse at his back, yet am embarrassed when he catches on and turns around.

"Yes, we do," he disagrees. "Still only yours on my back," he briefly explains while I stare at the newly developed muscles in his shoulders and back.

"I'm glad." I quietly admit, my mouth dry.

His eyes are full of amusement. "Have you went wild and gotten yourself a tattoo yet?"

"No." I swat at him, and he backs up against the counter and reaches for me.

"Are you okay with me touching you this way?"

"Yes," my mouth confesses before my brain has the time to agree.

He uses one hand to trail his fingers over the top lining of my tank top. "What about like this?"

I nod.

My heart is hammering through my chest to the point I'm convinced that he can hear it. I feel so in tune, so alive and awake, and starved for his touch. It's been so long, and here he is in front of me, saying and doing the things I used to love so much. Only this time, he is a little more cautious, more patient.

"I've needed you so much, Tess." His mouth is less than two inches from mine; his fingers are drawing slow circles on the bare skin of my shoulders. I feel drunk, my head is cloudy.

When his lips reach mine, I'm dragged back under. I'm taken to that place where only Hardin exists, only his fingers on my skin, only his lips caressing mine, only his teeth nipping at the corners of my mouth, only the soft groans sounding from his throat when I unbutton his jeans.

"Are you trying to use me for sex again?" He smiles against my mouth, pushing his tongue to cover mine so that I can't respond. "Teasing," he mumbles and presses his body completely against mine. My arms move around his neck, and my fingers lace through his hair.

"If I wasn't a gentleman, I would fuck you right here on this counter." His hands cup both of my breasts, his fingers hooking under the straps of my bra and tank top. "I would lift you up here, slide these hideous pants down your legs, spread your thighs, and take you right here."

"You said you weren't a gentleman," I breathlessly remind him.

"I changed my mind. I'm a half gentleman now," he teases.

I'm so wound up that I'm beginning to think I may combust and make a mess of the kitchen. I push my hand down his boxers, and my eyes roll back when he says, "Fuck, Tess."

"A *half*? What does that mean?" I moan when his fingers slide easily past the loose waist of my pants.

"That means, regardless of how badly I want you, how fucking badly I want to fuck you on this counter and make you scream my name so the entire block knows who is making you come"— he sucks at the skin down the column of my neck—"I won't be doing any of that until the day you marry me."

My hands freeze, one down his boxers, and the other on his back. "What?" I croak, clearing my throat.

"You heard me. I won't be fucking you until you marry me."

"You're not serious, are you?" *Please don't be serious. He couldn't be; we have barely spoken in months. He has to be teasing. Right?*

"Not even close to joking. No bullshit." His eyes dance with amusement, and I literally stomp my foot against the tile floor.

"But we aren't . . . we haven't even . . ." I gather my hair into one hand and try to make sense of what he's saying.

"Oh, you didn't think I would give up so easily, did you?" He leans in and touches his lips to my burning cheek. "Don't you know me at all?" His smile makes me want to slap him and kiss him at the same time.

"But you *did* give up."

"No, I'm giving you space just like you forced me to do. I'm trusting your love for me to bring you back to center, eventually." He raises one brow and brings out that smile and those evil dimples. "You are taking a long-ass time, though."

What the hell? "But . . ." I am literally at a loss for words.

"You're going to hurt yourself." He laughs and lifts his hands to cup my cheeks. "Will you sleep on the couch with me again? Or will that be too tempting for you?"

I roll my eyes and follow him into the living room, trying to understand how any of this could possibly make sense to him, or to me. There are so many things to talk about, so many questions, so many answers.

But for now, I'm going to fall asleep on the couch with Hardin and pretend that everything could be right in my world for once.

chapter seventy

TESSA

"Good morning, baby," I hear from somewhere nearby.

When I open my eyes, black ink in the shape of a swallow is the first thing I see. Hardin's skin has a deeper tan than ever before, and the muscles across his chest are much more prominent than they were when I last saw him. He's always been incredibly good-looking, but he looks better than ever now, and it's the sweetest form of torture to be lying here, against his bare chest, with one of his arms wrapped around my back and the other lifting to brush the hair back from my face.

"Morning." I rest my chin on his chest, giving me the perfect angle to admire his face.

"Sleep well?" His fingers are gently gliding over my hair, and his smile is still perfectly in place.

"Yes." I close my eyes for a moment to clear my brain, which has suddenly turned to mush at the sound of his raspy, sleepy voice. Even his accent feels more intense, more distinct. Damn him.

Without another word, he rests the tip of his thumb on my lips.

I open my eyes when I hear Landon's bedroom door open, and when I move to sit up, Hardin wraps his arms tighter around me. "No, you don't." He laughs. He pushes up from the couch and lifts his body, bringing mine with it.

Landon enters the living room, shirtless, with Sophia trailing behind him. She's dressed in her work clothes from last night; the black uniform accompanied with a bright smile suits her well.

"Hey." Landon's cheeks flush, and Sophia reaches for his hand and smiles at me. I think I catch a wink from her, but I'm still a little cloudy from waking up with Hardin.

She leans up and presses a soft kiss to Landon's cheek. "I'll call you after my shift."

The thick patches of hair on Landon's face are something I'm still getting used to, but the look is good on him. He smiles down at Sophia and opens the front door for her.

"Well, now we know why Landon didn't come out of his room last night," Hardin whispers into my ear, his breath hot against me.

Oversensitive and wound up, I try again to remove my body from his. "I need coffee," I argue.

Those must be the magic words, because he nods and allows me to climb off his lap. The loss of contact has an immediate effect on my body, but I force myself to make it to the coffeemaker.

I ignore the way Landon shakes his head while smiling, and I walk into the kitchen. The skillet from last night, full of uneaten vodka sauce, is still on the stove, and when I pull open the oven, I find the pan of chicken breasts still inside.

I don't remember turning the oven or stove off, but then again, I wasn't thinking much last night. My brain didn't seem to want to think past Hardin and the way his lips felt against mine after months of deprivation. My skin flames from the reminder of it, the gentle way he touched me, worshipping my body.

"Good thing I turned the heat off, right?" Hardin enters the kitchen, sweats hung low on his hips. His new tattoos accent the plane of his torso, drawing my eyes to the bottom of his sculpted abdomen.

"Uhm, yeah." I clear my throat and try to decide why I'm suddenly so hormonal. I feel the way I did when I first met him, and that worries me. It's always so easy to fall back into the dysfunctional pattern that is Hessa, but I have to keep my head clear here.

"What time do you work today?" Hardin leans against the counter opposite me and watches as I begin to work on cleaning up the mess.

"Noon." I pour the uneaten sauce into the sink. "Only one shift. I should be home around five."

"I'm taking you to dinner." He smiles, crossing his arms in front of his chest. I tilt my head, raising a brow at him, and turn on the garbage disposal. "You're thinking about shoving my hand into that right now, aren't you?" He points to the noisy disposal. His laughter is soft and charming and makes me light-headed.

"Maybe." I smile. "So you need to rephrase that into the form of a question."

"There's the sassy Theresa I know and love," he teases, sliding his palms across the countertop.

"Theresa, again?" I attempt to scowl at him, but a smile breaks through.

"Yes, again." He nods and does something un-Hardin-like. He grabs the small trash can from under the sink and starts to help me clean up the trash from the counter. "So will you please do me the honor of granting me your time to have a meal in a common place tonight?"

His playful sarcasm has me laughing, and when Landon enters the kitchen, he only glances at us and leans against the counter.

"Are you okay?" I ask.

Landon stares at the cleaning man in Hardin's body and glances back at me, baffled. "Yeah, just tired." He rubs his fists over his eyes.

"I would imagine." Hardin wiggles his eyebrows, and Landon shoves his shoulder.

I stare, feeling like I'm in some alternate universe. One where Landon shoves Hardin's shoulders and Hardin laughs, calling him an asshole, instead of glaring at or threatening him.

I like this universe here. I think I would love to stay awhile.

"It's not like that. Shut it." Landon adds ground coffee to the pot and pulls three cups from the cabinet and sets them on the counter.

"Sure, sure." Hardin rolls his eyes.

Landon mockingly says, "Shore, shore."

I listen to the two of them banter and take innocent digs at each other while I reach for a box of cereal in the highest cabinet. I'm standing on my toes when I feel Hardin's fingers tugging at my shorts, pulling them up to cover more of my exposed skin.

Part of me wants to pull them up farther or even take them off completely, just to see the expression that would come from it, but for Landon's sake, I decide against it.

Instead, I find the humor in Hardin's gesture and roll my eyes at him while unrolling the bag of cereal inside the box.

"Frosted Flakes?" Hardin asks.

"In the cabinet," Landon responds.

A clouded memory of Hardin bickering with my father over his eating all of Hardin's cereal comes forward. I smile at the memory and file it away. I no longer think of my father with pain in my chest; I have learned to smile at the humor he held and to admire the positivity he showed in the short time I got to know him.

I dismiss myself to the bathroom to take a shower for work. Landon is telling Hardin about his newest favorite hockey player's getting signed by an opposing team, and Hardin surprises me by staying at the kitchen table with Landon instead of following me.

AN HOUR LATER, I'm dressed and ready to begin my walk to the restaurant. Hardin is sitting on the couch pulling his boots on when I enter the living room.

He looks up at me with a smile. "Ready?"

"For what?" I grab my apron from the back of the chair and push my phone into my pocket.

"The walk to work, of course," he says as if it's the most obvious answer.

Loving the gesture, I nod and, grinning like an idiot, follow him out the front door.

Walking through the streets of New York with Hardin is slightly on the strange side. He fits in here, his style and the way he's dressed, but at the same time he seems to fill the street with his voice, his animated expressions lighting up the dreary day.

"The one, well, one of the problems that I have with this city is this . . ." He waves his hand through the air. I wait a second for him to elaborate. "The sun is hidden," he says at last.

His boots smack loudly on the pavement as we walk, and I find that I love the sound. I missed it. It's one of the smaller things about him that I hadn't realized I loved until after I left him. I would find myself alone, walking down the loud streets of the city, and miss the noisy way Hardin always stomped around in his boots.

"You live in rainy Washington—you can't bash New York's lack of sun," I counter.

He laughs and changes the subject, asking me random questions about the world of waitressing. The rest of the walk to work is nice; Hardin asks question after question about what I've been doing for the last five months, and I tell him about my mother, David, and his daughter. I tell him about Noah's spot on the soccer team at his college in California, and how my mother and David took me back to the same town that I went to with Hardin's family.

I tell him about my first two nights in the city, and how the noise kept me up all night, and how on the third night I climbed out of bed and took a walk around the block, and that's when I met Joe for the first time. I tell him that the sweet homeless man reminds me of my father in a way, and I like to think that bringing him food is helping him in a way that I couldn't my own blood.

This confession has Hardin reaching to pull my hand into his, and I don't try to pull away.

I tell him about how worried I was about moving here, and also that I'm glad he's here visiting us. He doesn't mention the way he refused to have sex with me and then teased me until I finally fell asleep in his arms. He doesn't mention his marriage offer, and I'm okay with that. I'm still trying to make sense of this, as I've been trying to make sense of the way I feel about him since he crashed into my life a year ago.

When Robert meets me at the corner, the way he does when we work shifts together, Hardin moves closer, holds my hand a little tighter. Neither of them say much; they just eye each other up, and I roll my eyes at the way men behave in the presence of a woman.

"I'll be here when you get off." Hardin leans in to press his lips against my cheek, and his fingers push my hair behind my ear. "Don't work too hard," he whispers against my cheek. I can hear the smile in his voice, but I also know a hint of seriousness is behind his suggestion.

Of course, Hardin's words curse my entire shift. We get swamped, with table after table of men and women drinking too much wine or brandy and overpaying for tiny portions of food on decorated plates. A child decides that my uniform could use a makeover: a plate of spaghetti, to be exact. I don't have time for a break the entire shift, and my feet are killing me by the time I finally clock out over five hours later.

As promised, Hardin is waiting for me in the lobby. Sophia is standing next to the bench he's sitting on. Her dark hair is pulled into a high bun, bringing attention to her stunning face. She's exotic looking, with high cheekbones and full lips. I look down at my dirty uniform and cringe, smelling the garlic and tomato sauce staining my shirt. Hardin doesn't seem to notice my soiled clothes, but he pulls a small chunk of something from my ponytail as we walk outside.

"I don't even want to know what that was." I laugh softly. He smiles and pulls a napkin—no, a tissue—from his pocket and hands it to me.

I use the tissue to wipe under my eyes; my smeared eyeliner from sweating at work can't be remotely attractive right now. Hardin leads the conversation, asking simple questions about my shift, and we get back to the apartment quickly.

"My feet are killing me," I groan, pulling my shoes off my feet and tossing them aside. Hardin's eyes follow them, and I can practically see the sarcastic comments forming behind that head of hair about my making a mess. "I'm going to put them away in a minute, of course."

"Thought so." He smiles and sits down next to me on my bed. "Come here." He gathers my ankles in his hands, and I turn to face him as he rests my feet on his lap. His hands begin to rub my aching feet, and I lie back on the mattress, trying to ignore that I've had my feet stuck in shoes for hours.

"Thank you," I half moan. My eyes want to close from the instant relaxation that comes from Hardin's hands massaging my feet, but I want to look at him. I have suffered through months without looking at him, and now I don't want to look away.

"No problem. I can deal with the smell to see that relaxed, fucking dreamy look in your eyes." I lift my hand, swatting at the air, and he laughs and continues to work his magic on my feet.

His hands move to my calves and up to my thighs. I don't bother to stop the noises falling from my lips; it's just so relaxing and calming to have him touching me, working the sore muscles of my body.

"Come sit in front of me," he instructs, gently pushing my feet from his lap. I sit up, climbing over his lap, and sit in between his legs. His hands grip my shoulders first; he presses his fingertips into the tense muscles and rubs every ounce of tension out of them.

"If you weren't wearing a shirt, this would feel much better," Hardin comments.

I laugh for a moment, but I'm silenced by the memory of his teasing me in the kitchen last night. Leaning forward, I reach for the bottom of my loose work shirt and tug it free from my pants. I hear the gasp from Hardin as I pull it, along with the tank top, up and over my head.

"What? It was your idea," I remind him, leaning back against him. His hands are rougher now, pushing into my skin with purpose, and my head falls back against his chest.

He mumbles something under his breath, and I mentally pat myself on the back for wearing a decent bra. Granted, it's one of the two decent bras I wear, but no one sees them outside of myself, and Landon, from a few embarrassing laundry mishaps.

"This is new." Hardin's finger pushes under the strap on one of my shoulders. He lifts the strap and drops it back down.

I don't speak. I only scoot back slightly, pressing back against his open legs. He groans, wrapping the span of his hand around the base of my neck, his fingers gently rubbing over the bottom of my jaw and back down to the delicate skin under my ear.

"Feels good?" he asks, knowing the answer.

"Mhmm" is the only coherent sound that I can muster. When he chuckles, I push farther into him, essentially rubbing my body against his crotch, and I bring my hand up to my bra strap and slide it down my shoulder.

His hand tightens on my throat. "No teasing," he warns, pushing the strap back up with the hand that was working on my shoulders.

"Says the master of the art," I complain, and push the strap down again. Sitting shirtless in front of him, removing my bra while his hand is still holding me in place, is making me crazy. I'm worked up, and Hardin is only amplifying my hormones by panting and rubbing himself against me.

"No teasing," I mock his words. I don't have the chance to get a laugh in at his expense before he puts his hands on my shoulders and turns my head toward him.

"I haven't been fucked in five months, Theresa. You're pushing every ounce of my self-control," he harshly whispers, just above my lips. I make the first move, pressing my mouth to his, and I'm reminded of the first time we kissed, in his dorm room at that damn fraternity house.

"You haven't?" I gape, thanking my stars that he hasn't been with anyone during our separation. I feel as if I knew this somehow, I knew that he wouldn't. Either that, or I forced myself to be convinced that he would never touch another woman.

He's not the same person he was a year ago. He doesn't use lust and harsh words to get to people. He doesn't need a different girl every night, he is stronger now . . . He's the same Hardin that I love, but he's much stronger now.

"I hadn't noticed how gray your eyes are," he'd said to me. That was all it took. Between the alcohol and his sudden kindness, I couldn't stop myself from kissing him. His mouth tasted like—what else?—mint, of course, and his lip ring was cool against my mouth. It felt foreign and dangerous, but I loved it.

I climb on Hardin's lap now, the same way I did so long ago, and his hands grip my waist, pushing me gently to move along his body when he lies down on the bed. "Tess," he moans, just like in my memory. It fuels me further, pushes me deeper into the overwhelming passion between us. I'm lost there, and I sure as hell don't want to find my way out.

My thighs straddle his torso, and my hands dig into his hair. I'm needy and frantic and rushed, and all I can think about is the way his fingers are running, so gently, down my spine.

chapter seventy-one

HARDIN

My entire plan is shot to hell now. There's no damn way I am going to stop her. I should have known I didn't have a chance. I love her—I've loved her for what feels like my entire life, and I have missed being with her in this way.

I've missed the sexy-as-hell noises that fall from those fuck-able lips. I've missed the way she moves her full hips, sliding them across me, getting me so fucking hard that all I can think of is loving her, showing her how fucking good she makes me feel both emotionally and physically.

"I've craved you every second of every fucking day," I say into her open mouth. Her tongue swipes across mine, and I wrap my lips around it, playfully sucking on her tongue. Tessa's breath catches. Her hands reach for the bottom of my shirt, and she pushes it up to my arms. I sit up, bringing her half-dressed body with mine, and make it easier for her to lift the shirt off me.

"You have no idea how many times I've thought of you, how many times I've stroked my cock, remembering the way your hands feel on me, the way your hot mouth felt on me."

"Oh God."

Her moan only spurs my words. "You've missed this, haven't you? The way my words make you feel, the way they make you soaking, fucking wet?"

She nods and moans again when my tongue moves down her neck, slowly kissing and sucking at the salty skin. I've missed this feeling so much, the way she can completely and entirely take me over, take me under, and pull me back to the surface with her touch.

I wrap my arms around her waist and turn our bodies so I can lay her underneath me. My fingers have her pants unbuttoned, and my hands push them down to her ankles within seconds. Tessa grows impatient and kicks her feet, tossing the pants to the floor.

"Take yours off," she orders. Her cheeks are flushed; her hands are shaking, resting on the bottom of my back. I love her, I fucking love her and the way she still loves me after all this time.

We are truly fucking inevitable; even time cannot come between us.

I do as I'm told and climb back on top of her, taking her panties off while she arches her back.

"Fuck." I admire the way her hips curve and her thighs just fucking scream to be grasped by my hands. I do just that, and she stares at me with those fucking blue-gray eyes that got me through hours of bullshit with Dr. Tran. Those eyes even brought me to call Vance a few times in the last few months.

"Please, Hardin," Tessa whines, lifting her ass off the mattress.

"I know, baby." I bring my fingers to the apex of her thighs and rub my index finger over her pussy, collecting the wetness there. My cock twitches, and she sighs, wanting more relief. I push a finger inside her and use my thumb to brush across her clit, making her writhe underneath me and causing the sexiest fucking noise I've ever heard when I add another finger inside her.

Fuck.

Fuck.

"So good," she gasps, her fingers gripping at the hideous flower-printed sheets on her tiny bed.

ANNA **TODD**

"Yeah?" I urge her, moving my thumb faster over the spot that drives her fucking crazy. She nods frantically, and her hand moves to my cock, sliding up and down in a slow but tight motion.

"I wanted to taste you, it's been so long, but if I don't get my cock in you right now, I'll come all over your sheets."

Her eyes widen farther, and I give a few more pumps of my fingers inside her before aligning my body with hers. She is still gripping me, guiding my cock into her, and her eyes close as I fill her.

"I love you, I fucking love you so damn much," I tell her and lean down on my elbows, pressing in and pulling out, pressing in and pulling out. She claws at my back with one hand and wraps the fingers of the other into my hair. She pulls at it when I shift my hips, spreading her thighs farther apart.

After months of improving myself, seeing the brighter side to life and shit, it feels so fucking good to be with her. Everything in my life revolves around this woman, and some people may say it's unhealthy or obsessive, crazy even, but you know what?

I don't give a flying fuck, not a single fucking one. I love her, and she is everything to me. If people have shit to say, they can take their judgmental bullshit elsewhere, because no one is fucking perfect, and Tessa brings me as close to perfect as I will ever be.

"I love you, Hardin, I always have." Her words make me pause, and another piece of me is glued back in place. Tessa is everything to me, and hearing her say this shit, and the way her face looks when I look down at her, is everything to me.

"You had to know that I would always love you. You made me . . . *me*, Tessa, and I will never forget that." I enter her again, hoping that I don't end up crying like a bitch while getting her off.

"You made me *me*, too," she concurs, smiling up at me like we're in some romance novel. Two lovers, kept apart for months, only to be wonderfully reunited in the big city. Smiles and laughs and plenty of fucking. We've all read it before.

"Leave it to us to have a sentimental conversation at times like this," I tease, planting a kiss on her forehead. "Then again, what better time is there for our feelings to come out?" I kiss her smiling lips, and she wraps her thighs around my waist.

I'm getting close now. My spine is tingling, and I can feel myself getting closer and closer to coming as her breaths get deeper, quicker, and she tightens her thighs.

"You're going to come," I pant in her ear. Her fingers tug at my hair, sending me to the edge. "You're going to come now, with me, and I'm going to fill you," I promise, knowing how much she loves my fucking dirty-ass mouth. I may be less of an asshole, but I won't ever lose my edge.

With Tessa calling my name, she comes around me. I join her, and it's the most relieving, fucking borderline-magical feeling in the entire fucking world. This is the longest I've gone without fucking someone, and I would gladly have gone another year waiting for her.

"You know," I begin, as I roll off her and lie next to her, "by making love to me, you just agreed to marry me."

"Hush." She scrunches her nose. "You're ruining the moment."

I laugh. "As hard as you just came, I doubt that there is anything that could ruin your moment."

"*Our* moment," she mocks me, grinning like a madwoman with her eyes firmly closed.

"Seriously, though, you agreed, so when are you going to buy your dress?" I push further.

She rolls over, her tits right in my damn face, and it takes everything in me not to lean over and lick them. She couldn't blame me; I've been sexually dormant for a long-ass time.

"You are still as crazy as ever—no way am I marrying you right now."

"Therapy only works for my anger, not my obsession with having you forever."

Her eyes roll, and she lifts her arm to cover her face.

"It's true." I laugh and playfully drag her from the bed.

"What are you doing?" she screeches when I lift her over my shoulder. "You're going to hurt yourself lifting me!" She tries to wiggle off me, but I tighten my arm around the back of her legs.

I don't know if Landon is here or not, so I call out a warning just in case. The last thing he needs to see is me carrying a naked Tessa down the hallway of this matchbox apartment. "Landon! If you're here, stay in your damn room!"

"Put me down!" She kicks her legs again.

"You need a shower." I slap my palm against her ass, and she yelps, swatting mine in return.

"I can walk to the shower!" She is laughing now, giggling and screeching like a schoolgirl, and I fucking love it. I love that I can still make her laugh, that she grants me such beautiful sounds.

I finally place her, as gently as possible, on the bathroom floor and turn on the water.

"I've missed you." She stares up at me from the floor.

My chest tightens; I fucking need to spend my life with this woman. I need to tell her everything that I've been doing since she left me, but now isn't the time. Tomorrow, I'll tell her tomorrow.

Tonight, I will enjoy her sassy remarks, savor her laughs, and try to earn as many forms of affection from her as possible.

chapter seventy-two

TESSA

When I wake up on Monday morning, Hardin isn't in my bed. I know he has some sort of interview or meeting, but he hasn't mentioned exactly what it's about or which part of the city it's in. I have no clue if he will return before I have to leave for work.

I roll over, clinging to the sheets that still smell of him, and press my cheek against the mattress. Last night . . . well, last night was amazing. Hardin was amazing; we were amazing. The chemistry, explosive chemistry, between us is still as undeniable as ever, and now we are finally at a place in our lives where we can see our faults, each other's faults, and accept them and work through them in a way we couldn't in the past.

We needed this time apart. We needed to be able to stand alone before we could stand together, and I'm so thankful that we made it through the darkness, the fighting, the pain, and emerged hand in hand, stronger than ever.

I love him, Lord knows that I love this man; through all the separations, through all the chaos, he has crawled into my soul and marked it as his, never to be forgotten. I couldn't have if I tried, and I did try. I tried for months to move along, day by day, keeping myself busy in an attempt to keep my mind from him.

Of course, it didn't work, and thoughts of him never strayed too far from my mind. Now that I have agreed to work things out, in our own way, I finally feel as though everything could work out for us. We could be what I once wanted more than anything else.

"You had to know that I would always love you. You made me . . . me, Tessa, and I will never forget that," he'd said while pushing inside me.

He was breathless, gentle, and passionate. I was lost in his touch, in the way his fingers traveled down the length of my spine.

The sound of the front door opening finally brings me out of my daydreaming and remembering last night. I climb out of bed, reach for my shorts from the floor, and pull them up my legs. My hair is a matted mess; letting it air-dry after the shower with Hardin was a terrible idea. It's tangled and frizzy, but I brush my fingers over it the best I can before pulling it back into a ponytail.

Hardin is standing in the living room, his phone pressed to his ear, when I reach the entrance. He's dressed in his usual style of all black, and his long hair is a wild mess, like mine, yet it looks perfect on him.

"Yeah, I know. Ben will let you know what I decide," he says while noticing me standing near the couch. "I'll call you back." His tone is short, impatient almost, and he ends the call. The annoyed expression disappears as he takes steps toward me.

"Is everything okay?"

"Yeah." He nods, looking down at his phone again. His hand runs over his hair, and I wrap my hand around his wrist.

"Are you sure?" I don't want to be pushy, but he seems off. His phone rings in his hand, and he looks down at the screen.

"I need to take this." He sighs. "I'll be right back." Kissing my forehead, he steps out into the hallway and closes the front door behind him.

My eyes travel to the binder on the table. It's open, and the edges of a stack of papers are sticking out from the sides. I recognize the binder as the one I bought for him and smile at his still having it.

Curiosity gets the best of me, and I find myself opening the binder. On the first page is printed:

AFTER: BY HARDIN SCOTT

I flip to the second page.

It was the fall when he met her. Most people were obsessing over the way the leaves were turning and the smell of burning wood that always seems to linger in the air during this time of year; not him, he was only worried about one thing. Himself.

What? I brush through page after page, looking for some sort of explanation to calm the chaotic thoughts and confusion. This couldn't be what I think it is . . .

Her complaining felt overwhelming to him, he didn't want to hear the worst parts of himself thrown at him. He wanted her to think he was perfect, the way she was to him.

Tears fill my eyes, and I flinch when some of the papers fall to the floor.

In a Darcy-inspired gesture, he funded her father's funeral the way Darcy covered Lydia's wedding. In this case, he was attempting to mask a family embarrassment caused by a drug addict, not an underage sister marrying spontaneously, but the ending was the same. If his life would become one from the novels, his kind gesture would bring his Elizabeth back to his arms.

I can feel the room spinning around me. I had no idea that Hardin had paid for my father's funeral. The small possibility of it crossed my mind back then, but I had assumed that my mother's church had helped with the expenses.

Even though she was unable to bear children of her own, she couldn't let go of the dream of them. He knew that, and he loved her even so. He tried his hardest not to be selfish, but he couldn't help thinking about the little versions of him that she couldn't give him. He felt for her more than himself, but he couldn't help but cry over their loss many more nights than he could remember.

Just as I decide I cannot take any more, the front door opens and Hardin walks in. His eyes go directly to mess of white paper printed with disgusting black words, and his phone falls to the floor, joining the chaos.

chapter seventy-three

HARDIN

Complications.

Life is full of them; mine seems to be chocked-fucking-full of them, overflowing and spilling out of the top in a never-ending surge. Wave after wave of complications collide with the most important moments and things in my life, and this moment is one that I can't allow to be drowned.

If I stay calm, if I stay fucking calm and try to explain myself, I can hold back the tidal wave that is bound to crash through this small living room at any moment.

I can see it brewing behind the blue-gray of her eyes. I can see the confusion swirling with anger, creating a heavy storm, just like the sea before the lightning flashes and the thunder rolls. The water is calm, resting, just barely rippling on the surface, but I can see it coming.

A sheet of white paper clenched between trembling hands and Tessa's ominous expression warn me of the danger ahead.

I have no fucking idea what to say to her, where to start. It's such a complicated story, and I am pure shit at problem solving. I have to get a grip, I have to make more of an effort to mold and shape my words, to form an explanation that will keep her from running, again.

"What is this?" Her eyes move across a page before she tosses it into the air with one hand and crumples the corners of the small stack left in her grasp.

"Tessa." I take a cautious step toward her.

She stares. Her face is hard, guarded in a way that I'm not used to, as her feet shuffle backward.

"I need you to listen to me," I beg, searching her clouded features. I feel like shit, complete and utter shit. We had just gotten back to us, and I had finally gotten back to her, and now this, after such a short time together.

"Oh, I'm listening, all right." Her voice is loud, her tone sarcastic.

"I don't know where to start; just give me a minute and I'll explain."

My fingers run over my hair, tugging at the roots, wishing I could trade her pain for mine and rip my hair straight from the scalp. Yeah, a fucked-up image.

Tessa stands, impatiently patient, her eyes moving from page to page. Her brows lift and drop, her eyes tighten and widen, as I begin.

"Stop reading it." I take a step and grab the manuscript from her hands. The pages fall to the floor, joining the other bullshit pooling at her feet.

"Explain it. Now," she urges, her eyes cold, a thunderous gray that terrifies me.

"Okay, okay." I shift on my heels. "Okay, I have been writing."

"How long?" She steps toward me. I'm surprised by the way my body retracts as if it's afraid of her.

"A long time." I avoid the truth.

"You'll tell me, and you'll tell me now."

"Tess—"

"Don't *Tess* me, motherfucker. I'm not the same little girl you met a year ago. You're going to tell me now or you'll get the hell out of here." She purposely steps on a page, and I can't find it in me to blame her. "Well, I can't kick you out, because it's Landon's place, but I will leave if you don't explain this shit. Now," she adds, showing that, despite her anger, she's still sweet.

"I've been writing for a long time, since the very beginning of us, but I didn't have any intention of doing anything with it. I was only venting, using the paper to figure out what the fuck was going on in my head, but then I had this idea."

"When?" Her finger presses against my chest, jabbing at me in what she must think is a forceful way, but she couldn't be more wrong. I won't tell her that, not right now.

"I started it after we kissed."

"The first time?" Her hands spread, shoving my chest, and I wrap my fingers around them as they push against me again. "You were playing me." She wrenches her hands from mine and digs her open hands into her long hair.

"No, I wasn't! It wasn't like that!" I say, trying not to raise my voice. It's hard but I manage to keep a somewhat subdued tone.

She paces the small living room, fuming and whirling.

Her hands clench at her sides before she throws them into the air, again. "So many secrets, too many secrets. I'm over it."

"You're over it?" I gape at her. Her body is still moving restlessly around the room. "Talk to me; tell me how you feel about all of this."

"How I feel?" She shakes her head, her eyes wild. "I feel like this was a wake-up call, the string that pulled me back into reality and away from the ridiculous hopes of the last few days. This is us." She waves her hand back and forth. "There is always some bomb waiting to explode, and I'm not foolish enough to wait to be destroyed. Not anymore."

"This isn't a bomb, Tessa. You act as if I was writing this to purposely hurt you!"

She opens her mouth to speak before closing it again, at a

loss for words, I'm sure. When she collects herself, she says, "And just how did you think I would feel when I saw this? You knew I would find out eventually; why didn't you just tell me about it? I hate the way this feels."

"The way what feels?" I ask with caution.

"This feeling, it's like a burning in my chest when you pull stuff like this, and I hate it. I haven't felt this way in so long, and I never wanted to feel it again, yet here we are." The sound of defeat is clear in her soft voice, and my skin rises in bumps when she turns away from me.

"Come here." I reach for her arm and pull her as close to me as she will allow. Her arms cross in front of her as I crush her against my chest. She doesn't fight me off, but she doesn't hug me. She stands still, and I'm not sure if the worst is over.

"Tell me what you are feeling." My voice comes out awkward and short. "What you are thinking?"

She pushes against my chest again, with less force this time, and I let her go. She bends down at her knees and picks up one of the pages.

I had originally starting writing this as a form of expression, and, honestly, because I'd run out of shit to read. I was in between books, and Tessa, Theresa Young at the time, had started to intrigue me. She started to annoy me and piss me off, and I found myself thinking about her more and more.

When she was in my head, there didn't seem to be room for anything else. She became an obsession, and I convinced myself that it was a part of the game, but I knew better than that, I just wasn't ready to admit it yet. I remember the way I felt the first time I saw her, the way her lips looked so pouty, and the way I cringed at her outfit.

The skirt she wore had touched the floor, and her flat shoes were causing the damn thing to drag across it awkwardly. She stared down at the floor when she spoke her name for the first time—"Um, yeah . . . my name is Tessa"—and I remember thinking she had an odd name. I hadn't paid much attention after that. Nate was nice to her, and I was irritated by the way she stared at me, judging me with those gray eyes.

She nagged at me every day, even when she didn't speak to me, especially then.

"Are you even listening to me?" Her voice breaks through the memory, and I look over at her to find her fuming again.

"I was . . ." I hesitate.

"You weren't even listening," she accuses, rightfully so. "I can't believe you would do this. This is what you were doing all of those times I came home, and you would put your binder away. This is what I found in the closet just before I found my father . . ."

"I won't make excuses, but half of the shit in there is from my intoxicated mind."

" 'Trash'?" Her eyes scan the page in her hand. " 'She couldn't hold her liquor, she stumbled through the room in a messy way, the way tasteless girls move when they drink too much to impress others.' "

"Stop reading that shit, that part isn't about you. I swear it and you know it." I pull the page from her, but she quickly snatches it back.

"No! You don't get to write my story and tell me that I can't read it. You still haven't explained anything." She moves across the living room, lifting a shoe from the rug near the front door. She pushes both feet into her shoes and adjusts her shorts.

"Where are you going?" I'm prepared to follow her.

"I'm going for a walk. I need air. I need to get out of here." I can tell she's mentally cursing herself for giving me any bit of information.

"I'll come with you."

"No. You won't." Her keys are in her hands, and she gathers her messy hair above her head, twisting it and tying it back to control it.

"You are barely dressed," I point out.

She sends me a murderous glare. Without a word, she leaves the apartment, slamming the door behind her.

Nothing was accomplished just now, nothing solved. The plan I had to control the complications turned into a fucking disaster, and now shit's even more complicated. I kneel down on the floor, forcing myself not to follow her, throw her over my shoulder while she's kicking and screaming, and lock her in her room until she's ready to talk to me.

No, I can't do that. That would be backtracking on all the "progress" I've made. Instead, I gather the scrambled pages from the floor and read over some of the words, reminding myself why I decided to try to do something with this shitty writing in the first place.

"What is that you keep trying to hide over there?" Nate leaned over, being nosy as ever.

"Nothing, man, mind your business." Hardin scowled, staring across the courtyard. He didn't know how he started sitting here every day, at this exact time. It had nothing to do with Tessa and annoying-ass Landon meeting at the coffee shop every morning. Nothing at all to do with that.

He didn't want to see the obnoxious girl. He really didn't.

"I heard you and Molly last night in the hallway, you sick fuck." Nate flicked the ashes off his cigarette and made a face.

"Well, I wasn't going to let her in my room, and she wouldn't take no for an answer." Hardin laughed, proud that she was so willing to blow him at any moment, even in the hallway next to his room.

What he didn't tell them was that he'd turned her down and ended up jerking off while thinking of a certain blonde.

"You're an asshole." Nate shook his head. "Isn't he an asshole?" he asked Logan as the third boy approached the rundown picnic table.

"Yeah, he is." Logan held his hand out for a cigarette from Nate, and Hardin tried not to look at the girl in the potato-sack skirt waiting to cross the street.

"One of these days you're gonna fall in love, and I'm going to laugh my fucking ass off. You'll be the one giving oral in the hallway, and the chick won't let you in her room." Nate got a kick out of mocking him this way, but he could barely hear him.

Why does she dress that way? he found himself wondering as she rolled up the sleeves of her long-sleeved shirt. Hardin watched, pen in hand, as she walked closer, her eyes focused on the sidewalk in front of her, and she apologized too many times when she bumped into a puny boy, causing a book to fall from his hands.

She bent down to help and smiled at him, and Hardin couldn't help remembering how soft her lips were when she forced herself on him the other night. He was surprised as fuck—he didn't take her as the type to make the first move and was fairly positive that she had only kissed her lame-ass boyfriend before. Her gasping and the way her hands were so eager to touch him made that pretty clear.

"So what's going on with the bet?" Logan nodded toward Tessa as she smiled widely, spotting Landon in all his nerd glory, backpack and all.

"Nothing new," Hardin instantly replied, covering the paper with one arm. How was he supposed to know what *was going on with the mouthy, poorly dressed girl? She had barely spoken to him since her crazy-ass mom and lame-ass boyfriend had showed up pounding on her door Saturday morning.*

Why was her name written on this paper? And why was Hardin feeling like he was going to break out in a full-on sweat if Logan didn't stop staring like he knew something?

"She's annoying, but she seems to like me more than Zed, at least."

"She's hot," the two guys said at the same time.

"If I was a dickhead, I would go against the two of you. I'm better looking anyway," Nate teased, sharing a laugh with Logan.

"I want nothing to do with this shit. This is all fucking stupid, really—you shouldn't have fucked his girlfriend," Logan scolded Hardin, who only laughed.

"It was worth it," he said, looking back to the sidewalk across the courtyard. She had disappeared, and he changed the subject, asking about that weekend's party coming up.

As the two of them bickered over how many kegs to buy, Hardin found myself writing down how afraid she'd looked on Friday when she nearly pounded his door in to get away from that creepy Neil, who tried to make a move on her. He's a bastard, and would surely remain pissed at Hardin for the bottle of bleach he poured on his bed Sunday night. It wasn't like Hardin gave a shit about her; it was the principle of the situation.

After that, the words just kept writing themselves. I had no control over it, and with every interaction I had with her, I had more to say about her. About the way she crinkled her nose in disgust when she explained to me that she hated ketchup. I mean, who hates *ketchup*?

With every small detail I learned about her, my feelings grew. I would deny them until later, but they were there.

When we lived together, it grew harder to write. I found myself writing much less often, but when I did, I would hide my latest writing in the closet in a shoe box. I had no idea that Tessa had found the damn thing until now, and here I am, wondering when I will stop complicating my damn life.

More memories flood my mind, and I wish I could just plug her into my head, so she could read my thoughts and decipher my intentions.

If she were in my head, she could see the conversation that led me to New York City to meet with publishers. It wasn't something that I had ever intended to do. It just happened. I had written down so many moments, so many memorable moments between us. The first time I said I loved her; the second time, when I didn't take it back. Thinking about all of these memories while cleaning up this mess is overwhelming, and I can't help the memories from setting up shop in my mind.

He was leaning against the goalpost, pissed and bruised. Why had he started a fight with those guys in the middle of the stupid-ass bonfire anyway? Oh yeah, because Tessa left with Zed, and he hung up on Hardin, leaving him with nothing but a sarcastic tone and the knowledge that Tessa was in Zed's apartment.

It drove him much crazier than it should have. He wanted to forget about it, block it out, and feel physical pain in place of the unwelcome burn of jealousy. Would she fuck him? he kept thinking. Would he win?

Was it even about winning anymore? He couldn't tell. The lines had blurred sometime, and Hardin couldn't exactly put his finger on when it happened, but he was aware of it, sort of.

He had sat down on the grass, wiping the blood from his mouth, when Tessa approached. Hardin's vision was slightly blurred, but she was clear, he remembered that. During the drive back to Ken's house she was fidgety, unsure, and acting as if he were some rabid animal.

She focused on the road and asked, "Do you love me?"

Hardin was surprised—hell, he was fucking surprised and not prepared to answer her question. He'd already proclaimed his love for her, then taken it back, and there she was, crazy as ever, asking if he loved her while his face was swelling and bruising.

Of course he loved her, who the fuck was he kidding?

Hardin avoided answering her question for a while, but holding back became unbearable, and he found the words spilling out. "It's you. You're the person that I love the most in the world." It was true, as embarrassing and uncomfortable as it was to admit. He loved her, and he knew from then on that his life would never be the same after her.

If she left him, if she spent the remainder of her life absent from his, he would still never be the same. She had altered him, and there he stood, bloody knuckles and all, wanting to be better for her.

The next day, I found myself giving the pile of crumpled, coffee-stained pages a title: *After.*

I still wasn't ready or actually considering publishing it until I made the mistake of bringing it to one of my group-therapy sessions a few months ago. Luke had grabbed the binder from under my plastic chair as I told the story of burning my mother's house to the ground. The words were forced—I hate talking about that shit—but I kept my eyes above the curious eyes watching me and pretended that Tessa was there, in the room, smiling and proud of me for sharing my darkest time with a group of strangers who were just as fucked-up as I am . . . was.

I had reached down to grab the binder as Dr. Tran dismissed our group. My panic was short-lived when I looked over at Luke and found the binder in his hands.

"What is all this?" he asked, his eyes going over a page.

"If you would have met me a month ago, you would be swallowing your fucking teeth right now." I glared at him, grabbing the binder from his grasp.

"Sorry, man, I'm not good at social etiquette." His smile was uncomfortable, and for some reason it made me feel as if I could trust him.

"Clearly." I rolled my eyes, shoving all the loose pages back into the pockets.

He laughed. "Will you tell me what it is if I buy you a root beer from next door?"

"How sad are we? A couple of recovering alcoholics, negotiating to read a life story." I shook my head, wondering how I got to this point at such a young age, but I was so thankful for Tessa. If not for her, I would still be hiding in the darkness, left to rot.

"Well, root beer won't make you burn any houses down, and it won't make me say hurtful things to Kaci."

"Fine. Root beer is fine." I knew he was going to Dr. Tran for more than couple's counseling, but I decided not to be a complete dickhead and call him out on it.

We walked to the restaurant next door. I ordered a shitload of food, on his tab, and I ended up letting him read a few pages of my confessional.

Twenty minutes later I had to put an end to it. He would have read the entire thing if I'd let him. "This is amazing, really, man. This is . . . fucked-up in some parts, but I get it. It wasn't you talking, it was the demons."

"Demons, huh?" I took a long draw, finishing off the root beer in my glass.

"Yeah, demons. When you're drunk, you are full of them." He smiled. "Some of this I just read, I know wasn't written by you. It had to be the demons."

I shook my head. He was right, of course, but I couldn't help but picture a creepy little red dragon-thing on my shoulder, writing the fucked-up shit that was on some of those pages.

"You'll let her read this when you finish it, right?"

I dipped a cheese stick into some sauce and tried not to cuss him out for ruining my amusing thoughts about little demon creatures. "No. No way would I let her read this shit." I tapped my finger across the leather binding, remembering how excited Tessa was for me to use it when she bought it. I fought the idea, of course, but now I love the stupid thing.

"You should. I mean, take some of that twisted stuff out, especially the part about her being infertile. That was just wrong."

"I know." I didn't look at him; I looked down at the table and cringed, wondering what the hell was going through my mind when I wrote that shit.

"You should consider doing more with it. I'm not expert on literature or Heningsway, but I know that what I read was really, really good."

I swallow, choosing to ignore the mispronunciation. "Publish this?" I chuckled. "No fucking way." I ended the conversation there.

But job interview after job interview, I was bored, so fucking bored—and I left each one feeling even less challenged than at the last, and I couldn't imagine sitting in any of those shitty offices. I wanted to work in publishing, I did, but I found myself rereading page after page of my fucked-up thoughts, and the more I read and remembered, the more I wanted—no, needed—to do something with it.

It just sat there, begging for me to at least try, and I had this idea in my head that if she saw it, after I could cut some of the harsh shit out, she would love it. It became an obsession, and I was surprised by the interest people seemed to have in watching someone else's road to self-recovery.

Fucked-up, but they ate the shit up. I emailed each potential house a copy via an agent I knew from my time at Vance. Apparently the days of bringing in a stack of half-handwritten, half-typed pages are over.

This would be it, though, or so I thought. I thought this book would be the grand gesture that she needed to accept me back into her life. Granted, I thought it would be months from now, when the book was printed, and she'd had more time to do whatever the fuck she's been doing here in New York City.

I can't sit here any longer. There is a limit to my newly found patience, and I've reached it. I hate, absolutely loathe, the idea of Tessa's walking around this massive city alone, mad at me. She's been gone long enough, and I have explaining to do, a lot of it.

I grab the last page of the book and shove it into my pocket, not bothering to fold it. Then I text Landon and tell him to leave the door unlocked if he comes in or goes out and head out of the apartment to find her.

I don't have far to go, though. When I step outside, I find her sitting on the front stoop of the building. She's gazing off into nothing, her eyes focused and hard. She doesn't notice me when I approach her. Only when I sit down next to her does she look up at me, her eyes still distant. I watch closely as they slowly soften.

"We need to talk."

She nods and looks away, waiting for an explanation.

chapter seventy-four

HARDIN

We need to talk," I repeat and look at her, forcing my hands to stay in my own lap.

"I would say." She forces a smile. Her knees are dirty, marked with angry red lines.

"What happened? Are you all right?" My plan to keep my hands to myself goes out the window as I reach for her legs, examining the wounds closer.

She turns away, cheeks red and eyes matching. "I tripped, that's all."

"None of this was ever supposed to happen."

"You wrote a book about us and shopped it around to publishers. How was that not intentional?"

"No, I mean all of this. You and I, everything." The air is humid, and I'm finding it harder than I expected to get the words out. "This year has been an entire lifetime for me. I have learned so much about myself and about life and about how life should be. I had this fucked-up view of everything. I hated myself, I hated everyone around me."

She remains silent, but I can tell by the trembling of her bottom lip that she's doing her best to keep a straight face.

"I know you don't understand, not many people do, but the worst feeling in the entire fucking world is hating yourself, and that's what I dealt with every single day. That wasn't an excuse for the shit I pulled. I should have never treated you the way that I did, and you had every damn right to leave me the way you did. I only hope that you will read the entire book before making your decision. You can't judge a book without reading from cover to cover."

"I'm trying not to judge, Hardin, I'm really not, but this is too much. I fell out of this pattern, and I didn't see this coming, and I still can't wrap my head around it." Her head shakes as if she's trying to clear the rapid thoughts that I see firing behind those beautiful eyes.

"I know, baby. I know." When I reach for one of her hands and wrap my fingers around it, she winces. I gently turn her hand over to examine the welts covering the skin of her palm. "You okay?"

She nods, allowing me to trace the wound with my fingertip.

"Who would even want to read it? I can't believe so many publishers want it." Tessa looks away from me, focusing on the city that somehow keeps moving around us, as busy as ever.

"A lot of people." I shrug, stating the truth.

"Why? It's so . . . not a typical love story. I've only read a little bit of it, and I can see how dark it is."

"Even the damned need their stories told, Tess."

"You aren't damned, Hardin," she says, despite the betrayal she must still be feeling.

I sigh, slightly agreeing with her. "In hopes for redemption, maybe? Maybe not, maybe some people only want to read about happiness and cliché love stories, but there are millions of people, people who aren't perfect and have been through shit in their lives, and maybe they want to connect with it? Maybe they would see some of themselves in me, and, hell"—I rub my shaking hand over the back of my neck—"hell, maybe someone could learn something from my mistakes, and yours."

She's looking at me now as I vomit the words onto the concrete stairs. Uncertainty is still clear in her eyes, pushing more words from my mouth.

"Maybe sometimes everything isn't so black-and-white, and maybe not everyone is fucking perfect. I've done a lot of shit in my life, to you, and to others, that I regret and I would never, ever repeat or condone. This isn't about that. This book was an outlet for me. It was another form of therapy for me. It gave me a place where I could just write whatever the fuck I wanted and what I felt. This is me and my life, and I'm not the only person out there who has made mistakes, an entire fucking book of them, and if people judge me for the dark content of my story, then that's on them. I can't possibly please everyone, and I know there will be more people, people like us, Tessa, that relate to this book and want to see someone admit their issues and deal with them in a real way."

Her lips turn up at the corners, and she sighs, shaking her head slightly. "What if people don't like it? What if they don't even take the chance to read it, but they hate us for what's inside of it? I'm not ready for that type of attention. I don't want people talking about my life and judging me."

"Let them hate us. Who gives a fuck what they think? They weren't going to read it anyway."

"This is just . . . I can't decide how I feel about this. What type of love story is this?" Her voice is shaky and unsure.

"This is the type of love story that deals with real fucking problems. It's a story about forgiveness and unconditional love, and it shows how much a person can change, really change, if they try hard enough. It's the type of story that proves that anything is fucking possible when it comes to self-recovery. It shows that if you have someone to lean on, someone who loves you and doesn't give up on you, you can find your way out of the darkness. It shows that no matter what type of parents you had, or addictions you were faced with, you can overcome anything that stands in your way and become a better person. That's the type of story *After* is."

" '*After*'?" She tilts her chin up, using her hand to shield her eyes from the sun.

"That's what it's called." I look away, suddenly feeling self-conscious about the name. "It's about my journey, after meeting you."

"How much of it is bad? God, Hardin, why didn't you just tell me?"

"I don't know," I honestly say. "Not as much as you think is bad. You read the worst of it. Those pages that you didn't see, the ones that are the true essence of the story, they are about how much I love you, how you gave me a purpose in life, and how meeting you was the best thing that has ever happened to me. The unread pages share our laughs along with my struggles, our struggles."

She covers her face with her hands out of frustration. "You should have told me that you were writing this. There were so many hints, how did I not see it?"

I lean back against the steps. "I know that I should have, but by the time I understood and began to change what I was doing wrong, I wanted it to be perfect before I showed you. I truly am sorry for that, Tessa. I love you, and I'm sorry that you found out about it this way. My intentions were not to hurt or deceive you, and I'm so sorry that you felt that way. I'm not the same man that I was when you left me, Tessa. You know that I'm not."

Her voice is barely a whisper when she replies, "I don't know what to say."

"Just read it. Will you please just read the entire book before making any decisions? That's all I ask, please just read it."

Her eyes close, and she shifts her body, making her knee lean into my shoulder. "Yes, I'll read it."

A fraction of air returns to my lungs, some of the weight is lifted off my chest, and I couldn't put my relief into words even if I tried.

She stands up, brushing off her scratched knees.

"I'll get something for you to put on those."

"I'm fine."

"When will you stop fighting me?" I try to lighten the mood.

It works, and she fights a smile. "Never." She begins to walk up the steps, and I stand to follow her. I want to go into the apartment and sit next to her as she reads the entire novel, but I know that I shouldn't. I use the small amount of judgment that I have and decide to take a walk around this dirty city.

"Wait!" I call after her when she reaches the top. I reach into my pocket and pull out a crumpled piece of paper. "Read this last, please. It's the last page."

She opens her hand and holds it out in front of her.

I take the steps quickly, two at a time, and place the wad of paper into her hand. "Please don't peek," I beg of her.

"I won't." Tessa turns away from me, and I study the way she turns her head to smile back at me.

One of my greatest wishes in life would be for her to understand, to truly understand, that she is rare. She's one of the few people in this world who know forgiveness, and when many would call her weak, she is truly the opposite. She's strong, strong for standing by someone who hated himself. Strong for showing me that I'm not damned, that I am worthy of love, too, despite growing up thinking the opposite. She was strong enough to walk away from me when she did, and she's strong enough to love unconditionally. Tessa is stronger than most, and I hope she knows that.

chapter seventy-five

TESSA

When I enter the apartment, I take a moment to gather my thoughts, which are shooting this way and that. When I reach the binder lying on the table, all of the pages are shoved inside, out of order.

I reach for the first page, holding my breath as I prepare myself to read. *Will his words change my mind? Will they hurt me?* I'm not even sure that I'm ready to find out, but I know that I need to do this for myself. I need to read his words and his emotions to see what was going through his mind all of those times when I couldn't read him.

That's when he knew. That moment was when he fucking knew that he wanted to spend his life with her, that his life would be meaningless and empty without the light that Tessa brings into it. She gave him hope. She made him feel as if maybe, just maybe, he could be more than his past.

I drop the page to the floor and start on another.

He lived his life for himself and then it shifted, it became much more than waking up and going to sleep. She gave him everything he never knew that he needed.

He couldn't believe the shit that came from his mouth. He was disgusting. He hurt the people that loved him and he just couldn't stop. "Why do they love me?" he constantly wondered. "Why would anyone love me? I'm not worthy of it." Those thoughts filled his head, haunted him no matter how much he hid from them; they always returned.

He wanted to kiss away her tears, he wanted to tell her that he was sorry and that he was a ruined man, but he couldn't. He was a coward, and he was damaged beyond repair, and treating her this way made him hate himself even more.

Her laugh, her laugh was the sound that brought him out of the darkness and into the light. Her laugh dragged him, by his damn collar, through the bullshit clouding his mind and infecting his thoughts. He wasn't the same man that his father was, and he decided then, as she walked away from him, that he would never let the mistakes of his parents control his life again. He decided then that this woman was worth more than a broken man could offer, and so he did everything in his power to make it up to her.

Page after page, confession after dark confession, I continue to read. My tears have stained my cheeks, along with some of the pages of his beautiful yet twisted story.

He needed to tell her, he needed to tell her how fucking sorry he was for the nerve he had to throw children in her face. He was selfish, thinking only of the way he could hurt her, and he wasn't ready to admit what he truly wanted out of life with her. He wasn't ready to tell her that she would make the most amazing mother, that she would be nothing like the woman who raised her. He wasn't ready to tell her that he would try his hardest to be good enough to help raise a child with her. He wasn't ready to tell her that he was absolutely terrified of making the same mistakes that his father had made, and he wasn't ready to admit that he was afraid of failing. He didn't know the words to express that he didn't want to come home drunk, and he didn't want his children to run and hide from him, the way that he did his own father.

He wanted to marry her, to spend his life by her side, reveling in her kindness and her warmth. He couldn't imagine a life without her, and he was trying to figure out a way to tell her this, to show her that he really could change, and that he could be worthy of her.

Time passes somehow, and before long, hundreds of pages are scattered on the floor. I am unaware of how much time has passed, and I couldn't possibly count the tears that have fallen from my eyes or the sobs that have escaped through my lips.

I keep going, though; I read every single page, out of order, scattered and disarranged, but I make sure to soak in every single confession from the man that I love, the only man outside of my father that I have ever loved, and by the time I reach the end of the stack of pages, the apartment has grown darker and the sun has begun to set.

I look around the mess that I've made and try to take it all in. My eyes scan the floor, resting on the crumpled ball of paper on the entry table. Hardin said that it's the last page, the very last page of this story, our story, and I try to calm myself before reaching for it.

My hands shake as I pick it up, unwrap the crinkled page, and read the words written there.

He hopes that she will read this someday and that she will understand just how broken he was. He doesn't ask for her pity, or her forgiveness; he only asks that she see just how much she affected his life. That she, the beautiful stranger with a kind heart, turned into his lifeline and made him into the man he is today. He hopes that with these words, no matter how harsh some of them are, she will be proud of herself for dragging a sinner from the pits of hell and raising him into her heaven, allowing him redemption and freedom from the demons of his past.

He prays that she will take every single word to heart, and that maybe, just maybe, she will still love him after everything they have gone through. He hopes that she will be able to remember why she loved him, why she fought so hard for him.

Lastly, he hopes that wherever she may be as she reads the book that he wrote for her, she will read it with a light heart and that she will reach out to him, even if these words find her years from now. She has to know that he hasn't given up. Tessa has to know that this man will always love her, and that he will be waiting for her for the rest of his life, whether she returns to it or not. He wants her to know that she was his savior and that he could never repay her for everything she has done for him, and that he loves her with his entire soul and nothing will ever change that.

He wants to remind her that whatever their souls are made of, his and hers are the same. Their favorite novel said it best.

I gather every last bit of strength left inside me and leave the scattered pages on the floor of the apartment, the last page of the book still in my hand.

chapter seventy-six

Two Years Later

Y ou are absolutely stunning, such a beautiful bride," Karen gushes.

I nod, agreeing with her. I adjust the straps on my own gown and look back into the mirror. "He is going to be so stricken. I still can't believe how fast this day has come." I smile, placing one last bobby pin into the thick wave of hair pinned up in ringlets and glistening under the bright lights in the back room of the church.

I may have sprayed too much glitter onto her hair.

"What if I trip? What if he doesn't show at the altar?" Landon's gorgeous bride has a soft voice, one so full of nerves that she may snap any moment.

"He will. Ken drove him to the church this morning." Karen laughs, reassuring the two of us. "My husband would have alerted us by now."

"Landon wouldn't miss this for the world," I promise. I know he wouldn't, because I saw his face and wiped away the tears under his eyes when he showed me the ring he'd picked out for her.

"I sure hope not. I will be really pissed." She lets out a nervous laugh. Her smile is so lovely, even with the anxiety buzzing beneath the surface of the beauty; she's holding herself together quite well.

My fingers gently brush over her dark curls, adjusting the

sheer veil on her head. I glance at her beautiful face in the mirror and lift my hand to touch her bare shoulder. Her brown eyes are filled with tears, and she's chewing nervously on her lower lip.

"It will be fine, you'll be fine," I promise. The silver of my dress shines under the light, and I admire the beauty of every detail behind this wedding.

"Is it too soon? We've only been back together for a few months. Do you think it's too soon, Tessa?" she asks me.

I've grown so close with her in the past two years, I could sense her worry when her fingers started trembling as she helped me zip my bridesmaid's gown.

I smile. "It's not too soon. You two have been through so much in the last few years. You're just overthinking this. I know a thing or two about that."

"Are you nervous to see *him*?" she asks, eyes searching my face.

Yes. Terrified. Maybe a little panicked. "No, it's only been a few months."

"Too long," Landon's mother says under her breath.

My heart grows heavy, and I press back the distant ache that accompanies every thought surrounding him. I swallow the words I could and maybe should say. "Can you believe that your son is getting married today?" I quickly change the subject.

My distraction works like magic, and Karen smiles, squeals, and begins to tear up at once. "Oh, my makeup will be a mess." She pats her fingertips under her eyes, and her light brown hair moves with her as she shakes her head.

A knock at the door silences the three of us. "Honey?" Ken's voice is soft and cautious. Approaching the bride's room full of emotional women will do that to a man. "Abby just woke from her nap," Ken tells his wife as he opens the door, his daughter on his hip. Her dark brown hair and bright brown eyes are striking, lighting up every room the little girl enters. "I can't seem to find the diaper bag."

"It's over there, next to that chair." Karen points. "Could you feed her? I'm afraid she'll throw mashed peas at my dress." Karen laughs, reaching for Abby. "Terrible twos have come a little early for us."

The little girl smiles, showing a full row of tiny half teeth. "Mama," the chubby toddler calls, reaching both of her little hands to grasp the strap of Karen's dress.

My heart melts every time I hear Abby speak. "Hi, Miss Abby." I poke the little girl's cheek, making her giggle. It's a beautiful sound. I ignore the way Karen and Landon's soon-to-be-wife stare at me with sympathy in their eyes.

"Hi." Abby buries her face into her mom's shoulder.

"Are you ladies almost ready? We only have about ten minutes until the music will start, and Landon's getting more anxious every second," Ken warns.

"He's okay, right? He still wants to marry me?" the worried bride asks her future father-in-law.

Ken smiles, eyes crinkling at the corners. "Yes, dear, of course he does. Landon's nervous as he could be, but Hardin's helping with that." Every one of us, myself included, laughs at this.

The bride rolls her eyes in humor and shakes her head. "If Hardin's 'helping out,' I better cancel the honeymoon now."

"We better get going. I'll feed Abby something small to hold her over until the reception." Ken kisses his wife on the mouth before taking the toddler back into his arms and leaving the room.

"Yes. Please don't worry for me, I'm okay," I promise the two women. I am okay. I have been okay with the long-distance kind-of-relationship with Hardin. I miss him constantly, yes, but the space has been good for us.

The worst part of being okay is that okay is far from happy.

Okay is that gray space in the middle where you can wake up each day and carry on with your life, even laugh and smile often, but okay isn't joy. Okay isn't looking forward to each second of your day, and okay isn't getting the most out of life. Being okay is what most people settle for, myself included, and we pretend that okay is fine, when we actually hate it, and we spend the majority of our time waiting to break out of just being okay.

He gave me a taste of how great life can be outside of okay, and I've missed it ever since.

I've been okay for a long time, and I'm not sure how to get out of it now, but I hope for the day that I can say *I'm great* instead of *I'm okay.*

"You ready, Mrs. Gibson?" I smile at the lucky woman in front of me.

"No," she says, "but I will be as soon as I see him."

chapter seventy-seven

HARDIN

"Last chance to bail," I say to Landon while helping him adjust his tie.

"Thanks, jerk," he fires back, pushing my hands away to mess with the crooked tie. "I've worn a hundred ties in my life, yet this one refuses to straighten out."

He's nervous, and I feel for him. Sort of. "Don't wear one, then."

"I can't just not wear a tie. I'm getting married." He rolls his eyes.

"That's exactly why you don't have to wear a tie. It's your day, and you're the one spending all this money. If you don't want to wear a tie, don't wear a fucking tie. Hell, if I was the one getting married today, they would be lucky if I wore pants."

My best friend laughs. His fingers twist and tug at the tie around his neck. "Good thing you aren't, then. I wouldn't come to *that* spectacle."

"We both know that I'll never be married." I stare at myself in the mirror.

"Maybe." Landon's eyes meet mine in the mirror. "You're okay, right? She's here. Your dad saw her."

Hell no, I'm not. "Yeah, I'm okay. You act like I didn't know she was coming or that I haven't seen her in the last two years." I haven't seen her nearly enough, but she needed the distance from me. "She's your best friend and your bride's maid of honor. This is no surprise to me." I pull the tie from my own neck and hand it to him. "Here, since yours is a piece of shit, you can have mine."

"You have to wear a tie—it goes with your tux."

"You know damn well you're lucky I'm wearing this thing in the first place." I tug at the heavy material covering my body.

Landon's eyes close briefly, and he sighs in both relief and frustration. "I suppose you're right." He smiles. "Thanks."

"And for wearing clothes to your wedding?"

"Shut up." He rolls his eyes and runs his hands down the sleeves of his crisp black tuxedo. "What if she doesn't show up at the altar?"

"She will."

"But what if she doesn't? Am I crazy for getting married so fast?"

"Yes."

"Well, thanks."

I shrug. "Crazy isn't always a bad thing."

He takes me in, his eyes searching my face for some sort of hint that I may unravel at any time. "Are you going to try to talk to her?"

"Yes, obviously." I tried to make conversation with her at the rehearsal dinner, but Karen and Landon's bride were stuck by her side like glue. Tessa's helping to plan the wedding was a surprise to me; I didn't know she was into that type of thing, but apparently she's pretty damn good at it.

"She's happy now; not completely, but mostly."

Her happiness is the most important thing, and not just to me; the world simply isn't the same when Tessa Young isn't happy. I would know, I spent an entire year draining the life from her while simultaneously making her shine. It's fucked-up and makes no sense to the outside world, but I have never, and will never, give a shit about the outside world when it comes to that woman.

"Five minutes, guys," Ken's voice sounds from the other side of the door. This room is small and smells like old leather and mothballs, but this is Landon's wedding day. I'll wait until after the reception to complain about it.

Maybe I'll just take my complaints straight to Ken. I suspect he's the one paying for this shit anyway, given the state of the bride's parents and all.

"You ready, you crazy bastard?" I ask Landon one last time.

"No, but I will be when I see her."

chapter seventy-eight

TESSA

"Where's Robert?" Karen looks around the small wedding party. "Tessa? Do you know where he ran off to?" she asks, panic in her voice.

Robert had taken on the task of entertaining the toddler while the women were getting their hair curled and faces painted on. Now that the wedding is starting, he's taken his role back on, but he's nowhere to be found, and Karen can't hold Abby while helping with the first part of the wedding.

"Let me call him again." I glance around the crowd, searching for him. Abby thrashes in Karen's arms, and she looks panicked once again.

"Oh, wait! There he is . . ."

But I don't hear the rest of Karen's sentence. I'm completely distracted by the sound of Hardin's voice. He's walking out from the long hallway to my left, his mouth moving in that slow way it always has, as he talks to Landon.

His hair is longer than it looked in the pictures I've seen of him recently. I can't help that I've been reading every single one of his interviews, every article about him, whether it's true or false, and maybe, just maybe, I've emailed a few heated complaints to bloggers who have printed terrible things about him and his story. Our story.

The sight of the metal ring in his lip surprises me, even though I knew it had reappeared. I had forgotten how good it looks on him in person. I'm taken, absolutely consumed, by seeing him again, thrown back into a world where I fought hard in and lost nearly every battle that was thrown my way, only to leave without the one thing that I was fighting for: him.

"We need someone to walk with Tessa; her boyfriend didn't show up," someone says. At the mention of my name, Hardin's focus snaps forward; his eyes search for half a second before he finds me. I break the connection first, looking down at my high heels barely peeking out from underneath my floor-length dress.

"Who's walking with the maid of honor?" the bride's sister asks everyone nearby. "There's too much going on," she says with a huff as she walks past me. I've done more than she has for this wedding, but her stress level would make you believe otherwise.

"I am," Hardin says, raising his hand.

He looks so put together, so devastatingly handsome in a black tuxedo with no tie. Black ink shows just above the clean white collar, and I feel a soft touch on my arm. I blink a few times, trying not to focus on the way we barely spoke last night and how we didn't practice walking together like we should have. I nod, clearing my throat and tearing my eyes away from Hardin.

"All right, then, let's go," the sister says imperiously. "Groom to the altar, please." She claps her hands and Landon rushes past, gently squeezing my hand en route.

Breathe in. Breathe out. It's only for a few minutes, less than that really. It's not that difficult of a concept. We are friends. I can do this.

For Landon's wedding, of course. Momentarily, I battle within myself to not think about walking down the aisle with him for our own special day.

Hardin stands next to me without a word, and the music begins. He's staring at me—I know that he is—but I can't bring my-self to glance up at him. With these shoes, I'm near his height, and he's standing so closely that I can smell the soft cologne clinging to his tux.

The small church has been transformed into a beautiful yet simple venue, and the guests have quietly filled almost every row. Beautiful flowers, so brightly colored that they may as well be neon, cover the old wooden pews, and white cloth is draped from row to row.

"It's a little too bright, don't you think? I think simple red and white lilies would have done the trick," Hardin surprises me by saying. His arm loops through mine as the snooty sister waves for the two of us to begin our descent down the aisle.

"Yeah, lilies would have been gorgeous. This is nice, too, for them," I fumble.

"Your doctor boyfriend cleans up nicely," Hardin taunts me. I look over to find him smiling, only teasing behind his green eyes. His jawline is even more defined than before, and his eyes are deeper, not as guarded as they always were.

"He's in med school, not a doctor yet. And yes, he cleans up nicely. You know he's not my boyfriend, so hush." Over the last two years I have had this same conversation with Hardin again and again. Robert has been a constant friend in my life, nothing more. We tried dating once, about a year after I found Hardin's manuscript in my New York apartment, but it just didn't work. You shouldn't date someone if your heart is owned by someone else. It doesn't work, trust me.

"How are you two? It's been a year now, hasn't it?" His voice betrays the emotion he's trying to hide.

"What about you? You and that blonde. What was her name?" This aisle is a lot longer to walk down than it looked from the hallway. "Oh, yeah, Eliza or something?"

He chuckles. "Ha-ha."

I like to give him shit about a fan-turned-stalker of his named Eliza. I know he hasn't slept with her, but it's fun to tease him when I see him.

"Baby, the last blonde I had in my bed was you." He smiles. My feet catch, and Hardin grips my elbow, steadying me before I fall face-first onto the white silk covering the aisle.

"Is that so?"

"Yep." He keeps his eyes toward the front of the church where Landon stands.

"You put your lip ring back in." I change the subject before I embarrass myself further. We walk past my mother, sitting quietly next to her husband, David. She looks slightly worried, but I give her credit when she smiles at Hardin and me when we pass. David leans into her, whispering something, and she smiles again, nodding to him.

"She seems much happier now," Hardin whispers. We probably shouldn't be talking as we walk down the aisle, but Hardin and I are known for doing things that we shouldn't do.

I've missed him more than I'm letting on. I've only seen him six times in the last two years, and each time only made me ache for him more.

"She is. David has been an incredible influence on her."

"I know, she told me."

I stop again. This time Hardin smiles while helping me continue down the never-ending aisle. "What do you mean?"

"Your mum, I've spoken to her a few times. You know that."

I have no clue what he's talking about.

"She came to a signing last month, when my second book came out."

What? "What did she say?" My voice is too loud, and a few guests stare at us for much too long.

"We will talk after this. I promised Landon that I wouldn't ruin his wedding."

Hardin smiles at me as we reach the altar, and I try, I really do try, to focus on my best friend's wedding.

But I can't keep my eyes or mind off the best man.

chapter seventy-nine

HARDIN

The reception of a wedding is its most tolerable part. Everyone is a little less uptight and easily loosened up by a few glasses of free booze and an overpriced complimentary meal.

The wedding was flawless: the groom cried more than the bride, and I am proud of myself for only staring at Tessa ninety-nine percent of the time. I heard some of the vows, I swear I did. That's about it, though. Judging by the way Landon's arms are wrapped around his new wife's waist and the way she's laughing at something he's saying as they dance across the floor in front of everyone, I would say the wedding went well.

"I'll take a club soda, if you have it," I tell the woman behind the bar.

"With vodka or gin?" she asks, pointing to the row of bottles of liquor.

"Neither, just the soda. No liquor."

She stares at me for a moment before nodding and filling a clear glass with ice and soda.

"There you are," a familiar voice says as a hand touches my shoulder. Vance is behind me, his pregnant wife next to him.

"Been looking for me, have you?" I sarcastically remark.

"He has not." Kimberly smiles, her hand resting on her giant belly.

"You okay? You look like you're going to fall over with that thing." I look down at her swollen feet, then back up to her sour expression.

"That thing is my baby in there. I'm nine months pregnant, but I *will* still slap you."

Well, guess her sass is still intact.

"If you can reach past that stomach of yours, of course," I tease.

She proves me wrong: sure enough, I'm slapped by a pregnant woman at a wedding.

I rub my arm as if she actually hurt me, and she laughs when Vance calls me an asshole for goading his wife.

"You looked nice walking down the aisle with Tessa," he says, raising a suggestive brow.

My breath catches, and I clear my throat, searching the dark room for her long blond hair and that sinful satin dress. "Yeah, I wasn't going to be doing any wedding-party shit outside of being Landon's best man, but it wasn't so bad."

"That other guy's here now," Kim says knowingly. "But he's not actually her boyfriend. You didn't buy that crap, did you? She spends time with him, but you can tell by the way they act that it's nothing serious. Not like you two are."

"*Were.*"

Kim grins at me, a cunning look, and nods her head to direct me to the table closest to the bar. Tessa is sitting there, silky dress shining under the moving lights. Her eyes are on me, or maybe Kimberly. No, her eyes are on me, and she quickly looks away.

"See, like I said, you two *are.*" Smug and pregnant, Kimberly laughs at my expense, and I down my club soda and toss the cup in the trash before ordering a water. My stomach is twisting and turning, and I'm acting like a little fucking child right now, trying not to stare at the beautiful girl who stole my heart all those years ago.

She didn't just steal the damned thing. She found it; she was the one to discover that I even had a heart to begin with, and she dug it out. Struggle after struggle, she never gave up. She found my heart, and she kept it safe. She hid it from the fucked-up world. Most important, she hid it from me, until I was ready to care for it myself. She tried to give it back two years ago, but my heart refused to leave her side. It will never, ever leave her side.

"You two are the most stubborn people I've ever met," Vance says while ordering a water for Kimberly and a glass of wine for himself. "Have you seen your brother?"

I look around the room for Smith and find him sitting a few tables down from Tessa, alone. I point to the boy, and Vance asks me to find out if he wants something to drink. The kid's old enough to get his own damn drink, but I would rather not sit and talk to Smug and Smugger, so I walk over to the empty table and take a seat next to my little brother.

"You were right," Smith says, looking over at me.

"About what, this time?" I lean back against the decorated chair and wonder just how Landon and Tessa can justify calling this wedding "small and simple" when they have some curtainlike shit covering each and every chair in the damn place.

"About weddings being boring." Smith smiles. He's missing a few teeth, one of them a front tooth. He's sort of adorable for a brainiac kid who doesn't care for most people.

"I should have made you bet money." I laugh, settling my gaze on Tessa again.

Smith looks at her, too. "She looks pretty today."

"I've been warning you off of her for years now, kid; don't make me cause a funeral at a wedding." I gently hit his shoulder, and he smiles a crooked and gap-toothed smile.

I want to walk over to her table and push her nearly-a-doctor friend out of his chair so I can sit next to her. I want to tell her how beautiful she looks and how proud I am of her that she has been excelling at NYU. I want to watch her get past her nerves, and I want to hear her laugh and watch her smile take over the entire room.

I lean toward Smith. "Do me a favor."

"What kind of favor?"

"I need you to go up and start talking to Tessa."

He flushes, shaking his head rapidly. "No way."

"Come on. Just do it."

"Nope."

Stubborn child.

"You know that customized train you wanted that your dad won't get for you?"

"Yeah?" His interest is piqued.

"I'll buy it for you."

"You're bribing me to talk to her?"

"Damn right I am."

The kid gives me a side glance. "When will you buy it?"

"If you get her to dance with you, I'll buy it next week."

He negotiates. "No, for dancing it has to be tomorrow."

"Fine." Damn, he's too good at this.

He looks toward Tessa's table, then back to me. "Deal," he agrees while standing up. Well, that was easy.

I watch as he walks over to her. Her smile for him, even from two tables away, knocks the breath straight from my lungs. I give him about thirty seconds before I stand and make my way to the table. I ignore the guy sitting next to her and find joy in the way her face lights up as I stand next to Smith.

"There you are." I rest my hands on the boy's shoulders.

"Will you dance with me, Tessa?" my little brother asks.

She's surprised. Her cheeks glow in embarrassment under the lighting, but I know her, and I know she won't turn him down.

"Of course." She smiles at Smith, and what's-his-name stands and helps her to her feet. Polite bastard.

I watch as Tessa follows Smith out to the dance floor, and I'm thankful for Landon and his new wife's love for slow and sappy songs. Smith looks miserable and Tessa looks nervous as they begin to dance.

"How've you been?" Doctor asks me as we both watch the same woman.

"Fine, and you?" I should be nice to the guy—he *is* dating the woman that I will spend my life loving.

"Good, I'm in my second year of medical school now."

"So what, only ten left to go?" I laugh, being as nice as I can be to a guy who I know has feelings for Tessa.

I dismiss myself and stride over to Tessa and Smith. She sees me first and freezes when her eyes meet mine.

"May I cut in?" I ask, tugging at the back of Smith's dress shirt before either of them can refuse. My hands immediately move to her waist, resting on her hips. I follow her lead and freeze, feeling overwhelmed by my fingers touching her.

It's been so long, too long, since the last time I held her. She came to Chicago a few months ago for her friend's wedding, but she didn't invite me as her date. She went solo, but we met after and had dinner. It was nice; she had a glass of wine and we shared a massive mound of ice cream, topped with chocolate candies and too much hot fudge. She asked me to come back to her hotel for another drink—wine for her, club soda for me—and we fell asleep after I made love to her on the floor of her hotel room.

"I thought I would save you from dancing with him, he's a little short. Terrible dance partner," I finally say when I can pull my head out of my ass.

"He told me you bribed him." She smiles at me, shaking her head.

"That little fucker." I glare at the traitor as he sits back down at a table, alone again.

"You two have gotten pretty close, even since I last saw you," she says with admiration, and I can't stop the blush rushing to my cheeks if I tried.

"Yeah, guess so." I shrug. Her fingers tighten on my shoulders, and I sigh. Literally fucking sigh, and I know she can hear it.

"You look very well." She stares at my mouth. I decided to put my ring back in a few days after I saw her in Chicago.

" 'Well'? I don't know if that's a good thing." I bring her closer to me, and she lets me.

"Very good, handsome. Very hot." The last words tumble from her full lips by accident. I can tell by the way her eyes go wide and she bites down on her lower lip.

"You're the sexiest woman in the room; always have been."

She tilts her head down, trying to hide in the mass of long, blond curls.

"Don't hide, not from me," I quietly say. Nostalgia fills me at the familiar words, and I can tell by her expression that she's feeling the same.

She quickly changes the subject. "When's the release date for your next book?"

"Next month—did you read it? I had an early copy sent to you."

"Yes, I read it." I take the opportunity to pull her to my chest. "I've read them all, remember?"

"What do you think?" The songs ends and another begins. As the female voice fills the room, we look into each other's eyes.

"This song," Tessa softly laughs. "Of course they would play this song."

I brush a loose curl away from her eyes, and she swallows, blinking slowly. "I'm so happy for you, Hardin. You're an incredible author, an activist for self-recovery and alcohol addiction. I saw that interview you did with the *Times* about dealing with abuse as a child." Her eyes well up, and I'm positive that if her tears spill, I may lose all composure.

"It's nothing, really." I shrug, loving her being proud of me, but feeling guilty for what it caused her. "I never expected any of this; you have to know that. I didn't mean for you to be embarrassed publicly by me writing that book." I've told her this so many times, and she always has the same positive response.

"Don't worry about it." She smiles up at me. "It wasn't so bad, and you know, you've helped a lot of people and a lot of people love your books. Me included." Tessa flushes, and I do the same.

"This should be *our* wedding," I blurt.

Her feet stop moving, and some of the glow disappears from her beautiful skin. "Hardin." She glares at me.

"Theresa," I tease. I'm not joking, and she knows it. "I thought that last page was going to change your mind. I really did."

"Can I have everyone's attention, please?" the bride's sister says through the microphone. That woman is annoying as hell. She stands on the stage in the center of the room, but I can barely see her over the table in front of her, she's just that short.

"I have to get ready for my speech," I groan, swiping my hand through my hair.

"You're making a speech?" Tessa follows me to the designated table for the wedding party. She must have forgotten about the doctor, and I can't say that I mind that one bit. I love it, really.

"Yeah, I'm the best man, remember?"

"I know." She gently shoves my shoulder, and I reach for her wrist. I planned to pull it to my mouth to press a kiss against the bare skin there, but I'm thrown off by a small black circle tattooed there.

"What the fuck is this?" I bring her wrist closer to my face.

"I lost a bet on my twenty-first birthday." She laughs.

"You actually got a smiley-face tattoo? What the hell." I can't help the laughter falling from my mouth. The tiny smiling face is so ridiculous, and so poorly done, that it's funny. I do wish, though, that I could have been there to see it done, and for her birthday.

"Sure did." She nods proudly, running her index finger over the ink.

"Do you have any more?" I hope that she doesn't.

"No way. Just this one."

"Hardin!" the short woman calls for me, and I carry out my intention of kissing Tessa's wrist. She jerks her hand away, not out of disgust but out of shock, I hope, as I walk toward the stage.

Landon and his wife are sitting at the head of the table, and his arm is wrapped around her back, her hands resting over one of his. Ahh, newlyweds. I can't wait to see them ready to rip each other's head off this time next year.

Maybe they'll be different, though.

I take the microphone from the ornery woman and clear my throat. "Hey." My voice sounds weird as fuck, and I can tell by Landon's face that he's going to enjoy this. "I don't like talking in front of a lot of people usually. Hell, I don't even like being around people usually, so I'm going to make this quick," I promise the roomful of wedding guests. "Most of you are probably drunk or bored to death anyway, so feel free to ignore this."

"Get to the point." Landon's bride laughs, holding up a glass of champagne. Landon nods in agreement, and I flip them both off in front of everyone. Tessa, in the front row, laughs and covers her mouth. "See, I wrote this down, because I didn't want to forget what to say."

I pull a crinkled napkin from my pocket and unfold it. "When I first met Landon, I instantly hated him." Everyone laughs as if I'm joking, but I'm not. I did hate him, but only because I hated myself.

"He had everything that I wanted in life: a family, a girlfriend, a plan for his future." When I look at Landon, he is smiling, and his cheeks are slightly red. I'll blame that on the champagne.

"Anyway, throughout the years that I've known him, we've become friends, family even, and he has taught me a lot about being a man, especially in the last two years with the struggles these two have had to deal with." I smile at Landon and his bride, not wanting to get too into the depressing shit.

"I'm going to end this shit now. Basically what I want to say is, I thank you, Landon, for being an honest man, and for giving me hell when I needed you to. I actually look up to you in a fucked-up way, and I want you to know that you deserve to be happy and be married to the love of your life, no matter how quickly you two put this together."

The crowd laughs again.

"You won't know how lucky you are to be able to spend your life with the other half of your soul until you have to spend your life without them." I bring the microphone down and lay it on the table just as I catch a glimpse of silver rushing through the crowd, and I hurry down from the stage to follow after my girl as the crowd drinks to my toast.

When I finally catch up to Tessa, she's pushing the women's bathroom door open. She disappears inside, and I don't bother to look around before following her inside. When I reach her, she's leaning against the sink, her palms resting on both sides of the marble.

She looks up into the mirror, eyes red and cheeks stained with tears, and turns to face me when she realizes that I've followed her.

"You can't just talk about us like that. About our souls." She ends her sentence with a whimper.

"Why not?"

"Because . . ." She can't seem to find an explanation.

"Because you know I'm right?" I egg her on.

"Because you can't say those things publicly like that. You

keep doing it in your interviews, too." She rests her hands on her hips.

"I've been trying to get your attention." I step toward her.

Her nostrils flare, and for a moment I think she may actually stomp her foot.

"You piss me off." Her voice softens, and she can't deny the way she's looking at me right now.

"Sure, sure." I reach my arms out to her. "Come here," I beg.

She obliges, walking into my outspread arms, and I hug her. Having her in my arms this way is more satisfying than any sex we could have. Just having her here, still drawn to me in the way that only the two of us understand, makes me the happiest son of a bitch around.

"I've missed you so much," I say into her hair.

Her hands move to my shoulders, tugging the heavy jacket off me, and the expensive cloth falls to the floor.

"You're sure?" I hold her beautiful face between my hands.

"I'm always sure with you." I can feel the vulnerability and sweet relief as she presses her mouth to mine, lips trembling, breathing slow and deep.

Too soon, I pull away, and she drops her hands from my belt. "I'm just blocking the door." I'm thankful for the chairs placed in women's gathering places, and I pull two of them over to the door to keep anyone from coming inside.

"We're really doing this?" Tessa asks as I lean down to lift her floor-length dress from the floor, up to her waist.

"Are you surprised?" I laugh into another kiss. Her mouth tastes like home to me, and I've been away from home, living in Chicago alone, for so long. Only small doses of her have been granted to me over the last few years.

"No." Her fingers hurry to unzip my pants, and I gasp when she grasps my cock through my boxers.

It's been a long time, too damn long.

"When's the last time you . . ."

"With you in Chicago." I urge her, "You?"

"Same."

I pull back, looking into her eyes to find only truth behind her claim. "Really?" I ask, even though I can read her face like an open book.

"Yes, no one else. Only you." She tugs my boxers down, and I lift her onto the counter, spreading her thick thighs with both hands.

"Fuck." I bite down on my tongue when I discover she's not wearing any panties.

She looks down, flustered. "There was a line with my dress."

"You're going to be the death of me, woman." I'm hard as a fucking rock when she strokes me, both of her small hands moving up and down the length of me.

"We have to hurry," she whines, desperate and soaking when I slide my finger over her clit. She groans; her head falls back onto the mirror, and her legs open farther.

"Condom?" I ask, barely able to think straight.

When she doesn't respond, I push a finger inside her and caress her tongue with mine. Each kiss holds a confession: *I love you,* I try to show her; *I need you,* I suck at her bottom lip; *I can't lose you again,* I push my cock inside her and moan with her as I fill her.

"So fucking tight," I whimper. I am going to embarrass myself by coming within seconds, but this isn't about sexual satisfaction for me, this is about showing her and me that we are truly inevitable. We are a force that can't be reckoned with, no matter how hard we try—or anyone else tries—to fight it.

We belong together, and it's truly undeniable.

"Oh God." She claws at my back as I pull out of her warmth and enter her again, this time completely. She stretches around me, her body adjusting to fit me the way it always has.

"Hardin," Tessa moans into my neck. I can feel her teeth pressing against my skin as my release climbs up my spine. I move one hand to her back, pulling her closer to me, lifting her slightly to reach a deeper angle inside her, and use my other hand to grope her full tits. She spills out of her dress, and I suck at the flesh there, tugging at her hard nipples with my lips, groaning and moaning her name as I come inside her.

My name comes in quick pants as I rub at her clit while driving into her. The sound of her thighs smacking against me and the counter is hot enough to have me getting hard again. It's just been so fucking long, and she's the most perfect fit for me. Her body claims mine, completely fucking owning me.

"I love you," she says as she comes, her voice strained as she loses herself with me, allowing me to find her. Tessa's orgasm seems endless, and I can't help but fucking love it. Her body goes limp, leaning into me, and she rests her head on my chest as she catches her breath.

"I heard that, you know?" I press a kiss to her sweat-beaded forehead, and she smiles a delirious smile.

"We're a mess," she whispers, lifting her head up so that her eyes can meet mine.

"An undeniable, beautifully chaotic mess."

"Don't go all writer on me," she teases, out of breath.

"Don't pull away from me. I know you've been missing me, too."

"Yeah, yeah." She wraps her arms around my waist, and I push her hair back off her forehead.

I'm happy, I'm fucking ecstatic that she is here with me, after all this time, in my arms, smiling and teasing and laughing, and I'm not going to ruin this. I've learned the hard way that life doesn't have to be a battle. Sometimes you're given a shitty hand from the get-go, and sometimes you fuck up along the way, but there is always hope.

There's always another day, there's always a way to make up

for the shit you've done and the people you've hurt, and there is always someone who loves you, even when you feel like you're completely alone and you're just out there floating along, waiting for the next disappointment. There is always something better to come.

It's hard to see, but it's there. Tessa was there, underneath the bullshit and self-loathing. Tessa was there beneath my addiction, Tessa was there beneath my self-pity and my shitty choices. She was there as I climbed my way through it; she held my hand the entire fucking way; even after she left me, she was still there, helping me through it.

I never lost hope because Tessa is my hope.

She always has been and always will be.

"Will you stay with me tonight? We can leave here now. Just stay with me," I beg.

She leans up again, pushing her breasts back into her dress as she looks up at me. Her eye makeup is smeared and her cheeks are red. "Can I say something?"

"Since when do you ask?" I touch the tip of her nose with my index finger.

"True." She smiles. "I hate that you didn't try harder."

"I did but—"

She holds up a finger to silence me. "I hate that you didn't try harder, but it's unfair of me to even say that because we both know that I pulled away from you. I kept pushing and pushing, expecting too much from you, and I was so angry over the book and all of the attention that I didn't want, and I let that rule my mind. I felt as if I couldn't forgive you because of other people's opinions, but now I'm angry with myself that I would even listen to that. I don't care what people say about us, or me. I only care what the people I love think of me, and they love and support me. I just wanted to say that I'm sorry for listening to voices that didn't belong in my head."

I stand in front of the counter, with Tessa still sitting in front of me, and I'm silent. I wasn't expecting this. I wasn't expecting such a turnaround. I came to this wedding hoping for barely so much as a smile from her.

"I don't know what to say."

"That you forgive me?" she nervously whispers.

"I forgive you, of course." I laugh at her. Is she insane? Of course I forgive her. "Do you forgive me? For everything? Or close to everything?"

"Yes." She nods, reaching for my hand.

"Now I really don't know what to say." I run my hand over my hair.

"Maybe that you still want to marry me?" Her eyes are wide, and mine feel as if they are going to pop straight from their sockets.

"What?"

She flushes. "You heard me."

"Marry you? You hated me like ten minutes ago?" She's truly going to be the death of me.

"Actually, we were having sex on this counter ten minutes ago."

"You actually mean that? You want to marry me?" I can't believe that she's saying this. There's no way in hell she's saying this. "Have you been drinking?" I try to recall if I tasted any liquor on her tongue.

"No, I had one glass of champagne over an hour ago. I'm not drunk, I'm just tired of fighting this. We're inevitable, remember?" she mocks, using a terrible English accent.

I kiss her mouth, silencing her.

"We are the least romantic couple that's ever been; you know that, right?" My tongue swipes over her soft lips.

" 'Romance is overrated, realism is in,' " she quotes from my latest novel.

I love her. Fuck, I love this woman so fucking much. "Marry me? Really, you will?"

"Not today or anything, but sure, I'll think about it." She climbs down from the counter, adjusting her dress.

I smile too. "I know you will." I adjust my clothing, trying to understand everything that's happening in this bathroom. Tessa is somewhat agreeing to marry me. Holy fucking shit.

She shrugs playfully.

"Vegas, let's go to Vegas right now." I dig into my pocket and pull my keys out of it.

"No way; I'm not getting married in Vegas. You're crazy."

"We're both crazy; who gives a shit?"

"No way, Hardin."

"Why not?" I plead, taking her face between my palms.

"Vegas is a fifteen-hour drive." She glances at me, then at her reflection in the mirror.

"Don't you think a fifteen-hour drive is long enough to think about it?" I joke, pulling the chairs away from the door.

Then Tessa truly shocks me by cocking her head and saying, "Yeah, I guess so."

epilogue

HARDIN

The drive to Vegas was a daunting one. The first two hours were spent creating fantasy scenarios about the perfect Vegas wedding. Tessa played with the ends of her curled hair, glancing over at me with flushed cheeks and a happiness in her smile that I haven't seen in so long.

"I wonder how easy it is, in reality, to be married in Vegas. Last minute. Ross and Rachel style," she questioned, her face buried into her phone.

"You're googling it. Aren't you?" I asked her. I moved my hand to her lap and cracked the window of my rental car.

Somewhere outside Boise, Idaho, we stopped for food and more gas. Tessa was getting sleepy, her head leaning forward and her eyes soft and heavy. I pulled into the crowded truck stop and gently shook Tessa by her shoulder to wake her.

"Vegas already?" she joked, knowing we were barely halfway there.

We got out of the car, and I followed her to the bathroom. I always liked these types of gas stations; they were well-lit and had full parking lots. Less chance of being murdered and whatnot.

When I came out of the bathroom, Tessa was standing in one of the many snack aisles. Her arms were already full of junk: bags of crisps and chocolates and too many energy drinks for her small hands to hold.

I stood back for a moment, just staring at the woman in front of me. The woman that would be my wife in just a few hours. My wife. After all we have been through, after fighting back and forth over a marriage that, honestly, neither of us thought would actually happen, we were on our way to Vegas to make it legal in a small chapel. At twenty-three, I would become someone's husband—Tessa's husband—and I couldn't imagine anything that could possibly make me happier.

Even being the bastard I was, I was getting a happy ending with her. She would be smiling at me, her eyes full of tears, and I would be making some stupid remark about an Elvis lookalike walking by during our wedding.

"Look at all this stuff, Hardin." Tessa used her elbow to point at the enormous number of random snacks. She was dressed in those pants—yeah, you know the ones. Those yoga pants and an NYU zip-up sweatshirt were what she was wearing on the way to her wedding. She was planning on changing when we arrived at whatever hotel we were going to check into, though. She wouldn't be wearing a wedding gown, the way I had always imagined in my head.

"You're okay with not wearing a wedding dress?" I blurted out.

Her eyes went a little wide, and she smiled, shook her head, and said, "Where did that come from?"

"I was just wondering. I was thinking about how you won't be able to have, like, the wedding that women are always obsessing over. You won't have flowers or anything."

She handed me a bag of some sort of orange-dyed corn puffs. An old man walked by us and smiled at her. His eyes met mine, and he quickly looked away.

"Flowers? Really?" she asked, rolling her eyes and walking past me, ignoring the way I rolled my eyes back at her. I followed her, nearly tripping over an unsteady child in light-up shoes wobbling by, holding the hand of his mother.

"What about Landon? Your mum and David? Don't you want them to be there?" I asked.

She turned to face me, and I could see the thought occurring to her in a different way. During the drive, our minds were both so clouded by our excitement over our decision to be wed in Vegas that we forgot about reality.

"Oh," she sighed, staring at me while I caught up to her.

We walked to the register, and I could tell what she was thinking: Landon and her mum have to be there when we get married. Have to. And Karen—Karen would be heartbroken if she didn't witness Tessa becoming my wife.

We paid for our junk food and caffeine. Well, she fought me and paid for it. I let her.

"You still want to go? You know you can tell me, baby. We can wait," I told her as I buckled my seat belt. She pulled open the bag of orange puffs and popped one into her mouth.

"Yeah. I do," she insisted.

It didn't feel right, though. I knew she wanted to marry me, and I knew that I wanted to spend my life with her, but I didn't want it to start this way. I wanted our families to be there. I wanted my little brother and little Abby to be a part of it, walking down the aisle, throwing flowers and rice and doing whatever crap people make the youngest family members do during weddings. I saw the way her eyes lit up when she proudly told me how much she helped with the planning of Landon's wedding.

I wanted everything to be perfect for my Tessa, so when she fell asleep thirty minutes later, I turned the car around and drove her back to Ken's house. When she woke up, surprised but not cursing me out, she unbuckled her seat belt, climbed into my lap, and kissed me, warm tears running down her cheeks.

"God, I love you, Hardin," she said into my neck. We stayed in the car for another hour. I held her on my lap, and when I told her I wanted Smith to throw rice at our wedding, she laughed, pointing out that he'd probably do it very precisely, grain by grain.

TWO YEARS LATER
TESSA

THE DAY I GRADUATED FROM COLLEGE, I was so proud of myself. I was so happy with every aspect of my life, except that I didn't want to work in publishing anymore. Yes, Theresa Young, obsessive planner of every detail of her future, changed her mind midway through college.

It started when Landon's bride didn't want to pay for a wedding planner. She was adamant about not hiring one, even though she had no idea how to start planning her wedding. Landon helped her, though; he was the perfect fiancé, staying up late to look through magazines with us, missing class to taste ten different cakes two different times. I loved the feeling of being in charge of such an important day for so many people. It was my specialty: planning and doing something for others.

During the wedding I kept thinking that I would love to do this more often, just as a hobby, but as the months went by, I found myself at bridal expos, and the next thing I knew, I was planning Kimberly and Christian's wedding.

I kept my job at Vance in New York City because I needed the income. Hardin moved to New York with me, and I refused to let him pay all of my bills while I tried to figure out what the hell to do, because though I was so proud of my college degree, I just no longer wanted to work in the field. I will always love reading—books are forever tied to my soul—but I simply changed my mind. Just like that.

Hardin gave me endless crap about this, since I'd always been so sure about my career choice. But as the years went on and I grew up, I realized that I didn't know who I was when I enrolled in WCU. How can people be expected to choose what they want to do for the rest of their life when they're just *beginning* their life?

Landon already had his job lined up: fifth-grade teacher at a public school in Brooklyn. Hardin, a *New York Times* bestseller at the young age of twenty-five, had four books published, and me, well, I was still working on figuring out my own path, but I was fine with that. I didn't feel rushed in the way I always had. I wanted to take my time and make sure every choice I made was set to make me happy. For the first time I was putting my happiness before anyone else's, which felt great.

I stared at my reflection in the mirror. There were so many times in the past four years when I wasn't sure if I would make it through college, and now here I was: a college graduate. Hardin clapped while my mother cried. They even sat together.

My mother walked into the bathroom and stood at my side. "I'm so proud of you, Tessa."

She was wearing an evening gown; it wasn't really suitable for a college graduation, but she wanted to dress to impress, as always. Her blond hair was curled and sprayed to perfection, and her nails were painted to match my graduation cap and gown. It was over the top, but she was proud and I didn't want to take that away from her. She had groomed me to succeed in life and be everything she couldn't, and now, as an adult, I understood that.

"Thank you," I responded as she handed me her lip gloss. I gladly took it from her, despite the fact that I didn't want or need to reapply any makeup, and she looked pleased when I didn't fight her on it.

"Is Hardin still out there?" I asked. The gloss was sticky and too dark for my liking, but I smiled anyway.

"He's entertaining David." She smiled along with me, and my heart filled a little more. My mother's fingers ran over the ends of her curls. "He invited him to that fundraiser he's speaking at."

"That will be nice." Things weren't as awkward between my mother and Hardin as they used to be. He would never be her favorite person, but over the past few years she gained a respect for him that I never would have believed was possible before.

I've gained a new respect for Hardin Scott, too. It's painful to think back over the last four years of my life and remember the way he used to be. I wasn't perfect either, but he held on to his past so tightly that he broke me in the process. He made mistakes—massive and devastating mistakes—but he paid his dues for them. He would never be the most patient, the most lovable and friendly man out there, but he was mine. Always had been.

Still, I had needed the distance from him after I moved to New York with Landon. We had been seeing each other "casually," as casual as Hardin and I could be. He didn't pressure me to move to Chicago, and I didn't beg him to move to New York. It was about a year after Landon's wedding that he finally moved, but we made it work by visiting one another when we could, Hardin more so than me. I was suspicious about his sudden "work trips" to the city, but I was always so happy when he came and wanted him to stay when he left.

Our apartment in Brooklyn was decent. Though he was making a lot of money, Hardin was willing to move into a place that I could help pay for. I worked at the restaurant between planning weddings and classes, and he only complained minimally.

We still weren't married, which drove him insane. I kept going back and forth on the subject. Yes, I wanted to be his wife, but I was tired of having to label things. I didn't need that label in the way that I grew up believing I did.

As if my mother was reading my mind, she leaned in and adjusted my necklace. "Have you set a date yet?" she asked for the third time that week. I loved when my mother, David, and his daughter came to visit, but she was driving me crazy with her new obsession: my wedding, or lack thereof.

"Mother," I warned. I would put up with her grooming me, and I even let her pick out my jewelry this morning, but I wouldn't entertain her when it came to this.

She raised her hands into the air and smiled. "Fine."

Her defeat came easy, and I knew something was up when she kissed my cheek. I followed her out of the bathroom, and my irritation dissolved when I saw Hardin leaning against the wall. He was lifting his hair up and wrapping a band around the long strands. I loved his hair long. My mother scrunched her nose as Hardin pulled his hair into a bun, and I laughed immaturely at her disgust.

"I was just asking Tessa if you two had picked a date for a potential wedding yet," my mother said as Hardin wrapped his arm around my waist and buried his face into my neck. I felt his breath against my neck as he chuckled.

"I wish I could tell you," he said as he lifted his head. "But you know how stubborn she is."

My mother nodded in agreement, and I was equally annoyed and proud that the two of them were teaming up on me.

"I know she is. She gets that from you," my mother accused.

David grabbed hold of her hand and brought it to his lips. "All right, you two. She just graduated college—let's give her a little time."

I smiled a thankful smile to David, and he winked, kissing my mother's hand again. He was so gentle with her, and I appreciated that.

TWO YEARS AFTER THAT
HARDIN

WE HAD BEEN TRYING to get pregnant for over a year now. Tessa knew the chances. I knew the odds were against us, like they always had been, but we still hoped. We hoped through fertility appointments and hoped through ovulation schedules. We fucked and fucked and made love and made love every chance we could get. She tried the most ridiculous wives' tales, and I drank some bittersweet, chunky concoction that Tessa swore worked for her friend's husband.

Landon and his wife were expecting a baby girl in three months, and we were the godparents of little Addelyn Rose. I wiped Tessa's tears from her cheeks as she helped plan the baby shower for her best friend, and I pretended not to be sad for us while we were helping paint Addy's nursery.

It was a normal morning. I had just gotten off a call with Christian. We were planning a trip for Smith to come visit us for a few weeks in the summer. He disguised the call as that, but he really was trying to pitch an idea to me. He wanted me to publish another book with Vance, an idea that I liked but pretended not to. I just wanted to fuck with him and pretend that I was waiting for a better offer.

Tessa came bursting through the door, still in her sweats. Her cheeks were red from the cold March air, and her hair was wild from the wind. She was returning from her usual walk down to Landon's apartment, but she seemed rushed—panicked, even—making my chest tighten.

"Hardin!" she exclaimed as she crossed the living room and walked into the kitchen. Her eyes were bloodshot, and my heart sank to the floor.

I stood, and she held a hand up, signalling me to wait a moment.

"Look," she said, digging into the pocket of her jacket. I waited silently and impatiently for her to open her hand.

A small stick was there. I had seen too many false tests in the last year to think anything of it, but from the way her hand was shaking and the way her voice cracked when she tried to speak, I knew immediately.

"Yeah?" was all I could say.

"Yeah." She nodded, her voice small but full of life. I looked down at her, and she lifted her hands to my face. I hadn't even felt the tears there until she wiped them.

"You're sure?" I said like an idiot.

"Yes, obviously." She tried to laugh but she broke into happy tears, and so did I. I wrapped my arms around her and lifted her onto the counter. I laid my head on her stomach and promised that baby that I would be a better father than either of mine had ever been. Better than anyone had ever been.

TESSA WAS GETTING READY for our double date with Landon and his wife, and I was flipping through the pages of one of the many bridal magazines Tessa left hanging around the apartment when I heard the sound. A nearly inhuman sound.

It came from the bathroom connected to our bedroom, and I jumped to my feet, rushing toward the door.

"Hardin!" Tessa said again. This time I was at the door, and the anguish in her voice was thicker than the first time she called for me.

I pushed the door open and found her sitting on the floor next to the toilet.

"Something's wrong!" she cried out, holding her small hands over her stomach. Her panties were on the floor. Blood covered them, and I gagged, unable to speak.

I was on the floor next to her in seconds, holding her face between my hands.

"Everything will be fine," I lied to her, reaching into my pocket and grabbing my phone.

The tone of our doctor's voice on the line and the knowing look in Tessa's eyes confirmed my worst nightmare.

I carried my fiancée to the car, and I died a little each time she sobbed during that long, long drive to the hospital.

Thirty minutes later, we had an answer. They were gentle when they told us Tessa had lost the baby, but that didn't stop the splintering pain that shot through me every time I looked at the complete devastation in Tessa's eyes.

"I'm sorry, so sorry," she cried into my chest after the nurse left us alone in the room.

I brought my hand under her chin and forced her to look up at me. "No, baby. You have nothing to be sorry for," I told her over and over. I gently pushed her hair back from her face and tried my best not to focus on the loss of the most important thing in our lives.

When we got home later that night, I reminded Tessa how much I loved her, how amazing a mother she would be someday, and she cried in my arms until she fell asleep.

I wandered down the hall after I knew she wouldn't wake. I opened the closet in the nursery and dropped to my knees. It had been too early to know the sex of our baby, but I had been collecting little things over the last three months. I kept them here in bags and boxes, and I needed to see them one last time before I disposed of them all. I couldn't let her see this. I wanted to shelter her from seeing the tiny yellow shoes Karen had mailed us. I would get rid of all of it and take the crib apart before she woke up.

The next morning, Tessa woke me up by wrapping her arms around me. I was on the floor of the empty nursery. She didn't say anything about the removal of the furniture or the empty closet. She just sat there, on the floor with me, her head resting on my shoulder and her fingers tracing over the ink on my arms.

Ten minutes later my phone buzzed in my pocket. I read the message to myself and wasn't sure how Tessa would react to the news. She peered up, her eyes focused on the message before her.

"Addy's coming," she read aloud. I held her tighter, and she smiled, a sad smile, and moved from my arms to sit up.

I stared at her for a long while—it felt that way, at least—and we shared the same thought. We both picked ourselves up off the floor of our would-be nursery and put smiles on our faces so we could be there for our best friends.

"We will be parents one day," I promised my girl as we rode to the hospital to welcome our goddaughter into the world.

A YEAR AFTER THAT
HARDIN

WE HAD JUST DECIDED to take a break from trying to conceive. It was winter, I remember clearly, when Tessa came bouncing into the kitchen. Her hair was pulled back into an elegant bun, and she was dressed in a light pink lace dress. Her makeup was different that day—I couldn't put my finger on it. She beamed as she approached me, and I slid out the stool I was sitting on and gestured for her to sit on my lap. She leaned against me; her hair smelled like vanilla and mint, and her body was so soft against mine. I pressed my lips to her neck, and she sighed, resting her hands on my parted knees.

"Hi, baby," I said into her skin.

"Hi, *Daddy*," she whispered back to me.

I cocked a brow at her; the way she said Daddy made my cock twitch, and her hands slowly traveled up my thighs.

"Daddy, huh?" My voice was thick, and she giggled, a silly and out-of-place laugh.

"Not the Daddy you're thinking of. Pervert." She playfully and gently swatted her hand over the bulge in my pants, and I put my hands on her shoulders to turn her to face me.

She was grinning again—then full-on fucking smiling—and I couldn't quite connect what she was saying.

"See?" She reached her hand into the front pocket of her

dress and pulled something out. It was a piece of paper. I didn't understand, of course, but I've always been known for not getting important shit the first time. She unfolded the paper and placed it in my hand.

"What *is* that?" I stared at the blurry text on the page.

"You're ruining this moment so terribly right now," she scolded me.

I laughed and lifted the paper to my face.

"Urine test positive," it read.

"Shit." I gaped, my hand tightening around the paper.

"Shit?" she laughed, excitement clear in her blue-gray eyes. "I'm afraid to get too excited," she quickly admitted. I reached for her hand, crumpling the page between us.

"Don't be." I kissed her forehead. "We don't know what will happen, so we should be as excited as we fucking want to be." My lips pressed against her head again.

"We need a miracle." She nodded, trying to joke, but she came off so serious.

Seven months later, we had a blond little miracle named Emery.

SIX YEARS AFTER THAT
TESSA

I WAS SITTING at the kitchen table in our new apartment, tapping away on my laptop. I was planning three weddings at once, and I was pregnant with our second child. A little boy. His name was set to be Auden.

Auden was going to be a big boy—my stomach was swollen, my skin stretched once again with pregnancy. I was so tired toward the end, but I was determined to stay on task. The first of the three weddings was only a week away, so to say I was busy was an understatement. My feet were swollen and Hardin griped about me working so hard, but he knew better than to push it too much. I was finally making a decent income and building my name. New York City is a tough place to break into the wedding scene, but I had finally done it. With the help of a friend, my business was growing and my phone and email were full of inquiries.

One of the brides was panicking: her mother decided at the last minute to bring her new husband to the wedding, and now we had to adjust seating arrangements. Easy enough.

The front door opened, and Emery stormed past me and down the hall. She was six now. Her hair, an even lighter shade of blond than mine, was twisted into a messy bun; Hardin had done her hair for school this morning while I was at the doctor's office.

"Emery?" I called as she slammed her bedroom door. The fact that Landon teaches at the school Addy and Emery attend makes my life easier, especially when I'm working so much.

"Leave me alone!" she cried out. I stood up, my belly touching the counter as I shifted. Hardin came out of our bedroom with his shirt off and tight black jeans hanging low on his hips.

"What's with her?" he asked.

I shrugged. Our little Emery looked as sweet as her mom, but she had her father's attitude. It was a combination that made our lives very interesting.

Hardin laughed a little as Emery yelled out, "I can hear you!" She was six and already a tornado.

"I'll talk to her," he said as he walked back into the bedroom. He returned with a black T-shirt in his hands. Watching as he pulled the shirt over his head, I had a flashback of the boy I met during my first week of college. When he knocked on Emery's door, she huffed and complained, but he went inside anyway.

As he closed the door behind him, I walked over to the door and pressed my ear to the wood.

"What's going on with you, little one?" Hardin's voice echoed through her room. Emery was a fighter, but she adored Hardin, and I loved the way they were together. He was such a patient and fun father to her.

I reached my hand down and rubbed my belly, telling the little guy in there, "You're going to like me more than your daddy."

Hardin already had Emery; Auden was mine. I told Hardin this often, but he just laughed and said that I'm too much of a pushover with Emery, and that's why she likes him more.

"Addy is being a brat," Hardin's mini-me huffed. I imagined she was pacing around the room, pushing her blond hair back from her forehead like her father.

"*Is* she? How so?" There was sarcasm in Hardin's voice, but I doubted Emery would catch on.

"She just is. I don't want to be her friend anymore."

"Well, baby, she's family. You're stuck with her." Hardin was probably smiling, enjoying the dramatic world of a six-year-old.

"Can't I have a new family?"

"No." He chuckled, and I covered my mouth to laugh quietly. "I wanted a new family for a long time when I was younger, but it doesn't work like that. You should try and be happy with the one that you have. If you had a new family, you would get a new mommy and daddy and—"

"No!" Emery seemed to hate that idea so much that she didn't let him finish.

"See?" Hardin said. "You have to learn to accept Addy and the way she can be a brat sometimes, the way that Mommy accepted Daddy being a brat sometimes."

"You're a brat, too?" her little voice questioned.

My heart swelled. *Hell yes, he is*, I wanted to say.

"Hell yes, I am," he said for me. I rolled my eyes and reminded myself to warn him about cussing in front of her. He doesn't do it nearly as much as before, but still.

Emery went into a story about how Addy said they aren't best friends anymore, and Hardin, being the incredible father that he is, listened and commented on every line. By the time they were finished, I had fallen in love with my brooding boy all over again.

I was leaning against the wall when he came out of her bedroom and closed the door behind him. He smiled when he saw me.

"Life in first grade is tough," he laughed, and I wrapped my arms around his waist.

"You're so good with her." I leaned into him, my belly blocking me from getting too close.

He turned me sideways and kissed me, hard.

TEN YEARS AFTER THAT
HARDIN

"REALLY, DAD?" Emery glared at me from across the kitchen island. She tapped her painted fingernails on the granite and rolled her eyes, just like her mother.

"Yes, really. I told you—you're too young to be going to something like that." I picked at the bandage over my arm. I had just gotten some of my tattoos touched up the night before. You'd be surprised how much some of them had faded over the years.

"I'm seventeen. It's a senior trip. Uncle Landon let Addy go last year!" my beautiful daughter exclaimed loudly. Her blond hair was straight, hanging down past her shoulders. She whipped it when she talked; her green eyes were wildly dramatic as she continued to state her case regarding how I'm the worst father *blah, blah, blah.*

"This is so unfair. I have a 4.0, and you said—"

"Enough, honey." I slid her breakfast across the island, and she stared at her eggs like they were as involved in ruining her life as I was. "I'm sorry, but you aren't going. Unless you want to reconsider not letting me be a chaperone."

"No. No way." She shook her head with attitude. "Not happening."

"Then neither is this trip for you."

She stormed off down the hallway, and within seconds Tessa was walking toward me, Emery behind her.

Damn it.

"Hardin, we already discussed this. She's going on that trip. We already paid for it," Tessa reminded me in front of Emery.

I knew this was her way of showing me who's in charge here. We had a rule, only one rule in our house: no fighting in front of our kids. My children would never hear me raise my voice to their mum. Ever.

This didn't mean that Tessa didn't still drive me fucking crazy. She was stubborn and sassy, both lovely traits that only grew stronger with age.

Auden came walking into the room with his backpack on his shoulders and headphones in his ears. He was obsessed with music and art, and I loved that.

"There's my favorite child," I said. Tessa and Emery made snorting noises and glared at me. I laughed, and Auden nodded, the official teenage boy "hello." What can I say? His sarcasm was advanced for his age, just like mine had been.

Auden kissed his mum on the cheek and grabbed an apple from the counter. Tessa smiled, her eyes softening. Auden was affectionate, where Emery was all sass. He was patient and soft-spoken, where Emery was opinionated and headstrong. Neither of them were better than the other; they were just different in the best ways. Surprisingly, the two of them got along very well. Emery spent a lot of her free time hanging out with her little brother, driving him to band practice and going to his art showings.

"It's settled, then. I'm going to have so much fun on this trip!" Emery clapped her hands and pranced to the front door. Auden said his goodbyes to us and followed his sister out the front door for school.

"How did we become the parents of two kids like that?" Tessa asked me while shaking her head.

"No fucking idea." I laughed and opened my arms for her. "Come here." My beautiful girl walked toward me and leaned into my arms.

"It's been a long road." She sighed, and I brought my hands to her shoulders and rubbed them.

She sank back, relaxing immediately. She turned to me, her blue-gray eyes still holding so much love for me after all these years.

AFTER EVERYTHING, we made it. Whatever the hell our souls are made of, they are the same.

acknowledgments

Wahh, here we are! The END. The freaking end of this crazy ride that has been After. This one is going to be the shortest, because I've already said everything in the others.

To my readers, you have stayed with me through everything, and we are now even closer than ever. You're all friends to me, and I love how much you support me and the books. We truly are our own family. We took something that started as a whim for me and turned it into a four-book series. That's just nuts! I love you all, and I will never be able to stop telling you how much I appreciate and care for each and every one of you.

Adam Wilson, the best editor in the entire universe (I know I say a variation of this every book), you helped make these books what they are, and you were a great teacher and friend. I texted you too many times, left too many comments on the side, but you always responded and never complained! (You deserve an award or thirty for that.) I can't wait to work with you again!

To the production team and copyeditors, especially Steve Breslin and Steven Boldt, and to the S&S sales team—you rock for working so hard on this series!

Kristin Dwyer, you're awesome, dude! Thanks for everything, and I look forward to working together for our entire lives, hah. (I only mean this in a slightly creepy way.)

Everyone at Wattpad, thank you for always giving me a home to come back to.

My husband, for being the other half of me and always encouraging me in every aspect of my life. And to Asher, for being the best thing to ever happen to me.

Connect with
Anna Todd on Wattpad

The author of this book, Anna Todd, started her career as a reader, just like you. She joined Wattpad to read stories like this one and to connect with the people who wrote them.

Download Wattpad today to connect with Anna:

📖 imaginator1D